INCREDI

MOSHOESHOE
and the
LIGHTNING BIRD

By

JW LANGLEY

MONTAG

First Montag Press E-Book and Paperback Original Edition January 2022

Montag Press ISBN: 978-1-957010-03-8
Design © 2022 Amit Dey

Montag Press Team:

Author Photo: Alex Baker photography
Cover: Malky Currie
Editor: Charlie Franco

A Montag Press Book
www.montagpress.com
Montag Press
777 Morton Street, Unit B
San Francisco CA 94129 USA

Montag Press, the burning book with the hatchet cover, the skewed word mark and the portrayal of the long-suffering fireman mascot are trademarks of Montag Press.

Printed & Digitally Originated in the United States of America
10 9 8 7 6 5 4 3 2 1

Dedication

To Dianna, for your relentless love and support.

And to Helgard (Fridge), Ashton and Matthew (Red Room), Barney (5FM), Preacher (Shaft) and Nick (Zeplins)– DJs who made magic every time they had the floor.

Praise-songs for Incredulous Moshoeshoe and the Lightning Bird

'Langley's blend of pop culture, humour, politics and horror is a blast and reading it is to be air dropped directly into a wild world, fizzing with energy and ideas. While the rest of us keep mining the same old monsters time and again, he opens up a rich cave of folklore too long ignored. Recommended.'

Peter Laws,
Fortean Times columnist and
author of *Purged* and *The Frighteners:
Why We Love Monsters, Ghosts, Death & Gore.*

'A unique and thoroughly engaging tale, sardonically animated and richly crafted as only JW Langley can. It's Africa, her lore, and her people, through an imaginative lens of irreverent reverence.'

Ashton Nyte,
The Awakening, author of *Waiting for a Voice.*

'The motto of the Montag Press Collective is 'Books Worth Burning,' and Jonty Langley's modern African folk-tale *Incredulous Moshoeshoe and the Lightning Bird* fits the bill perfectly. In its brilliant mélange of traditional African folk characters such as the Tokoloshe and the eponymous Lightning Bird himself with a cross section of diverse twenty-first century subculture figures, from Goths to racist punk cops, from Marxist-antifascists to Afrikaner politicians, *Incredulous Moshoeshoe* (what a sublime name!) *and the Lightning Bird* has literally everything that the firemen from Station 451 would hate. Which makes it the perfect book for you — who follow Montag and Clarisse into the forest — to pick up. And memorise.'

Charles S. Kraszewski,
author of *Accomplices, You Ask?*

'This is the book Stephen King would have written if he was possessed by the mischievous spirit of Douglas Adams, and was also an African, a poet and more than a little mentally disturbed.'

Helgard deBarros,
author of *the Second Skin*, and
founder of The Fridge nightclub.

'This is a terrific book. JW Langley plays with language like a dolphin plays with waterspouts – not many writers could come up with a simile like, "Fat and slow as a successful lion". *Incredulous Moshoeshoe* riffs on music, theology, politics, and much else besides. I don't know whether to describe it as divine humanism or humane divinity. Either way, it's brilliant.'

Mark Woods, former Editor and
Consulting Editor of *The Baptist Times* and
Methodist Recorder, author of *Does the Bible Really Say That?*

'To borrow a phrase, this guy can *"preach like a motherfucker"*. Italics mine, because it's a line I wish I'd written.

'The soul-flaying juxtaposition of sun-scoured sand and silverblack glitter perfectly evokes the searing unknown and dim-remembered familiarity permeating JW Langley's aggressively alien South Africa. Like a child possessed by dark and alien things, the novel wears a skin that can only hint at what writhes inside. Incredulous Moshoeshoe navigates a world both modern and ancient, as open as a drawn gun and as closed off as beaten wife. There are old stories here, told in a new and incomparable manner that demands as much as it promises.

'A relentless, kinetic tale of monsters inhabiting the darkness within and without, rich with spitfire dialogue and unforgettable characters. Memorable as dancefloor blowjob.'

Paul d. Miller,
author of *Albrecht Drue, ghostpuncher.*

Acknowledgements

Thanks to Ash for being willing to be in it and to Penny Miller for literally writing the book on South African myth and legend. Thanks to Bee for being the best beta reader and to Helgard for the encouragement and catching errors like a champ. Thanks also to Charlie, who put up with the most appallingly formatted manuscript in history, and to Lolly for introducing me to Alternative music – which literally changed my life and made this book possible. Thanks to my Dad for filling my childhood with the sound of typewriters and my Mom for telling me I could do anything. And to my brother because he's fucking hilarious (and if anything in this book is amusing, it's probably my subconscious trying to make him laugh).

"Okay, but lightning birds? What the hell? And vampiric?" Jon Power said. "Are we looking for Dracula or the Tokoloshe?"

"Africa's got monsters," Incredulous said. "Just like Europe."

"Ja," said the pastor.

"I just always believed they were human."

"This one is, sometimes."

Foreword

Notes on a playlist,
by Incredulous Moshoeshoe

UtterSin, the DJ, is a man of rugged countenance, never lighted by a smile. That is to say, he is one good-looking Goth. When he asked me to create (or 'curate' – which is what all DJing is, I think, though a real DJ would never say it, because only people who want to be punched in the face say that word in that way) a playlist for the 30th Anniversary of Club Manderley, I was hesitant. After all, how does one encapsulate the spirit of a club in just one set, however long? And an entire genre – one as sprawling and influential as Goth, with all its incarnations and subgenres – well, it's frankly impossible.

But he *is* very handsome. And, it must be said, a legend of our scene. So, I have tried to do him – and Club Manderley – justice.

There will be some who find some of my choices odd. The Cure, it must be said, cannot always be called Goth (though I maintain that often they can). Similarly, the inclusion of Soft Cell may be controversial. But the particular track I've chosen by Mr. Almond et al. is at least as alternative, as dark, as any Depeche Mode track, and I'd argue they have a place here, too.

For the most part, however, I have stuck to the classic (if not classical) understanding of Goth – the darker side of the Romantic tradition, expressed in music unbound in any exclusive way to either rock or electronica, but that every person who ever lit incense sticks next to their black candles, every kid who snuck off to clubs like Manderley or the Fridge, every Goth would recognise the moment they heard it. Music that felt like home.

As for the order – I'm not going to pretend this playlist flows. But I hope it tells a story.

bit.ly/IncredulousPlaylist
DJ Mosh

Playlist

The kiss

The public ablution block smelled of sulphur. Something to do with the anti-malarial drugs used by tourists backing up from the pre-Apartheid drains perhaps, or tap water sucked out of the fertilizer-saturated Letaba river. She wasn't expecting incense, and she didn't care. She hadn't chosen the location for its aesthetics. She hadn't chosen the location at all.

White porcelain urinals slowly bled the inedible breath-mints in their bowls as a slow trickle of water kept the urine in the bottom fresh. Clear hand-soap dispensers above the basins, consecutive refills layered like volcanic sand sold to tourists in the Tswaing crater embalmed several large crickets – never removed, just drowned and re-drowned in different shades of soap. Archaeologically fascinating, but making a nonsense of any serious ambition to be clean. Hunting spiders, perfectly camouflaged against the wooden shower-cubicle doors, waited just below the door hooks, fang-surprises for fluffy tourist towels. *It was not*, she thought, *romantic*. But, then, she wasn't stealing into the men's bathrooms at two in the morning to be won over.

In the dark, warm air outside, the cicadas had entered one of their odd silences, as if the bushveld were holding its breath, waiting. A hyaena, probably attracted by tourists throwing scraps of meat and charred bone over the fence from their campsites, was baying. They always sounded far too close for her liking. Even as a little girl on holiday with her mom, when every meat-eater spotted was a victory; even at kills, she had always found the scavengers' cries more disturbing than her family's excitement at death. Wild, cackling groans and whoops, the vicious high-pitched laughing barks that punctuated sounds of cracking bones. Not that she went in for that sort of thing, but if there were a hell, that would certainly be part of the soundtrack.

She stood in the bathroom and looked around, thatched roof, South African National Parks tiles, flickering neon tube-lights swarmed by mosquitoes and moths, the insects surrounded by a stalking ring of spiders, mantises, and geckoes. Four shower stalls lined a wall opposite the basins and their grisly ornaments, and one of their doors was closed. Steam rose from behind it and the sound of shower water, mixed with something that was either whistling or singing.

The hyaena gave another low "wooh...ih!" and Alida started, her heel clicking on the tiles as she steadied herself. The shower noises and the singing stopped. Glancing back at the mosquito-screen door, she considered leaving. Walk straight back out. *Go back to your chalet. No shame in a no-show.* She was just turning when another "woo...ih!" seemed to come from closer than it possibly could have done. Was it the thought of the walk back in the dark, of the unseen hyaena with its big, corpse-dog eyes, its scuttling, un-mammalian gait, its black-stained mouth, that made her hesitate? Stories of hyaenas mauling tourists inside camps could have rooted her to the floor. But, then, so could the sight of a beautiful and very naked man.

The shower door opened and there he stood, wet, naked, and smiling, a white towel dabbing his shining, dark brown skin, his eyes completely black in the low, flickering light.

"You came," he said.

"I did. I don't know why."

"I think you do," he said and pulled her to him, her wispy blonde hair standing on end as he whispered in her ear, "Don't be afraid." And she wasn't.

All thought of the hyaena melted under a rain of kisses and her head filled with the sound of his breathing and the friction of his skin. As he undressed her, she was vaguely aware of a rising wind outside. The promise of a storm after the heat of the day. She liked a good storm.

Incredulous Moshoeshoe was depressed. Which was not unusual, to be fair. That's what Goth does to people. Not the music, obviously, but the certain, undeniable, unshakable knowledge that the music, the style you love, is never, *ever* coming back.

But tonight, his depression had motivation. He was tired, he was grumpy, and he was hating himself for being convinced. But she *was* beautiful.

Incredulous didn't usually do readings for total strangers. The occult, he always reasoned, was like a drug to some people.

Only idiots dealt it to customers they didn't know. That's how people got killed. Dealing to a stranger *in your own home*, he would say, meant not only that you deserved to be killed, but that at some level you wanted to be.

So, Incredulous was depressed. He must have been.

He didn't usually work on a Sunday, much less a pitch-black Sunday night. But this agitated white girl who had appeared at his door half-an-hour ago had seemed genuinely frightened. And beautiful. And if her fear and beauty had seemed real, her credit had proved to be equally sound. Depression, Incredulous would sometimes say, after a few drinks (Absynthe, Snakebite, or, for some reason, *Klippies* and Cream Soda), was very much like being in love.

Card tapped, payment made and formalities dispensed with, he had agreed to don his ceremonial gear (white girls always felt more comfortable when you did) and had brought out the ritual objects of divination, the "bones", as generations of Europeans had been pleased to call them. Shells and teeth from various animals. Beads and stones that fell in certain ways resonating with the energies of the earth and the past. An assegai, the traveling salesman from Maputo had assured him, that had once belonged to King Shaka. Plus his GoPro to record the session.

The music she had interrupted by nearly battering down his door was booming again from his flat-screen and surround. An improbably large, dark baboon in a cage (a gift from a friend up North, a violation of his rental contract and a helpful prop) moved edgily, eyeing the stranger with suspicion.

"You like Bauhaus?" he asked the girl, as the bassline dum... dum... dummed ponderously and the guitar effects clicked, echoing like splintering ice. Her big, blue eyes registered confusion.

"The... like, the architecture?"

Incredulous sighed, managing to keep his facial expression a good mix of bright, open, and professional.

"No," he said. "Well, actually, yes, but I meant the band."

He gestured towards the screen mounted on the wall beyond the divination mat. Peter Murphy, bottom-lit and clinging like a bat to a mesh fence on stage, looked cadaverous, manic, glorious. Bela Lugosi *wished* he was that Goth.

"Um, I don't know them," she said and Incredulous nodded, sighed, turned it down a little.

Of course not.

"Before we begin," he said, "can I get you a drink?" She brightened a little, her faith restored by his politeness where it had been undermined by a subculture, like a parent interviewing their child's reassuringly middle-class coffin-kid boyfriend. It had always been the same when he turned on the elite-school manners. *He's terribly well-spoken, isn't he?*

Blah. It was all too easy.

"I'd love something, yes. Please. Do you have a –" she paused a fraction too long, looking at the 'bones', the woven grass mats hanging on the wall, the wooden mask above the TV. *Don't say it,* Incredulous thought. "A Redbush tea?" *Oy vay.*

"No," he said deliberately, "I have Earl Grey?"

Who even drinks that stuff?

"Um," she said, "could I just have a Coke?"

Incredulous opened the fridge in the kitchen and asked with his back to the girl in the living room beyond the counter, "Why do you call it 'Redbush'? You're Afrikaans, aren't you?"

"I saw it on a packet when I was in England," she laughed.

"Ah."

"And I thought I'd lost the accent. Is it still very strong?"

"No, no. I just knew." he smiled, "It's magic."

She grinned, relaxing, and he handed her the bottle.

"Your coke."

She drank half of it in one go and he apologised, "It may be almost as warm as Rooibos. Or, *redbush*. Sorry. No ice!"

"That's okay," she giggled, and Incredulous sat down next to her on the couch, sipping a cider into which he'd dripped a teaspoon of blackcurrant.

"Before we get started," Incredulous asked, "May I ask your name?"

"Chanel."

"Hello, Chanel." He offered a hand and she shook it with mock solemnity. "My name is Incredulous," he said, handing her a business card. "Incredulous Moshoeshoe. You pronounce the end bit 'shwe-shwe', even though it's spelled 'shoe-shoe'. Buying boots on account brings out *all* the comedians."

"I'm sure!" she smiled.

"Now, Chanel, what can I do for you?"

"I was told that you could find things out." Her eyes suddenly serious with some of her earlier panic returning, urgent and contained.

"For that, you could hire a detective. Komatipoort's a border town. There are plenty."

"No," she said with force. "They can't tell me this."

"And what do you think I have that they don't?"

"That... magic, the one you mentioned." She attempted a smile with her mouth only.

"What is it you need to know?"

"I want to know if my sister is okay. I want to know if she's okay right now. *Tonight.*"

Thunder cracked like a gunshot and the flash from outside drew long, weird shadows pulled themselves across the sulphurous ablution block.

Alida pushed him away, sweat prickling her chest, her heart pounding. The thunder was scaring her half-to-death.

'Fuck *me!*' she thought and smiled.

The thunderstorm was going to be a noisy one. *Good.* Getting caught was one of her fantasies, but not this one. She scrunched her fingers in his thick hair as he made his way down her torso, the neon tube, its bloodsuckers, and predators swimming unfocussed above her half-closed eyes. She could hear the rain outside, the drops gathering momentum into the kind of rush of sound you get when God holds a shell to his ear. Not that she believed in him either.

Alida closed her eyes and when she opened them, the neon tube in the ceiling had given up the ghost. She was in darkness. The rain sang and hissed in rhythmic waves. *Was the shower on again?* The kisses had evolved into small, delicious, biting things and every time the lightning flashed, she saw him in a pornographic photograph. His skin. His red mouth. His arms, now enfolding her, beating the air in a kind of savage ecstasy. His teeth.

A jolt of fear in the dark. She called to him across the chasm of the storm,

"Dulu?"

He said something in her ear, running his sharp nails down her back, sending sparks of electricity through her body, still inside her. Still hovering above her. *That was crazy.*

"Dulu?" she said again, but his voice was drowned once more in thunder and the punishing rain that was systematically obliterating the dust and heat of the past day. Abruptly, she tried to pull away, tried to sit up, to stop, but he was there above her, in erratic strobe slow motion, seeming higher than he could have been, his voice somehow inside her ear,

"Don't worry, baby." His breath was hot, melting her fear. "I'm here."

His hands ran across her skin as light as feathers, barely touching her, bringing her out in goose pimples.

"I thought you liked the storms?" he asked, but he was not waiting for a reply. His mouth was on her collarbone, her shoulder, her neck. He was a post in the ground, as tall as the sky, his hair rich and thick, like thatch.

As he bit her, gently, insistently on the throat it seemed that every follicle tingled, every hair and softest hint of down stood all on end, anticipating and charged. His mouth was hot, harder than she expected, his too-long fingernails traced painful, pleasing furrows, up and down her back, pinging her taut nerves like strands of high-tensile wire, her ears humming.

Flashes of electricity from outside illuminated his face and Alida thought (as much as she could think anything) how very beautiful he was. His strong jaw and hooked nose, his hands with their perfectly manicured, long nails working magic on her back, her neck, her thighs. His strong arms lifting her against the shower wall. The shower *was* still on, lashing deliciously at their skins, spraying like cloudbursts ricocheting off hot stone. He lifted her onto his shoulders, pressed her back against the cubicle wall, pressed his face into her, kisses and licks and bites. His teeth occasionally and almost painfully pressing into the skin. She could feel her pulse on his lips.

If anyone had come in, she wouldn't have noticed. Her only thought was for him not to stop, to continue for the rest of her life.

⌐━━━⌐

Incredulous connected himself, in a sort of theoretical way, to the spirit (if not the spirits) of the people his grandma had called 'his ancestors.' He threw the strangely magnetised beads and shells, the bits of ivory and bone onto the mat, and the baboon screamed, throwing itself against the cage door. Chanel let go of his hand with a cry.

"Dammit, Ziggy!" he shouted. "Fuck!" he threw an unimportant piece of occult paraphernalia at the cage and Ziggy wheezed and shook the bars.

"I'm sorry. Are you alright?" Incredulous said, looking down at the bones on the mat as he spoke, his eyes wide.

"I'm fine," said Chanel and looked at the bones.

Incredulous had looked alarmed before the noise with the baboon. He was trying to hide it now.

"Please, Incredulous," she said. "What do they say?"

~

In the lightning, the water, and the delirium, the shower over Alida became the rain. The black ceiling, with its distorted shadows, invoked by lightning, became the thorn-trees and black sky outside; the thunder every thrust upward; her little whimpering cries drowned out by the storm. Opening her eyes, she saw among the confused shadows racing 'round the tiled walls what looked like wings. Feathers. Great wings beating. Feathered glory. A poem from school. She closed her eyes, abandoned to the water, the thunder, the lightning swirling louder 'round and 'round her head.

The hyena broke the spell. Its unmistakable 'woo...ih!', savagely playful and not outside.

"Jesus Christ, Dulu, there's something *in* here!" she hissed, trying to be quiet as if the animal might hear her words and understand. Dulu didn't reply. Lightning flashed with a wild panic. She was alone.

"Dulu!" she screamed, and immediately regretted it. She tried to be silent, to scramble onto the little concrete ledge intended as a seat, trying to hide her feet from anything low-slung and prowling outside the stall. Her feet slipped on the tiles as she scrambled and she let out an involuntary cry as her knee scraped raw on the edge. Her tears and shower water were getting colder. She gritted her teeth and tried to hold her breath.

She tried to be quiet. The rough edges had cut the soles of her feet and she saw her blood swirling with every lightning flash. Naked and paralysed with nightmare images of an animal outside the cubicle door, she tried not to move, tried not to think of what had happened to Dulu. The storm lulled. It was dark. She waited for the lightning.

Crack.

A violent flashbulb illuminated silver drops of water, nightmare shadows moving on the ceiling, and Dulu, somehow seemingly above her, reaching down to her. Incoherent, unthinking relief flooded her as he scooped her under his arms and drew her to him.

"Shh, baby. It's alright. There's nothing there."

She began to cry in earnest.

"Oh God, Dulu, I thought... I thought..."

"Sshhh. It's alright."

Alida's eyes were closed, her head weeping against Dulu's powerful breastbone. In a brief flicker of lightning, she didn't see him smile.

⌒

"Is she alright?" Chanel asked.

Incredulous looked back at the symbols on the mat, and into his subconscious, hoping and wishing to see something else.

"No," he said. "No, I am sorry, but I don't think she is."

⌒

Dulu was beside her. Above her. Inside her again. Hot, painful, reigniting her with confusion, hunger. Her vague fingers were pushing at him to get off, to get him out of her, to get his breath out of her ears, off of her shoulders, her face. She heard him laugh, felt his mouth on the nape of her neck, then on her thighs. The beating of wings and the sinking of teeth into the blood river running to the centre of her. Dizziness, racing heart, a smell of burning and bright, incandescent light. The bathroom aflame, halogen. Whiteness, feathers, shining white as the sun. Red, like blood. Black like a curtain, an eclipse. Alida thought of Sunday school, when she was a child. Of God, in Heaven, the Temple, and the Ark. Of lightning, thunder, an earthquake, and an eclipse. Of Jesus, white as lightning, no, no, white as wool. Dove's feathers. Lamb's wool. And as her mind descended into softness, the room exploded into crackling arcs of nothing.

Preacher Man

"**D**o you believe in Jesus?"

Jon Power smiled into the dark, blinking at the shadows behind the marquee, willing his eyes to adjust after the too-hot lights.

"*I said, do you believe in Jesus?*"

Jon took a deep breath of the cooler air and wondered if the question counted as rhetorical if everyone not only knew the answer but shouted it back at the stage?

"*And do you love Jesus?*" the voice on the PA continued from inside. "*I said, do you love Jesus?*"

Whooping, applause, and cries of, "Yes, Lord!" made it through the thick plastic flaps as a *bakkie,* with headlights dimmed, pulled up, effectively silent against the thunder of sound exalting from the marquee.

"*Then show Jesus how much you love him! Show him now!*"

The *bakkie* killed its lights completely and a silhouette got out of the car. A big, neckless beast of a silhouette, the offspring of a heavyweight boxer and a medium-sized truck. It loomed out of the shadows towards him and Jon slipped his right hand from the pocket of his khaki shorts in preparation.

"*It's time for your money,*" said the voice on the PA and Jon chuckled.

"Yes, it is."

"Well, at least they got that right," agreed the former silhouette.

"*It's time for a sacrifice to God! A thank-offering of praise! Praise Jesus with your giving now!*"

"You've not got any prettier, Caiaphas," said Jon. The dark-skinned, scar-faced, man-mountain in front of him smiled.

"And you've not stopped hanging out with these pricks."

"*While the stewards come 'round, let's give the Lord a thank-offering of praise, come on! You know he loves a cheerful giver. Thank you, Jesus...*"

Jon Power stepped forward and hugged the big man, pounding on his back with affection while the crowd inside applauded their largess and their Lord.

"How've you been, my friend? And why are you so late? You nearly missed me."

"I'm good, bra-Jon, I'm good. And *ja*, sorry about the time. That's why I came myself. I was sorry to hear..."

"Me too, my friend, me too."

"For what it's worth, they say it wasn't your..."

"I know, Caiaphas. Thank you." But Jon Power did not have the look of a man who knew it wasn't his fault. This much was clear, even in the shadows.

"Ja, well, bra. These things happen. But there are people who don't so much understand."

The muffled praise music and buzz played on, the soundtrack to baskets being passed 'round for an offering. Jon put his hands in his pockets and turned to look at the horizon. There were no stars.

"Broeders?" Jon said after a while.

"Yes."

"Is it just about the girl? Or do they know more?"

"We're not sure yet. But they were watching you already. Ever since we stepped up operations when Mandela died. Or. You know. Pretended to."

"And now he's going to die again."

"Yes, bother. And with this other shit with the girl, it's getting too hot, bra." Caiaphas said. "You're going to have to take a holiday."

"A holiday where?" Jon said.

"Kruger. We've made your booking. If you leave early tomorrow you can be there for the opening of the gates."

"Seriously? Now? I've committed to these people, Caiaphas."

"They are Christians. Let them forgive you."

"Fuck off, Caiaphas," Jon said, louder than he had intended.

"Sorry, man. You know I don't mean –"

"I know."

"But, Jon, they suspect too much. It isn't safe. It's not just about you."

"I know, I know."

"Thank you, brothers and sisters, thank you. The seed you've sown will come back to you one hundredfold, amen?"

"Alright," said Jon, "I'll leave tomorrow. Look, I've got to go."

"You're still doing this crap tonight?" asked the big man.

"Yes."

"With everything that's happened."

"Yes, friend."

"Why?"

"You don't like the money?"

"You know there are other ways you can be useful to us..."

"I'm not interested in those. You know that."

"I meant up front. Same skills. Different cause."

"I think it's the same cause."

"Ja, bra, ja. I know. I just mean ..."

"Our next preacher tonight is a true man of God and what he has to say is going to bless your heart..."

"Caiaphas, I have to go. Here." He handed the thick roll of R200 notes without ceremony into the other's big hand, heavy and silver in the reflected light.

"They'll know where I've gone, anyway, Caiaphas. My car is easy to spot."

"A nephew of mine will take you. He called me tonight. He's got some business there tomorrow. You'll like him," Caiaphas smiled.

"Ja? How so?"

"He's... sort of religious."

"Let me hear you give a big Holy Spirit Handclap..."

"Like me?"

"FOR JON..."

"Ja, bra-Jon, sure. Like you."

Jon didn't like the smile.

"Fuck. Alright. I've got to go. Send me word. Amandla. I'll pray for you."

Caiaphas laughed from the cab of the *bakkie*. "Don't bother! Amandla!"

"POWER!"

The applause and cheering in the tent thundered as Jon Power stepped through the opening and onto the stage. The lights were bright and the music loud. The buzzing sound had increased from a hum to a chorus of unintelligible noise. Half the audience was praying in tongues. Standing before the fervent, cresting wave of sound and light and belief he bowed his head, emptied his conscious mind, and asked the Spirit to help him.

Perhaps it was the bad news. Or the good feeling of handing over money he knew would be well used. Or the freedom of a final sermon. Whatever it was, Jon Power preached like a motherfucker that night – like a man anointed. He preached up a frenzy, preached up a storm. Beyond the horizon, in the sky, a ribbon of cloud flashed and glowed. Then he heard the thunder.

Noxious (the demon's game)

In his mind, Jon Power stood at the end of the bed. That was where the horror had begun.

He stood outside, the blaze of sun wringing pops of sweat from his brow. He felt old. Remembering the previous morning like a too-often copied scene from a book, a film. He cupped his hands around the glass of hot, sweet, Rooibos tea as if to warm them. As if he were still there. He could not shake the memory. It clung to his back like his khaki shirt, wet with perspiration. The deliverance was over, if such things are ever truly over, but he sifted through the layers of action and reaction, like an archaeologist slowly brushing bones out of dust. He sipped his tea and waited for the religious cousin. Remembering.

She had been very young.

In the economy of abomination, Jon Power's darker concerns were melodramatic, high-risk, high-yield investments. Next to the routine horrors that take children from parents and make men of greater faith than his renounce their God – hunger, cancer, habitual cruelty – the enemies Jon fought might anywhere else have seemed fantastic luxuries. But in Africa, they are common as dust or dung or good people complicit in terrible things. In Africa, the European missionaries would say, the spiritual realm is somehow closer to the surface of life – more real. Not even cynics or Anglicans ever bothered to deny it.

Jon had never felt the need. The devil was real. And those who could only see him reflected in the barrel of an American rifle or the bonnet of a German sedan were just afraid to turn around to look at him directly. Jon was not afraid. But he never took the experience lightly.

The house had been quiet. He remembered that. No roaring or thunderous noises from inside the walls. Not then. Just the strange emptiness that seems to seep from the pores of people living with a truth they no longer mention. You see it when you visit the dying. Jon had felt it in too many living rooms, sat opposite wives with split lips and arms in clumsy slings. You taste it in some churches. It hums with taut nerves and subconscious waiting. A desperation to keep everything alright that hides its whitened knuckles under sofa cushions and wedding bands.

The maid (in Komatipoort the word had not accumulated the embarrassments it had in the more progressive suburbs of the cities) opened the door and smiled tightly at him, ushering him into the cool, high-ceilinged house. Paint flaking in corners, but spotlessly clean.

"Where is she?"

"Who? The *miessies*?" The maid smiled hard.

"The little girl. Beauty."

"She's in bed, master." Other words had escaped censure here too. "But, master..."

"It's alright. The *miessies* has asked me to come and pray for Beauty. What's your name?"

"Me, I'm Sophie, master."

"Call me Jon, Sophie. I'm a pastor."

"You are very welcome, Pastor," she sighed, uncoiling slightly. "The miessies is out. But you can go through and see Beauty. She is in the second room on the left. I'll show you."

Old houses in Africa are built to be as cool as possible against the inferno of Summer outside. At noon, near the Tropic of Capricorn, the sun is as merciless and heavy as a physical presence beating on the roof, this one felt icy.

Sophie stayed a pace behind as Jon moved down the passage. His limbs felt heavy as if he were walking through water – sinking, like Peter. Like a magnet forced to press against a matching pole.

The girl was coffee-coloured, perfectly still, healthy-looking. She was the same age as his niece. Primary school. She was lying as still as a carved stone on top of the bedclothes of a small single bed. She smiled at him as he entered.

"Close the door, Sophie," Jon said gently. "Hello, Beauty."

"Good afternoon."

"How are you feeling, my girl?"

"Well," she said, without emotion. "I'm well. The weather is sunny, I have a roof over my head and parents who dote on me. I am well. Very well, thank you."

John sighed with recognition.

"Nothing wrong?" He did not mirror the small girl's eventual adult smile.

"Why do you ask?"

"Your parents are worried about you. Your mother asked me to see you."

"Are you a doctor?" Beauty smiled sweetly, all eyelashes and dimples, looking at a spot on the wall.

"No."

"I know."

"But I can help you, Beauty."

The girl turned her head for the first time and faced Jon. Nothing in her manner or features objectively pointed to anything but sweetness. No distortion or grotesquery. But as her eyes met Jon's he felt the familiar catch in his breath, the hollowness in his stomach. His skin crawled with a thousand microscopic claws.

"No," she said, spacing the words deliberately and decisively, "You. Can't."

She almost whispered.

"I know what you are," said Jon. He had not broken eye contact since they had begun talking.

"I am a little girl. No more than eight years old."

"Seven."

"Seven, then." She looked quickly away but the smile remained nailed onto the little face. Curls of hair haloed over the baby-blue pillow behind her. "We are seven."

"We?"

Beauty's throat tightened in a laugh, her mouth tentative around the sound.

"Is that funny?"

"*Everything* is funny."

"It is better to go to a house of mourning than to go to a house of feasting," said Jon, and Beauty's head turned to him, her smile drained away.

"And death is the destiny of every man," the girl's voice said. Then, smiling again and looking long into Jon's eyes, her lips parted, the girl on the bed whispered, "The living should take this to heart." She laughed again.

Jon Power felt nausea bead on his throat, his chest, and he looked around. He was in a guestroom. Blue lace trimmed the lampshades and curtains. An old lady chair crouched in the corner. Deep, cream carpet. Behind small panes of glass, Jon could see a garden in sunshine, green and slow and mammal hot, like all Lowveld gardens in Summer. Buzzing, fluttering things all around the flowers and long, thirsty leaves. The tapping of several bees, hard bodies bumping into the small glass squares, tapping fingers with no body. Jon's mind knew well enough to stay out of the garden.

Legion

The girl was looking at him.

"Who are you?" Jon asked.

She was silent. Smiling still.

"I command you to tell me in the name of Jesus Christ, Son of God, whose blood covers me. Who are you?"

"We are a rag-tag band of misfits," the girl said cheerfully, and though the room was icy cold, she was sweating. So was Jon. A flurry of sound began to build at the window. Like the first drops of rain growing into a shower. It was that of hard insect bodies butting against the glass – a skittering shower of hail. And now the faint buzzing of a fourfold legion of wings.

"And what do you want?" he asked the thing inside the girl.

"What do we always want? What have we ever wanted?"

"I've never understood that," said Jon.

"Guess."

"To defile? To destroy? To cause pain?"

"Prejudice."

"What, then?"

"We want a home."

"Somewhere warm?" Jon's tone was neutral, unconfrontational. "Somewhere alive?"

"You've been reading the wrong books," the little girl's mouth said, and as Jon glanced at the window, he saw more bees, a small electron cloud.

The door opened behind him. He spoke as he turned.

"It is the only book we have." Sophie's face was shining with sweat at the door. Beauty was perfectly still bar her face.

"There are better books," the voice in Beauty said.

Jon ignored it. "Do you need blood to have a home?"

The voice laughed too loudly. Jarring. Sophie caught her breath but stayed at the door.

"Is there blood in the forest? Is there blood in the stones? Is there blood in the air?" Beauty's mouth said.

"No," said Jon.

Another laugh, and then Beauty's mouth whispered, "There will be."

Jon Power recognised the words. He had heard both stranger and more subtle terms pour from the faces of much younger children. From people who had never learned the languages they spoke. Babel had its own form of Tongues. As he allowed himself the luxury of chatting and asking questions, he prayed. Wordless, fundamental prayers, invoking greater wisdom, emptying himself.

The buzzing was getting louder.

"Perhaps you do want a home," said Jon, thoughtfully. "But what you do to it..."

"We do what any owner does."

"You destroy."

"We make adjustments, yes. We strengthen for a harsh world. We make realistic alterations. We… extract value."

"You defile what God has made precious."

"Nothing is precious beyond its use. No one is precious beyond what they do and what has this done?" the girl's hand gestured head, shoulders, knees, and toes.

Jon Power said, "All have sinned. But this girl is under God's grace. You cannot harm her. She would have to harm herself."

"She will. You always do. You love it."

The buzzing was becoming loud, the bees against the window like a hundred drumming fingers.

"Usefulness is finite," the thing inside the girl said to Jon, "Even he says this. He uses you. He measures your worth, weighs you. This is the *Plan*." The voice emphasised the last word with something like pleading.

"She is precious by being born."

"Sentimentality."

"I claim nothing," Jon Power said.

"Look at her." The girl's voice was hard to disentangle from the roaring bees, queenless and swarming – an ordinary summer event.

"What good is she? She has done nothing. Offers nothing. And she will do terrible things. I can show you them." the demon asked in a little girl's voice, with all its specificity of age and accent.

"Behold," said Jon, "the Lamb of God, who takes away the sin of the world."

Beauty's body was racked by a fit of coughing. A tiny drop or two of vomit spotted her chin. Little fragments from a child's lunch. Sophie, who had been motionless at the door, ran forward.

"Stop that," said Jon, as the coughing continued, the girl's lungs wheezing. Sophie stepped back and the child began to convulse, asphyxiating. "In the name of Jesus Christ."

The coughing stopped. Jon was standing and took Sophie to the old chair in the corner and helped her sit. She was trembling, her eyes wide.

Some people expect a spectacle. Ritual is for them. Jon Power did not believe authority needed a uniform or a badge, despite his past.

He turned back to the little body with its painted-on smile.

"We are not afraid of you," the mouth said.

"No. You are not."

The demon laughed a man's laugh, but stopped abruptly as Jon spoke.

"But you fear Him who is in me. Don't you?"

Beauty's head turned away in silence.

"Sophie." Jon realised the maid was probably the girl's mother. White families in rural areas could be proprietorial with children. And adults. Her face glistened with sweat, her eyes wide and black-pupiled with fear.

"Yes, Pastor?"

"Close the door."

"Yes, Pastor."

"Sophie, I need you to promise me that you won't open the door while I pray for this girl."

"Yes, Pastor."

"Sophie, look at me. You need to know that as soon as I start praying, there will be many reasons for you to want to open the door. You must not."

"Alright, Pastor." Sophie looked afraid. Jon was glad of that. People prayed harder when they were afraid.

"Sophie, are you a Christian?"

"Yes, Pastor."

"What church?"

"Caris Chapel, Pastor."

"You pray in tongues?"

"Yes, Pastor."

"Good. I want you to pray for Beauty and me. In tongues. I do not want you to stop, the whole time I am praying. Can you do that for me?"

"Yes, Pastor. Will she be alright, Pastor?"

"Greater is the one who is in us than those who are in her. The Spirit wants to set her free. We must ask God to cast out the unclean spirits."

As soon as they started praying, Jon reciting Scripture and invoking the Name, Sophie pouring out a language only for the Lord, her eyes closed, it began. The phone outside the room began to ring. Sophie looked up at Jon, who continued to pray over the girl but fixed her eyes with his, shaking his head.

The phone rang and rang and rang, piercing through the sound of their praying, piercing even through the sound of the bees, now an engine hum outside, a thickening dark mist at the window.

The girl's eyes rolled back, white in their brown sockets, as Jon continued to pray.

The phone began to ring again, and this time it did not stop for three or four minutes. It seemed longer. Insistent that they needed to answer – pleading. And when the ringing stopped there was a rapping at the front door. Loud and urgent, shaking the room as if already in the house. A child shouted from the garden beyond the window, but Jon fixed Sophie with a look and they continued to pray.

He felt as he always did when the Spirit worked through him, an uncluttered calm. In the early days, he had mistaken it for complacency or a lack of passion and had felt guilt for the peace. As if he were not properly engaged. *Everyone wants to earn love.* But he had learned, through counsel from more experienced intercessors than himself, that this was normal. In the noise of orchestrated distraction and of praying loudly in the language of Heaven, he felt clear and calm and quiet.

Words he'd heard before but never understood washed in waves from his throat. He prayed with peace. Confident. In his heart, he also felt the words of his mind's prayer.

Lord, God of Hosts, you are here. Holy Spirit, You are in me. The blood of Jesus, the blood of Jesus covers me.

"Fuck!" Beauty cried. "You're hurting me!"

I am washed and covered by your blood. I ask it in Your name, release her, Lord. You say if we ask in your name we receive and I ask, Lord, save her.

The spirits in the girl would have no choice but to leave if he and Sophie continued to pray in faith. He never faltered in this knowledge. A faith that must have seemed like self-confidence.

We do not do this in our strength. Our prayers are meaningless without You. Save her, Lord. Hear us.

His faith was in the power that made the sea and formed the mountains and breathed life into every human child from the beginning until the end. The one who would bring low the oppressor. The one who breaks the yoke.

The child had shaken.

Then the child convulsed and quivered as the beast inside her clawed and clung onto the inward apparatus of her flesh in an effort to resist being cast out again into the dry, cold air.

The child spat and swore and, yes, screamed. And a thousand distractions and urgencies seemed to whirl around the room. A few bees somehow found their way in and died stinging Jon and Sophie on their open skin.

But the spirit had left the girl.

Small and exhausted and warm to the touch, Beauty slept, curled up, and Jon had been certain she was safe as any human being can be.

And in that night, she had died.

Jon heard from Sophie's aunt that someone had called an *ngaka*, a pagan spirit healer from the local *kraal*, to come and help her. Some elements in the household had not believed that this man, who did not even look like a priest, could have had any effect.

Jon did not know if it had been some toxic herb or some rough rural magic, reopening the door to the child's body, which had been responsible. But the child was dead. He never considered the strain of the deliverance itself.

And responsibility, he was told, was being laid on him. A posse was being put together, partly made up of those who were already watching him. The people, he knew, were unquiet.

Mandela was really dying.

The country was on the edge of something sharp and new. There was a hunger everywhere for enemies. He could feel it laying in the shade of the baking trees and spitting convulsively from the pipes of windmills rusting on the edges of the town. It was in the air, like the unclean spirit that had killed the girl, and was prowling now. It was looking for a host.

Angry hearts, fearful minds, and the homes where sin is welcomed in are open doors for spirits wishing to do harm. This country was full of them.

Jon Power tried to dispel the pangs of guilt as he waited for the relative his friend was sending. He should have stayed. Should have checked on her. He tried to quiet his anger at the family, the house, that chose to keep the mother in servitude and pretended to care enough for the child to justify a lynching. They had probably called Beauty their 'daughter'. He spat.

The funeral was happening as he waited for the car to pick him up. After that, the ungrateful and unrighteous, and unreformed would come for him.

A car shimmered into view in the distance and resolved like something rising out of water. The something was a *bakkie* but modified. Pimped – if the pimp in question had mainly served a clientele of necrophiliacs. It was stretched, canopied, and shiny black. It had silver chrome trim in motifs of flowers and skulls. The grill was custom, resembling teeth. Its canines pointy. As it came to a halt, the hubcaps slowed enough to show the bat-wing designs across their diameters. There are, in South Africa, more practical vehicles.

"For fuck's sake," the pastor said.

He resented the car. He resented the creature climbing out of it with a surly look on its weird face. He resented leaving. He felt disinclined to pray. But he did anyway.

Black No. 1

"*Incredulous Moshoeshoe, Magic Negro*"

Jon Power turned the business card over, frowning.

"*Bones thrown, curses lifted, spirits contacted, tokoloshes wrangled.*"

Jon looked back up at the owner of the card – long dreadlocks, black; long fingernails, painted glitter black; long, shiny boots, all straps and sole, also black. Leather leggings, mesh shirt, stylised cowboy hat, and Apartheid-era ethnicity, all black.

"What's a 'Magic Negro'?" he asked.

"A mythical creature. Soon to be extinct. Don't worry about it. I assume you're Jon?"

"Yes. I promise."

"What?"

"Well. I assume you are... *Incredulous*?"

Incredulous sighed, lengthening the word unnecessarily, his slightly English accent evident more in his tone than pronunciation, "*Yess.*"

"Incredulous... *Mo-shoe-shoe*? *Shoo-shoo*? As in, hot? Or, *I like footwear so much I forget to pluralise?*"

"As in, *bite me.* Your name's *Power.* A bit on the nose, big guy."

Jon Power laughed. "Fair enough," he said, throwing his small pack into the back cab of the large black bakkie.

Moshoeshoe was not finished. "The name has history," he said. "Moshoeshoe," he said, careful to pronounce each 'shwe', "was a great man. He was..."

"Moshoeshoe was the founder and greatest leader of the Basotho nation. When cannibals roamed South Africa, he kept his people safe on top of *Thaba Bosiou*, Mountain of Night, near Maseru. Beautiful spot. You been?"

"No."

"You know he was ultimately betrayed by white men. Maybe because he made too many assumptions about them, based on their race."

"Okay," Incredulous said, unwillingly impressed.

"That said, your uncle Caiaphas is not a Sotho. This I know."

Not once had Jon Power lowered his gaze from Incredulous, who filed the tanned, irredeemably uncool fortysomething with the potbelly and the all-khaki ensemble away for later classification.

"Our family became..." the witch doctor paused, searching, "...detribalised. Ideology, you know? Marxism became the creed. Big family. Lots of marriages. Almost intentional mixing of tribes and tongues. We're a Leninist Babel, my peeps."

"Makes sense," Jon Power said.

"If you say so," Incredulous said. "Politics bores me."

"Of course," said Jon. "It's already helped you. You don't need it. Or you think you don't. But whitey is waiting. This shit right now will be when he takes it all back." The 'all' was stretched out and raised in pitch. Incredulous looked unimpressed.

"Whatever, man. Uncle Caiaphas sent me to pick you up," he said. "Wants me to take you on a job with me. Wasn't specific about where to take you. Just 'away'. Any idea why?"

Jon eyed the painfully effeminate coffin kid in front of him, trying to reconcile the shiny black Vespa with its eighteen-wheeler relative. "No clue. But Caiaphas isn't *often* wrong."

He paused as if to say that Caiaphas was human and as open to failure as any man. "He didn't tell me you were..."

"A Goth?" interjected Incredulous.

"No..."

"Educated abroad."

"No, not that. I mean..."

"Ooh, ooh! I know! Black!"

"Bugger off, man."

"*Dominee!*" Incredulous affected his campest Afrikaans accent. "That's no way for a minister of the Lord to talk."

Jon took a deep breath.

"He didn't tell me you were a *sangoma*."

"An *isangoma*, actually. I am *very* pretty, but I am a man."

"A witch doctor."

"Not the term I prefer. To be honest, I'm not crazy about *Isangoma* either. Hence the cards. I have the gift, I know the lore, but I feel I have very little in common with your average backwater bone-thrower. Wouldn't you agree?"

"You call it a gift."

"What would you call it, Dominee Power?"

"I would call it playing with the Devil."

Incredulous rolled his eyes. "Well, this is going to be fun. Get in the car."

⌒⌒⌒

Incredulous had not grown up in South Africa. This may have accounted for his disdain for the place. He and Jon Power drove through a haze of tan and khaki – and other words that basically just meant brown. It was hot. Too hot. And they spoke little over the music, which Incredulous had turned high for that purpose. He disliked his uncle and he disliked helping him. But it's hard to say no to family. Particularly family with paramilitaries and caches of weapons all over the fucking country. *It was 2018, for fuck's sake. Not 1981.*

Of his early childhood, Incredulous remembered little. His grandmother, *Gugu*, in a hut already anachronistic by the 1980s, throwing bones and telling the young Incredulous the legends of their people and the peoples beyond – the extended family, the pan-Africanist dream returned to the religion of its soil. Dusty farm roads turned into bush-veld just like the one the dominee and he were driving, and interminable hours sitting under trees, while his parents met with people he was instructed immediately to forget. White police and Bible lessons in a farm school both hot and dark that smelled of guano.

His later years in London, an adolescence of semi-stardom and acting as visual aid and mascot for his parents' campaigning – that he remembered better. And also his parents' fighting. His inevitable resentment of *Struggle* fundraiser politics and the cloying African mystique ascribed to his family by white liberals in spectacularly unattractive clothes.

While Jon's fondest memories were of open fires, starry skies, and the distant calls of jackals and hyaenas, Incredulous smiled at thoughts of strobes and smoke machines in Goth-Industrial nightclubs, his discovery of the dark-Romantic aesthetic of the Sisters of Mercy, Nine Inch Nails and a host of other bands about as white and far from his South African roots as was possible outside of Norway. And he had dabbled in the Norwegian scene a little too.

Jon Power didn't know any of this. He just got a taste of the music as they drove.

"What the hell is this crap?" Jon Power asked after half-an-hour of excruciatingly polite listening.

"The Lowveld."

"No, man. What is this... *music*?" He spoke the last word tentatively as if it were far from confirmed.

"It's Clan of Xymox," said Incredulous, staring straight ahead as thorn tree after windmill after thorn tree sailed past in waves, on a sea of khaki. Brown. The sun was high and hot and the only people out moved slowly, like figures caught in a rainstorm with a long way to go. Shabby donkeys drifted by and flocks of ragged children with sticks and absorbing games in ditches and fields. Signs bearing leaping Kudu, spiral horns majestic in their spring, alerted motorists to the danger of wildlife crossing and served as a secondary warning, peppered as they were with bullet holes of varying calibres. The soundtrack – classic goth, all tortured, crypt-deep vocals, and mournful basslines – was not a natural choice for the scenery. You could almost smell the smoke machine.

"It's *kak*," said Jon after another track.

As a DJ on the Alternative circuit, particularly after returning from the UK, Incredulous had commanded respect as a true artist. But DJing gets old faster than DJs do. The constantly rotating crowds of scenesters and unholier-than-thou uber-Goths, the Norse-God-bothering metallers, and the drunk, thick as hog-shit bike rockers wore you down. After a while, you knew exactly how to play them. How to warm a floor and fill a floor and kill a floor for the next set, the next demographic to please and appease. Incredulous had started setting himself challenges.

Tonight, I will make Goths dance to Creedence. This set, covers only. Let's see if I can actually, literally, make them cry. Line up Something I Can Never Have and Crowds. Play a little Marvin Gaye and see if we can keep those Nu Metallers dancing.

After a while even the challenges got dull. The girls became so well known it seemed unhygienic to keep passing them around and anyway they had turned from groupies into friends. Old lays are like that in the club scene. They sneak up on you. Before you know what's happened you respect them as human beings and you're going 'round to talk and play board games. It's disgusting. He had had to leave.

"Ag no, man," said Jon, grimacing at the iPod in the dock. "What's this now?" He had rolled his window down and was shouting over the roar of the hot air. Incredulous had responded by turning up the music.

"It's Sopor Aeternis!" he shouted.

"Superman's turnip?"

"Sure." Sometimes it's best not to bother.

Jon looked satisfied, shook his head, and stared out the window, the OTT shrieking silenced every time he ducked his head into the airstream like a farm dog might. A lot of Goth is misunderstood and worth defending and explaining. Some of it is not.

The upshot of his stellar DJ career was that Incredulous had longed for something more exciting, more spiritual even, than the power to make hundreds of black-clad forms writhe in pleasure to music they didn't even know they loved. As an *isangoma,* he had connected with his roots. He had kept up the DJ work, but by day he visited the markets where *muti* was sold, chatting to the salesmen, all of whom remembered his maternal *Gugu.*

He cut an unusual figure, to be sure. Goth is about as big in black circles in South Africa as Phil Collins and fondue sets. That is to say, you'd be surprised how many people were into it, but there'd be a reason for your surprise. In more traditional majority contexts, like those that have rediscovered indigenous religion and committed themselves to the Azanian cause, it's about as big as Aryan nationalism. But the Moshoeshoe name carried credibility, his *Gugu's* reputation more still, and enough vendors and practitioners of South Africa's *real* oldest profession ignored his looks. So, as his interest in the subject grew from genealogical to semi-professional, the grudging respect shifted from his family to that strange-looking Moshoeshoe boy himself, looks like a queer, terrible fucking taste in music – don't they all these days – but hey, he knows his shit. *Our* shit.

The owners of the little stalls eventually welcomed his visits, his willingness, absent in so many of their own sons and grandsons, to stop and sit and talk. To discuss fading arts – an endangered craft. They shared recipes and tales and legends and began to teach him, in person and by doing, what no person, no matter how talented by blood, can learn from words alone.

The grind of his night job was made easier by his newfound interest. Playing *Living Dead Girl* for the fourth time on request to a bafflingly full floor, he felt less trapped than he had done in months. And he even started trying new forms of divination, reading the bodies on the floor on a slow strobe as if they were the shells and bones of his *Gugu*.

He was, like so many strippers, waiters, and DJ's before him, putting himself through school. He was getting into the family business.

He remembered more of the lore and legends than he had ever been conscious of imbibing. Stories and songs and, yes, spells – names and lyrical descriptions of creatures never likely to appear in textbooks came back to him as he chatted with his now ancient G in her little room in his aunty's house. She and the aunties, cousins, sisters from other parents, had helped him to awaken latent abilities, the talent for understanding portents and reading a medium for divination. He'd been eager. He'd enjoyed it. It was easy somehow. Like reading once you finally understand the letters and the way they work together. But this was a new, dark alphabet. Bones. Chicken entrails. Pieces of dead predators. The spirits of the dead. It was all so fucking *Goth*.

After a while, he started incorporating it into his look. Aesthetics are as important in getting people to believe your readings as they are in getting sulky twentysomethings to dance. The profound Eurocentrism of his subculture had mashed more easily and excitingly than he had imagined possible with the darker aspects of his African roots. Incredulous, while respectful of the ancestors and their magic, was not above making an impact. And his necklaces of 'bones,' his dancefloor moves, augmented with elements of spirit dances and rituals, his purchasing of pet snakes and a baboon, all added to his mystique and cache in the clubs. People started asking him for readings. Soon, Satanists, and weekend Wiccans would defer to him in conversations, not just an Uber by virtue of his status as a DJ, but as one of the hardcore. People who didn't just wear darkness as a fashion choice – people who lived it.

That was exactly the kind of stupid shit that made him want to quit. And, eventually, he had. There were still those who remembered the legendary DJ Mosh (the Goths had hated it, but pretty much everyone else in the scene had lapped the metal-centric name up), as an *isangoma*, Incredulous felt for the first time that he was doing something useful. As an *isangoma*, he had respect from people he respected. As an *isangoma*, he was going some way to filling the spiritual void left by England and Catholic school and way too much cocaine. As an *isangoma*, he was connecting with his family, his past, his country in a way that had been denied him by his parents' choices and his own personal aesthetics.

As an *isangoma*, he was having to baby-sit a religious maniac on a trip to the fucking game reserve. Ugh. And a religious maniac with an unsettling knowledge of black African history who, from the look of him, probably killed animals for entertainment. Incredulous could have done without that.

But, then, with sweat running down his leather-clad legs and pooling in his boots, he could have done without a lot of things.

"Do you have any 80s?" the *dominee* asked. "Something nice, man. Like Wham."

Yup. A lot of things.

Just like Heaven

The Kruger Park is where God lives. Well, he frequents Mpumalanga generally. But his house is in Kruger. This is because God, being God, has limitless choice in the matter of where he might hang his hat and kick off his shoes – assuming he has a hat or wants shoes. That is the point, He is God, so He gets to choose. The Ultimate Subject, the First Cause of choice, the Supreme Free Will is not limited by where He might find a job. He had a Job. You can read about it. God needs no passports and no special permissions and He never pays tourist rates.

God, being God, knows all the most beautiful places in the entire expanding universe He created, has no need for oxygen or temperatures beneath 2,000°C, and has a superb grasp of fundamental aesthetics. And He chooses to live in Kruger.

This is because the Kruger Park (Or *South African National Parks Board Kruger National Park* as it is called by no one, anywhere, ever) is easily the most beautiful place, not only on planet earth but in the entire universe. Consequently, accommodation rates, in season, are a bit pricey. Though not too pricey. God wouldn't want the most beautiful place he ever created to be inhabited solely by the super-rich. God is just, and He dislikes bankers. He has decreed that the Kruger Park remains State-owned, administered by a conservation-minded, history-respecting Parks Board that still today will not let tourists get out of their cars or drive off designated roads.

If this state of affairs ever changes, that will be a sad thing indeed, primarily because the Kruger Park will have been laid as low as Kenya's Mara, but also because it will be a sign that the Lord has decided to move elsewhere. And that hits you right in the property values.

For the moment, though, Kruger remains beautiful. A 220 mile long, 40-mile-wide stretch of loveliness, mostly comprising land as virgin as an evangelical teen. That is to say, parts of it have, at times, been interfered with, but that time is mostly forgotten and everybody involved is terribly sorry. Now it's very much, 'look and don't touch.' And people get pretty tense if you transgress.

Long, yellow grass on savannah plateaus gives way to thirsty crowds of ancient trees, knotty giants whose canopies shake one day with slinging baboon play, and with the force of hot, pre-storm winds the next – and, on unspecified days in between, playing host to lazy leopards, tails flicking in the dappled light. Small mountain *koppies* like burial cairns of stones deposited at the feet of an ancient race of giants are reached by roads of tar and dirt that curve past watering holes of every imaginable size and level of danger to the animals who drink there. Most are too far from any road ever to be seen.

Birds, from the visitors of shadowy death, the eagles, with their immense wingspans, to minute waxbills, insectile in their smallness and improbably blue, with every *Loerie*, hornbill, roller, and vulture in between, make foreign skies seem like dead places. And in the Kruger Park, you see large mammals in the natural habitat their ancestors have known for hundreds of thousands of years. Not caged. Not imported. Not reintroduced or paraded for tourists or fed in special spots at certain times to assure their visibility. Just hunters and hunted, living their beautiful, terrible lives against the ubiquitous background of singing cicadas and the occasional click or ping of a car-bound camera.

The sky is big enough for stars in Kruger, the air clear enough to smell an elephant before you see it, and the scent of rain on the grateful earth in this place is more wonderful than anywhere else on a planet full of beauty. It is nature, wild and free and as it was intended, Africa as it should be.

"Fuck, I fucking hate this fucking boring, fucking place."

Incredulous spoke mainly to himself as he drove, his head leaning against his door frame, his Lennon-loving shades shielding his eyes from the flapping of his dreadlocks.

"That's because you're going too fast," said Jon.

It did not slow their progress.

They'd had trouble at the entrance and Moshoeshoe was annoyed.

Jon Power had burst out of the car, the closest thing to a smile that Incredulous had so far seen on his face, saying something about "taking care of this".

If care had been taken, it had been a waste of energy. Jon had been in the reception office a very long time.

Incredulous leaned against his car, ignoring the open stares of the cleaners as they arranged the sand around thatched ablution *rondawels* with splay-fingered rakes, semi-conscious zen gardeners in khaki uniforms decked with green epaulets and 40-degree heat.

Incredulous' car was coiled like a shining black snake in the shade of a Maroela tree and through his black sunglasses (an '83 shade of Eldritch) the entrance gate with its high thatch roof and anachronistic barber-pole boom trembled in the heat. Tired tourists alighted from cars and took their booking forms into reception, returning minutes later to stroll into the shop or pass under the boom, their papers authorised. Jon had still not emerged after half an hour.

Inside the reception area, he was struggling.

They had come at a bad time. The computer system was down. The manager had her day off. The reception clerks were on lunch. A lone, rather junior and stupid-looking security guard had been left processing entries, and for some reason, he had taken a dislike to Jon.

Perhaps it was the smile. Jon Power did not use it much and he may just have lost the knack. Maybe it was his two-tone khaki shirt, his farmer's bearing, his warm hello in a local language that had turned out not to be the security guard's own. It's always a tricky business with 11 official tongues to choose from. Whatever the cause, the guard had initially refused Jon entry and had subsequently made him wait.

Jon had tried polite friendliness. He had tried reason and he had tried threats. All to no avail. There is a level of stupid, a degree of mulish that cannot be coerced, and the security guard had nowhere to be. Jon Power, on the other hand, had an eye on the clock. It would take two hours to reach Letaba, where

Moshoeshoe had said they had to spend the night, and it was already half-past three. At six, the gates to the camp would close.

Visitors to the Park had to be in camp by six, or... Or? Jon had no idea what would happen if they were late. He'd been coming to the Park since he was two years old and he had never had cause to find out. Kruger does that to people. Ordinarily libertarian, free-will types with minds of their own submit body and soul to the order that preserves beauty. Opening hours are like the constraints of a sonnet to such people.

The security guard's name badge said 'Isak'. His actual mouth said nothing at all to Jon Power.

"Boet, could you please take another look at my reservation, *please*, man."

Stony silence.

Shiny brown face with puffed-out cheeks and sulky mouth. Shiny bald head. Shiny boots. Polite to other customers, even friendly. But Jon? There was more chance of getting help from the stuffed Elephant head on the wall. The pastor stepped into the white glare, leaving the black glare behind him. He motioned to Incredulous to come and give it a try.

If anything, that made it worse. The surly guard went from obstructive to destructive, banging staplers and books on his desk with a force that knocked a vase onto the floor. The noise brought a smarter-looking ranger in from the backroom, sleepy-eyed and puzzled. Recognition flashed across his face as he took in the scene of angry shiny-head, Jon and Incredulous.

A conversation ensued in a language neither Jon nor Incredulous understood and, with much ill-feeling, the guard stomped off to a car beyond the gate, slammed the door, and sped off at what seemed to Jon to be more than the regulation 50 km/hour.

The sleepy ranger apologised, stamped their reservation, and wished them a pleasant stay.

When, a few hours later, they had arrived at Letaba, a bald head, still shiny despite an evident black cloud above it, was sitting in the guard hut at the still open wooden gates that barred entry after hours to cars and wild animals alike. He scowled darkly as they sailed past, Incredulous flipping a long, black-nailed finger out the window.

Cantus

Praise song for Incredulous Moshoeshoe

There are things you need to know about Incredulous Moshoeshoe.

That force of nature. That force of human will. That black tsunami of magic and reason in dark lipstick and lace.

Yes, there are things you need to know about Incredulous Moshoeshoe.

You think you know. You think because you know about his birth, about his origins in heroism and struggle, you know all about him. You know, or think you know, about his descent into the hell of unimaginative people, away from the soil that birthed him, because you have seen the pictures. Because you have bought the clothes and worn the wet mascara of his people, but you do not know.

You are like an émigré returned into the bosom of his mother earth to find that everything is more expensive than it was before, you are in no position to judge the real cost.

He it was, who crossed the oceans when a child to power.

*He, who tamed the tongue of the empire, who learned
its ways and cast them aside.*

He it was, who became like a god to men, a pillar of fire to women.

*Incredulous Moshoeshoe! Filler of floors! Hero of cool
and uncool alike!*

Black Goth! Black Briton! Black magician of the ancestors' way!

*Silver-fingered, steel-tongued teller of the ancient tales,
Incredulous Moshoeshoe!*

*You think you know about Moshoeshoe because you read a tale, you
heard a whisper of his prowess, like a cat, about his powers, like a
jungle magnate, stacking up the curses and the charms like so many
murders and acquisitions, and you think you know because the
people talk about his magic like a fairy tale.*

Well, the magic is real.

*But there are things you need to know about Incredulous
Moshoeshoe.*

There are things he, too, must know.

Bloody kisses
(A death in the family)

L impopo is not London. And it certainly isn't Camden. The province in South Africa's north-east, known in part in Jon Power's heyday, with Mpumulanga, as the Eastern Transvaal, is barely South Africa – if the South Africa you have in mind is upmarket Jozi gyms and Cape Town clubs. If Incredulous had seemed striking but, initially at least, unremarkable in the Alternative scene of Camden in the late 90s, flitting between British and South African clubs like an overpaid bat, he seemed somewhat more than striking in Limpopo, which had yet to resign itself fully to the fading of the 70s. Here, bats were still routinely burned out of their nests.

And while the Kruger Park is an oasis of quietly-managed, mod-con-intensive beauty in the retrograde province that depends on it for revenue, and though it is filled with foreigners from distant continents and futures, there is still something backwoodsian, something you're-not-from-round-here-esque about some of the places in Kruger where people mill about and congregate.

Perhaps it's the fact that many Limpopo locals frequent the Park. Or, perhaps, it is the spirit of the place, the years of hard-line, out-of-the-way resistance to change, and a suspicion that central government neither knows nor cares what local power brokers and homogeneous communities of privilege do. Perhaps that is the spirit that quietly possesses the more easy-minded of its visitors. Whatever the reason, there is an inherent conservatism about the place that finds expression in the people moving through it, wherever they come from.

That conservatism was currently staring at Incredulous Moshoeshoe and forgetting to eat its ice cream before it dripped on its shoes. Letaba rest camp is beautiful, welcoming, and cool, but many of the people who visit it as daytrippers are, as a rule, not.

The rings through Incredulous' nose and lip flashed like unforeseen lightning in the baking sun, and his black leather trousers shone like burnished belligerence. Kohl-lined and mascara'd into long-lashed extravagance, his eyes wore green contacts, and they, too, caught the sun. Bones and shells, bird claws, and coloured stones hung from a leather *riem* around his neck. It would have been a brave man who put money on there being anyone within 100 kilometres who looked even vaguely like Incredulous.

People nudged each other. Some pointed. A couple of burly white men in green-tan farm shirts, unbuttoned navel-deep, laughed aggressively over their lunchtime beers. It irritated Jon Power.

"You're making friends quickly here, Moshoeshoe," he said, his own eyes hard, hidden in the shade of a disgraceful old leather Stetson. There had been a brief month when hats like his had been in fashion, but Jon Power had missed it. He was not exactly metrosexual. More hobosexual.

Ordinarily, it was he who would have been on the receiving end of this kind of middle-class White South African bonhomie.

"I don't need any more friends," said Moshoeshoe, walking ahead of the pastor towards a congregation of yellow cars and flashing blue lights.

"Everybody needs friends," smiled the preacher, making little effort to keep up with the uncomfortably warm-looking Goth striding ahead of him.

"These people?" Moshoeshoe asked, lifting his chin at a large family in the parking area, checked midway through embarking or disembarking by the sight of the flamboyant black dandy.

"These people," said Jon quietly, "need a reason to say or do one damn thing to help you if one of those *boerseuns* decides to teach you a lesson."

"The day I need help from these people," Incredulous said, "please, for the love of God, kill me. Come on. We may be too late."

They were.

More police vans than Jon had thought existed in this part of the country were parked under the Maroela trees that cast their shade around an ablution block. Or what had been an ablution block. The charred walls were mostly standing, but the thatched roof was gone and an ugly morgue truck was parked with its jaws open, waiting by the charcoaled doorway.

Bored junior officers in their blue uniforms sat with their car doors open, sleeping or chatting, waving off flies. Some played music from their phones. None seemed to notice Jon and his attention-magnet companion. Like police everywhere, there was very little in everyday life that seemed strange to them. And besides, they had had their stimulation for the day. The air of boredom that usually accompanies the aftermath of tragedy lapped about the place. If there had been crowds, they, too, had succumbed to boredom and evaporated in the heat. Sirens, if there had been sirens, had been drowned out by quiet conversation, birdsong, and the intermittent buzzing of lazy flies.

A worried-looking group of senior officers, sleek and fat and hard-eyed, stood at the entrance to the ablution block, shooting glances of unaccustomed concern at another group, comprising Parks Board officials, men in suits, and a blonde woman in a simple trouser ensemble. Jon clocked at least two bodyguards for the woman, white men, built like rugby-playing cement trucks, all reflective sunglasses, and Terminator faces.

"What is this, Moshoeshoe?" Jon asked, eyeing the bodyguards uneasily.

"This is a fuck-up," the *isangoma* said, his whole manner subdued.

Jon glanced sideways at Incredulous.

"You alright? Seriously, what is this?"

"I'm fine. This is a murder."

One of the junior officers, who Jon would have sworn had been asleep, sprang up suddenly behind them and laid aggressive hands on Incredulous' shoulders.

"What do you know about it, then, eh? Hey, boss! I've caught you a suspect!"

Jon Power pulled back his fist and scanned the scene for the quickest exit, factoring in the likelihood of carrying a six-foot-nothing coffin kid as squirming living-deadweight, but someone checked his arm.

A startlingly good-looking man in an immaculate if slightly flashy suit smiled at him with the calm of immense strength and confidence.

"Not a good idea, my friend." His accent was not South African. Or, not fully. "Come." He had strong, handsome features, more refined than the bodyguards, and a soft, almost musical way of speaking. His hard jaw and slightly hooked nose were set in dark brown skin and he was accustomed to being obeyed. His red tie, thought Jon, probably didn't signal a very deep sympathy with socialism. With a small motion, he sent the officer back to his car and propelled Jon and Incredulous, one in each hand, towards the group with the woman at its centre.

It all happened so fast, Jon Power only became fully conscious of developments when he was standing before her. That's what fixers do. They fix without you noticing that they're fixing.

The woman had stopped talking and was looking up inquiringly at the handsome black man in the black suit with the red tie. His accommodating smile seemed surgically implanted and he didn't seem to sweat, even in the heat.

"I think this is the man you were looking for, ma'am."

"What?" protested Incredulous. "No, no! I was not even here last – "

"Last night?" the woman asked, her voice empty. "Last night when my daughter was killed?"

Dominion

Limpopo Herald, Sunday Edition

Aak de Nau death ruled 'accident'

Nelspruit - Police have ruled the death of Alida Aak de Nau, daughter of Public Protector, Elena Aak de Nau, an accident. Ms. Aak de Nau's body was found following a fire that destroyed a building in the Kruger National Park camp of Letaba and was identified using dental records. Alida Aak de Nau was 19 years old.

Arson investigators had been involved in the initial inquiry into the fire which is believed to have killed the prominent opposition politician's daughter, but subsequent investigations pointed to lightning as the cause. The blaze destroyed a public ablution block in the country's most popular tourist destination.

SA National Parks chief executive, Justine Piennaar, said that a full investigation into lightning safety in thatched huts would be undertaken, but that tourists need not be concerned over safety standards. "The Kruger National Park is a beautiful place with international-standard facilities.

We take every precaution to ensure safety in the Park, but we cannot protect people from acts of God," Piennaar said on Monday. "Our hearts go out to Ms. Aak de Nau's family. I have personally spoken to the Public Protector and, while she is devastated, she is satisfied that the death of her daughter was not due to any human malice or negligence."

Police have declined to comment on rumours that many in the staff community at the camp believe the death to have involved supernatural methods. "We are thinking more of lightning than the tokoloshe," Piennaar said during a lighter moment in today's press conference.

In her role as Public Protector, Elena Aak de Nau has led many high-profile investigations that have proved embarrassing for the ANC government, particularly since former President Nelson Mandela's death in 2013 was proven to be a hoax. Her appointment in January 2012 as Public Protector was seen by many commentators as a move towards building bridges between Aak de Nau's People's Democratic Federal Party and the ruling ANC.

Insiders have warned, however, that Mrs. Aak de Nau, who has one surviving daughter, Chanel (18), has made many powerful enemies through her campaigns against graft, bribery, and corruption. Aak de Nau's PDFP has made surprising advances in recent polls, largely attributed to their courting of the Christian vote and through their recent 'Demand Change Nau' poster campaign.

Alida Aak de Nau will be buried on Tuesday following a private funeral at Sola Deo Gloria Tabernacle church in Pretoria. President Jacob Zuma and several high-ranking government ministers are expected to attend. Police have been requested to keep picketers from the Radical Youth Movement away from the ceremony. RYM Chief Cadre, Scientist Likota, called the heavy police involvement in the investigation of Alida Aak de Nau's death "a classic case of capitalism protecting its own" and "a waste of workers' money on protecting the white ruling elite". The firebrand RYM leader said he would be raising questions in Parliament about what he called "a white conspiracy to defraud the nation of taxes and further line the pockets of the rich."

The Public Protector could have been carved from soapstone, like the pink and cream striped smooth bowls and curios sold on the road to the Park. Soft-looking, smoothed as if by a gentle hand, but more mineral than mammal. Even her voice had a brittle, powdery quality as she waved off her attendants and motioned to Incredulous follow her into the shade of a large sausage-plant tree, its pendulous fruits hanging threatening and heavy, waiting to fall. Jon Power followed, unbidden and undeterred by the woman or her flashy fixer.

"You are the one Chanel spoke to last night." She spoke it as fact, not question. "She told me this morning. She is... confused."

"She didn't seem confused to me."

Elena Aak de Nau's face gave away nothing. Immobile by necessity. A politician on a wave of loss.

"You may be right." The lines of her face relaxed very slightly. "I may not be the right person to..." she broke off and looked to her right, towards the vista of the riverbank, giant trees and smoothed animal drinking paths. "It is important to me that nothing," she hesitated, "*untoward* results from this accident."

"Ma'am," Incredulous began, "I don't believe this was an accident."

"No," said the Public Protector, impassively. "You don't. Chanel told me. Your reasons?" She asked as she would ask a shadow minister in her party for polling figures. Like an equal, but an equal whose position was far from unassailable. It had the effect of making one feel both elevated and on edge. Incredulous hesitated before speaking, gently.

"I see things."

"How?"

"In ways my grandmother taught me."

"A witch?"

"If you like."

Aak de Nau laughed with the softness of dry grass tearing in strong hands.

"I don't." She turned to Jon. "And you," she said, her eyes fixed on his, "Mr. Power. What are you doing involved with this... occultist?"

Jon Power had felt safe up to that point in his role as an impartial and anonymous observer. The mention of his name sent a shock of questions from his neck to his brain and down to suddenly cold hands. *Who else knew he was there?*

"Me?"

Aak de Nau nodded. Jon shifted uncomfortably; his fragile frame of reference pulled out from under him like a mixed metaphor.

"How..?" he asked, feebly.

"I have known about you for some time, Mr. Power. Or do you prefer 'Reverend'?"

"I'm not ordained."

Another brittle laugh.

"Aren't we all a priesthood of believers, Mr. Power? Apart from my other duties, I take a keen interest in certain... *religious* matters." She tasted the word slowly and seemed not to like it. "You are a player whose name and face have come across my desk before. Naturally, my people notified me that your name had been registered at the entrance to the Park. Your name has come up in connection with a number of exorcisms. In Limpopo."

"Every one of those people gave consent in –" Power started.

The public protector raised her hands with a smile as cool as an air-conditioned lounge.

"I'm on your side, Mr. Power. Or, rather, we're on the same side. We both want to see Satan lose his grip on this country. That's what you want, isn't it?"

"Yes." Power spoke with the matter-of-factness afforded by encountering a fellow believer.

"So do I. There is a plague on this country that we never talk about in Parliament. The old police squads set up to deal with it have been disbanded by our *rainbow nation*," – again she seemed not to like the words being in her mouth and spat them out like luke-warm filth. "Satanism, witchcraft, and the occult are rampant."

Incredulous chuckled, more as a matter of principle than actual amusement. Aak de Nau ignored him.

"It's not enough that this *government...*" – the word pealed like recently rung quotation marks in her mouth – "...is dragging us into socialism, corruption, and moral collapse. It's not enough that their supporters harass and attack those of my party who want to see change. No, they also want to see this country brought to its knees spiritually as well." She was warming. No longer the grieving mother, but a politician slipping comfortably into more familiar waters and being carried by the welcoming stream.

"Now we allow witchcraft to salt the foundations of our national monuments and false gods to be worshipped in Parliament. It's a curse, Mr. Power. And its effects are felt at every level. God's judgement is upon us."

Incredulous thought that this woman could easily lead churches or countries, given the chance. Her words seemed to lift and carry one in unintended directions. Jon Power, he noticed, listened impassively.

"It is always hard to serve God," said Power, matter-of-factly.

"Yes," the Public Protector smiled, "But it will be harder still if this country slips into chaos."

"You mean..."

"I mean that when Mandela goes, this country could plunge into civil war, Mr. Power."

"It didn't the first time," he said. "People have been predicting doom when the old man dies since he went into prison. And when we all thought the worst had happened, nobody died. Literally."

"That wasn't real. People can sense that."

"Can they, though?"

She ignored him. "This time, when he *really* goes, there will be chaos."

"Alright. But I suspect that you and your family have more pressing matters to deal with."

"Perhaps," she said, coolly. "But I have reason to believe that my daughter's death was not an accident."

Jon glanced dubiously at Incredulous and, recognising his thought, she continued,

"No, Mr. Power. Not because of what some deviant witch doctor says. It's not unconnected to our former President preparing, if he has any wisdom left, to meet his maker. I have enemies, Mr. Power. Violent enemies."

"You also, if I may say so, have friends."

"Indeed, Mr. Power. And they were not wrong about you. And you have aged well since the last photograph we have on file. Angola, was it?"

Incredulous perceived hardening in the *dominee.*

"Maybe."

"Oh, I think it was. The Truth and Reconciliation process may have conveniently erased many people's memories, Mr. Power, but records still exist."

"It was a long time ago. I am just a pastor now."

"Just a pastor? Really? You must be a true man of God to have such modesty. You are becoming very well known for your work in the field of deliverance, aren't you?"

Incredulous interjected, "This place does remind me of that movie." He sang half a bar of the banjo theme.

Aak de Nau turned a glacial smile on him. "Ah, Mr... it *is* 'Mr'? Mr. Moshoeshoe." She pronounced it to rhyme with pooh-pooh, and the smile hung like icicles on her face. "Your services will not be needed here. This is a crime. It requires an investigator. Not a necromancer."

Jon Power spoke before Incredulous could.

"Why me?"

"Because I need to act quickly and you are here. Because my sources tell me you need to be away from Komatipoort for a while. Because they also tell me you could do with some influential friends with the trouble you have. And I am not without influence."

"What trouble would that be?"

"Beauty and the Beast?"

Jon Power said nothing.

"Do you know what I mean?"

"Yes."

"Good. I think, then, we understand each other."

"Why don't you just ask the police. Judging by the number of cars here I can't imagine you'll have trouble getting top priority," Jon said.

"The police are idiots." The man in the shiny suit and red tie smiled at this. Aak de Nau continued, "Corrupt from top to bottom. If I waited for them to look into it I could wait years and hear nothing or get whatever answer I wanted in a day, complete with suspect, shot while trying to escape. I want the truth."

Jon Power nodded.

"I need you to tell me what happened to my daughter. I need you to do it quickly, and I need you to do it quietly. I don't need to tell you of the potential for unrest if the wrong information got out..."

"No."

"My supporters... certain... elements..."

"Yes."

"If a white girl, *my daughter*, is seen to have been murdered by my enemies..."

"The RYM?"

"Obviously, Mr. Power. They are very powerful. With your interest in the rulers and principalities, the dark powers of this world, I am sure you know that."

"Oh, please," Jon said impatiently, his cool slipping for the first time during their conversation. "They're a joke. They wouldn't have done this. Why would they?"

"You may not have noticed, Mr. Power, but they don't like my party and they don't like me. And they probably wouldn't like you, considering the colour of your skin."

Jon held his tongue.

"The point is, Mr. Power, you may believe them incapable, but many of my supporters do not. The past few years have not been kind to this country, and particularly not to my people. If the idea got out... well, I could not be held responsible."

Elena Aak de Nau's control seemed to flicker for a second. "It cannot happen, Mr. Power. If the RYM are responsible, I want you to find the individuals and turn them over to me. No police. No public attention. My daughter's killer will face justice, I promise you. But I need someone I can trust," she flashed a look at Incredulous, "and I cannot trust someone who consults the dead. You understand."

"Yes." He did. "But what if it is not RYM?"

"Then," she said, suddenly artificially sweet, "I will naturally let the law take its course. I am looking for justice, Mr. Power. My only concern is that it does not come at the cost of peace."

Jon Power nodded.

"And in exchange for your help, I can offer you the full support of the administration and courts in your unfortunate experience in Komatipoort. A tragic accident, but one that freedom of religion should protect if only the people with understanding and insight can be put on the case."

Jon Power's face was set. "Thank you."

"No, thank *you,* Mr. Power. My people will contact you."

Jon Power made to move back to the car when she continued, "Oh, and Mr. Power?"

"Yes?"

"Keep an eye on this," she motioned towards Incredulous with distaste, "investigator. He has been engaged by my daughter and she has the means and the will to keep him investigating. I need you to go with him."

"And what if I don't want him with *me*?" said Incredulous.

The large man in the shiny suit moved so quickly Incredulous was on the ground before Jon could spin 'round.

"You will accept it." smiled Aak de Nau.

Jon Power helped Incredulous back to the car. To the evident pleasure of the onlookers, he was bleeding from a cut under one black-rimmed eye. A mother in a floral tent of a dress laughed with her blue-eyed toddler and handed her another *koeksister*.

"Nice people, you Christians," Incredulous said.

"We're not all the same," said Jon, helping Incredulous into the passenger seat of his black stretched *bakkie*. A bunch of people had already been staring at the vampire-batmobile. Now they had a show.

"Well, I guess this makes us partners. I bags Turner. You can be Hooch."

"I haven't decided anything," said Jon, the baking heat of the car making him sweat. "But we can both be Turner. I'll be Ike."

Incredulous smiled, closing his eyes and leaning back in his seat as Jon started the car. "Not bad, Dominee."

Jon Power smiled briefly, reversed the car, and began to pray.

Vision thing

In the seventh year of the reign of President Zuma – or was it the ninth, I'm so bad with dates – after Nkandla, anyway, but before the hearings and the indictment and the plane crash. Before all that, the Word of the Lord came to me.

The Lord said to me that I had been right to run from Komatipoort, that He did not require me to be punished, and I received peace about the deliverance and about Beauty. He said that it wouldn't kill me to call my Mom and that I should get checked out for prostate cancer. The Lord is nothing if not practical.

I prayed fervently for Beauty, for her spirit or her soul, or whatever it really is. I did not know if there was any point, but I believed that it could do no harm. I felt nothing from the Lord and heard nothing about Beauty and whether she was saved. I asked forgiveness once again for the men I have killed and those I have failed. And I wept before the Lord and He gave me peace.

I prayed for the poor of our land and for justice. I prayed for the captives to be set free and the strongholds, principalities, and powers of Mammon to be thrown down among the idols of the past, and I prayed for the soul of my friend Caiaphas, that he would meet the

Lord. And the Lord showed me that my cause – Caiaphas' cause – was just, and I felt free to continue in its service. But the Lord cautioned me through Scripture to be careful and to guard my lips. I also read a Proverb about giving alcohol to the sad and the poor and I was amused.

I was uneasy before the Lord about the necromancer and offered to the Lord my willingness to withhold from him and any people detestable to the Lord, my help. But the Lord was silent. Which was a bloody nuisance.

But the Lord my God spoke to my spirit and told me I might seek justice for the murdered girl. And when I asked Him how and with whom He was silent again.

I decided to stay another night and booked into the camp with the diviner.

We slept early and I dreamed.

The Lord showed me a picture that I understood. A man was eating at the wedding banquet. A rich banquet. And another sat with nothing. The feasting man praised the Lord with a mouth full of food and the food that fell from his mouth rotted on the floor. And a great tsunami of blood rose up against the man.

Then the Lord showed me a picture I did not understand. A wave of blood stood poised at the tip of our continent. The shadow of a bird. And the sound of thunder.

I gave thanks to the Lord and prayed that I would have wisdom with the necromancer and that my car would continue to run smoothly.

I spent the next day in the necromancer's car in the Park, giving thanks to the Lord for his creation and for some time alone. In the evening we decided to investigate as the police were gone.

I prayed before we went, and prayed for Moshoeshoe's soul and that we would have victory in our endeavours.

I asked also for a victory for the Bulls on Saturday, but I promised to the Lord that my faith would not require it.

God is good.

Night Shift

The cicada rhythms filled the air like maracas on a scratch-loop. Cicadas: aside from the pitch-shifted biplane of the mosquito or the click-hiss of a beer can sweetly opening, no other sound more epitomises the bushveld night. Jon and Incredulous crunched down the sand path to the ruined ablution block, the cicadas forming a background to the sounds of the camp at night. The occasional clang of the big tin bins. A car door closing or a muffled laugh. Crickets and nightjars and the distant, almost musical moan of a lion.

The night was moonless and the sky was unfathomably big, shot through with stars. Eyes accustomed to the dark, they walked quickly, silently, to the scene of the crime. The air was warm and still and laced with charcoal fires. Jon Power felt calmer for a day in the bush. Moshoeshoe felt calmer for a day in the camp coffee shop. A day with Wi-Fi.

The ablution block loomed, a jagged void in the salt-spray of stars, seeming larger and somehow more present for the destruction visited on it, as some people do. The smell of wet smoke and the clicking of charred timber. A blackened, blistered door which had grown a fresh padlock and a police notice. The melted, shattered windows with their scorched rims made the place look eyeless.

Jon did the breaking-in with ease and Incredulous made no comment. It wasn't the night for it. The building seemed to sigh as they shut the door. The ceiling was made of stars.

"What are we looking for?" asked Incredulous, his voice echoing too much in the large, tiled room.

Jon did not answer.

"Well, come on super-sleuth," Incredulous whispered. "The lady chose you. Where do we start?"

Jon looked around. Dried ash-mud and pieces of timber. The space where the body had lain, almost apologetic for its emptiness. Melted tiles in the shower cubicle.

Jon Power felt uneasy in his spirit and could not discern whether the recent presence of death, the breaking of laws, or the proximity of a diviner was the cause. He found it hard to pray. The occultist intruded on his thoughts.

"Why did she choose you anyway? Who are you?"

"I'm a pastor."

"That is not the reason," Incredulous replied, and Jon cut him off before he could continue.

"I was an investigator," he said.

"Police?"

"More military."

"'*More*' military? What does that mean? The army?"

"Something more… clandestine. It didn't have a name."

"Where?"

"Angola. For a while, a long time ago."

Incredulous whistled.

"Angola? Should I be worried? You going to cut my throat with piano wire?"

"I don't have any piano wire."

Jon had meant it as a joke but Incredulous had not laughed.

For a while they were quiet, their soles crunching through ash and the occasional submarine pulse of a Scops Owl.

"What kind of investigator?" Incredulous asked at length.

"Special forces."

"I didn't think you people had MPs."

"Only when things went," Jon hesitated, "very wrong." He shifted a charred beam caked in grey ash with his shoe. "I wasn't an MP. I was more… informal."

"So, you have a lot of experience? A lot of 'cases'?" Moshoeshoe fired the last word like a rubber bullet. Power seemed not to notice.

"I did enough. Wait."

"What?"

"What's that up there?"

Jon was pointing high up one of the remaining walls. A black pattern with lighter patches was just visible in the ambient light that trickled through the window sockets.

"Bat droppings?"

"You're a Goth, you say?"

"Hilarious. What, then. Insect nests?

"No."

"It could be blood?"

"Nobody said anything about blood. She was supposed to have died in a fire."

"Wait. Let's try this..." Incredulous pulled a small torch from his bag.

"No lights," said Jon, with a firmness that irritated Incredulous. The *Isangoma* flicked the slightly odd-looking flashlight on. The pastor-investigator shut his eyes and clenched his jaw, but there was no flood of incriminating light, nothing streaming out of the windows to alert any wandering security guard. Just a strange glow.

"It's a blacklight. UV. You know, like on CSI," said Moshoeshoe, his teeth, eyes, and a few ultraviolet facial tattoos glowing, ghoulishly. "From my nightclub days. Got loads for checking stamps at the door."

Jon Power nodded vaguely. Nightclubs had never really been his natural habitat. Incredulous aimed the purple glow at the wall.

"Yes," he said. "Weird. It's blood. It's glowing. How the hell did it get up there?"

"Hard to tell," said Jon, "unless we can get a better look at the spray pattern."

"Okay, hold this." Incredulous passed the blacklight to Jon and pulled out his phone. "I need to get a picture."

A high-pitched keening cry seemed to come from a long way off. A bird of the African night.

"*Hammerkop*," muttered Jon, mildly puzzled, staring blindly into the black dome above him. "They're not usually noct—...." Suddenly, his mind caught up with what Incredulous was doing, but he was too late.

The camera pinged, its flash hardening the soft black shadows around them into the crisp shell of a building in an instant, hurting their eyes and making the darkness above them seem infinitely deep. The stars switched off.

Something in the dark startled into a panicked scramble, toppling masonry from the high-point of the remaining wall above them. A reptile that had found a safe place to rest, or a bird. The force of its panic sent the burnt rampart of the upper wall into a teetering collapse. A loud crash.

"We need to go," said Jon to the space behind him. Incredulous was at the door, holding it open.

They kept to the shadows of huts and buildings as they made their way back to their chalet. The rush of feet they had anticipated materialised only as a sleepy guard, who peered through a window in the charcoaled structure, swore, and walked irritably back to his post to sleep.

"Should we go back?"

"No," said Jon. "No point. Nothing to see. Well, nothing more."

"More than what?"

Jon Power walked for a while without answering, crickets and the sounds of noisy sleep from open windows they passed filling the time. Eventually, he said,

"It's just strange. The fire seems to have been the hottest near the body. Actually, in the shower."

"Yeah?"

"Well, that's not how a thatch fire works. Not from a lightning strike. But the shower cubicle had basically melted. Ceramic tiles. Melted. Do you know what kind of heat that would take?"

"Yes, of course. Doesn't everyone? Massively into arson, me."

"Well trust me. That's weird. And then there's the blood. So high. Arterial spray."

"I'm no expert," said Moshoeshoe, "but I'm pretty sure that's not normal for a fire, right?"

"No."

"Do you think the public protector was telling us everything?"

"No."

They didn't see the stranger until they were basically on top of him.

"What the actual fuck!" Incredulous shouted.

An old man, about as broad as he was tall, had stepped out of the shadow of one of the chalet huts. Toothless and pale, he caused both men to recoil. He wore an old, filthy khaki shirt, unbuttoned almost to the waist, and his white flabby chest was crisscrossed in what first appeared to be hair but, when he stepped into a dirty puddle of light, turned out to be a network of scars. Burns and cuts. Hundreds of them. He spoke Afrikaans.

"The Lord killed that girl, you know," He said. "It was the Lord. You guys should pay attention. Be aware. The Lord is not made a fool of. Children who stray from the path will face his wrath, no matter who their parents are."

Jon Power's Afrikaans was good. Incredulous Moshoeshoe's just good enough to get the gist. The pastor replied,

"I'm sorry, uncle. What do you mean? What girl?"

"Don't you fucking talk shit to me," the old man replied, spittle forming white flecks at the corner of his mouth. It was like he was looking through them. His eyes seemed to elude the light. "You and this black heathen. I fucking know you, and him, you piece of shit. Filth. I know you. Filth! You're both going to die, like her, because you mock the Lord. You wait. You watch!"

A crunch on the sand path behind them broke the spell and made them jump. The man fell silent, looking at the ground, not making any move to leave.

"I see you've met Piet," a large silhouette said in a friendly voice, an unfamiliar accent. "Don't listen to him. He's a little simple."

The silhouette stepped forward into the little pool of light where Incredulous and Jon had stopped and the sounds of the bush seemed to flood back as if a fader had been gently pushed up.

Incredulous started to say, "Hey, you, you prick..." but Jon Power touched his arm and silenced him.

"Good evening," he said, offering a hand. "I'm Jon Power. We met this afternoon."

"Mine's Kabila. Jean-Pierre Kabila. I'm sorry about earlier..."

"Sorry? Oh, well that's fine then. You fucking hit me!" Incredulous was trying not to sound whiny.

"I apologise. My employer... Well, she likes a show of force, and she doesn't like you. I had very little choice."

"It's not a problem, Mr. Kabila. You know this man? Is he unwell?"

"He's fine. He helps with some of the *practical* aspects of our campaign." The man with the hooked nose and the beautiful suit seemed to shudder as he said the word. Practical. His face was smooth, his clothing incongruously immaculate for the bush, his fingernails extraordinarily long and well-manicured. He had about him a sense that he had not always known civility. It clung close like an old-fashioned cologne. "He's harmless," Kabila said, "but a little strange when he drinks. I hope he hasn't upset you?"

The white man called Piet did not look up even once as the black man was talking. Pig-like eyes, watery and weak, focused on the shadowy ground at his feet, his slack, empty mouth making habitual chewing motions while the taller, better-dressed man spoke.

"No, no. We were just a bit startled."

"Out for a stroll?" Kabila smiled, his large black eyes glittering with amusement.

"Are you?"

"My chalet is here. No bathroom, sadly. All booked up by the time we got here. I've been abluting. There's a small ablution block behind the restaurant that not a lot of people know about and most of my party haven't seen. It's clean. Funny what passes for luxury here."

"In Kruger?" asked Jon.

"Sure."

Piet started to mumble something, still looking at the ground, and Kabila silenced him, poking a slender, long-nailed finger into the man's chest.

"Nobody wants to hear what you have to say, Piet. Go to bed."

The pathetic creature shuffled off.

"I'm sorry gentlemen. It's best not to listen to the defective. Or to gossip. You won't believe the kinds of things I've been hearing from the labourers in this camp."

"I can't imagine," said Jon.

"No," smiled Kabila. "No, you can't. Best not to give oxygen to the fire, don't you agree?"

"Yes."

"Well, then, I will bid you good night. Will we be seeing you tomorrow?"

"Quite possibly."

"Sweet dreams."

Kabila took Jon's hand and squeezed it. Every hair on the white man's neck and arms stood on end.

When he and Incredulous got back to their chalet, a human form seemed to be roosting in the shadows by the door.

Some kind of stranger

She was drunker than a Christian girl had a right to be. But bad Christian girls are hard to find. And she did not, Jon Power thought, look entirely good, morally speaking. Nor was she entirely unattractive. Some (not a respectable pastor, you understand) would have said she had a body lovingly moulded from still-wet clay by very grateful hands. Some might have described her hair as being long and golden-white as savannah grass in winter and her eyes as 'round and big and blue enough to have been drawn by a Japanese animator.

She was a cliché in a pretty summer dress, with her head expectantly and unhappily in a bucket bin.

When Jon Power and Incredulous had returned to their chalet (little more than a hut with *twin* beds, Jon Power had been quite insistent, eyeing Incredulous in a dubious sort of way as they booked in), she had been there, curled on the *stoep*. Incredulous went immediately to her side and gently woke her. Drunk girls were waters where he habitually swam.

Jon stood back, inhaling the scent of the bushveld and staring at the infinite concave of sky above him, trying to take his thoughts about the girl captive. He was always weaker when he was tired.

Taking thoughts captive – impure, unhelpful thoughts – that was the advice he had received as a young man and it had stood him in good stead. But some were wily and evasive. Some thoughts would not be captured without a fight. They had to be subdued, blindfolded, and made to dig their own grave before being beaten righteously to death with their own shovel.

Incredulous sat down next to her and Jon walked straight past them into the chalet, muttering about teenagers and drinking and parents and discipline, allowing the mosquito mesh door to spring back with a slam behind him. Insects congregated around the stoep light like tow trucks around a dangerous intersection.

"Who is she?" the pastor asked from inside the chalet.

"She's drunk. She is…"

"She can't stay here," the pastor interrupted. He made the declaration and turned to find the girl now inside their bedroom, the isangoma behind her.

"We may need to talk to her," Incredulous Moshoeshoe replied.

"If you think I'm sharing a room with you and some…" He did not get to finish his sentence.

"I'm Chanel Aak de Nau."

Jon Power was silent for a long while, looking at the girl, then the floor, then back at her again.

"You're…" Jon Power lingered on the word, hanging uncomfortably between optimism and realisation.

"I'm Alida's sister. Yes."

"And your mother..."

"Is Elena Aak de Nau. The woman who threatened, instructed, or employed us, or whatever the fuck it is she did, to investigate," said Moshoeshoe.

"Please watch your language," said Jon reflexively, instantly regretting it.

"Or what?" Moshoeshoe, squared up to the older man, looking at him as if for the first time. Grizzled and greying beard. Hard jawline. Sunken eyes and a strong brow. Short-cropped, almost military hair, also dusted with grey. At this moment, suspended in apparent surprise and self-doubt, the preacher seemed somehow less imposing.

"Chanel is *my* client," he said, his face inches from the pastor's.

"I'm sorry," Jon said quietly. When he sat heavily down on the Parks Board bed (never a very good idea, even for the young), Incredulous could no longer maintain his irritation and sat down as well. Jon Power leaned over to the little fridge and opened it. He threw a beer to the isangoma, looked at Chanel, the black rings under her red eyes, skin-like stretched tissues and decided she'd had enough.

"Miss Aak de Nau," said Jon Power quietly, "I'm sorry. I thought you were a drunk teenager from one of the campsites."

"Well, I am still a little drunk," she said, more steadily than Jon expected. "And I am a teenager. I was looking for Mr. Moshoeshoe. I have something to tell him."

"Where have you come from?"

"Komatipoort."

"For your mother?"

"For my sister."

"And why are you *here*?" He indicated the small room, their chalet – what generations of visitors to the Park had called a 'hut'.

"I'm worried about Paprika."

"Allergies, or just over spicing?"

Neither Incredulous nor Chanel laughed.

"Papps is my friend. Paprika Hendl. She was Alida's friend really. I called her today when I heard about Alida. She and Alida were close. She's not replying to my calls and none of her friends have heard from her either."

"Look, Chanel," Incredulous said, gently, "I told you this afternoon, I'm already looking into your sister. I promised you that. I need to focus …"

"Papps was here, with Alida, the week before she died. The camp office said she checked out a few days ago. But I can't get hold of her. I'm worried, Incredulous."

The men exchanged glances.

"What can I do about it, though?"

"Can you do another reading?"

"I'll leave you alone for a while," said Power, as he pushed the creaking mesh door open, stepping out into the night.

She's lost control

Paprika Hendl's diary

   He promised me tomorrow. At the Krone. The drive took forever, but he was insistent. Privacy. He's going to meet me there. Been driving all day. Battery dead, not spoken to Alida, not to anybody. I guess I should get used to being separate from them. I'm so excited I can hardly breathe. The next time I write, I will stand above all the posers and the fakes, forever. Tonight he'll give me what she didn't deserve. Tonight, I will be reborn.

The Egoli Krone Hotel ("two stars, free DSTV") in Roodepoort is not a great hotel. I know that. But I've stayed in some shit-holes and I survived. Of course, I did.

   This little bitch wouldn't know the difference. A little nervous. Light smell of sweat and the anticipation of sex in the air. They do like a bit of rough.

   Not that I'd describe myself as rough. But to a white girl, it doesn't matter how well-groomed you are. You could be Operations

Director at Anglo or Vice President, when she's in bed with you, she's riding Shaka fucking Zulu. Bayete, Inkosi.

The location is less than stylish but necessary.

She's been waiting, a little miff, for about an hour. I tell her I've had business, which is not a lie, and that I've flown to get here. And she is relieved, if not happy to see me. She's lit candles. So many fucking candles, she must have had to bring them in a valise, and the crappy little room is rank with patchouli incense. Merde. These fucking people.

She says "Hello baby," and "How are you, precious?" and how she was afraid I'd changed my mind. She says she's happy I haven't. She thinks she's in a novel. She thinks she's in a franchise movie. She deserves what she is about to get.

She says, "So do you want to start right away, or do you want to play around a bit first?" She's acting playful, but I can smell she is afraid. Turned on and afraid. If I didn't have to do this, perhaps I still would.

The Highveld thunderstorm is roaring outside and she jumps a little with the flashes and bangs.

"Jis," she says, "It's hectic, hey?"

Yes, I say. Come here.

And she does. Makes to kiss me and I let her. Why not? She's running her tongue along my teeth. Ha. Oh no, girl. That is not the way this works.

She's begging me to fuck her and I say yes again because I am kind like that. Because I am a one-man pan-African outreach. Because I've been told to. Because this is how it works. And I fuck her like Samuel Jackson. I fuck her like Joseph Kony.

She is frightened but still able to enjoy it and it takes some time. She thinks she is passing through the storm.

She has come. I have come. And we are sitting, facing one another on the floor. She says, like a stupid child, "The carpet..." And I tell her not to worry. It's not our carpet. And besides. It won't make a difference.

She says, "I'm ready." Brushes sweaty strings of hair from the nape of her neck and leans back, head to one side, eyes closed.

They open when my wings unfold.

They widen and she cannot scream, will not scream, because they are strange and beautiful and surprisingly agile, long feathered tips flexing. Red and black. I beat them once, gently, and all the candles go out.

She asks, in the darkness, quietly, unable to move from where I hold her, squirming from the sharp claws in her skin, "Are you an angel?"

She really is very stupid.

"No, Paprika. I am not."

"Good," she says, and I can hear her smile with all the certainty and mental structure of a pentagram on a high-school book bag.

"Make me into one of you," she sighs.

What I make of her is a meal.

And in the ensuing and highly contained electrical storm that follows, I make a bit of a mess. If it's not too Eurocentric a reference, I am the Keith Moon of monsters.

This is the real me.

Peepshow

Jon re-entered the room gingerly, looking around as if he expected to see sigils on the walls and levitating furniture.

"Black mass over," smiled Moshoeshoe, "it's safe to come in."

"You..." Jon Power paused. Chanel was wiping tears from her face, sitting where he'd left her.

"We made contact," said the isangoma.

"With ... ?" Jon Power was still standing at the door. He tried not to look around the room for chicken entrails.

"With a phone."

Incredulous was gentler than Jon had expected.

"What's wrong?"

Chanel said, "Papps is dead."

"Wait, what?"

"I called her phone again. This time someone answered. A black dude. That's not unusual for Papps," Chanel smiled, "She is a lot like Alida in some ways. But this guy sounded different. I asked him who he was and he just asked my name. Asked if I had spoken to Miss Hendl before last night. If she had mentioned anyone, any plans."

"A boyfriend?"

"The police. He called Papps 'the deceased' and I said, 'What? Is Paprika dead?' and he hung up. Her phone was off after that, but I eventually got through to Mrs. Hendl and she was crying. Papps was found dead in a hotel this evening. An hour or two ago. The place was on fire but they managed to get it under control."

"I've been there," said Moshoeshoe. "It's basically made of asbestos."

"I am so sorry, my girl." The pastor in Jon came out automatically in these situations. "Would you like me to pray with you?"

"You're kind, pastor, but I am fine. I haven't seen Papps in a long time. As long as I've not seen my sister. I had only made contact recently because I had started to get worried about Alida. And now this. It's probably just a coincidence, but it's still..."

"There are no coincidences."

Incredulous and Jon spoke the words at the same time and immediately looked embarrassed.

"I don't think so either, Mr Power. Mr Moshoeshoe and I," She was tired and pronounced it like footwear to Jon Power's evident pleasure, "think we need to go to Skukuza. Tonight. To... investigate."

"Well, we can't. Gates are closed. And anyway, why could this not wait until tomorrow?"

"Alida's body will be stored there. They have a small hospital. A morgue. They will keep her there until gates open tomorrow and then they will transport her back to Nelspruit for better examination."

"An Aak de Nau death will be taken to Pretoria."

"Whatever. Point is, they are going to move it."

"We could go tomorrow, first thing."

"That will be too late," Incredulous said.

"People don't wait long to bury the dead in the Lowveld," the girl agreed.

"No, they don't," he agreed. "They'll bury her tomorrow if they can. They've already ruled it an accident I think."

"Then we need to see the body tonight if we're ever going to get the chance."

Jon Power laughed. "But this is my point! Why would we want to see the body?"

"Well, you said it yourself, there are no coincidences," the girl said. "Papps was with Alida this week. Now she's dead. This was not an accident."

"If there's a connection, a similarity..." agreed Moshoeshoe, "then, first of all, we are looking at murder. Second of all, it may have nothing to do with the RYM."

"Have either of you," Jon Power asked, "heard of coroners? Police? We could learn everything we need from their reports."

"Do you think they will let you just read their reports?" Incredulous replied with matching sarcasm.

"Yes." The dominee said it simply and without any trace of doubt.

"And what if..." Incredulous was hunched forward, his dread-locks like bead curtains across his face.

"And what if the report has been tampered with?" Chanel interrupted. Incredulous nodded.

"My mother is important," she said.

"Debatable, historically speaking."

"You know what I mean. Chances are, this gets covered up."

"She did say she wanted you to investigate because the police would uncover either exactly what she wanted or exactly what her enemies did," Incredulous Moshoeshoe said. "You know there's no objectivity when it comes to politics in this country."

"And what if it was something to do with her?" Chanel said.

"Oh, come on now!" Jon's eyes were not laughing as he chuckled. "Elena Aak de Nau, opposition politician, and hotel murderer? Anyway, she was *here* yesterday!"

"If Papps had anything to do with my sister's death, Mr. Power, my mother would have the desire and the influence to hurt her. She hated Alida being friends with Papps. She gave up on me a long time ago, but she and Alida were closer. Generally." She said the last word as if remembering something but pushed on. "Mr. Power, if she thought Paprika had got Alida involved in something – and she often worried about Papps's influence on Alida – there is no coroner in South Africa who she could not reach."

"But what point is there?" the white man asked. "We're not doctors, not morticians. What would we even look for? We don't know…"

"We don't know anything," Incredulous interrupted. "That's the point. But two deaths in three days, girls who knew each other, both in fires. There's got to be a connection. And anyway. You were an investigator. You telling me you've never examined a body before?"

"No," Jon Power said simply.

"Well then. Right now, all we have is a hot fire and a spray of blood. We need more."

"A spray of what?" Chanel asked.

"Nothing, I'm sorry. The point is, Dominee, that we're not going to see Paprika's body or the Joburg fire. But maybe we could learn something from Alida's remains."

Jon Power sighed with resignation. "Alright. Alright. Let's assume that there is a connection – though let's remember there might not be. There's still nothing we can do. The earliest we can leave is first thing tomorrow, and the body will be gone by the time we get to Skukuza."

"Exactly," said Moshoeshoe, rising.

"What now?" asked Jon Power, lightly. "What do you see? A vision? A sign in the stars? Or maybe a way to examine a body after it's been buried for a day?"

"I see," said Incredulous, packing bits and pieces into a shiny black messenger bag, "that we need to get to Alida's body tonight. I see we need to sneak out of this camp. And I see a fat old white *doos* sitting on his arse instead of getting a move on."

Jon Power chuckled and creakily got to his feet. Decisive orders had always given him more cause for respect than a man's rank or lack thereof. It was one of many reasons he had had to leave the permanent force, apart from his vocations. He started to pack his bags. "Well, Ms. Aak de Nau," he said, turning to the girl, "are you ready to break the law?"

⸺

"What, *exactly*, are you asking me to do?" Chanel was standing now, beside the car, significantly more together than she had been when she woke up on their *stoep*. And significantly less compliant. It was far from imperceptible now that her mother was the granite-willed woman who had sent Jon Power to investigate.

"We are asking," Incredulous said, taking a breath and repeating what he had already repeated several times, "for you to distract the guard."

The light above the little hut at the wooden gates shone yellow in the night, an improbably dense quantum cloud of insects surrounding it like too many electrons. The shiny bald head stared straight ahead, out of the camp. The sound of a radio, thinly tuned to a soccer game commentated in Venda or possibly Xhosa or some other language Moshoeshoe did not speak, drifted over to them in waves as they sat in the idling car, its lights dimmed behind a hedge of aloes and succulents in the darker shadows.

"How?" she asked, arms. crossed. "*How* would you like me to distract him?" She was going to make them say it.

"Well..." Incredulous shifted uncomfortably in the seat next to her, casting imploring looks at Jon Power in the back seat.

"You know..." said Jon Power. "*Distract* him."

"How?"

"You know..." said Incredulous, achieving nonchalance with the ease and effectiveness of Richard Dawkins trying to sound pleasant.

"I don't, actually," she said.

It was never this hard on TV.

"We want you to use..." Jon said with care, "your feminine wiles."

"Are you asking me to prostitute myself?" she asked, managing to sound shrill and reproachful in an angry whisper.

"No, no! Of course not!"

"Chanel, *no*!" agreed the dominee. "But if you could maybe use your, um... influence... You're a very pretty girl, you know, and maybe..."

"Maybe what?"

"Maybe you can convince him."

Incredulous had not managed to. The surly face and puffy little cheeks he recognised from the gate had darkened when he had sauntered up, casual as he could, to the little guard hut.

They had not lightened when Incredulous had offered a couple of hundred Rand. Nor had the forecast seemed more promising when he had offered a few thousand. When Incredulous appealed to his better nature, hail, thunderstorms, and possibly showers of frogs seemed to be on the horizon. First-born sons shivered. The camp gate was closed. It was illegal and against orders to allow anyone to pass outside the camp. The gate would open at 6 am, not before. Incredulous had returned, defeated.

"Chanel," Jon said, "Have you ever kissed a man you didn't love?"

"What?"

"I am asking you. Have you ever..."

"Yes," she cut him off. "But..."

"And was that all that bad?"

"Mr. Power, that is not..."

"Ah, Chanel, not 'Mr', it's *Reverend*. The reverend is asking you for just a little sacrifice..."

"A little sacrifice!"

"Yes."

"This is disgusting. When you see it in movies, you never think about it, but it's disgusting. What if he … ?"

"Absolutely not. If he asks you to do anything immoral you should say no and we will find another way. But if you can... Well, I mean, if you can convince him. If you can flirt..."

"*Just* flirt?"

"Sure. And maybe touch a little..."

"*Touch!*" Chanel shouted, making the guard look over in their direction.

They all kept very still and he went back to staring out at the bush, a sentinel of stone.

For a while, it was all crickets and cicadas and the occasional call of a nightjar.

"Well, not if you don't want to," whispered Jon, eventually. "But you want to find out what happened to Alida, don't you?"

"Yes."

"And we need to get out."

"Yes."

"Well, then, maybe if you could try..."

"Hmph."

Chanel closed the door more loudly than she needed to. More loudly than one needed to on a tank. The sound was shortly followed by the clicking of impractically high heels on paving as she made her way to the guard's hut.

She had not been gone long before she returned, smiling.

"He's going to let us through?" Jon said, excitedly.

"No, *Reverend*," she smiled. "Well, not just yet. He says he will. But he asks for *you*."

A slow and heavy tread carried Jon towards the hut.

Incredulous and Chanel could not see very well through the gaps in the succulent hedge, but they could hear that the soccer channel had been switched to one playing music. And through the window of the hut, once or twice, they saw Jon Power moving. There was a grim rhythm in it. Dancing. They could hear clapping. Incredulous was sure that he had seen a great deal of bare pale skin, but Chanel had said he was imagining it.

Still, when he came back ten minutes later, Jon Power had a look in his eyes like the one they wore on his return from Angola. A look that said he had seen things. Done things. Terrible things.

Incredulous could not have been happier.

With lights and engine off, Incredulous and Chanel pushed the car through the gates under the smiling and benevolent gaze of Isak the security guard, who reminded them not to start the car until they were two kilometres from camp. Over his shoulder, glancing back to the dim, receding light, Incredulous thought he could make out a happy wave.

Garden of Delight

Jon Power sat in the driver's seat, steering, while the other two pushed, neither speaking nor offering to help. And though both Incredulous and Chanel felt exposed clinging to the outside of the car in the infinite black of the bush – vulnerable and *watched* even – neither of them thought it wise to ask for any. It was *very* dark. And they were very exposed, walking in the warm night air of a game reserve well stocked with predators.

The rolling crunch of the tyres and the sound of their breath could not completely blot the sounds of birds, of far-off hyaenas and jackals, the occasional heart-palpitating rushes crashing through the bush as startled, startling animals ran.

After a while, neither Incredulous nor Chanel bothered to look around into the darkness. Doing so just seemed to turn up the volume. Occasionally, though, they would look at each other and smile.

Two rather fretful, sweaty kilometres out of camp in the pitch dark, all the rangers' stations left behind and the lights dimmed, they started the car and made their way towards Skukuza. For several hours, neither the Isangoma, nor the beautiful girl with the improbably blonde hair mentioned their departure from the camp. The pastor's face seemed to forbid it. But Jon Power was not thinking about the guard or his dance. He was troubled in his spirit. He was sensing a warning. He switched the headlights to dim, just to be extra safe.

The crash was inevitable.

To Incredulous, it felt familiar, somehow. Though he couldn't have told you why.

The only light was the flickering rays of their headlamps, in which the steam from their hard-driven radiator rose in a white cloud. The black bonnet was buckled against the sickly green of a fever tree. For a moment, the hiss of steam, the unsteady trickle of liquids, and the clink of relaxing metal were all they could hear. It would be minutes before the sound of the bush would stalk back in.

Jon Power had been driving faster than he should have been. The smooth tarmac of the Kruger Park roads, worn fine over decades of millions of tyres going at moderate speed, give one false confidence.

They had turned off the tar because they'd seen, far in the distance on the main road to Skukuza, the lights of a car. Probably a night patrol or rangers moving between camps. Either way, unwelcome. And Jon Power had not reduced his speed significantly at all, comfortable as he was with dirt roads and the rhythmic rumble and dust they create. The road was a river loop and would take them far enough from the main road for safety if the rangers didn't stop.

Soon they were hemmed in with trees, which in places arched right over the roadway 'til they passed as through a tunnel. Occasionally the ambient light threw up a vision of great frowning rocks, guarding the road. It did not illuminate the bird standing in the middle of the road, though, until it was too late. A *Hammerkop*, bigger than Jon Power had ever seen, standing in silhouette against the desaturated tan of the path before them. At least he thought it was a *Hammerkop*. It had the hammer-shaped head for which it had been named, but it was darker than the familiar chocolate brown all bushveld people know. Almost black against the road. Light seemed to glint off its small black eyes as it turned, in slow motion, towards the car and – Jon Power swore later – flew directly at the windscreen.

A forest

Now they were walking. Miles from anywhere, in the Kruger Park night. Walking without a car to jump into.

You do not want to be walking in the Kruger bush at night unless you have a rifle. A rifle, several big, athletic men with bigger rifles, and a good supply of slow-running fat people. Just in case.

The Kruger Park is not a zoo. It is also fairly rare as a game park in that its more interesting species are not fed by Park officials to make them easier to locate for tourists. Its lions, leopards, hyaenas, and wild dogs hunt all over the Park. Mostly at night.

If you can forget about the very respectable selection of deadly venomous snakes (from lazy Puffadder to terrifyingly aggressive Black Mamba), and it's probably best that you do, the bush around you is, at night, still full of active predators. Animals that would proactively seek to kill you, as opposed, say, to the hippos, buffalo, rhino, and others who might trample or gore you out of fright rather than hunger. And the predators have better eyesight, keener senses of smell, and infinitely better hearing than any human being. If they want to kill you (which statistically few of them are likely to, but tell that to your evolutionary memory) there is very little you can do about it.

Even without most of this cheery knowledge, Moshoeshoe, the city boy, was less than comfortable as they walked. Every step the little group took seemed to him, as it did to Jon Power, unnecessarily loud. It would have been comical if he was not imagining carnivore eyes behind every shadowy bush.

The rushing rustles in the dark undergrowth that had been terrifying to hear on the tar road with a car nearby took on more urgency the further they got from its wreck.

Moshoeshoe wasn't sure when exactly the white girl had started holding his hand. Perhaps as he helped her from the car. But she was holding it still. It pleased him.

"So, what's the plan, Dominee?" asked the isangoma, not unkindly.

"We're closer to Skukuza, so we'll try to make it there."

"Wouldn't we be safer climbing a tree or something?"

Jon Power laughed. "No."

"How far is it, do you think?"

"Along the road, a few hours by foot."

Incredulous said pointedly, "And by car?"

"I said I was sorry, man. That bloody hammerkop. Straight at us!"

"Yeah, well."

They walked in silence for a while. The thrilling liquid pine of a Nightjar and the sonar pop of a Scops Owl gave the blue-filtered light a marine quality. The night breeze had an uncharacteristic chill in it. All three humans felt the wildness watching them and said nothing. The air smelled of nitrogen.

Somewhere overhead, a hammerkop keened.

⌒〜⌒

There was a glow at the foot of the rock. A small fire, making long shadows dance and stretch across its rough surface between the flickering and fading waves of orange light. It seemed to have been abandoned, its illumination struggling to reach very far into the darkness. The looming shape of the rock, a monstrous baby's bauble discarded on the bushveld floor, painted out the stars and cast shadows even from the feeble sliver of a new moon. It had hidden the fire from them until they were almost past it, like a child protecting a secret.

The clearing had been recently inhabited. Incredulous could feel it. So could Jon. They hesitated at the edge of the light, like wild dogs. Chanel shivered as she stepped into the wavering glow.

"There's no one here," she said, peering into the deep shadows that lay like pools around the island of light.

The two men stepped slowly forward.

Jon Power felt his spirit uneasy. He stood poised, legs slightly bent, ready to fight or step aside. The sense of warning was profound. Strong. Something beyond being out and exposed in the bush at night. Something even beyond finding other people. People who didn't belong there. His heart was pounding like erratic thunder.

"What is this place?" he asked of no one in particular. Around them, the bush was almost completely silent and dark.

Incredulous Moshoeshoe had his head bent low, his dread-locks casting weird shadows on his face as he listened, watched for movement. His eyes were lost in pools of shadow.

"*Ntimu,*" he said quietly.

Jon Power nodded. Chanel asked, 'what?' with her eyes.

"See the trees?" he said.

"They're just trees. I don't see anything strange..." Chanel said.

"Except..." said Jon, "For the berries. None of the berries have been touched. None of the leaves either."

"It's a cemetery," said Incredulous. "Even animals avoid it. There are spirits here." He glanced at the pastor, expecting a snort of derision or a contradiction, but Jon Power's face was as immobile as the rock.

"And it's not safe," said Jon, his eyes peering into the dark-ness at the boulder's summit, his ears straining for the tell-tale rumble of a leopard, the scent of a lion.

"But it's got a fire, it's protected on one side and it is shielded from the road if the rangers come back," said Chanel.

"That fire," said Jon, "is one of the reasons it's dangerous. If we found it, there's no reason the rangers won't. Or worse."

"Worse how?" she said.

"Fires don't make themselves."

"No," Incredulous said, still glancing around. "And whoever made this one has blasphemed this place. We should leave. And we should put out this fire."

"Please don't."

The voice had come from outside the circle of light.

"Please help us."

Moonchild

An old man stepped out of the shadows. He spoke with the portuguesified accent of Mozambique and looked a healthy 70, if an exhausted, worried one. His face was furrowed and in his right hand, close to his side, he clutched a *kierie*.

Behind him, edging closer, a small group of men and women stood. Jon Power recognised the signs of the Illegals. Migrants trying to reach the golden promise of wealth in Johannesburg or even the better life promised by a border town. Sturdy but worn-down shoes. Plastic bags filled with clothes. Hats or headcloths habitually worn, even at night. Dirty, layered clothing. A look of determination and distrust.

"How far have you come?" he asked.

"Beira." The man replied.

"That's a long way."

"Yes."

"How can we help you?"

The man looked at the three faces, his eyes shifting around the clearing, too, uncertain.

"You said you wanted help," Jon said again.

"You are not the police?" the man asked.

"Do we look like police?"

"What are you doing here?"

"We saw the light. Your fire."

The man winced, mentally berating himself. Then he called into the gloom.

A woman came out, a child on her back, wrapped close to her with a blanket. The woman looked frightened, a wildness in her eyes not in keeping even with the alarm of meeting strangers, even as illegals. When Jon addressed her, she did not reply. He gestured to her, looking at the old man, asked what was wrong with her. The old man pointed to the child.

It was completely still. Dark skinned, a full head of thick, shiny hair, and healthy-looking. A boy. Healthier than the woman. But that wasn't that unusual. The child's eyes were black. He was perfectly still.

Jon spoke to the woman, "Your child is sick?"

The woman shook her head hard, her eyes swivelling wildly around, her mouth tightening and untightening in obvious fear. She started moaning in soft, Mozambican Portuguese that Jon Power understood, "Not mine. Not mine." She began to cry.

One of the younger men caught her as her knees buckled beneath her. Jon noticed that the man – 20-something and wearing a white vest from which grew powerful bough-like arms. – stepped in front of her. As if he were avoiding the child. Jon Power felt a cold shiver run down his neck to the tips of his fingers. For a moment he stood, the woman crumpled like a shopping bag at his feet, the child as serene as green leaves on a windless night.

Chanel rushed forward to help. "Don't just stand there!" she shouted at Jon as she took the woman's hands. The woman had been laid on her side, the child still on her back, clinging at what looked an impossible angle. Moshoeshoe was still standing perfectly still, his face a mask, blank, as Chanel called to him for help. He didn't move. Neither did the men, women, and children in the woman's party, now standing in a small semi-circle at the edge of the clearing.

"Fine," Chanel shouted. "Don't help. What is wrong with you people?"

She unwrapped the blanket holding the child on the woman's back and made to catch him as he fell. She didn't need to.

The child stayed exactly where it was, clinging to the woman's back, and Chanel stopped, mentally recalibrating. *Why and how. What?*

"What..." she muttered quietly, her eyes wide and her face altered by confusion and something more primal.

Under the blanket, where the boy's hands and knees gripped the woman's sides and back, her clothes were torn and soaked with blood. The child showed no signs of distress or injury. Little fingers, chubby legs, sturdy and bloodless. Unchipped. But the woman's skin seemed to have been ripped. Not deeply, but enough to cause bleeding and tears to her clothes. It looked like the child had dug into her flesh. Grown into her.

"What the hell has happened? What..." Chanel shouted. The group of migrants stood silent.

"Help us, please," the old man said.

Incredulous Moshoeshoe stepped forward. "Tell me."

The old man told them.

They had arrived a few hours earlier, worried about walking too long at night, their scent being picked up by lions. They had chosen the spot because of the rock and the clearing and had all been tired and wanted to sleep for a few hours before starting off again at dawn, away from the main roads. They had sat for a while 'round the fire, eating their meagre rations. One of their number had told a story. The story had held them, 'round the fire, sufficiently breathless. And then they had slept. The woman had been on the first watch.

She'd woken the group after walking a little way beyond the clearing to gather some berries from the trees. She'd collected enough for them all and was hungry. She had eaten a few as she walked back to the clearing. According to what she had told them, she'd heard a small voice in one of the trees behind her.

She had managed to stifle her scream, but when it spoke again, she realised it was a child.

The little face had nestled above head-height in one of the trees. He was naked, clinging to a bough. Big eyes, following her slowly. Night ants making their path across his back without breaking their progress to and from the limb's end.

He had seemed unworried. No distress. Just those big eyes, watching without fear or friendliness. A lost boy? A refugee or a wild child? There had been cases, but the woman would only have heard vague tales.

She had asked him where his parents were, but he had not responded. Offering him a berry and eating a few herself, she had tried to coax him for a while, and then, without any discernible reason, the child had climbed willingly into her arms. When she put him on her back, he had clung comfortably up and had accepted being wrapped close to her in the way of so many of Africa's poor.

Her companions, when she woke them, were, as one might expect, troubled that a child would be abandoned in such a position and confused that it looked so healthy. *Where were the parents?* They had formed little parties going out into the bush but found no one.

It was only when they returned and tried to take the child down from the woman's back to feed and clean him that they had become aware of something wrong. The child would not budge. His grip was like iron and nobody – not the old women or young men – could make him let go. They had started gently, and become less gentle as they struggled. When the strong young man in the vest had wrenched at the child, the woman had cried out in pain, her clothing and skin tearing with the force. The blood from her pulled skin soaking away quickly, they had simply wrapped the child to her again.

The woman had become hysterical, crying and screaming, pleading with the group that was now backing away from her, slowly but definitely. Only as they heard Jon Power and his friends approaching had they hidden.

"Then you arrived," the old man said.

Jon Power had become quiet. He stood at the edge of the clearing, looking out into the bush. Chanel seemed to be in shock. The woman was still lying on her side. Chanel sat with her, stroking her hand.

Incredulous said quietly to Jon, taking him aside, "You're going to think I'm insane, but I think I know what this is."

"What?"

"It's a forest spirit. An *Ntimu* forest spirit."

"Ag don't talk crap, man!" Power exclaimed too loudly. Several eyes turned warily towards them and he lowered his voice. "What are you talking about?"

"It's a legend. A myth. A lot of tribes have it. It says that the cemetery forests are holy places. The only people allowed to go into them are the priests of the tribe. Male descendants of chiefs and elders, because that's who is buried here."

"Ja, but so what. Mumbo jumbo. You don't believe…"

"I don't know what I believe. I assumed those stories were myths. Allegories. Wisdom. But you believe in the supernatural, don't you?"

"Yes, but…"

"And I have gifts I can't explain with science. I know things. I *can* read the bones."

"It's an abomination," Jon Power interjected.

"Maybe. Whatever. But the point is, what if other things are true. Do you believe in spirits?"

"Yes."

"Do you believe they can manifest?"

"Yes, but…"

"Then maybe they can take on flesh."

Jon Power was quiet for a while.

"So, what do we do?"

"Well, I'm trying to remember what my grandmother taught me, but…"

Both men turned at the sound of a commotion. The young man in the vest was shouting in Portuguese and had pulled the woman to her feet. He had a kierie in his hand and from Jon's meagre Portubican he could make out a few phrases about not waiting any longer. Before either man could intervene, he had swung the kierie back and, with a scream from Chanel, brought it down with sickening speed and force on the baby clinging to the woman's back.

The heavy wooden staff broke in half and the man recoiled, clutching his hand, now looking genuinely frightened.

"Do something," Jon Power whispered to Moshoeshoe.

"Translate for me."

Jon Power did his best,

"This man is an Isangoma," he said. "A witch doctor. He can help your woman, but only if you do exactly what he says. Do you want his help?"

The people looked unconvinced.

Incredulous pulled the velvet bag of 'bones' out of his pocket and threw them on the ground, elaborately doing a reading at the feet of the stricken woman. The baby blinked impassively, but he felt it watching him.

Jon Power translated again, "This woman is barren. She has had no children because of something that happened before. She has no people and has joined you only recently."

He felt deeply uncomfortable giving words from unclean spirits and divination. But he had always been able to set aside qualms when there was a job to do.

The people had begun to talk and the old man said, after some consultation, "It is true," he said. "What must we do?"

"Ask them if they have any livestock," Mosheoshoe instructed Jon.

"A chicken."

"Come," he said to Jon, indicating the man in the vest and the woman, who seemed almost catatonic, swaying where she stood. "Ask him to bring the berries she gathered, and whatever other food they have."

"They want to know why they should sacrifice their food for her."

"Tell them that they have blasphemed a holy place and that if they kill her, the child or some other spirit will pursue them all. They will never leave the Park alive."

Jon Power consulted with the old man and the others. "Alright," he said.

"Good," Incredulous said. "Tell him to bring a knife."

"No!" Chanel shouted! "He's just a baby!"

Incredulous 'rounded on her. "Listen to me," he said, quiet as stone. "This is not a baby. You know that, deep down. This is something else, and if we don't do something soon, it is going to kill this woman."

"But …" she said hopelessly.

"The knife is not for the child," he said gently. "You have seen that I know things. Will you trust me?"

She looked long into his eyes.

"Okay."

The old man asked, "Will she die?"

"I hope not," said Incredulous Moshoeshoe, and led Jon Power and the strong man with the fruit and food into the forest. Moshoeshoe held the knife.

Jon Power was disturbed. But not in the way he had expected. As Moshoeshoe performed a ritual that involved going into a kind of trance before a tree where he had laid out all the food, he felt nothing. No fear, no unease in his heart. The Spirit seemed quiet in him. *Have I sinned against You?* he thought. He banished the Unforgivable Sin and thoughts of God ceasing to strive with him and tried to pray.

Moshoeshoe was kneeling on the ground, the chicken's feet clasped in his hands, the knife glinting in the starlight as he addressed the child staring impassively at him. The woman was clinging to the tree.

"Free this sister," he was saying. "She meant no harm. This is all these people have."

There was a long pause in which all were silent and the sounds of the bush broke through. A hyaena far in the distance. A keening night bird. An owl.

The child spoke.

"For too long people have shown no respect to this place. Why should we be tolerant?"

The voice sounded like musical wooden sticks, tapped rapidly together.

"Because we offer you gifts," Incredulous said, unsure of himself. He knew the folklore. He knew the stories. He didn't know the exact tone to adopt when talking to an actual forest spirit made woody flesh.

"Gifts that are ours. Gifts that are small."

"Do you get so many these days?"

The tree at whose feet they knelt was whipped by a sudden wind and it shook and creaked like a shout, a scream.

"Maggot. Worm. Filthy monkey thief, you show no respect!" The child's face was immobile but its eyes blazed. The woman carrying him whimpered and Incredulous removed the blanket.

The child's fingers were hidden, sunk deep, now, into her sides. The blood seemed to spill from the wound and then retreat, sickeningly. The boy breathed deep, satisfied. Sucking up life through his fingers.

"I mean no disrespect!" Moshoeshoe said, kneeling and putting his head to the roots of the tree.

The woman's whimpering abated slightly, then ceased. Incredulous peered up through his dreadlocks at the child's face.

"I do not know the muti. I do not know what to do, oh great Ntimu."

"Maggot." Just the word. Almost an agreement, hard wooden sticks banging rhythmically together.

"Oh, for Christ's sake," Moshoeshoe said.

"Him." The child smiled and Incredulous felt at a loss. *Had he been mistaken? Was this the province of the pastor?*

"We lost much because of him. It is good that you blaspheme him."

"Will you then please accept our sacrifice?"

The child's head turned with a clicking sound that turned to a slow splintering sound as it reached 180 degrees and then turned back to look at the black man, clad in black, kneeling before it.

"Kill the woman."

"No."

"She will die, anyway. We have our roots in her. She disrespected our Mother."

"No. I will give you what is right. This life." Incredulous raised the chicken, hypnotised and calm, above his head.

"We want a woman. A mongrel, half foreign and worthless, but her pain will please us."

"It is too much."

"Too much?" An explosion of shaking from every tree in the grove, wind throwing leaves and dust up in eddying whirls of anger. "Do you know who you address? Kill her for us!"

"No."

The forest stilled.

"Then, maggot," the child said, "why should we grant your request?"

Incredulous moved closer, until his mouth, black and glinting with unfaded lipstick, was against the child's ear. "Because if you don't, I will tell the servant of Christ over there that you are not a spirit but a god. And he will burn your fucking forest to the ground."

The child was silent, closed his eyes, and dug deeper into the woman who screamed and screamed and stopped, abruptly.

"If she dies," Moshoeshoe said, standing up, towering over the child, "you will be ash on the wind before the sun comes up."

The child opened its eyes and stared at Incredulous for a long time.

"A bird, then," the child said with half a smile. "Fine. It is fitting that you would kill a bird. It may be your only chance."

Incredulous shrugged off the cryptic smile as just the kind of bullshit gods would be likely to say when you humiliated them and congratulated himself on avoiding all the religions of this strange country. He raised the chicken, looked into its eyes, and apologised to it. Then he slit the bird's throat deeply so that its head folded back like a bottle of water, and he held it over the roots of the tree. Poured out a warm and wriggling libation. As the life drained from it, so the berries on the ground seemed to shrivel and dry. The food mouldered and sank into the earth.

Slowly, like a spider or a lizard or the stop motion capture of a vine, curling, the child climbed off the woman's back and up into the tree.

Incredulous Moshoeshoe unclenched his ass and felt sweat run down the inside of his leather trousers.

"Ho. Lee. Shit," he said.

The man in the vest was embracing the woman, picking her up, and carrying her to the clearing. Jon Power put his arm around Moshoeshoe's shoulders as they walked back.

"Well done," he said. The pastor wouldn't have seen it in the dark, but the Goth was smiling.

No time to cry

"What are you going to do for food?" Jon Power was smiling, as was the old man. His people were fussing over the woman, bringing her water and chattering more loudly than perhaps they should have done. Relief and joy had flooded through the clearing like a wave, making all of them forget the sounds beyond of lions and incongruous birds.

"We'll trap and hunt," the man said.

"You'll poach," Jon said, but it was hard to put any feeling into his disapproval.

"It won't be hard. We're not far now, and we've been told the rangers don't go into the area we are going at this time of year."

"I'm glad," said Jon. "I hope you all find what you need."

"As do I. But will we find peace?"

Jon's face must have been quizzical because the man explained, "Mandela is sick. We all know the story of when people thought he had died the first time. All the doomsday prophets were proved wrong."

"Praise Jesus," Jon Power said.

"Yes, that was a foolish thing. But I think maybe this time he will die. And this time it will not be peaceful. Many say there is a war coming."

"War? Who would fight a war?"

"On the illegal trail, you meet people," the old man said. "Gun runners. We are not the only thing being smuggled through Kruger."

"Meaning?"

"Just that others have seen many shipments of weapons carried into the country. Not just handguns, sir. Mines. Mortars. Rockets."

"Who are they going to, these weapons?"

"Both sides."

Jon thought of Caiaphas. "What sides? I think you're imagining things, old man. South Africa is peaceful. The struggle is over. The good guys won."

"There are many of your race who don't think so," the old man said. "And their organisations, the societies they were part of – they didn't disappear when their government fell. And neither did every one of the victors assume that their victory would last."

"You're talking about the *Broederbond*. How would you know about that?"

"I lectured in political science in Maputo when it was still LM."

Jon Power laughed. "Well, pleased to meet you, professor. I'm sorry you've fallen on such hard times."

"Ah," the professor said, "Civil war fucks everything up."

"Yes," said Jon Power, his fading smile turned to look into the night.

"You didn't ask me, pastor, about the other side in any South African civil war."

"No..." said Jon. He never finished his sentence. A high keening call above him unsettled him and he lost his train of thought.

He looked up and heard a powerful beating sound, like a slow troop helicopter or distant thunder. It came faster and louder than he could have anticipated, not that there was anything he could have done.

Everything dies

The thunderous beating became closer and louder and, in a confusion of dust and wind and sparks, the little group was thrown into disarray.

Squinting against the ash and dust and stones being thrown around like confetti, Jon and Incredulous saw a gigantic bird, jet black with red flashes under its wings. It swept down around the boulder. Men and women scattered and the beast – it must have been a full 20 feet across its wings, body the size of a man – made straight for the centre of the crowd, where Chanel had stood talking with the woman they had helped.

Half-blinded by the detritus blown up by each powerful beat of its wings, Jon could hear, between the roar of air and a cry at once strangely familiar and blood-chillingly new, people screaming. It took him back.

Soldiers talk about training taking over. About how a mind, once broken open and filled up with drills and rules, will always snap back into those drills when they are needed. That is not what happened to Jon. Experience makes a difference, certainly, and Jon had been in enough fire-fights and bloodbaths in the sub-Saharan bush to never want to see another one.

He wasn't scared. But he had spotted an enemy. And enemies had won too often, lately.

Jon Power stood up and shielded his face with his left hand as he ran towards a young girl and her grandmother – spectators all along to the evening's drama – catching each around the waist and lifting them in a spectacularly ungraceful pirouette as he ran back to the thorn tree he'd come from. Back to cover. He dumped them, dazed and clinging to each other in the flying dust, motioning for them to stay there, where the huge wings would not be able to go.

Looking back into the clearing he saw the woman Incredulous had just saved from the Ntimu god. She was standing upright, not bothering to shield her face, and electricity made arcs and small jumping orbs of fire across her skin. Her clothes pulled at her body as if trying to stand on end and her face was empty. The fight gone.

As long black talons plunged into the woman there was an explosion of light, bolts, and spheres of electricity pulsing through her, bouncing off her, and Jon was reminded of the smell of napalmed bodies. A pulse of thunder, a rush of air from a monstrous wing, and she was lifted with a sickening jerk into the blackness. It was then that it began to rain.

Fine drops fell on Jon's face as he looked into the cloudless black sky. A single drop landed on his lip and he reflexively licked it away. The warm, metallic taste of blood.

Then silence. The thunderous beating faded and they stood in stunned emptiness.

"Is everyone..." Jon Power was interrupted by the crunching thud of a body dropping out of the blackness and splitting wetly in the dust.

Screams and a small handgun produced. The man in the vest fired it aimlessly into the sky in the manner of blind, powerless people everywhere. He ran to the body.

In a second the huge black wings and confusion were back, as the bird made another pass, a few feet from the ground. The man in the vest stood and faced the bird and emptied the handgun at it. It didn't even slow down.

He broke into a run, aiming for the sacred forest. A flash of white and a sound like tearing filled the skull of every person there. The smell of burning and a prickling all over the skin. Charred and blackened, frozen rigid, the man fell to the ground.

Chanel screamed and ran to him, Incredulous trying but failing to hold onto her, to keep her sheltered in the dark. The bird swept past again and caught her by the back, her scream filling everything as she was jerked upwards. Jon Power ran forward and jumped in time to grab her foot, slowing the bird, which hovered, beating the air. He looked up and saw Chanel's face, peaceful, unconscious, and beyond it to the face of the bird, its hooked beak. He could only see the gleam of a pair of very bright eyes, which seemed red and cruel and mocking.

Searing pain filled his hand, his arm, his body, as Chanel's form jerked and bucked and the air around him sizzled. With a swiping motion, the bird slashed at her neck with its beak, blood fountaining into its open mouth, raining over everything and running down her thrashing form onto his hands. With an electric jolt, he let go, and as he fell he heard a crack as the bird folded her frame almost in half and dropped her near where the other body lay.

The night had been absolutely clear and still and yet the sound of bursting, grinding thunder was all around them. A single arc of lightning, followed by another, and another, and another struck the people in the clearing, rooting them to the ground for a second and dropping them, smoking, in the dust.

The girl and her grandmother sat quietly, making no attempt to move. They had been told to stay. Lightning from the sky struck vertically at the centre of the thorn tree, turning it instantly into a towering canopy of flame. And still, they sat. The bird swept down and seemed to fold in half and half again until the silhouette of a man was striding forward towards the pair, embers raining down on them.

Jon tried to run towards them but was repelled by an explosive burst of charge that partially blinded him.

Through burning eyes, he saw the silhouette raise a hand and slash at the pair. Throat height. The figure leaned in, bending towards them for a time, then standing, walking towards him, a black outline against the flames, wiping its mouth.

Oh Jesus, thought Jon, unable to tell if it was a prayer or blasphemy. *Oh Jesus, help us.*

The man seemed to unfold again and climbed over Jon on wingbeats, rising into the air.

It was all impossible and it was happening.

Incredulous, crouching down, his eyes screwed up against the dust and smoke and ash, made it to the centre of the clearing, to Chanel's body. She was dead. Pale and almost bloodless, fingers blackened and hair charred.

He stood up, face upward, looking for the bird, and was hit by a bolt of lightning which sent him flying into the grass.

When he stood up, the bird gave a liquid cry and disappeared.

Both men followed the sound of its wings and the small arcs of lightning in its wake, standing side by side. The rubber soles of Incredulous' enormous boots had melted. Seven people lay dead around them.

"Jesus…" Moshoeshoe said.

"I know."

Stunned and slightly deafened, neither man noticed the bakkie bouncing through the veld behind them until it stopped and dipped its headlights.

They turned and made out a huge, neckless beast climbing out of the cab.

"Come on!" it shouted. "We have to go!"

Something fast

"Caiaphas?"

"Uncle?"

Jon and Incredulous stood where they were. Dust drifted from where the bakkie had slid to a halt. Cicadas and crickets resumed their hiss.

"Come on. We don't have much time. I heard the noise here from ten Ks away. Rangers' people will have heard it too."

"It was a bird, Caiaphas..." said Jon.

"And she's dead," said Incredulous, looking back at Chanel.

"You can tell me in the car all about that," Caiaphas shouted. "We have to go!"

Painfully, feeling unnaturally slow, the two men walked to the car and climbed in. Caiaphas Molefe looked at the clearing. The bodies and smoke. He wondered what had happened, but he was not shocked. This was not his first massacre.

He looked up at the sky. There were dark, rolling clouds overhead, and in the air, the heavy, oppressive sense of thunder.

"Right," he said. He slammed his door and put on his brights. "Let's get the fuck out of here."

Caiaphas Molefe drove heart-stoppingly fast. The bakkie rose and fell with stomach-defying regularity, flying over dips and bumps in the dirt road, skidding around corners, throwing Jon and Incredulous numbly about in the back seat. The beast of a car kicked stones and dust up from under its spinning wheels and the engine roared like an angry animal. Jon watched the rapid flickering of thorn trees and Mopani bush throwing wild, swinging shadows as the headlights veered left and right. He said nothing for a very long time.

Back on the tar, the engine's roar now full-throated and brutal, Jon said, "What are you doing here, Caiaphas?"

"It's a pleasure, bra-Jon. No trouble." He was glancing back to where they sat, alarmingly ignoring the road for seconds at a time, smiling.

"Thanks. But how...?"

"I've got tracking software in my nephew's car." Incredulous said nothing, his face to the window, staring out at the circulation patterns of dead branches against the lightening sky.

Caiaphas said, "I've been pretty close the whole time, just outside the Park. And I've had my people in that woman's operation reporting back to me."

"That wasn't necessary."

"You know what's coming, Jon. You know when he goes it will just take one thing. We must be ready. Plus, I don't trust her. White people."

"I know. But..."

"I saw you were leaving camp after hours. When the signal went dead, I came to find you. I found the car and made arrangements to have it cleared away. It will be gone by morning. And then I heard the noise and saw the flashes in the sky. What the hell was that? Broeders? Cross-border shit?"

"You wouldn't believe me."

"Was it Jesus?" Caiaphas chuckled.

"No."

"Then try me."

"I don't know what it was." Jon Power said, quiet enough that his old friend fell silent. The car sailed down the tar road, lights dimmed to avoid attracting too much attention, warm air pouring through the windows with the smell of grass and leaves and air as thick and clean as rain.

"I think I do." Incredulous seemed to have woken out of his trance. He was sitting up, his face uncharacteristically marked by uncertainty. "At least, I might."

"Oh, yes?" Caiaphas was smiling, but Jon saw no amusement in his eyes.

"I think so. I think it was …"

"What you think, boy, is not important. What you know is nothing. These are men's things. You best be quiet."

"Hey, Caiaphas," Jon interrupted, wanting to defend him. "Leave him alone."

"With love and respect my brother, I tell you I will speak to him as I please. This chickenshit is like his father. My sister did him no good by letting him grow into… into this." Caiaphas jerked his chin up at the rear-view mirror, indicating the nearly foetal young man in shining black leather curled on the back seat.

"He handled himself alright back there."

Caiaphas grunted, unconvinced.

"No, really, Caiaphas. He was alright."

The big man gripped the steering wheel tight and released it a few times.

"Well," he said. And said nothing more.

They passed through the gates without a problem. A quiet nod to the guard on the gate, who had already opened it before they slowed. Caiaphas made the sign of the fist at the window and the guard reciprocated.

"So, Jon, are you going to tell me what happened back there?"

Jon did.

⌒⌒

"You're right," said Caiaphas. "I don't believe you."

"I'm not lying."

"Well," the big man said again. He fell silent again. Sometimes it's best not to try too hard to fit the impossible into your worldview. Some men can leave thoughts unfinished.

Caiaphas turned on the radio.

… of unrest in Mamelodi, with protests turning violent in several areas. The Mandela family have thanked people for their prayers for the former President and called on all parties for calm. Elena Aak de Nau issued a statement today, saying that South Africa's minorities would not stand idly by as chaos…

Caiaphas switched the radio off, irritably. For a while, they drove in silence.

Trees sailed past, the rhythmic hum of the wheels and his exhaustion sending Jon into an anxious sleep. When he woke, a question that had grown just behind his conscious mind came out.

"What happened back there, Caiaphas?" he said. "How did we get through the gates? How did you get to us? How will you get the car…"

"We have people everywhere, brother. We had some of our men stationed here when we knew you'd be here and when we heard about the woman. We had them take shifts."

"You can't have that many people. Not in every place."

"We have enough. And others can be bought."

"And the people who you can't buy?"

"For them, we have these." Caiaphas reached under the passenger seat next to him and unfastened a catch. The seat flipped forward, revealing a cache of guns and hand grenades.

Jon Power felt sick. He must have looked it. Caiaphas said,

"What did you think the money was paying for, bra-Jon?"

"I know, I know," he said. "But it was always as a precaution. To make sure we were ready. To make sure…"

"Never again. I know, bra. I know."

Incredulous was pressed up against the door of the car, as far from the weapons as he could be.

"What the *fuck*, uncle?!" he shouted. "What the hell is all that for?"

"War, boy," Caiaphas said, now facing the road. "There is a war coming."

Cantara

A psalm of Jon Power

How glorious are your ways, O my God.
How steadfast your love!
You have delivered me from the hand of the evil one
And your mercy has followed me, even unto this place.

You provide for me a vehicle in the face of the enemy.
Swift safety from winged death.
My enemies surround me and attack me but you are there.

How strange is your mercy, O Lord.
From the unclean and the unbelieving you bring forth fruit.
Life-giving help you bring from the hands of the unworthy.
Solace and safety from the despised among the brethren.

Even in my distress and my weakness,
Yea, though I consort with sinners and the unclean

You rescue me. Your grace abides with me.

Woe to those who never recognise your sovereignty, Lord!
Woe to those who spurn your help.
Bring them, Lord, to a knowledge of you!
Bring them to your house of worship for thanksgiving and praise!

I cry out to the Lord with weeping.
How long shall the innocent die?
When will their blood be avenged?

The Lord is faithful and just. He will not fail.
With broken tools, he makes the world perfect.
From shattered pots, he pours the oil of his mercy,
And all will be made new.

I lift my face unto the Lord and cry out.
For strength and justice, I cry.
Arise O Lord, and bring your justice.

And let your servant be your sword.

Red flags and long nights

The hotel was beautiful. An old landowner's estate, now catering to fly-fishing weekenders from the city.

Caiaphas made a few calls and had taken roads seemingly at random to make sure they were not followed, and they had slept as he drove, and ended up in a little town called Dullstroom, in a place neither of them could afford. Caiaphas "knew someone" on the staff. Caiaphas always knew someone.

There had been one room – Caiaphas had left them at the hotel and gone to spend the night at his contact's place – with one expansive bed. Jon Power had tried to stay up as long as possible, but his exhaustion had finally defeated his homophobia. And for him it *was* a phobia, a discomfort, rather than a hatred. The men had climbed into bed in total silence.

They did not sleep well.

Jon Power woke to the sound of clicking and bright light in his eyes, his hand jerking reflexively under his pillow for a handgun that wasn't there. Old habits die hard. He consciously let go of the adrenaline tension years of army life regularly triggered on waking and opened his eyes. Saw the space beside him. The pillow with its mascara smudges. Felt all the tension flooding back.

"Morning, sunshine!" Moshoeshoe was sitting at a little table on the other end of the expansive room – really a self-contained unit with a lounge and writing area, plus its own fireplace, something that had proved necessary for warmth in the night. This was what tourism marketers called 'the highlands'. Everyone else called it ball-freezingly chilly.

"Morning," Jon mumbled, sitting up and taking it in. "Nice place," he yawned, staring at the sofas with appreciation and the extensive coffee-making facilities with something approaching lust. "What time did we go to sleep last night?"

Moshoeshoe didn't look up from the screen of his laptop. "We went to bed about one," he said lightly. "But if you meant actually sleep, that was *much* later." He looked up at Jon, pointedly, and in a camper-than-a-rainbow-pup-tent tone, said, "You were *wonderful*," and bit his lip.

For a second, Jon felt dizzy. Then amused. He didn't smile. "Of course, I was," he said, getting up. "Let that be a lesson to you."

Incredulous chuckled. "Coffee?"

"I would kill for a coffee," Jon shouted from the huge, impressively if impractically marbled bathroom. "I would maim for a coffee. I would …"

"Do something extreme for a coffee. Yes. I get it. Milk, two sugars?"

"Ja! How..?"

"White South Africans," Moshoeshoe almost rapped the phrase, extending the final syllable in a mock Sandton accent.

"You're properly British, hey?"

"I don't take sugar if that's what you mean."

"If that's a thing," Jon said, stepping into the room and making his way across the plush carpet to the sofa where Incredulous had put his coffee.

"It's a thing."

"So, listen, last night."

"Nothing happened, dominee. I'm straight."

"No, man."

"I know," Incredulous smiled.

"That thing. I… I know you're going to find this hard to believe, but… I think it was a demon."

"Nope," Incredulous said brightly, still tapping at his keyboard, occasionally clicking something and pausing to read.

"Nope, what?"

"Nope, I don't find it hard to believe. I'm an isangoma. And nope, it's not a demon."

"Oh really?"

"Ja, really." The younger man mocked the pastor's thicker accent. "I have consulted…"

"If you've consulted the spirits, please forgive me if I ignore you," Jon Power interrupted. "Spirits lie. They are evil. They are not on our side. If it's supernatural it's either the Holy Spirit or the Enemy. That's it. If you consulted with them, that will only…"

Incredulous cut him short, "I consulted the internet."

"Oh."

"Yellow Moepels."

"Oh?"

"It's a website."

"Oh. Sorry." Jon said, sidling sheepishly up behind the isangoma, looking at his screen. "Yellow what?"

"YellowMoepels.co.za," he said, clicking the site's home button. He showed Jon Power the homepage.

Yellow Moepels – *roots and fruits of esoteric South African knowledge*

"Essential reading for the modern sangoma and isangoma. Searchable, forums, wiki section, and even a news blog. Pan-tribal, cross-referenced entries and well moderated community-sourced knowledge on everything from spells and healing herbs to tribal legends. That's the bit I'm on now."

Incredulous clicked one of the many tabs open on the browser.

Jon was impressed.

Lightning bird
See also, Izulu (Pondo), Impundulu (Xhosa), Mamasionoke (BaSotho)
Categories, Familiars; Monsters; Elementals; Pan-African myths; Birds; Shape-shifters; Humanoids
Tags, Vampiric; Pondo beliefs; Sotho beliefs; Xhosa beliefs; Seducers; Lightning; Hammerkop

"You believe this kak?" Jon asked, not unkindly.
"You believe in six-day creation?"
"No, but…"

"Yeah well, I never believed this, much, either. If you found out six-day creation was literally true, would that blow your mind?"

"Not really, no."

"Well, this is a little harder for me to swallow, but hey. I tell the future by throwing bones. What you gonna do?"

"Okay, but lightning birds? What the hell? And vampiric?" Jon Power said. "Are we looking for Dracula or the Tokoloshe?"

"Africa's got monsters," Incredulous said. "Just like Europe."

"Ja," said the pastor. "I just always believed they were human."

"This one is, sometimes. Look, here, it says it can take on the form of a beautiful man. Will often seduce women. Drinks their blood and can control lightning. You've got to admit, that sounds like the thing that killed…" Incredulous trailed off.

He had been trying to be cheerful and together all morning. Mostly he had been successful. He had hardly known the girl. But he had also never seen people die before. Never like that. Never like anything.

Jon Power was not, in contemporary terms, a sensitive man. In the 80s, compared to other commandos in Angola, sure. But with a big black mess of mascara and moepels, whatever they were? He put a hand gingerly on the crying isangoma's shoulder.

"I'm sorry. You liked her, hey?"

"It's so stupid," Incredulous said, looking away, out of the window, down the brown, rusty valley. "I only met her a couple of days ago. I just felt like maybe…"

"I know, man."

"It's not just her."

"I know. How many?"

"Thirteen? Fourteen, including…"

"Chanel."

"I just wish I could have done more. I feel so, so…"

"Angry."

"Yes."

"That won't ever go away," Jon said. "You just have to make sure it motivates you to do something. Don't let it turn you bitter and useless."

Incredulous said nothing.

Jon put his hand on his shoulder. "You did all you could. You mustn't let yourself feel responsible. It's okay to cry."

Incredulous looked at the pastor for a long time. "Do you want to braid my dreads?"

"Ag, bugger off, man! I was trying to help." Jon stood up, embarrassed.

"I know, I know. Sorry. I'm just not African enough yet. All this earnestness. It freaks me out. But thank you. I will try."

"Okay." Jon dropped into a voluminous chair and stared at the ashes of the fire.

"I'm assuming your advice comes from your time in the army?"

"Ja."

"That fucked you up properly, didn't it?"

"It usually does. And if you've seen what I've seen…"

"Okay," Incredulous elongated the 'oh' and closed the laptop in a business-like fashion. "But before you go all *Da Nang* on me, let's get back to last night. You saw what I saw. That was a bird. You're probably a twitcher, so…"

"Are you calling me a *moffie*?" Jon said. After a three-second pause, he smiled, slyly.

"Ha ha." Incredulous said the words, rather than laughing. But he was smiling.

"I'm not a twitcher, but I know my birds. That was nothing I've ever seen. Similar colouring to a Bateleur, but bigger than anything… normal."

"Exactly."

"Did it say something about Hammerkops?"

"I saw the word, it's associated with the lightning bird. I didn't know what it meant. Why?"

"I kept hearing them at night. They're not night birds. And that one that flew at us, that caused the crash."

"And ruined my car. Yes."

"So, it could have been...?"

"I'll check." Incredulous opened his laptop again and clicked a few times. "It says there are a few stories about Impundulu having their own animal familiars. But it's not a common theme."

"But possible?"

"Yes."

"So, if it…" Jon Power swallowed, unused to talking about the corporeal in the terms he regularly used to talk about the spirits. "If it was opposing us, it might have sent the Hammerkop?"

"Perhaps. Which means I may have been wrong."

"About?"

"About you just being a bad driver."

"Gee, thanks. And you are sure they said Hammerkop?"

"Hammerkop. Brown bird, head like a hammer, hangs around water?"

Jon nodded.

"Yellow Moepels says there's a definite correlation, but there are differences of opinion as to what the relationship is between the lightning bird and the Hammerkop."

"That thing we saw last night was not a Hammerkop."

"No," said Incredulous Moshoeshoe, slowly getting to know more than he was comfortable with about birdlife. "No, it wasn't."

Jon got up to turn on the TV.

"Mpumulanga police are looking for two men to help them with their enquiries into the deaths of Alida and Chanel Aak de Nau. Incredulous Moshoeshoe and Jonathan Power were last seen in the Kruger National Park, where Chanel Aak de Nau's body was discovered last night. Several unidentified bodies, believed to have been illegal migrants from Mozambique, were also found."

Jon turned off the TV just as a powerful pounding started thundering at the door.

Neither man moved.

Doctor Jeep

Incredulous and Jon remained immobile. Frozen in shock and fear. Eventually, the pounding stopped and a key fiddled in the lock outside. The door opened.

"Hello, boys!" Caiaphas stood, smiling and expansive in an expensive suit, filling the door.

"Uncle, Caiaphas, for fuck's sake!"

"Don't take that tone with me, boy. I'll rip your arm off and slap you with the wet side."

Jon laughed.

"I trust you've seen the news?"

"Yes," Jon said grimly.

"Well, then you'll know we have to go. Come on, boys. It's time to move."

"Where are we going?"

"We're going to get you a car."

Incredulous shoved things into his bag, irritated at his uncle. Irritated at how shaken he was. Irritated at having to confront as concrete realities things he had only ever believed in theoretically, like Anglicans and angels. Irritated that he'd brought only one change of boots and that fucking fake Shaka spear.

Jon Power packed his rucksack methodically. Neatly. Old habits, yes.

A short drive down the horrifically yuppified main street and 'round the back of the town took them onto a long, straight, terrible road into what used to be called 'the location'. Towering floodlights for mass protection and control loomed like gigantic water birds, fishing in their shadows. Houses of every level of poor jostled for space. A few men in filthy overalls eyed them indifferently as Caiaphas's slick Execu-bakkie sighed past them and a skeletal yellow dog only jumped out of their way just in time to avoid becoming yet another corpse on the roadside.

"Don't say I don't take you to all the nice places, eh," Caiaphas laughed.

"Lovely," agreed Incredulous.

Jon Power just watched the parade of expensive cars and hovels. A sense of peace, of self, returned to him. For the last twenty minutes of the drive, he was able to pray. By the time they reached the old municipal wrecking yard, he felt refreshed. God was sovereign. God was good. God would guide him through.

"Here," Caiaphas said, pulling into the drive and 'round the back of a rusted industrial building.

It was bizarre.

Crowded around them, in an arc at least ten layers deep, crouched about a hundred old vehicles of varying levels of official. Ambulances. Military registered 4x4s. Old yellow police vans and garbage trucks. Electric milk vans and hearses and fire engines and military people transports. It could have been a museum if the proprietor hadn't looked so much like a cartoon paedophile. Museums have rules about those sorts of things.

"Mr. Molefe," he said, his eyes shifting from face to face standing in his lot. His pink face was gaunt, his eyes yellow, his teeth incongruously perfect.

"Guyck." The syllable settled any doubts Jon or Incredulous might have had about the power dynamic between the two.

"Always nice to see you, Mr. Molefe. I got your message. I have a few… things for you to see." He sounded like a madam in a particularly low-rent brothel. A Natal Sharks cap almost hid his greasy red hair and he wore a pair of overalls flecked with motor grime, unzipped to his crotch, an old Not My Dog t-shirt hanging from his ribcage.

"Good. We need something clean, eh?" Caiaphas smiled patronisingly. "In every way, nê."

"Yes sir."

Guyck led them along the rows of formerly official vehicles, pointing out comparative virtues. Jon Power knew a little about vehicle maintenance, particularly military vehicles, and soon engaged the twitching, shaky mechanic. Incredulous got bored and wandered off towards a small collection of hearses.

"Hey, fuckface!" Caiaphas shouted after him. "Don't go too far! And don't touch anything. You'll break a nail!"

Incredulous gave him the opportunity for a good long look at one back-lacquered specimen in particular and disappeared in the sea of dusty blackness.

"Why do you give that kid so much shit?" Jon asked.

"Oh, you like him now? You switching to 'traditional African religion', bra-Jon?"

"Hey. Just curious. Not my business. Just that he's family."

"Ja, Jon. That's part of the problem. That boy is everything that is wrong with his generation. No politics. No ideology. No sense of where we've come from, what we've won. How much we still have to work. To fight."

"I know, but still…"

"Nah, brother. Look at him. That's not what a man looks like. In Uganda they would execute him, just to be sure."

"Caiaphas, you old-fashioned devil. I had no idea you were such a conservative."

"Oh, you love the gays, now, preacher man? Your Bible saying something new about them that you hadn't read before?"

Jon laughed. "No. It's still a sin. But so is gossip. So is greed."

"And what are we going to do to the greedy when the war comes, bra-Jon?"

"You know for me it is a last resort, Caiaphas. Something we pollute ourselves with for the sake of a greater good."

"Maybe for you. For me, it's because I have a long memory. A lot of people don't these days. But I do."

"Me too, old friend. Still. Go easy on him. I think he and the girl last night were a thing. He watched her die."

"Good," said Caiaphas.

"Good?"

"You may need him. He might be helpful with a bit of hate in him. A sense of vengeance. Who knows, maybe he turns out not to be completely useless."

You don't know the half of it, thought Jon. "Yes?"

"A contact sent me these last night." Caiaphas handed Jon his phone and indicated to swipe through a set of pictures. They were of white men in khaki uniforms and camouflage, standing next to huge caches of weapons. Not just handguns and rifles, but cases of ammunition, rocket-propelled grenades, and military vehicles of every description. The last two photographs showed rows of tanks, artillery, and several drones on a runway. The horizon was lined with thorn trees.

Jon shuddered. "What is this, Caiaphas?"

"Those were taken this week. The Broeders are better armed than we ever anticipated. The old contacts with GunCo have been paying off. Our guy says he's also heard talk of Mossad and Israeli weapons trainers in some of their camps. The worse Mandela gets, the more activity we're hearing about. And now this shit with that woman."

"What about it?"

"If that gets perceived as a race crime… Well, that's all they'll need."

"I thought you wanted a war."

"Brother, you know better than that. But if they want one, I'm going to be ready."

"Well, I don't want any weapons."

"Tough shit, brother. You're taking some. A couple for you and that boy. A box of booby-trapped grenades I need you to deliver to my contact in Pretoria."

"Booby-trapped grenades?! Are you insane?"

"Relax, brother. They can't hurt you unless you throw them. Timers are all fucked up."

"Shit, Caiaphas."

The man-mountain smiled. "You said you wanted the girl's body or autopsy or what-what last night?" Years of knowing Jon had taught him that when arguing seemed futile, changing the subject was powerful and effective, like the prayers of a righteous man. Yeah, he'd been to church too. He just didn't like it.

"Yes," replied Jon.

"Well, the second girl's been buried. No point. Accidental death, signed and sealed. But the Aak de Nau girl is in Pretoria. An administrative hold-up."

"Coincidentally where you want me to take your booby-trapped grenades."

"Coincidentally."

"If the body's in Pretoria, it will be in a high-level morgue."

"I know some people there."

"Of course you do."

Incredulous wandered out from among the hearses, his nails and trousers glinting and black as the cars' paintwork, shimmering in the gathering heat. He was holding a cell phone to his ear, talking and smiling.

"The old jeep will be good for you two, I think, Jon?"

Jon nodded and watched Incredulous sidle up to his uncle. "Okay, mom. Bye. Love you too. Here."

He handed the phone to his uncle, who flinched as he put it to his ear.

Two minutes later, he handed the phone back to his nephew and rolled his eyes at Jon. "Change of plans," he said. "Which one do you want, boy?"

Incredulous smiled.

Twenty minutes later, Jon was in the passenger seat of a newly polished, particularly stylish hearse, as black and gleaming as Caiaphas's furious eyes.

They pulled out of the junkyard, with Incredulous lifting a finger at his uncle in salute and Jon Power smiling wryly. Caiaphas stood passively by his bakkie, a hand lifted chest height, giving a single wave. Guyck was suppressing a smile next to him.

Incredulous turned to Jon, plugging his iPod into the car stereo. It had better speakers than he would have expected from a hearse. "What do you want to listen to, dominee?"

"Do you have any Cat Stevens?"

Incredulous nodded. "I can live with that."

They hit the highway at an inappropriate speed for a cortege, heading for Pretoria.

⌐———꒛

The album had lasted an hour – a greatest hits, rather than an original release, which Incredulous Moshoeshoe usually eschewed – and all through it neither man talked. Caiaphas had counselled them to take back roads, indirect routes, and Incredulous had done just that, a slow meandering that avoided highways or populous areas. They wanted to be entering Pretoria as it grew dark and the shift workers neared the end of a long day.

Sad Lisa may have done it. The piano line was always guaranteed to bring up thoughts of old loves, dead friendships. His more narrowly alternative friends might have been surprised that Incredulous even owned the album. Had they seen his tearful eyes, if they had managed to remove his sunglasses without a fight, they would have smirked.

"Are we going to talk about it?"

Jon Power was deep in his thoughts, a different set of images and memories playing on his mind. His eyes were dry.

"What?" he said, eventually.

"Are we going to talk about what happened last night?"

"We did. Your Pampoentjies."

"Moepels. Yellow Moepels."

"Sure."

"You believe it was a magic bird."

"Looked a lot like it."

"This doesn't bug you?"

"It bugs me plenty. But so what? It bugs me that people go to hell. Happens every day. It bugs me that people get demon-possessed. Mostly through doing crap that you do. But hey, it happens. Can't save everybody."

"This is different from spirits. God."

"Yup."

"Do you think it killed Alida Aak de Nau?"

"The burning inside the building? Possibly?"

"And the others?"

"Possibly."

"*How can you be so calm about this shit?*" Incredulous shouted and instantly regretted it.

"Look, Moshoeshoe…"

"Incredulous."

"Incredulous. Fine. Look, you're not a religious man."

"No."

"But you believe you can tell the future – consult with the ancestors, whatever the hell it is you do with those bloody bones."

"I don't know how it works, but it works."

"Of course it does," said Jon. "But there will be a cost."

"People would have called most modern science witchcraft a hundred years ago."

"That's nonsense, obviously, but I get what you're saying. There are things we don't understand. Things that sound crazy, but aren't."

"Sure."

"Like God."

"That *is* crazy," Incredulous laughed.

"Ja, ja. Everyone's clever until they meet the devil."

"You think what we saw last night was the devil?"

"Maybe. Maybe not. That's not the point. Whatever it was, it killed all those people. Maybe Alida, maybe Paprika Hendl. The question is not what it is or who it killed."

"Well, then what is the question?"

"Why it let us live."

Gush forth my tears

"You did it?"

"There were complications."

"I know. Were you seen?"

"It was unavoidable." There was not a hint of apology in his voice.

"Witnesses?"

"You said to let them live."

"I didn't expect…"

"I did what I was told."

"You could have thought."

"That is not how this works."

Transcript of Elena Aak de Nau press conference

"Ladies and gentlemen.

"Thank you for being here. As you will understand, this is a very difficult time for my family. We would ask that you please respect our privacy and allow us time to grieve and space to make sense of what has happened, not just to my daughters, but to our whole family.

"Alida and Chanel were wonderful daughters. They were very different souls, with very different personalities, but they were both, in their own ways, the best daughters a mother could have hoped for and I will…

"I will…

"I'm sorry. Excuse me. I will miss them, very much…

"Both of my girls were fiercely independent, strong women who made their way in the world without ever asking anybody for a handout. That should have meant that they had happy, successful, peaceful lives, but this world is not like that. This country is not like that.

"There are those in this country who find a strong woman a threat. Those who see any woman as a possession, an object, a thing to be controlled and used for their own ends. Those who see all people as fair game, as targets for violence and crime.

"I want to say to those people, *you will not win*. You can take the life of one, two, thirty, a thousand innocent people. But eventually, we will rise up. Eventually, we will say to those who commit these crimes and to those who allow the conditions for crime to flourish, *no more*.

"To those who hoped that personal tragedy would sap my will to fight, I say, sorry. To those who would, through complacency or malice, allow the killing of women, the murdering of

farmers, the targeting of white people or any minority,
I say, your time is up.

"To the ANC, I say, your time is up. You had your chance and
you blew it. You let women like my daughters die on your watch
and you did nothing. You let racial tensions get out of control
and you did nothing. You let crime become an epidemic in this
country and, You. Did. Nothing.

"To my supporters, I say: calm. There is no evidence yet that
my children were targeted by our enemies. Let the police do
their jobs. Let justice be done. This is a time of uncertainty for
our country. A time when all we have worked for hangs in the
balance. I call for peace. But let us remain watchful.
Let us be prepared.

"God rewards those who are prepared. He favours those who
are courageous against the odds. He is mighty to
save his people.

"My daughters' lives were taken in hate. Their deaths
will not be in vain.

"Thank you."

Song to the siren

Jon Power was depressed. Goth will do that to you.

Not that the genre itself is depressing – that's a common misconception. But it's an acquired taste, like racism, casual violence, or reality TV. Nobody's born loving it and only a few have a natural predilection. The rest of us have to learn like we learn to drink beer or like girls.

Jon Power had not had the time to learn and he wasn't the ideal candidate.

He was no fan of Easy Listening, but the music Moshoeshoe was playing was Awkward Listening. It was Complicated Listening. Difficult Listening.

"What is this?" he asked. A lone, echoing voice, strangely accented and flat as a crypt-top intoned, *Give me the power*, as a sad droning chord progression rose in the background. Skeletal fingers played an arpeggio on an orientally flavoured guitar.

"It's Corpus Delicti," Incredulous shouted over the slow-revving drums and effect-drenched guitars.

"Of course it is," Jon said.

"You like?" Incredulous asked, his window open, dreadlocks whipping wildly 'round his head in a happy storm of sunlight and sound. His eyes were protected by the biggest, blackest sunglasses Jon had seen outside of a welding shop. And even then, he wasn't sure…

He was trying to be polite. Caiaphas' unnecessary hostility to the boy had reminded him of some of the men in his unit. Men for whom cruelty was not merely the practical means to the end of obedience and subjugated will that armies rely on. Men who, left alone in the bush, separated from others, succumbed to the worst weaknesses of violence. Men he had investigated. Men he had prosecuted and eliminated. Men he was always afraid of becoming.

"It's…" Jon searched for the word and immediately felt like a parent, "passionate."

Moshoeshoe laughed.

"Well to be fair, most of their stuff sucks. But this was a great club song back in the day. Here," Incredulous said, flicking through the iPod, "Try a little Type O Negative."

Jon tried it. His body rejected it.

"Wait, this is a different band?"

Behind his glasses, Incredulous rolled his eyes.

"Oh come on."

"And neither of them is that group, what are they called, the ladies of chastity…?"

"Sisters of Mercy."

"But it's the same guy. I mean, different band names, but the same guy singing. Like the music in Erasure and Yazoo."

"Erasure and Yazoo do *not* sound the same!" Incredulous was incensed.

"Ja, but you know what I mean."

"It's deep voices and a slightly gloomy tone. You think Leonard Cohen is the same guy too?"

"Don't you have any 80s?"

"The Sisters were 80s!"

"You know what I mean."

"Wait. Let me play you some Diary of Dreams."

The name made Jon wince but he hid it. "That sounds nice."

It wasn't half bad. Like Depeche Mode, slowed down and robbed of all that mattered to them.

"Is he saying *can you believe my testicles*?" asked Jon.

"Are you trying to be annoying?" asked Incredulous, not taking his eyes off the road, occasionally swerving to miss pot-holes the size of bird-without-wings-baths. Hearses handle better than you'd think.

The Darkwave electronica boomed and the anguished vocals soared above the roar of the hearse's engines and the air they were tearing through. Jon smiled out of his window at the highland browns and reds, the long stretches of nothing.

"Yes," he chuckled and tried to keep from singing along.

The old yellow police car had surprised Jon as they drove past it. Sitting under the kind of roadside trees where one could fall asleep and dream of ghosts of the past. They must have been the only car for hours. Any policeman doing their traffic monitoring from there must have been lazier than most, or doing something else.

Incredulous swerved to miss a pot-hole at least a foot deep and four or five feet across. The hearse's wheels squealed like Ned Beatty as he struggled to maintain control, keeping them on the road. An answering squeal of a police siren rose behind them and blue lights flashed against a backdrop of wheel-spun dust, rising in the rear-view mirror like a swarm of locusts.

Incredulous slowed the hearse and pulled over to the side of the empty road, quietly saying, "Fuck," as he did so.

Jon began to pray.

Roadside heretics

The police car crouched behind them for an uncomfortable length of time, a sickly yellow in the thin, cool sunlight. The sun had hidden behind a cloud and there was a bite in the air.

Neither Jon nor Incredulous moved for a while, the music booming loudly. Jon reached towards the radio and was slapped by a black hand, heavy with rings and nail polish.

"No," he said quietly. "My car."

All men over a certain age understand this, no matter what their cultural background, and Jon Power submitted. The music pulsed moodily. They sat where they were. One did not, as a rule, do anything in the presence of police that police might not expect, or like. Moshoeshoe turned off the ignition and they were immersed in tense silence.

At length, a figure emerged from the driver's side of the boxy yellow police car. An old model. Innovation takes its time to work through the South African system, like everywhere.

The figure stood by the canary can with its lights and B number plate, a portly man, stretching. Another figure emerged, shortly after from the passenger side and slipped behind the car before Incredulous could get a clear look at him in the mirror. The first man was clearly a policeman. Which was briefly a relief.

Fat and slow as a successful lion, he approached the driver's side of the hearse, slowly peering into the windows at the back, then at Incredulous Moshoeshoe's profile up front. Then he stood up, pausing. Looking around? Deciding what to do? He had all the time that power and isolation give a man, and the crotch of his crumpled blue trousers filled Moshoeshoe's window.

He whistled loudly enough to hear through the glass, slow and confident, and knocked asking Incredulous to please get out of the car.

Jon knew it was prejudiced, but he had expected Afrikaans. The policeman had a monster of a moustache and the clear devil-blue eyes of a white-supremacist drill sergeant. Jon's own eyes, to a stranger. His potbelly testing the buttons of his shirt beyond reasonable expectation, his hair thin and tightly stretched as the concept of universal rights far away from a big nation's capital, he spoke an almost neutral English. Traces of South African heaviness weighted his pronunciation, but if he'd been wearing an *I heart Sydn*ey t-shirt or a maple-leaf cap one might have thought differently.

"Good afternoon," he said, a little too loudly. "Would you please get out of the car?"

The policeman whistled as Incredulous unfolded into the sunlight, glorious in his shining darkness.

"Henk" he shouted over his shoulder, not taking his eyes off the dark face, the darker make-up, the dreads, and shells and dark, long-lashed eyes. The PVC trousers. As cops went, he was standard issue, if younger than his frame had initially suggested. Jon thought he was probably 36 or 37, heavy with sitting around all day, dissipated with fleecing passing motorists in quiet places for whatever it was he wanted.

Incredulous thought he was an officious little prick. But then he was prejudiced against normies.

The man called 'Henk' emerged from behind the car and approached, a slow drawl of a walk in the silence. His head was shaved at the sideboards, long up top. His arms were covered in tattoos. Up close, some of them were clearly prison jobs. He and the policeman exchanged glances. The policeman nodded and Henk smiled. He was holding a heavy wooden stake about five feet long. It was sharpened to a wicked point. Over his arm, cradled in his elbow, was a length of rope.

"Please take off your glasses, sir," the policeman said into Incredulous' face. His breath smelled of cigarettes. Tuna. Klip-drift. "Yes," he smiled. "I thought so." He jerked his head lightly at Henk. "We're very lucky you came this way this morning. Honoured. Aren't we, Henk?"

"Ja." Henk was smiling too. Neither man's eyes had left Moshoeshoe since he had left the car.

"Hey," Jon broke in, "Can I ask why you've stopped us? We weren't speeding."

"You swerved and skidded past that pot-hole." The police-man's eyes were cold. "Dangerous."

"Ja," said Henk again, fingers flexing at his sides. *Nervous-ness? About what?*

"I'm sorry, are you even a policeman?" Jon asked.

"Don't you worry about that, *boytjie*." The officer was *not* Australian. "He's helping me," he paused as if thinking, "helping me keep this road safe." He smiled. "Sir, please go with Henk to the car. There's something you can help us with." He indicated with a slight flick of his eyes for Jon to follow the tattooed deputy.

"I'm not sure…"

"Just *go*, man! I want to talk to your friend."

There is a quiet way of speaking that is far more aggressive, more threatening than shouting. Jon obeyed.

His back receded silently with Henk. Incredulous was alone with the officer. In the empty silence. It sounded like there wasn't another car, another human being for miles. Full of quiet and the occasional bird. The sighing of breeze through grass. The sun had come out again.

The policeman's manner had warmed, awkwardly. He offered Incredulous a cigarette. "Fransie," he said.

Incredulous took the cigarette but looked blank. Images of men in blindfolds and pockmarked walls filled his head. The man in the crumpled uniform explained.

"It's my name. Francois Vermeulen. People call me Fransie."

"Thanks, Fransie. Are we going to be here long?"

The smile disappeared from his face. "Are you in a hurry?"

"No, no. Just a question." Incredulous inhaled more deeply than he should have and coughed like a ten-year-old.

Fransie laughed and patted his back, the large fleshy hand lingering a little longer than Moshoeshoe liked on the mesh of his shirt.

"Come on," he said, motioning the taller, slimmer man towards the back of the hearse. "Please open it up."

Incredulous obliged. A scent of old flowers slid from the interior, landing at their feet and splashing up to their faces.

"A real hearse, hey?" Fransie said.

"Yup."

"Get inside and lie down, for a moment, please."

Jon Power arrived in the shade of the tree next to the cop car as slowly as he could, dragging feet in the yellow, gravelly dust, aware with every step of Henk's eyes on his back. Of Henk's hand on the heavy stake. Of Henk's apparent need for rope.

"A nice spot," he said to the man in the wifebeater vest and camo long shorts.

"Not so nice for some of the motorists who come past here," Henk said. He still had the rope and the sharpened stake. Jon shivered.

"Why?"

"Bad things happen here sometimes." Henk's eyes were empty, his mouth open. Occasionally he glanced back at the hearse. Jon thought Henk looked like he would rather have been there than here with him. It was comforting, in a way.

He thought about what to do. He could take string bean here, that was certain. But not if he was tied up. And the cop had a gun. He breathed deeply and reached for the Calm. He might have called it the Holy Spirit, but he didn't. This was from before. Sitting in a dugout position, waiting for a target. Waiting for a firefight. The Calm was essential if you weren't going to be blinded by fear and unconsidered decisions. If you weren't going to die. The Calm made you wait.

"In my experience, bad things don't usually just happen. Bad people make them happen. Nothing is inevitable." he said, as casually as he could. "We all have a choice …" His voice had risen at the end of the phrase, like a question. *Dammit, Jon,* he thought.

Henk stopped and looked at him with disdain. "What are you, a philosopher?"

"I'm a pastor."

Henk laughed. "My Pa was a pastor." His accent was Afrikaans. Farm boy. "I don't believe anymore."

"Why?"

"Because of bad men. And science, you know?"

"Science?"

"Ja. Science. They have proved there is no God. I guess that makes your job pointless."

"I'm not sure …"

"I don't want to talk," Henk said abruptly. He had been glancing at the hearse and now seemed annoyed. He paced 'round to the back of the police car and Jon could hear him opening the doors to the little cage where suspects under arrest were locked up.

"I want to do this before another car comes," he said. He sounded resigned. As if it were a chore to be done, his heart not really in it.

"Okay, go ahead." Jon edged as far from him as he could without being obvious, trying to stay out of the conversation now. "Don't let me get in your way."

"No," Henk said. "You are part of it. Come." He was motioning Jon to the prisoners' compartment. He was holding the stake like a spear.

⸻

Jesus, thought Incredulous Moshoeshoe as he slid along the raised platform in the back of the hearse, trying all the time to keep his eyes on Fransie.

He had been about to object to the policeman's request when he had noticed the gun. Unsheathed with a speed and silence that had taken his breath away. He was cold with fear.

He felt the hearse's suspension creak as the fat man clambered in.

"Fransie, no…" he said, but the mass of panting blue fabric was already clambering up beside him, the revolver waving around alarmingly.

"Ag, don't worry, man. It won't take long."

And with that, the fat man seemed to pirouette in the air and land on his back next to Incredulous.

Resting his head on the black meshed shoulder of his companion, he lifted the gun between them, not pointing at Incredulous per se, but nestling between their faces. The policeman's other hand was fiddling in his trouser pocket.

Incredulous closed his eyes.

In some contexts, ten seconds is nothing. History. Sexual stamina. Pregnancy. But in others, it is very long indeed. Incredulous still had nightmares about DJ sets where factors beyond his control resulted in dead air. Ten seconds of that hideous, shaming silence can break a strong DJ. In his early days, he had committed the sin a few times and had felt how long a sixth of a minute can take. Felt the awful judgement of peers and punters as he fumbled for another track. Ten seconds in that context could be a year.

Ten seconds in the back of a hearse, with a large white policeman jiggling about next to you with his gun in your face, is longer.

An electronic click in front of him made Incredulous open his eyes. A phone, at the end of Fransie's extended arm, hovered above them. On its screen, Incredulous saw Fransie smiling, and his face, grey, with screwed-up eyes, as if waiting for a balloon to pop.

"Selfie!" Fransie giggled and then barked. "Come on, man, your eyes were closed! Open them!"

"Okay, okay! Just don't…"

Fransie wasn't listening. He grinned, clicked, and was wriggling out of the coffin-cab, fiddling with his phone before Moshoeshoe could decide whether what he was feeling was nausea or relief.

"Ag, thanks, man!" Fransie said. "I'm a big fan! Are you maybe going to do a gig 'round here?"

Incredulous lay motionless in the back of the hearse for a while, trying to process what was happening.

"Ummmm, no…" he said slowly to the plush ceiling. Like the backrest of a white sofa. Tasteful.

Fransie chuckled, "Hey come on out, man, I know you're a goth, but don't get too comfortable in there, hey!" His accent was becoming more South African with every word. Like blood rushing to an unbent limb. Incredulous was getting pins and needles. He clambered out, sheepishly.

"Ja, man, I'm more of a Punk guy, Fokofpoliesiekar, NOFX, and that stuff, but I used to live in Jozi and I heard you at the Underground. You were amazing. When I saw your name on the dispatch this morning, I said to Henk I hope you come this way. You were the best, man."

"Thanks, Fransie."

"No, man, it's true. Everyone always said so. Even Henk, and he hates Goths."

"Henk?" Incredulous was still in a daze.

"Ja man. Henk!" Fransie laughed at the ditsy DJ standing awkwardly before him. *Artists, eh?* "Henk with the tattoos back there. My boyfriend."

"Ohhhh...." Incredulous smiled.

"Ja we loved you, man. Where've you been? You haven't played in years now, hey? I tell you, this place is nice, but the club scene is shit."

"Yeah, I do the occasional gig, but not a lot..." Incredulous' mouth was on autopilot.

"I heard you joined a blood cult." Fransie was smiling, happily munching on a Tex Bar, crumbs of chocolate dancing in his moustache.

"No... No, it's more a ..."

"Ag wait until the guys at the station hear that I met you! We've got a few metalheads, some rockabillies. There's even a young guy who's into that Emo shit. You like that stuff? I can't get into it. It's like Punk for girls." Fransie laughed contentedly, looking around at the beautiful emptiness.

"And this report…" Incredulous said, tentatively.

"Ag, it's kak, isn't it? I said to Henk, I said, 'That Goth wouldn't kill a woman. He basically *is* a woman!'" Fransie laughed as if he had said something very funny, and Incredulous decided to laugh along with him.

"It is kak, yes."

"I thought so. Everyone knows it was the Likota and the RYM who killed those poor girls. Our Commandos are preparing for action. The moment Ms. Aak de Nau says the word…" Fransie patted his side-arm. A thought seemed to occur to him. "Hey, whose side will you be on?"

"Side?"

"You know. Black or white. You're black, but, you know…. One of us."

Incredulous bit his tongue-piercing. "Thanks," he said and smiled what he hoped was a non-threatening, almost white smile.

"No, we knew it wasn't you. Your friend, though. The Christian. We're not so sure about him…"

～

Jesus, Jon Power prayed. He didn't have words. Just the name he had called on in the worst of times. Just the name.

He walked slowly towards the man with the stake, who watched him blankly as he trudged. Arriving at the back of the van, he winced to see it laid out with brutal-looking tools.

"What are they for?" he asked, his voice faltering despite himself.

"For you," Henk said, and Jon Power felt his muscles tighten and his fingers go cold as blood rushed to prepare him for fight or flight. Henk continued, "To carry to that pot-hole."

"Look, I'm sure there must be something…" Jon started without listening and then pulled up. "Wait, what?"

"To that pot-hole. The one you swerved by."

"Why?" Jon's body was confused. It was in good company.

"I *said*, man. It's dangerous here. You *mos* saw. That pot-hole is dangerous. Bad things happen here. We've had five crashes here in a month. Local government won't fix it, so we sit here in case something happens. We want to put up a sign to warn people but Fransie's back is bad and he sucks at practical stuff anyway. You're going to help me put this stake into the ground on the side of the road. We'll nail the sign on the stake once it's in nicely." Henk nodded towards a board lying in the grass a few feet from the police car.

"And the rope?" Jon asked.

"Oh," smiled Henk. "The rope's to tie you up with."

⌒⌒

"Wait, what the *hell*, Fransie?"

Incredulous was standing with his arms slightly raised in front of him, like a tennis player with the ability to swat away bullets, waiting for the policeman's serve. Jon Power stood next to him, his wrists bound with red and white nylon rope.

Fransie waved the gun at the men, still smiling that inane smile.

"Hey, I don't know why you're so pissed off," he said. "We aren't going to report you. We're not even going to kill you. We're just going to rob you!"

"Fransie, we need to get to Pretoria."

"Ja, cos I'm going to take your car from you. Cos that will be easy to sell. No man, don't be stupid. We just want some money. And any valuables."

"Valuables."

"Ja, something we can use. Mr. Christian here was involved with Mrs. Aak de Nau's daughters. Probably fucking them, hey!" He laughed. "They're all like that. And the dispatch said he pulls in big bucks on his tours of little *dorpies*. Rolling with high-fliers and pulling in long dollars, he's got to have something. And we need something. Sorry, Mosh."

In the time-honoured tradition of all grown-up DJs, Moshoeshoe winced at his stage name.

"Why Fransie? What do you need it for?"

"A shitstorm is coming, bru. We need guns. We're gonna fight. We're gonna take our country back. And guns aren't cheap."

Jon thought for a moment. "Ummm…"

"What's it, Jesus Freak? You want to pray for us?"

"I don't give a shit about your souls. I want to offer you something. Something you morons might like."

Fransie and Henk were intrigued enough to ignore the sleight.

"Ja?"

"How would you like some *real* weapons? For when things get real?"

The white men smiled.

"You've got to promise only to use them if it comes to war. You promise that?"

"Sure, sure. What are we talking about?"

Incredulous and Jon heard a hollow boom of the hand grenade about a mile down the road.

Incredulous didn't know how to feel. He flicked Adrian Hates and his merry band back on and opened the window to enjoy the drive.

Alice

Alice Bechdel-Smith was talking to her girlfriend. It wasn't easy.

"What?" Lily shouted. It was muffled. Like a teacher in a Charlie Brown movie.

"I said I'm sick of talking about your old boyfriends!"

Alice was shouting. She wasn't angry. This wasn't an argument. Just an observation, a thought that had popped into her mind like a bubble. Ephemeral and light and exactly the kind of thing she would usually say immediately, without having to repeat it.

She was shouting and repeating herself because Lily was wearing a diving bell helmet on her head, so she sort of had to.

Lily opened the glass hatch in the front of the brass monstrosity. It made her walking vaguely unstable for a few steps, but she recovered. This was not her first underwater rodeo.

"Well, we don't have to," she said. She felt like her lips were sticking out of the diving bell's window, comically, like a camel's or a giraffe's. *You know,* she thought, *the way giraffes look in diving bells.*

"What do you want to talk about?" Lily asked. She was an even-tempered girl, a dream to go out with if you could get her to pay attention long enough to pay a bill or for dinner occasionally.

They were walking down a dusty roadside. It had been an hour since they'd seen a car and the sun was dropping quickly now. It was getting cold. Still, Lily didn't complain. If it rained, she was dressed for it.

So was Alice, though she was going to feel it more. Lily's outfit cascaded in pleats of brass and rubber, as if Phileas Fogg had fucked a frog-man. Lily's outfit was, between the cannibalised wetsuits and drysuits, pretty much waterproof. Alice's had been born to get wet. A genuine Victorian bathing suit, all boning and binding and pleats and skirts, it looked like a strangely demure yet short dress, bunched at the calves with ribbons and frills. All black. All heavy, strong material. It would have drowned Penny Heyns in 30 seconds. If it rained, it would be heavier than the diving bell. Alice had been walking in it for hours.

She adjusted her bonnet (basic black, broad) and looked up the road.

"I don't know," Alice said. "ISIS?"

"The goddess?"

"Fighting that middle-class stereotype, my love."

"The dog on Downton?"

"You're fucking killing me."

"Not the terrorists. Surely."

"Yup. Them."

"I preferred them when they were called Al Qaeda in Iraq," Lily said.

"The brand change worked for them."

"You're happy for them?"

"I'm interested in branding," said Alice.

"I'll heat the iron."

"Haha. There's something about them. Been thinking about them ever since I read that paper."

"I'm dating a spy nerd."

"A foreign policy nerd."

"Sure, sure."

"Ssshh, my love!" Alice said with an exaggerated finger to her lips. "They'll hear you!"

"I'll report myself to HR the moment we get back to work," Lily said.

"Noted. Twenty points to the Hufflepuff Caliphate."

"Ta. What about the artists formerly known as Al Qaeda in the East?"

"Well, to my knowledge, none of your old boyfriends are Muslim extremists. Or extremists at all. Neither are mine, as far as I know. So that's a fairly safe topic."

"If you were really gay, you'd not have ex-boyfriends." Lily pouted exaggeratedly, imagining her lips extending beyond the window of the diving bell again.

"If I were really gay, I'd be dating someone who looked a lot more like a dude."

"Homophobe."

Alice skipped in front of Lily and kissed her. It was not easy, but she managed it. People bleat about walking 500 miles or swimming across oceans. They have never tried to kiss a delicate-faced girl with skin like caramel through the tiny, sharp-edged brass window of a 120-year-old helmet. That is real love.

"Ouch," said Alice.

"Love hurts."

"Anyway, that's my point."

"What?"

They were walking automatically, they had been for many miles. More kilometres. The sun was weak and a little above the horizon in front of them.

"Isis. They're not terrorists, are they?"

Lily turned her head to face Alice. Carefully.

"What?"

"Don't get me wrong, they are arseholes. War criminals."

"If there is a 'but' coming, I am going to be annoyed," Lily said.

"But ... no, listen, but ... terrorists are operating with a focus on civilians, right, to terrify them and pressure governments. Terrorists are not the same as armies."

"Isis isn't an army. It's not even a militia. They're a bunch of terrorists. They cut off children's heads."

"That was never proven."

"You sound like the lamest PR girl ever. 'Actually, no, we never beheaded children. We crucified them.'"

"I'm not an Isis apologist!"

"I think you are. Is that a burkini you're wearing?"

"Fuck off."

"Ha."

They walked in silence for a bit. Lily looked at the trees lining the road ahead, the pinks and blues of the eucalyptus, tall and stately grey smudges in circular cut-out.

"I just think 'terrorist' is a loaded term. We don't call official armies terrorists when they do the same thing," Alice said.

"If they're official armies they are not terrorists!"

"Alright, Fox News!"

"Oh, that is unfair."

"I just don't think that a loaded term like terrorist should be applied simply because you don't have matching uniforms or fighter jets. It's that whole 'give us your planes, you can have our baskets' thing in *The Battle of Algiers*."

"The battle of what?"

"Algiers. Have I not shown you the Battle of Algiers?"

"Nope."

"I must."

"Nope."

"Why not?!"

"You're not going to radicalise *me*."

Alice risked her face and crumpled her bonnet again to kiss her girlfriend, dancing a little as she pulled away from her, twirling into the road. "You're a 'known associate' now. Might as well join my jihad." She danced more, bowing to her lady.

"Move around all you like," Lily said. "That's not going to fool a drone. And my colouring is not going to help."

"Again with the race card."

Lily laughed. "You, madam, are a bitch. I will not write to you from Guantanamo."

"You'll be fine. They'll give you a Quran to read. It will be like being back at home."

"My parents are *Methodists!*" Lily said.

"You don't fool me. I know an Arab when I see one."

"You don't know my people's struggles."

"Didn't your people vote the Nats in the 40s?"

"That was the *Cape* Coloureds. We're from Pretoria."

"Sure, sure," Alice said.

A low rumble like thunder made both women turn and glance back along the road. A hearse was barrelling down on them.

"No way."

"Way."

"Do you think …"

"What?"

"Do you think it's … in service?"

"Is its light on?"

"Shut up. Not like a taxi, I mean, is it on the way to a funeral? Is there any point … ?"

"Can't hurt to try!"

"Which one of us would have a better shot?"

Alice looked at Lily and down at her own clothes.

"Yeah, that's a crap-shoot."

"A what?"

"Let's both do it. No leggy business this time." Alice turned to face the oncoming hearse, her not-Arab, not-Cape-but-Coloured girlfriend skipping ahead until she was 30 meters behind her.

"Of course not," Lily called, trying to sound hurt and extending a fine, fishnetted leg from a slit in her diving suit.

"Come on," Alice said to the approaching car shimmering on the road. "Two nice, ordinary, 19th century girls out hitch-hiking, not offering anything more than entertaining company."

"Who could resist?"

"Hopefully not the dead."

Alice rubbed the rosary in her pocket. She felt calm. They waited for the car.

Clown

"In fact, actually, they are the criminals!" Scientist Likota shouted. The crowd approved. "They tell us we are stealing, but what is a mine if not stealing from the earth?" His accent was heavy, pan-working-class black South African, resonating. They cheered. "My enemies," he said, "infiltrators and agents – they are your enemies also. They are bourgeois, capitalist running dogs. But we will defeat them! Amandla!"

The crowd roared its *Amandla* back to him and he gave the black power salute and walked briskly backstage. Within 45 seconds he was in the back of his late-model Mercedes Benz.

"That go alright boss?" the driver asked.

"Exceptionally," Likota said. The accent had gone. The Palestinian solidarity scarf was crumpled on the seat next to him. "Any messages?"

"No, boss."

"Wonderful. What's our ETA?"

"This traffic, about an hour."

"Gosh," he sighed. "My kingdom for a helicopter."

"Only a matter of time, boss," the driver grinned.

Likota smiled benevolently and closed his eyes. "Music," he said gently.

The driver hit a button and Thelonius Monk skittered out of the speakers and softly bounced off windows and doors. "Thank you, Houk."

"Of course, boss."

The sedan pulled out into the Joburg traffic and headed towards Pretoria.

Lucretia had been dancing at the Vivaldi for about three months. It had not become less boring.

The stripping had become easier, true, and the punters had become familiar, if occasionally tiresome, fixtures in her life – bored, unlucky, stupid, and ugly more than threatening. Like a fumbling uncle at a New Year's party. But the music, God, the music. She had thought it was a joke initially. That Mario, the slightly greasy owner, would grow out of it. He hadn't.

"It's a USP," he'd pontificated to her in her third week when she raised it. It was certainly U. SP was doubtful. Though, how much of an SP, U or otherwise, one needed to encourage men to come and watch beautiful women take their clothes off was debatable.

Mario had been something of a big deal in the Johannesburg advertising scene. He'd chucked it all in for dreams of becoming a rock star, but his tendency to start odd little personal vendettas with clubs, promoters, and bands had brought it to an end. "It's what will set us aside from the rest of the market. You'll see." Lucretia hadn't.

She'd seen that she was trying to roll her hips, shake her tits, and generally grind out a living to classical music. And that was hard. More than that, it was boring. Classical wasn't her thing. It's hard enough feeling sexy while a dozen middle-aged men pretend not to be interested in your body (on a weekday) or 150 of them are shouting as if they're at a rugby match (on a weekend night). When the music has no groove, has no soul, has no *sex*, it's like dancing in broad daylight to tunes from a phone.

"It's *classy*!" Mario had shouted at her from a stagefront table one slow day, her face peering at him from between her calves as she bent double to a Beethoven's 4th piano concerto, two customers studiously ignoring her over their beers and chips in the corner. The scent of salt and vinegar filled the air.

The Vivaldi had, despite Mario's predictions, attracted the same clientele as all the other upper-end strip clubs in Pretoria, though Mario's advertising contacts had brought in a more moneyed crowd from time to time. Yuppies, musicians, political fixers and managers had all lined up to watch the girls and drink the over-priced beer. Lucretia had given dances to them all. Not one of them had ever mentioned the music.

It was one of the fixers who had introduced her to Scientist Likota.

"Don't frown like that, baby," he'd soothed as she spun her long, auburn hair behind her like a rotor blade. She was sitting astride him in one of the little lapdance booths by the bar. The DJ was spinning Mahler. The fixer continued, trying to get her to warm to the subject, "He's a public servant."

"He's a prick," she said. "And he's dangerous."

"He's an exceptionally good politician and a better customer," Mario said, later that day, during a quiet period when he was conducting a 'quality control spot check' as he called it.

"He's a phony! The way he talks on stage, at his rallies, in the news. It's nothing like when he comes in here."

"And I guess all the guys you dance for really do remind you of the boy who took your virginity?"

"That's different."

"How?" he asked.

"I'm a stripper. He's a whore."

Mario laughed. "Ah, baby, you're just prejudiced because you're a boer *plaas meisie.*"

She flicked her head and slapped him in the face with her hair. "Song's over," she said, lifting her perfect behind from her boss' lap. She flicked her g-string into her hand with the heel of her tall, exceptionally pretty shoe, and flounced out of the booth, managing to infuse a bare ass with strong-willed irritation.

A few months later she was giving the same aggressive treatment to the firebrand in question. She stepped out of the booth and flicked a tiny lacy thing into the air and caught it in her left hand, fixing Scientist Likota with an icy stare.

"Thank you, baby, I hope you enjoyed that," she said with all the human warmth of a frozen chicken.

"Hey, don't be like that!" He reached out a hand but stopped short of putting it on her hip when she shot a look at a beef-slab of a bouncer, towering by the door.

"Okay," he said, producing R800 in cash and holding it out to her. She glowered at him. "Take it," he said. "I'm sorry for suggesting…"

"For suggesting what?" she pouted.

"For suggesting that you were a racist. I knew you'd hate it."

She took the money. She was naked, save for a light dusting of glitter on her C-cup breasts, shimmering down a narrow waist and dusting the smooth, white skin of her thighs as if with stars. An attendant appeared from between the molecules of the air and took the money for her, depositing it in her tip jar (20% to the house). Chopin's Minute Waltz came on and she smiled.

"This song?"

"No," he laughed. He'd been there before.

Her face softened a little. "Did you mean it?"

"Mean what, baby?"

"You know what." She'd adopted a coquettish pose, one leg crossed around another, teetering, hands behind her back. He liked it. She knew he did.

"Well, you know who your daddy is."

"Nobody is supposed to," she said. She didn't look as severe as she should have.

"Ah but it's my business to know. Have you seen the news lately? For every moderate like Aak De Nau out there, there's a man like your daddy, waiting to start a race war."

"My daddy's a prick."

"That doesn't mean you don't agree with him on some things, though."

"You know what colour you are, right?" she said, uncrossing her legs.

"Coffee. With a dash of milk. And lots and lots of sugar," he said.

"So how can I be a racist?" 'Air on a G String' had begun. It always made her smile in that context. She began to dance.

"Well, you're at work. I represent a lot of people I don't like. But some of them have way too much money to let that change a damn thing."

She was on her knees, arching in an elegant concave up his body, brushing it with her breath and hair up to his ear. She whispered, "I love my job. And you're special."

That had been six months after she'd first danced for him, which had been on the day of Mandela's first death. It's how she remembered that particular anniversary. She wasn't sentimental. The world was, though.

The world mourned. Leaders gathered. Selfies were taken and sign language was faked. And that was not all.

A test for the country was how the powers that be had sold the truth when it had come out. An unsuccessful attempt to spend his declining years in peace, free from use as a living justification for the Party. A simple medical clerical error that had set wheels in motion that were too big for any hospital to stop. Some people bought it, some people didn't. And then people moved on.

Mandela's glorious resurrection had been received with a measure of coolness by the international community and a ratcheting up of tension in South Africa. Old racisms, never dead, just hidden beneath the blankets of the Rainbow Nation, emerged, sleepy and grumpy. Violence had erupted again. The likes of Scientist Likota and the newly invigorated Broederbond agitated and infuriated the country into a state of high alert and the father of the nation had calmed the nerves of the masses.

For my sake, he seemed to say, don't let this happen. And it had worked, for a time.

An unspoken agreement to hold back, to cease active hostilities while the old man was alive had existed for a time. Now, as his health was failing, there were rumours of sides being taken, ploughshares being beaten into swords, blank cheques written by the New South Africa bouncing, and weapons being cached.

Against this background, Lucretia had met Scientist Likota – bogey-man of White South Africa. Inarticulate, inflammatory, impressively influential, and terrifyingly stupid.

Except he wasn't.

"It's a populist act, my sweet," he'd told her on one of their early, 'proper' dates, outside the club. "It's what the people want."

"I don't want it. You say terrible things."

"Do I?" he smiled. "I like to think of it as 70 percent reasonable leftism, cloaked in 25 percent down-home, uneducated, man-in-the-street ignorant anger. With about five percent cut-loose insanity, just to guarantee some headlines."

"Seventy percent?" she teased. "Really?"

He laughed. "Fine. Maybe 60. But my column inches and my polling suggest that it's working. And I'm the only one pushing this government in the right direction."

She leaned over and kissed him. They were in the back of his car, heading into Waterkloof and the moneyed suburbs of Pretoria. "I disagree with your statistical analysis and your politics, but I *love* your column inches."

"Oh, yes?"

"Yesssss," she growled, lightly. "Want to do some intensive polling?"

Scientist had laughed again and pulled her closer. That night they made love for the first time. The head of the Radical Youth Movement, committing what would have been a crime under Apartheid.

They had been married, secretly, in the Spring. It was an odd kind of marriage. No living together, no public recognition. But it had meant something to them – even if they couldn't put their fingers on it. Someday, when his political career was more stable, they'd move in together. Make it public. Make his shift into the centre. Until then it was dancing to make ends meet – South African journalists love to follow a trail of money to a scandal. And Likota marrying a white girl would have been quite a scandal.

Tonight, years of secret assignations and successful obfuscation later, was their anniversary.

She had booked out a private function suite at the club as she often did – Mario had been happy for the money, happy for the new high roller needing his place to show discretion towards Likota's seemingly unquenchable taste for one particular white girl. He had offered an entrance through the Ultra-VIP room and a balcony overlooking a sweep of veld running into the twinkling jewellery of distant Joburg, visible from its high vantage point in Centurion. Only the little button on the bedside table – linked to a discrete switchboard in the club, where that room's booked 'performer' would be listed – gave any impression that this was anything other than an upmarket hotel room. Only about a third of the girls used the room. The rest remained poor.

Lucretia was in the communal dressing room in the main club when she received a text from the switchboard.

He was early.

O Fortuna was surging into life as she strode through the heaving club, her soft, relatively conservative dress marking her out as a punter or the wife of a punter rather than one of the girls tonight.

She walked quickly so that the initial choral intensity had subsided into the quiet, building anticipation that came before what she liked to think of as Orff's money shot by the time she reached the Ultra VIP room. She smiled at the huge, immaculately suited doorman as he stepped aside. She could vaguely hear the money shot explode as she passed the second, inner, doorman, and shut the inner door behind her.

The lights were low and the sliding door to the balcony was open. A brief flash of lightning silhouetted a man's shape against the sky.

"Scientist?" she called out.

Her hair was standing on end.

⌐———⌐

Centurion is not a pretty suburb. It used to be called Verwoerdburg and is still about as beautiful as a satellite town named after the architect of Apartheid was ever likely to be. There is not an arboreal nursery in the world big enough to make a dent in its air of treeless, concrete horror, its walls high and hostile.

At night, it could be quite pretty. And there's good drinking to be had if you know where to find it. More than that, if you have money, there are places in Centurion where you can be made very comfortable. Places out of the public eye, where a well-known face can be given the peace and quiet he desires.

These things were occurring to Scientist Likota as he alighted from his car and said goodbye to Houk.

"I'll call you when I need you, comrade," he said, the stiff formality of his role returning as potential public scrutiny flooded back into his mind. He adjusted the Palestinian scarf and gave a black power salute to the press photographers crowding the velvet rope. His security detail and the club bouncers had to wait as he said a few words to the press.

"It is a black man's *duty* to affail himselve of some luxuries that have always been held by the white man. It is good for a black man in today's South Africa to watch white women and black women dance. I belief this is what our struggle was for. Equality. Amandla."

Thirty percent, he chuckled to himself as he strode into the club and made his way for the Ultra VIP.

God, he hated the music in this place.

⌒

It wasn't Scientist.

"How, how did you get past the bouncer? Who are you?"

"I didn't. I'm Dulu."

"Get out!"

"I don't want me here any more than you do."

There was a pistol in the nightstand. Even with high rollers, you couldn't be too careful. Especially with high rollers. She lifted it out and pointed it at the man. "Get…" she said, "Out."

Dulu smiled, a little sadly, and flexed his fingers. A flash. Lucretia dropped the gun, crippled in pain. Her muscles felt like they were on fire. Her ears screamed. Thousands of amps passed through her with the weight of a thousand more volts, and then, like that, stopped.

Lucretia crumpled, but before she could hit the floor she was caught.

"There, there," a voice said. "It's okay. Everything's going to be fine…"

⌒

He looked like a vulture.

A bird of some kind. Of course, he can't have done. Can't have been, but it felt…

Scientist Likota's thoughts were confused. Jarred by the sight of a looming figure over Lucretia's limp body. *Was he kissing her? Was he wearing a cloak?* He… it… seemed to flex and grow and of course, that couldn't be happening. He stood still. Unable to move, wanting to run away, to run to her. To do something.

The figure flexed again and the head turned an impossible distance 'round to look at him. Scientist thought of an owl from a picture book he would read to his nieces. Burning eyes in a dark face stared at him, a streak of red and a hooked nose. Slowly, the head rose, the clothes of black and red almost pulsing as the face rose higher, impossibly high, and there was a noise like the wind. A beating of air.

It wasn't human. Likota was sure of that. But that was where his brain stopped, where his mind refused to go further, a roadblock of uncomprehending terror. The door opened, the security man wondering what the noise was. He stood dumb for just a second – a second too long – and the door slammed shut behind him and the bird made an impossibly tight circle in the air of the high-ceilinged room and swept down on the doorman before he could pull the handgun from his holster.

The sound of his neck snapping was clear above the thunderous rushing. And then the bird, the man alighted in front of him. Took a confident, almost human step too close.

His face ... did he recognise ... ? No. Of course not. And yet ...

The burning eyes stared deep into his and a long-nailed hand caressed his face.

Likota gave a short cry, the first sound he had made since entering the room, as three sharp nails drew lines of blood along his left cheek. The eyes never left his. One of the nails hooked into his scarf and tore a small bundle of threads from it. Dulu held it up in front of his eyes, a knot of fibre clinging to a sharp yellow point. The face Likota thought he knew came closer until he could smell the metallic breath and feel it on his mouth. The man kissed him. A soft, quiet kiss at first and then a sharp pain. He had been bitten.

He pulled away sharply, hand to his mouth. He was bleeding. Still staring into the eyes, not daring to look away for a second.

The lightning bird turned its back on him and scooped up the girl from the floor. In a single motion, the man unfolded into a bird and passed up, out of the balcony doors and over them into the dark, night sky. There was a rumble of thunder, and then silence.

The room was quiet. A single black feather lay on the floor where Lucretia had been. He felt his cheek stinging and glanced at himself in a mirror.

"Jesus," he muttered, looking at the security man.

They would think…

He burst out of the suite door and into the passage. It was quiet.

Scientist Likota called Houk and told him to meet him at The Vivaldi's private entrance. Then he called Caiaphas Molefe.

My girlfriend's girlfriend

"Ugh," Incredulous said. "Steampunks."

"Steam-whats?"

Jon Power was confused. For the last half hour, Incredulous Moshoeshoe had been explaining in excruciating detail the differences between Goths and Emos, Punks, Metalheads, Industrial people (who would never be called 'rivetheads,' however much they campaigned for it), EBMers, and the like. Ugh. Plus the different types and factions within the Goth scene itself and the catch-all term 'Alternative', that seemed to span the subcultures like the boughs of a mighty oak. Or in the South African scene, a thorn tree. Draped in black shwe-shwe fabric. With some toothless dude taking a piss on the bough, whistling *Sarie Marais*.

Now, this. Steampunks. Visions of saunas and safety pin earrings. He shuddered.

"Steampunks," Moshoeshoe said wearily. "It's a Goth thing, really, not a punk thing at all. The old school and new school punks – none of them have anything in common with

Steampunk. It's closer to Goth. The people into it are more gentle Goths than any kind of punks."

"So, the music sounds like…" Jon Power was trying to understand. Incredulous pulled a face. Jon soldiered on and then gave up. "Could you play me some?"

"There isn't any Steam Punk music."

"But you said the whole alternative scene is defined by music."

"*Was*," Incredulous said. "It was. But it's dying. Atomising like all good postmodernisms should. The scenes get more and more niche as everybody tries to be the king of their small kingdom."

"Like Protestant churches," Jon said.

"Yeah, I guess."

"And Steampunk comes from what, then? Where?"

"Pinterest. And Tumblr."

Jon looked blank but didn't bother asking anymore.

"We should slow down. Offer them a lift," he said.

"What? Why?"

"Because they're girls, man. And this is South Africa. And…" he chuckled, "*look* at them."

Incredulous understood what he meant. Diving bell, bonnet, huge cases with brass cogs, and copper tubes glinting in the sun.

"Yeah, but…"

"But what? Don't you have any fellow feeling for your people?"

"Those are *not* my people."

"Well, slow down anyway. Offer them a lift. If they're Goths, they're going to get a kick out of your car."

"Fine. But if they start spouting Victorian bullshit, they *will* be getting kicked out."

Incredulous slowed down.

Alice stepped up to the passenger window and peered in, possible pervert vs length of walk calculations whirring behind her eyes.

"You girls want a lift?"

"Maybe. Where are you going?"

"Pretoria."

"Same," Alice said warily. The dangerous dance of the hitcher.

"Fine. Jump in the back."

"Does the door open from the inside?"

"I wouldn't imagine so. Not much call, ordinarily speaking."

"Hmm."

"Don't you trust me?"

"No."

"Why not?"

"You're driving a hearse. And you're stopping for hitchhikers. The hearse I can live with. But what kind of person stops for hitchers?"

"A kind person?" Incredulous said, regretting stopping already.

"Or a rapist."

"I'm not going to attack you," Incredulous said patiently.

"That's what all the rapists say."

"I don't think they do," he said, looking out at the warm browns and yellows and the deepening purples of the horizon. "Also, I'm not sure jokes about rape are okay."

"Who said I was joking?"

Incredulous lowered his sunglasses and gave her an irritated look.

Alice mused, "Plus, I think the problem is jokes that say rape is okay. Know what I mean? Like the punchline, the ideology behind the joke is saying that rape is acceptable or not a big deal or something people secretly want. Not every joke involving rape is like that. It's like jokes about race."

"You think racial jokes are okay?" Incredulous said, turning to her, his glasses slipping further down, like underlining to his question.

"Sure. Some of them. Just not the ones that have racism at their heart, as their message."

"There are other kinds of racial jokes?"

"Sure. Well. They're about racism. Or involve race. A joke that makes a racist the victim, the butt, that's fine. Like a joke about rapists."

If there had been more traffic, twenty cars would have sailed past while they spoke.

"I can't imagine it."

"Your lack of imagination is not really what should define acceptable expressions of comedy."

"Are you a comedienne?"

"A comedian. Yes. I dabble. In between songs. We're a kind of steampunky comedy music act."

"Wow."

"Yeah, a freelance hearse driver slash rapist is in a position to judge me for my career choices," Alice said.

"You have a funny way of asking for a lift," Incredulous said.

"See? Funny. It's my business. Anyway, I'm still not sure. We'd be trapped in the back there."

"Sure, but we can't climb in either. And those are big windows. If you wanted to attract attention, you would be easy to see. Plus, passengers moving in the back of a car like this – people will remember. I'd say you're pretty safe."

"I'm not sure if I should find the fact you've thought this through comforting or disturbing."

"I don't care," Incredulous said, flexing his fingers on the steering wheel. "We just thought you might like a lift."

Alice glanced up the road ahead, long and straight.

"Okay. Thanks."

The women climbed into the back of the hearse, pulling the door closed behind them.

It was twenty minutes and four times as many miles down the road that Lily took off her helmet, allowing her to see properly the face in the rearview mirror, and to properly be seen.

"*Lily*?"

"*Incredulous*?"

"Oh, for fuck's sake."

"Shit."

~~~

Incredulous Moshoeshoe had switched off the Cat Stevens. He'd switched to Bauhaus. *Stigmata Martyr* had always suited his blackest moods, in the non-ethnic sense of the adjective. It wasn't that it was musically heavy. A man with Incredulous' breadth of taste had played and listened to far harder, heavier music. It just had a mood. A sense of darkness. Of something genuinely sinister in the powerful bass groove, something with fangs and claws in the scratching guitars. Peter Murphy intoning something weird over a Catholic blessing at the end and phrases like 'look to your crimson orifice in holy remembrance and scarlet bliss' helped. Incredulous didn't believe in God, but annoying Him made him feel stronger.

He cranked it high.

Jon Power felt fine, but he didn't like it. Bit dramatic, all this B-movie shouting. The song reached its crescendo and Incredulous turned it down.

"How are you, Lily?" he said in a strained, polite voice, glowering at her in the mirror.

"Wonderful."

"I didn't know you were a farmer."

"I'm not a farmer," said Lily.

"Are you a farmer's prostitute?"

"Fuck off."

"It's just that we picked you up in the middle of farms, and, you know…"

"What?"

"You're a bit of a prostitute."

"Fuck you, man!" The pretty coloured girl shouted and kicked at the partition between the coffin compartment and the cab. She and Alice were sprawled against the left-hand wall, propped up against their big, elaborate steampunk guitar cases, all brass and leather and unnecessary cogs, which rested against the opposite wall.

Alice shouted, "Hey!" as much to her as to Incredulous. "Come on. Incredulous, Lily tells me you used to date an ex of hers."

"Yes. It *had* been a very good relationship."

"And she stole your girl, humiliating you."

"That's not the point. She…"

"She took your woman and she's a woman. And you can play the nancy boy all you like but I have heard stories about you and I know you're *all man*." She said the last two words in an American accent, erect with sarcasm. "You didn't like that. It made you feel less of a man and played on your deepest fears that you were so unsatisfying that you turned her away from dick. You didn't. Lily told me that she always worried that Amelia was never happy with her because she had had you."

"Deepest fear is a bit much…"

"Blah, blah, boring. How long ago was this?"

"I'm not sure. I haven't thought about…"

"Liar. How long."

"Eleven years and three months."

"That's a long time."

"Yes."

"When last did you talk to or even think about Amelia? This year? Last?"

"I'm not sure."

"Exactly. Have you considered your animosity towards Lily is automatic, not real?"

Incredulous mumbled something and Lily laughed.

"Baby, don't be a bitch," Alice said firmly, stroking her girl-friend's hand. "I love you, but you're being rude. They're giving us a lift." She raised her voice, clearly addressing Jon Power. "Thank you."

"Nothing to do with me," he said, desperately trying to stay out of it.

"Okay," she said and continued at Incredulous, "This is a weird coincidence and naturally it's uncomfortable. But it doesn't have to be. Why don't you guys talk? Let Lily sit upfront with you. We've been with each other for hours. I could do with a break."

Lily slapped her arm and Alice held her slender wrist, kissed her hand.

"I love you, baby. But you're batshit insane. Why don't you talk to the nice DJ? I'll be safe in the back with his friend. Won't I, Nothing To Do With Me?"

"Sure," Jon replied, opening his hands slightly in the universal sign of male capitulation.

Incredulous pulled over and they switched 'seats'. It wasn't easy with the helmet and guitar cases.

"What are you?" Jon asked, not unkindly, sitting across from the girl in the black bathing suit. Alice understood what he meant.

"Singers. We're called the Diving Belles. Lesbian Steampunk stuff, mostly."

"Incredulous tells me Steampunk isn't a genre."

"Incredulous is an old man."

"Is he?"

"In DJ years, sure. He's older than you."

"DJs are like dogs?"

"In so many ways."

Jon Power laughed.

"When's your concert?"

"Our gig is tomorrow. Elyzzium."

Jon Power looked blank.

"It's a big alternative club in Pretoria. With two zeds. It's gross."

"Do you go there often?"

"Sure."

Jon Power thought of some of the churches he'd attended over the years.

"I can understand that."

Alice smiled.

"Yeah. It's better than nothing. And it's a lot better than anything in the Highlands."

"You don't strike me as the kind of girl who fits in in the Highlands."

"I moved back because my mom got sick. My day job can be done remotely. I try to get back to Pretoria every few months. I've got to dance."

"Sure," he smiled.

"If you don't mind me saying, you don't strike me as much of a dancing man."

"I dance. Not to this crap," he said, waving his hand vaguely around the air that was currently full of Rosetta Stone, "but I dance."

"What kind of thing?"

"You wouldn't know it."

"Try me."

"You're a child."

"I'm 29."

"Exactly. It's mostly 80s stuff."

"Bon Jovi 80s or Soft Cell 80s?"

"I like Bon Jovi," he said, and she groaned. "But I prefer the synth stuff. Depeche Mode. Men Without Hats."

"I love those bands! They play them all the time at Elyzzium."

"Don't be unkind."

"I'm not! It's pretty standard, synth stuff at a gothy club."

"Seriously."

"Yes!"

"Why? I know you're a child, but do you remember the 80s? I mean from a social studies class or something? Not dark. Not dark at all."

"I don't know. Maybe it's tradition. When the Alternative scene formed around bands like the Sisters and the Cure there was a lot of that synth stuff around. The kids listening to Siouxsie would also have loved Violator. Most of Depeche Mode's stuff. And when you consider Vince Clarke was in Depeche Mode and Erasure *and* Yazoo… Well, all I'm saying is that it's not a million miles from A-HA to some of the darkwave stuff. And Marc Almond *is* Sheep on Drugs. Only more fucking deviant."

"I literally do not understand more than half of what you're saying."

Alice laughed.

"All I'm saying is it's a thing."

"Okay."

"Anyway, what are you boys doing? Are you also a DJ?"

"I'm a pastor."

"Oh, dear."

"You disapprove of Christians?"

"I love Christians. It's Protestants I have a problem with." She was smiling.

"Oh no," Jon smiled back. "A blerrie *Roomse gevaar*?"

Alice chuckled. "Guilty. And you? A Bible-bashing, prosperity-preaching, right-wing nut-job?"

"Are there any other kinds of Protestant?"

"Lol. No." She pronounced 'lol'. It confused Jon Power. "So, seriously, what kind of pastor are you?"

"Prosperity. We prefer 'faith', but it amounts to the same thing."

"You believe all that stuff?"

"I believe the Bible."

"So do I. But that stuff…"

"I believe it *all*. From Genesis to the maps."

Alice Bechdel-Smith laughed. She said, "Ha."

"I can't claim that as my own. Stole it from another faith preacher."

"Well, out of his abundance he can afford to sow a good line into your ministry, no?"

Jon Power laughed.

Alice asked, "And are you crazy right-wing, too?"

"Depends what you mean by crazy."

"I mean do you think my girlfriend and I are sinners for loving each other? Do you think Jesus was a capitalist? Are you super into guns?"

"Do I look American?"

"Don't avoid the question. We've still got a long way to go. I'm interested."

"Well, I'm a Communist, if that helps?"

"Ha!" Alice said again. "Really?"

"Yup."

"*Rooi gevaar?*"

"Guilty."

"How does that square with the prosperity? All that concern for the poor."

"You're a Catholic? Have you seen the Vatican?"

"Have you heard of Dorothy Day?"

"I like her. She's wrong about a lot, but I like her. I like real Liberation Theology more."

"Oooh, Latin American stuff. Like Oscar Romero?"

"And others..."

Alice was not sure she liked the way he said that phrase. It felt cold, like a weapon. Steely.

"So how does that work, though? All the wealth? You give the change to the poor after you've bought your jet? Not very Liberation."

Jon Power smiled. "I guess there's about as much change to give as those Liberationists living in poverty have to give. It's easy to advocate redistribution when you've got nothing to redistribute."

"Trickle-down theology!"

Jon Power laughed. "I redistribute just fine. There are systemic and localised ways to do it. I don't have a jet."

Alice smiled.

Jon said, "What's a smart Catholic girl like you doing dressed like that?"

"It's as reasonable an outfit as yours."

Jon Power looked at his clothes. Khaki from head to toe. Short-sleeved shirt. Shorts. *Velskoenne.* Long socks. He hadn't shaved in a week. He was bristling.

"This is not what they wear in your steampunk clubs?"

"Not so much."

"You don't like it?"

"Not really."

"Isn't it as reasonable an outfit as yours?"

Alice smiled. "Sure."

Jon Power looked out of the window at the cars rushing murderously on the highway alongside them. A flash of bright headlights reflected in the paintwork of another car reminded him of the events of the previous night.

"That wasn't good," said Alice.

"What?" Jon asked, lifted lightly from his thoughts.

"Whatever it was you were thinking about. We were getting along so well. Did you remember I was a lesbian?"

"I think of little else."

Alice chuckled. "Arse."

"No, really. It's so endlessly fascinating. And you're sitting there. All … *lesbian.*"

"Alright, alright."

"No, really. Tell me everything. We could start with diet. What limitations does a penis-intolerant diet put on your daily routine?"

"Okay, you're not obsessed, I get it. Refreshing. But I'm interested. Do you have a problem with us?"

"A problem? No."

She considered him.

"Hmm. What does that mean?"

"It means why would I have a problem with you?"

"You don't think it's a sin?"

"I didn't say that."

"Aha!"

"Are we back on 1980s music?"

"No. 1880s morality."

"It's older than that."

"You think I'm going to hell because I'm gay?"

"No. I think you're going to hell because you're Catholic."

"Be serious."

"Okay," Jon said. "I have no idea if you're going to hell."

"Because you think homosexuality is okay."

"No."

"Arg!" She said the word again. Jon laughed again.

"Explain yourself, Pastor!"

"It's not myself. It's Scripture. I think it makes it pretty clear in some places that homosexual acts are sinful."

"So I'm going to hell."

"Is Jesus your personal Lord and Saviour?"

"I wouldn't put it in that…"

"Oh come on, Vatican II, you know what I mean."

"Sure. Yes. I love Jesus. I have faith."

"Then you're not going to hell. The fact you do some sinful stuff – that's an issue for you and God. Like all sin. If you think it's *not* a sin, well that's an issue for your priest."

"That's profoundly unsatisfying," Alice said.

"I'm sorry."

"Gay marriage?" she asked, like checking off questions on a list.

"I haven't met the right boy. This is all so sudden."

"Should the government allow it, as a rule?" she persisted.

"I mean, if it's a rule, that would make it awkward for straight people..."

"Pastor!"

"I don't care."

"But it undermines the family."

"So what."

"Your people..."

He interrupted her. "I don't think we know each other well enough for you to know who my people are."

"Fine. Pentecostals. Evangelicals. Fundamentalists. They think gay marriage is unbiblical."

"It is. So are microwaves."

"So, you'd marry a gay couple?"

"No."

"Because they're sinners?"

Jon Paused. "You've got me there. I was going to say 'because they're heretics', but they might not be. I mean, if they thought we should ignore Scripture, they would be. But they might just interpret it differently."

Alice smiled again, for the first time in several minutes. "Pastor Jon, you old softy! You're a pluralist!"

"Nope," he said simply and emphatically. "No, truth is truth. Conflicting statements can't all be true. But I can believe that people of good conscience, who love God and believe in the Bible can come to different conclusions."

"You just believe some of them must be fundamentally wrong."

"Obviously."

"Well, well, Pastor. It's nice to meet you." She held out a hand and Jon shook it. "I hope you don't think me rude."

"No, my girl."

"'My girl'?" she parroted. "I'll assume you didn't mean that in a patronising misogynist way."

"Assume what you like."

Alice grinned. "Well, we've covered theological capitalism and homophobia. What about guns?"

"They have their uses in a war," Jon said.

Both of them fell quiet then. Minds on recent news reports, private worries about a public problem, flickering like street-lights as they entered Pretoria.

Last exit for the lost

Despite what Capetonians tell you, Pretoria is not "*snor* city." And despite what Joburgers tell you, it's not a last bastion of racism, clinging on by its white-knuckled fingers to outdated modes of thinking. That's the Eastern Cape. And most of the Free State. Actually, there's a lot of clinging going on, even today.

Pretoria is pretty *verlig*, actually. Tshwane, as it is now known, has a fantastic music scene, a chilled vibe, and clubs that don't suffer from narcissistic personality disorder. There are hipsters, sure, but they're like crime and bad driving. You just have to get used to them. They aren't going anywhere. Pretoria is also very pretty, though, with more trees per square metre than most of South Africa's big cities. You should go there. You'll love it.

Incredulous kissed Lily on the cheek as she got out of the car. It was easier with the helmet off. They seemed friendly enough. Jon had shaken hands with Alice and climbed into the front passenger seat, fastening his seatbelt as Moshoeshoe reversed out of the suburban driveway.

"You guys are friendly," he said, arching an eyebrow at Moshoeshoe.

"Shut up. She's a nice girl. We talked. It was a million years ago. She invited us to their gig tomorrow night at Elyzzium."

"I'd rather get punched in the kidney by Steve Hofmeyr."

"Wow."

"I know," the pastor said. "Her girlfriend is nice."

"You approve? The scandal!"

Jon Power exhaled deeply and shook his head. Had he been Alice Bechdel-Smith, he would have said "sigh".

They bedded down in a crappy hotel on the side of a highway. Its name conjuring up sitting in a perfectly engineered racing car, the experience felt like sleeping in a large filing cabinet. One room each and a dawn start. It's always good to hit the morgue early.

⤚⤙

The morgue was unremarkable. As was its attendant – a friend of Caiaphas's in an apron and cheap shoes. Disappointing. On TV they are always so cool.

"Will you be taking us to the mortician or the medical examiner or whatnot?" Incredulous asked, peremptorily.

"I beg your pardon?" the nondescript apron-filler said.

"I mean when do we meet him? Or is it her? I can't wait!"

"I… I don't understand… I'm the morgue assistant on duty…"

"Sure, sure, brother. No offence. I'll wait 'til we get to your 'lair'." Incredulous was grinning happily. Jon Power rolled his eyes down the grimy government corridors and stairs.

"Here we are, ma-gents," the morgue assistant said, seeming to loosen up a little. "We can talk here. I'm Pauly. This is the Frank Peretti Ward. Some church donated to it about 30 years ago, so that's when all the equipment was updated. All the suspicious deaths come through here at some point, from Pretoria, Centurion, and any of the *bundus* where they can't hack it."

"This." Incredulous said it flatly but it was clearly a question.

Pauly glanced at Jon Power, nervously. Jon shut his eyes and nodded slightly, as if to say, *yes, my friend here is an idiot.* He had an incredible urge to slap the back of Incredulous' dreadlocked head.

"Problem?" he asked.

"Well…" Incredulous said, looking around, more crestfallen than a coat of arms at the bottom of a stairwell. "I mean… Where is the incongruous music? The sardonic wit? The subcultural coolness and gallows humour?"

Pauly looked nervous again, confused. He glanced at Jon Power, who closed his eyes again.

"I… I'm a Jehovah's Witness," Pauly said as if that explained everything. It sort of did.

"This is fine, Pauly. Thanks for giving us your time. Can you tell us about the bodies?"

"Mr. Molefe said you'd want to talk about the Aak de Nau girls?"

"And a woman called Hendl."

"That makes sense," Pauly said.

"Why?"

"All three bodies showed evidence of bleeding to death. All three were, coincidentally – if you believe in that sort of thing – burned."

"Burned?"

"To varying degrees, yes."

"So you think they're connected."

"Well, not because of that."

"How so," asked Jon.

"Well, bodies get burned all the time to cover crimes. The first Aak de Nau girl's body was almost cremated. Hendl and her sister look more like electrical burns. I see that sort of thing in a lot of people trying to rip power for free from Eskom. And torture deaths."

"You see a lot of those?"

"Some. These were different though. More like lightning, to be honest."

"Must have been weird to have two lightning deaths in a week though?"

"Are you kidding? This is the Highveld, bud. Lightning death happens more than drowning, and there are a *lot* of pools here."

Incredulous didn't say 'Yeeesh', but he wanted to. Growing up in Britain, where one peal of thunder counted as a 'storm' that everyone would talk about the next day, he had never become used to South Africa's epic, cataclysmic thunderstorms. And though he had been a paranormal investigator for a few years, this was his first morgue. He thought he was hiding that fact pretty well.

"I have a question," he said.

"Yes?"

"You're the only guy here? There isn't a more interesting, cool girl or a funky guitar-playing guy with a limp? Something?"

"I'm going to have to ask you to leave," Pauly said.

"Fair enough."

"Sorry, Pauly. We appreciate your time. Were there any other commonalities?"

"Well, yeah. A couple. One means nothing. The other means something I don't understand."

"Great."

Pauly grinned. "Hey, I'm basically a butcher here. Too much crime. Too much death. This isn't CSI."

"So, what was the thing you didn't understand?" Jon asked impassively.

"Phthiraptera."

"Bless you," said Incredulous.

Pauly shot Jon a look and continued irritably, "Phthiraptera are bird lice. The second Aak de Nau girl and Hendl were both covered in them. They're not generally found on people."

"And the first death?"

"That's weirder. Finding the lice themselves on a body – that can happen from working a poultry farm or racing pigeons. The first Aak de Nau girl had eggs in her scalp and her groin and even inside her ear piercings."

"First," Incredulous said, "That's disgusting." His stomach had turned right about the time the word "eggs" was mentioned. "Second, how did you find them if her body was so badly burned?"

"Well, your delicate sensibilities aside, I know because my first lab job was with the food inspectorate."

"What?"

"You know. Restaurants. Chains. We had to look for infestations in cooked meat. I worked a lot of chicken cases."

"And they…" Incredulous was quite pale.

"Yup. You get to know the signs."

"That is absolutely…" Incredulous said but was cut off by Jon.

"So helpful. Thank you, Pauly. Are these the only bodies you've seen these on recently?"

"There was another, but it's unconnected."

"Humour me."

"It was a bouncer at a strip club. I noticed a few of them on him, but not nearly as many as the women. And he didn't bleed to death. His neck broke around the time as he had a heart attack."

"That's odd."

"Yeah, but you know these places. Politicians. Organised crime. Sports teams. Things get out of hand. This one looked like a kidnapping of one of the girls. I haven't got 'round to analysing the trace evidence from the scene. They found some fibres and blood outside, but it's not a priority with the Aak de Nau pressure, you know?"

"I know."

Pauly nodded.

"Yes, I heard. Mr. Power, Mr. Moshoeshoe, you are in a heap of shit, if you don't mind me saying."

"You heard the news."

"Yes. It's only because Mr. Molefe has been so good to me that I haven't turned you in. This is not the time for this sort of thing to take place. You know what could happen, right?" he paused, worry all over his spotty young face. "With the country, I mean."

"I know, Pauly. That's why we're trying to figure it out."

"Well, unless the real killer is a chicken-farming pyromaniac, I'm not sure I can be of much use."

"There are other factors, Pauly. But I appreciate it. The best thing we can do is find the real killer before people start firing shots."

"You didn't hear?"

"Hear what?"

"A military-grade bomb went off near Dullstroom yesterday. They're saying it was a RYM bomb. They say the Broederbond is gathering force again. If Mandela goes…"

"He went once. It was fine."

"This time it's different. You must see…"

"I know."

The neon lights buzzed above them and they were quiet for a bit.

"What was the other thing they had in common?" Incredulous Moshoeshoe asked. "The thing that didn't mean anything."

"Just something pretty common in dead people their age. A club stamp on the wrist. UV. It's a bat."

"You know what that means?"

"A club?"

"Ever been to one with that symbol?" asked Jon.

"Have you ever *met* a Jehovah's Witness?" Pauly said.

Talk about the weather

"*Shit on my face.*" Incredulous Moshoeshoe said it slowly, like a whistle of amazement. Jon Power just looked at him. They had stopped for petrol in Pretoria central. Moshoeshoe seemed a little jumpy. Jon was calm. This was where he did what he did, most of his life.

"Indeed."

"Seriously though," Incredulous said, staring into the distance, his mind on something.

"What?"

"The lice. The bird lice."

"Yes."

"I mean," Incredulous said after a pause. "Is this real? I mean, is it possible that what we saw, that what we read about – Lightning birds…"

"It looks that way."

"You're okay with this? I mean, apart from what's real, apart from any rational, scientific considerations. Your faith?"

"What makes you think that my faith is apart from rational, scientific considerations?"

"No need for an apologetics talk, Ravi Zaccharias. You know what I mean."

Jon Power sighed and looked around. A Total forecourt full of petrol attendants, all hustling for business. A Pretoria street, made of dirt and boredom and 70s concrete architecture. Brand new German sedans and thousand-year-old trucks and buses vomiting smoke and fumes and thick, dead air onto the streets and pavements around them. Noise and shade and sunshine and innumerable people shouting, laughing, working, and grifting. *That* was real.

He looked up through his windshield at the sky, closed his eyes for a second, and thought of God, eternal, benevolent, omnipotent. Of Jesus, the Lamb, crucified, alive, answering his prayers, lifting his chin, extending grace. Good things to men who didn't deserve them. That was real. That, too. Both of them. At the same time. Incarnation is a paradox. Strength is holding them together.

"I can believe it," he said. "But I don't have to like it."

Their petrol attendant was shaking their car, making space for every last drop of fuel.

"Meaning?"

"Meaning we need to put a stop to this."

"Now, *there's* a Bible-belt response I can respect."

"Good," Jon said. "It's time to get going."

"Where?"

"Somewhere we can talk. Somewhere we can decide how we kill this thing."

The petrol attendant was wiping the windows he had just washed, rubbing them with paper towels until they shone. Jon gave him his card.

"Should we involve someone else?" Moshoeshoe asked. It was a reasonable question.

"Who? The police are after us. Aak de Nau's people too, probably. And with Mandela properly on the brink this time and the shit on both sides building up, no one can help. Not without exposing themselves unnecessarily."

"True. But will we be enough? If we don't kill it, if we don't stop it ..." A cloud of worry passed over Moshoeshoe's face. "It could mean war."

"Mmm," Jon rumbled. An idea that had been skulking around the perimeter fence of his mind was preparing to make a dash into the light.

"I mean, the victims are the worst possible. The worst luck." Incredulous shook his head.

"I don't believe in luck," Jon said and was about to expand on the belief (or lack thereof) when the bubblegum tones of Enola Gay by OMD broke through the traffic noise. He answered his phone. The petrol jockey who had just returned stood patiently, leaning against a no cell phones sign.

Mr. Power?

"Yes. Pauly?"

Hi. Sorry to bother you so soon, but I just got some info you might find interesting.

"Yes?"

That bouncer? He did have slight electrical burns. I didn't notice them at first but they are there.

"Okay."

And Mr. Power?

"Yes?"

The blood on the fibres.

"Yes?"

It's Scientist Likota's.

Jon was silent for a while. Long enough for Incredulous to look at him inquiringly. He asked, "You're absolutely sure?"

Yes sir.

"You know what…"

I know what that information could do, Mr. Power, yes. I am trying to keep it quiet, but the Spieëlding case will eventually come up. I can't keep it… "

"The what case?"

Spieëlding. Lucretia Spieëlding is the kidnapped girl. Stripper. I'm getting a weird amount of pressure to fast-track the investigation, considering what she is.

"It's not what she is," Jon said. "It's who she is."

I don't understand.

"It's okay. But it's important that you delay that news getting out for as long as possible."

Okay.

Pauly rung off.

"Shit," Jon said.

Incredulous looked inquiringly at him. "Problem?"

"You could say that." He signed the slip the petrol jockey brought him and reached into his pocket for a tip.

"What?"

"The kidnapped girl."

"Ja?"

"She's the daughter of Herman Spieëlding. The current head of the Broederbond."

Jon handed the jockey an unusually large tip and pulled out into the dazzling sunlight and traffic that was the odd blend of aggressive and lazy, peculiar to cities like Pretoria. It was comforting. They drove in silence until they reached the place Incredulous had suggested for lunch.

⌒⌐⌐⌐

"One," Incredulous Moshoeshoe said after a bite of an amazing veggie pita, "the Broederbond is a thing?"

Bob Marley played over the speakers of the shady place, a '100% gluten-free zone', according to the slogan on the wall. It was all earth tones and weed-chic. The beer wasn't very cheap.

"Two," he said, "So what?"

Bob Marley also gazed beneficently down from a mural and up from the menus. *Irie.*

"Three, How the fuck do you know who he is, much less who his daughter is? Four, Why do you drink that shit? Doing your bit to preserve stereotypes in a post-racial South Africa?"

Jon Power sipped on his Castle, thinking. He drank from the bottle, the chilled glass with its beer-flattening droplets of water like a crust of pearls sat lonely and abandoned on the hand-painted wooden table.

Every little thing's gonna be alright, Bob said.

"One," Jon Power said, "Yes. It's a thing. Very much a thing. In fact, the New South Africa made it stronger by driving it deeper underground. It used to be about influence. Today it's paramilitary, para-security, para-espionage. Certain European and North American powers are pretty heavily invested."

Incredulous looked at him blankly.

Jon continued, "I know him. Spieëlding."

He took a deep slug of his Castle. "Four, I drink this because it's the best beer in the world. Seven, I don't have to play by your numerical rules." he smiled. "And two, don't be so thick. Likota on one side, the Broeders on the other, Mandela about to pop his clogs, not just symbolically this time. With all the tension around? Tension we have added to? What the hell do you think is going to happen when the Broeders find out their girl is missing and that everybody's favourite clown to hate is implicated?"

Incredulous sipped contemplatively at his Black Label.

"It's still a very white beer. Afrikaans, even."

"Well, it's a good thing I'm not a racist."

"Ah, aren't you?" Moshoeshoe asked, cocking a pierced eyebrow. "Then how is it you're buddy-buddy with the head of an organisation that makes the Apartheid government look like Noam Chomsky?"

"He worked with me in… in my previous profession."

"Your sort-of military one?"

"Ja. A lot of them were in pretty high positions then. They had intentionally targeted that sort of work. He was… alright."

"Alright?" Incredulous looked a lot like his name. "I got the impression you weren't a fan of racists. You're involved with my uncle and he's not a million miles away from Likota and those assholes."

"Your uncle's organisation is there to prevent us going back into…"

"Into the bad old days. Yeah, yeah, I've heard it all before. I think they like to play soldiers."

"You don't know what it was like."

"Oh yeah, white man?" Incredulous' eyes had gone dark. He said, "Tell me how you suffered."

Jon Power was silent for a long while.

"I committed sins that I cannot forgive. I was put in a position where I was part of the problem. And then I decided to be part of the solution. In both positions I did things ... I'm trying to do the right thing. Not to make up for it, I can't, but so that, if I ever have to do something terrible again, I will be on the right side."

"Can't you just ask your God for forgiveness?"

Jon Power looked contemplative. Calm. "I have. But who fucking knows, you know?"

"Dominee," Incredulous chuckled, "That may be the best answer I've ever heard from a Christian."

"Well that just means the *world*," the pastor deadpanned. "Shall we hold hands?"

Incredulous laughed. LKJ grumbled from the speakers and a couple of waiters returned from their prandial herbal respite from the rigors of workaday life. "Okay, so how is the head of a far-right secret society plotting the downfall of multicultural South Africa 'alright'?"

Jon shrugged. "Sometimes people are more than their beliefs."

Incredulous grunted. They ate in silence for a while. Eventually, he spoke.

"So, are we thinking that the victims are not random? That they were specifically targeted."

"I would say so."

"And the work of this … Impundulu?"

"It looks that way."

"Without wanting to get into the how of things," Incredulous said, "let's talk *why*. Why would a mythical creature …"

"Supernatural," Jon corrected him.

"Ugh. A *semi*-mythical creature … want a civil war in South Africa?"

"It's demonic," Jon said. "The forces of darkness don't need a rational reason for anything. Satan hates you. He hates me and he hates everything God created. He wants to destroy. To cause chaos."

"Hmmm," Moshoeshoe said dubiously. "But if you're just in it for the unalloyed joy of fucking shit up, why go to all that trouble? Why be so specific?"

"That's easy. Maximum impact. White South Africa's matriarch has her family violated publicly. The Broederbond similarly attacked privately. Both assuming the RYM are to blame. The RYM are spoiling for a fight, and your Uncle and his friends –"

"*Your friends*" Incredulous corrected him.

"Fine. *Our* friends will mobilise the moment it looks like the Broeders and Aak de Nau's crowd are making a move. They've been preparing for this since the early 90s and they've only got better equipped. If you wanted to destroy a country, destroy the maximum possible lives, this is how you would do it. There are already small incidents. Our box of grenades for one. And the Broeders are not like Aak de Nau. If they discover the Spieëlding girl is gone, if they think it was the RYM …"

"Or if she turns up dead and it's linked to Likota," Moshoeshoe interjected.

"Yes. Then that will start a chain reaction that will force Caiaphas's hand. People will take sides. It will explode. A satanic triumph."

Incredulous mmm'd, "I'm not convinced."

"By my logic?"

"By the presumption of the existence of a personal source of evil."

"You believe in Lightning birds, but not in the Devil."

"I don't believe in a fucking thing. I trust what I see. I don't believe in ESP, but I can tell you your future right now if you like."

"I don't like."

"Well, I don't know if I believe in Impundulus or whatever, but I've seen one. So I guess I don't need to."

"Okay. Well, then, how do we stop it? You said the bird takes human form."

"Yeah."

"So, if we stop it, if we kill it, we would have a human to blame, right?"

"That would be helpful," Incredulous said. "I never understand that shit in horror movies, you know? And things like *Supernatural*, where they're chasing a monster or a demon and they have to contend with all these people who don't believe it exists. Like, come on, guys, just make something up, right?" Incredulous grinned briefly at Jon Power and then saw how far from his frame of reference his current audience was.

Jon blinked at him.

The isangoma continued, "We could call it a serial killer, a psychopath operating alone. Plus clear our names. Worst case scenario, we could at least stop the escalation."

"That's a plan, my man, Stan."

"Please don't do that."

"Sorry."

"The question is how," Incredulous said. "This isn't a vampire."

"I thought you said …"

"I know, Dominee, I know, but it's not like there are rules for how you kill it. No garlic or wooden stakes or holy water or crosses. For all we know, it can die just like any animal. Or is impervious, like a spirit."

"Okay. What do we know? It's a bird, sometimes a man. It can control lightning, maybe more meteorological stuff, it drinks blood, yes?"

"Yes."

"But pushing it off the edge of the endangered species list is more of a mystery."

"That's about the size of it."

"Well, there's only one way to find out. And that depends on finding it."

Enola Gay started beeping again. Jon looked at his phone. It was Elena Aak de Nau.

Pale empress

P*astor?*

"Ms. Aak de Nau."

Are you surprised to hear from me?

"A Little."

I'm sorry about the statement. I know you were not to blame.

"I understand. If the story is one multiracial pair operating on their own, maybe it can slow the escalation. Prevent the escalation."

Nothing is going to prevent that Mr. Power. But we might be able to prevent a war.

"Meaning…"

Meaning I want you to continue with your investigation.

"We have discovered…" Jon Power paused.

What, Mr. Power?

"We've discovered something strange. Your daughter… Daughters…"

Something occult?

"You know?"

My people's report from the scene of Chanel's death. There were strange… anomalies.

"Mrs. Aak de Nau, that night, I saw…"

I don't want to hear it, Mr. Power. You're investigating with an occultist and whoever is to blame – some RYM thug or someone else— whoever it is, has an unhealthy obsession with magic or ancestor worship or some demonic practices. I don't want to hear about what they've done or what you and your friend think they can do. I want you to find them.

"Yes, ma'am."

Do you have any leads?

"Some. I'm busy talking to people at the morgue."

You will be hearing from me.

She rang off without another word, like an American on TV.

"Goodbye," Jon Power said, pocketing his phone.

"And?" Moshoeshoe asked.

"And the Aak de Nau dogs are off us for a while. She knows it wasn't us."

"Which explains why the cops have been so scarce."

"Ja," Jon said.

A dreadlocked white boy with surfer yellow hair and t-shirt bearing the logo of Rasta Al Dente floated up, his eyes slits in an unshaven face.

"You guys irie?"

"Nah, man. We're fine," Jon said, wafting him away with a chuckle.

"You're a prick," Incredulous said.

"*Me*?" Jon asked, glancing off at the white boy. He was standing under a ceiling fan, watching its blades like a bemused kitten.

His phone rang again.

"Oh for fuck's sake, buy low, sell high!" Incredulous said, pulling out his phone in the time-honoured manner of people in bars who want to make it clear they have other friends.

Jon answered.

Mr. Power? It's Pauly. I've found something.

"What kind of thing?"

The Hendl girl. And the Aak de Nau girl. They had those traces of UV ink on their wrists. Some kind of stamp. We have an up-to-date list of local club stamps though. It doesn't match anything we have on file, but I thought you'd like to know. I'm sending you a picture. It's not Gibbs quality but it should give you an idea. Also, Hendl seemed to have been exsanguinated before.

"How's that?"

Well, not entirely, but she's definitely had blood taken, pretty regularly, from some places not usually used for that purpose by clinicians.

"You mean *recreationally?*"

We see weirder stuff all the time.

"Thanks, Pauly."

Of course, Mr. Power. Any friend of Mr. Molefe's will get my help, but it's nice to meet another religious person. Think of this as my present to you.

"Merry Christmas, eh?" Jon said.

No, Pauly said, *Not really. I'm a…*

Jon didn't wait for him to finish. He thanked him, hung up, and opened the message.

"You know any idiots who think they're vampires?" Jon asked.

"A few. And some who wish they were enough to get into blood play. There's a bar you can go…"

"I'd rather not hear about that, thanks."

"It could be helpful for the investi—"

"Even so. You live in that world. I don't want to."

"Suit yourself, Dominee," Incredulous said and sipped on his beer.

"Here, look at this," Jon said, holding up his phone, Pauly's message open.

The picture was well illuminated, if not *terribly* illuminating. A cross between a number six and a B, next to a squarish N or incomplete Roman II. Jon passed it to Incredulous. "Ideas?"

"Yes," Incredulous smiled.

"Don't tell me, this is another arcane African occult symbol."

"Nope."

"What then? Runes? That crap is all Greek to me."

"Close. It's Cyrillic. Russian, based on Greek. Invented by one of yours."

"Cyrillic was invented by a former Apartheid special services operative with Communist sympathies?"

"By a man of God. A priest."

"Wonderful news. I'll call my prayer chain. What does it say?"

"Well, it's not so much what it says – this here is Be." Incredulous drew a Б on his paper menu. "And this is Pe," he said, drawing a П.

"And?"

"It's Russian for B and P. I think. At least that's what it's supposed to be. It's a marketing thing, meant to evoke something Slavic."

"Slavic?"

"Well. Transylvanian. Accuracy is not as important in these things as the idea."

"What idea are we talking about?"

"It's a Borgo Pass. Like a special pass to get into exclusive events or areas at clubs."

"Borgo..?"

"It's from Dracula. Bit of an in-joke."

"Oh good grief, what kind of loser...?"

"It's aimed at the ubers, to keep the dilettantes out."

"Give me strength. Does that mean that the clubs this pass is for are..."

"Yup. If we're going to follow the trail, you're going to have to be touched by the hand of Goth."

Black planet

I was looking handsome. She was looking like an erotic vulture.

The Pixies track growled exuberantly from the boarded-up windows and the open door. Against the wall were perched several vultures of the most erotic persuasion, survivors of a Victorian funeral fashion house fire and girls who put the MDMA into BDSM.

I was all dressed up in black, she was all dressed up in black.

They were smoking and talking, laughing more than the cartoon image of coffin kids Jon Power held had led him to expect they might. They were from different subbacultures.

The days of clubs catering to a purely Goth audience were long gone. A return to the heyday of the Alternative scene, when all the subcultures had to mingle – that's what was happening now. Goths and Industrial freaks, Synth Poppers, Metalheads, and EBM aficionados all sharing a space. Even subculture denizens from the lighter side – Punks and the classic alternative crowd – all congregated in the black-walled layer cake that was Elyzzium. With two Zs.

I was wearing eyeliner, she was wearing eyeliner.

Incredulous looked spectacular. His dreads flew heavily behind him as he strode towards the door, Jon, Alice, and Lily trailing behind him. Incredulous was all shining PVC, rubber, and latex – blacks and deep reds, straps, and artful cutouts revealing toned dark flesh.

The bouncer was a minor mountain of a man, wider than the door and almost as tall. Long ponytail, gentle beard. Softly spoken.

"Mosh!" he exclaimed warmly.

"Jimmy!" Incredulous said. "You're working this gig?"

"It's not the worst. Not like the old days."

"Nothing is," Incredulous smiled.

Jimmy waved Lily and Alice through, stopping Jon Power.

"Ummmm..."

"It's okay, Jimmy, he's with me."

"Buuuut..."

"I know. It's khaki. It's what he wears."

"Sorry Mosh. There's a dress code."

"What? What the hell kind of place are they running here?"

"Like I said. Not like the old days."

"Well, shit."

"Sorry. Management's orders. I've got a box of shit by the door if you like?"

The door lady, like all door ladies in alternative clubs, was pretty, friendly, and bored, with something of Middle Earth about her. She showed Jon and Incredulous into a room adjoining the coatroom. They were in there for a while.

Twenty minutes later, the door lady smiled as Jon Power came out of the storeroom behind the bag and coat-check.

"Sweetie, that is *divine*."

Jon Power was in a mesh shirt which made him look and feel more exposed than if he had not been wearing a top at all. He didn't have a bad body for an older guy, but he was not basking in the glow of appreciative glances. Were he a man to cower, cowering is what he would have been doing. Looking sheepish seemed a reasonable compromise.

The trousers they had given him were leather – red in a shade called oxblood, very different from the hue beloved of conservative British politicians and moneyed students with a penchant for being punched in the face. The platform boots he was wearing seemed more complicated than they were, and shone like the newest of newly minted classic fascist footwear. The road from towering to tottering is paved, apparently, in slightly camp, damp togs.

Incredulous looked pleased. The women less so.

"Incredulous tells me you're doing some snooping, Pastor," Lily said.

"Investigating."

"Indeed. Well, you look better, but not good enough for anyone to buy you belong here."

"I thought this was all about rejecting codes of belonging."

"Perhaps once. At least a part of the scene. Now it's a fashion-scenester clusterfuck just like any subculture, Punk, High Art, the Church…"

"Indeed," Jon Power said.

Lily smiled. "Come with me."

The club was dark, a layer of fog from the smoke machine creating a soft-focus haze and disguising the horrible floors.

Deep, pounding beats reverberated through Jon Power's chest as he tried to ignore the almost mechanical screams of the vocals and the writhing bodies on the strobe-addled dancefloor. *Gosh*, Incredulous thought. *It's good to be back.* He smiled a peaceful smile at the glittering darkness tumbling around him.

"In here!" Lily shouted to the pastor over the noise pulsing from the dancefloor.

"This is the ladies!" Jon shouted back.

"It's not such a big divide here!"

It wasn't. The long passage between stalls and basins had several men among the women fixing make-up, adjusting outfits, talking, and, in the time-honoured tradition of club bathrooms across all cultures, crying. Lily pulled him through them with handheld aloft, somewhere between a dancer guiding a twirling partner and a tour guide pushing through Venetian crowds. Jon bumbled bewilderedly past a man with a beard and heavy mascara who seemed to be performing an ENT examination on a pretty girl in a velvet dress using only his mouth.

Safe inside a cubicle, he asked, "So guys can come in here if they're…?"

"If they want to. Lots of the guys in skirts and make-up here are straight."

"Sure, sure," Jon said, trying to sound nonchalant. "They just get a sexual thrill out of wearing women's clothing."

Lily laughed. "Some of them, I guess! Others just think it's pretty." She smiled sweetly. "You've not spent a lot of time around the alt scene, have you?"

"I must warn you, I'm a man of God," he chuckled back. "I will not abide you attaining arcane truths about me from the spirits."

"Ha. Mea culpa."

"Wrong kind of man of God."

"I will avoid accentuating your Roman nose, then."

"When?"

"When I do your make-up."

Jon started away from her visibly.

"Hey, hey, hey, man!" he said, smiling weakly, shortening the final syllable in the time-honoured tradition of English-speaking white South Africa when it's a little nervous. "Chill! I mean, won't I look weird?"

"Not in here."

"Ja, but is it essential? I mean, there are plenty of guys in here without make-up on. I clocked at least ten on the way to the toilet."

"Sure, but you're not going to be able to speak to everyone if you look like them. And I assume you want to speak to as many people as you can, yes?"

"Sure, but..."

"But nothing. You don't imagine this is some kind of class-free hippie commune, do you? Peace and love and acceptance may have worked for the old-school Alternative crowd, but this is a culture like any other. We have a hierarchy and we have factions."

"Can't I pretend to be from a non-make-up-wearing faction?"

"Let me explain. Have you seen the Lord of the Rings movies?"

"Sure. Great Christian allegories, Tolkien stories."

"Wonderful," Lily said impatiently. "So think in terms of the races in those. The traditional metalheads are like the dwarves. Beer drinkers, simple, a little dumb and aggressive but not fundamentally malicious."

"Okay," Jon said dubiously, a hundred backward masking talks running through the back of his mind and creating suspicion by friction.

"They're really sweet," Lily said, watching his face, patient. "Just boys. Even the girls. They don't wear make-up, but the other groups don't respect them."

"Why?"

"Because their music is silly and old and mostly appeals to 14-year-old boys? Because they are unsophisticated? Because they have no sense of irony or shame and most of them will still happily dance to Alice Cooper?" She shuddered.

"Another Christian," Jon Power said.

"Fine. But they won't get listened to. Plus, dressed like that, no one will think you're an old-school metalhead. They will think you're a cop. How fast does your hair grow?"

"Regular speed?" Jon said, self-consciously fingering his widow's peak.

"Well, that's no good. Unless you can grow a mane you can swing about when you headbang or have a Blind Guardian tee in your pocket, they're out. Do you have a Blind Guardian tee? Hmmm?"

"Okay, okay! What are the other factions?"

"Well," Lily said, "there are the hobbits – that's how I like to think of the Alternative crowd, the people who like a little bit of it all and have no particular allegiances. They're sweet and naïve and, because so many of them are in high school, short. You can see the girls in their stripey stockings and fingerless gloves and tutus. Some of them wear fairy wings."

"Sweet."

"They are. And they carry no social weight whatsoever unless they are DJs or former scene kingpins. You are neither. And anyway, a lot of them wear make-up. Not happening."

"Right. Who are the Orcs in this metaphor?"

"They are the Black Metal crowd."

"Like Incredulous."

"No, smartass. Not like Incredulous. This is almost an exclusively white thing. Black Metal is a kind of hybrid of Goth and Metal. You know, Cradle of Filth. Dimmu Borgir. That sort of thing."

"I really don't."

"Okay, well let's just say that Black Metal doesn't heart Jesus, okay? It's pretty much satanic. Or wants to be. Most of them aren't serious about it in any religious sense but as a culture, it's darker. Not just aesthetically. Lots of nice people in it, but the vibe I get is always a little bit … not unsafe, but not safe either, if you know what I mean? The Orc thing is just because they wear make-up but it is grotesque and overdone. You know Immortal?"

"I feel like my answer is going to be wrong."

"True," Lily smiled. "Anyway, they're kinda like an updated church-bothering Kiss. Old now, but the Black Metal Orcs love them. We may get you to pass for one of them."

"Sounds delightful. Who are the Elves?"

"The Elves are the Goths."

"I thought Elves were all about light."

"In this scene, nobody's about light. It's 50 shades of black in here. But the Goths, particularly the more uber you go, are more poised. A little more refined and cultured. Or, again, they want to be. Airs and disgraces, the uber Goths."

"Like an aristocracy…"

"Yup. Though not universally loved."

"So, just like an aristocracy."

"Sure," Lily said. "And while the Orcs are about accentuating ugliness, the Dwarves don't care and the Alternative scene is too much fun…"

"You might say it was Hobbit-forming…" Jon Power interrupted.

Lily laughed. "Okay. Listen. Alternative is too fun to let you pay much attention to that stuff, but the Goths are trying pretty hard for beauty."

"Those girls looking like Morticia Addams. and the ones with half their heads shaved and rings through their noses?" Jon snorted.

"It may not be your aesthetic, but yes. You're not going to find the serious self-conscious Goths chugging beer and crushing cans on their heads or raising their arms to guitar solos. And they, too, wear make-up. Often understated, often not. Regularly quite beautiful and avant-garde."

"So, which do you want me to be?"

"Hold still," she said. "I'll show you."

Now I'm feeling zombified

"Hail whatshisname," Jon Power said to Incredulous Moshoeshoe with a hangdog expression on his face. At least, Incredulous thought it was hangdog. It was hard to tell through the black and white make-up, but the pastor's voice had enough Bill Murray in it to kill a cheerleader.

"Satan?" Incredulous said, grinning.

"That guy," said Jon.

Incredulous laughed. A big, hearty, plosive sort of laugh that went on longer than was kind.

Jon Power had had his hair sprayed jet black with a temporary spray dye. His face was covered in a sort of claw silhouette in black with the spaces filled in in white. His pupils had been reduced to pinpricks with white disposable contact lenses and a sprung silver ring hung from his nose, making his eyes water more than the contacts.

Moshoeshoe had been holding court in a corner of the club and regained composure quickly, turning to his friends.

"So sorry. This is my buddy," he paused for a fraction of a beat, "Orloch." He's from Joburg.

Appreciative nods for the intimidating spectacle Jon made were exchanged and kudos were added for being from the big city. If South Africa has an inferiority complex about its grasp on global culture, its capital city has similar feelings towards its big sister Jozi.

Incredulous introduced Jon Power, who sat down in a ratty old sofa that had probably seen its first body fluids when Goth was still young. Some of these kids could have been conceived on this couch. The pastor watched a parade of youth that was more hell-*ish* than hellish – wasting its time and innocence, ostensibly playing listlessly with the dark forces that he had dedicated his life to fighting. They were making a game of it. Inverted crosses everywhere. Pentagrams. Debased, twisted images. He was annoyed at his lack of revulsion.

Incredulous felt content. At peace, the way some men do in strip clubs or rugby stadiums. He could see the large dancefloor, the centre of a coliseum rising three storeys with people leaning over railings to watch the dancers below. The usual mix of pseudo-industrial fans, Goths, and alternative kids danced to an old Rob Zombie track he could remember being sick of in 2006. The Living Dead Girls arched their backs and beckoned in the air above and in front of them, conjuring a closer connection with the music and looking damn fine doing it. One of the boys was on his knees, shirt off, in the manner of an old friend he still missed, a suicide victim in a culture that loved to dance with death. He beat his chest and punched the air around him in complicated patterns before jumping to his feet, shadowboxing with the speakers.

They faced the speakers. The dancefloor was not where you came to chat or pick up partners or to make out. All faced either the speakers or the DJ, himself lost in the music on the first floor. All were absorbed in the song, consumed in the joy of being part of it as smoke and strobe and well-appointed beams of red lasers were orchestrated by a second DJ, working lights because it made the song better.

In a corner of the bar, a beautiful, impressive pixie with curly hair as black as bat pupils held court. The Gothfather.

"Hello, Ashton," he said, sauntering up.

"Darling!" The pixie's voice was deep, subterranean, echoing of warm and ancient stone. The acolytes around him seemed to be flung off like water off a black dog with a thoughtless shake. Ashton's frame was slight but he radiated confidence and power. It's good to be king.

Ashton Nyte was – is – a singer, South Africa's great gothic Rockstar. So much more than that as well, but here the crowds that knew him knew him for his booming bass that shot up octaves at a whim and pierced the listening heart with sweetness. He was pretty fucking good, and not just for a goth.

The men chatted. Equals, though in times past their roles had been disjointed by the power of the Rockstar and the DJ. Different planets, similar orbits. Incredulous had always thought that Ashton, The Awakening, his band, was too good for the tiny scene over which he presided.

"How are you, brother?" the Rockstar asked.

"Well. Well," Incredulous said.

"Why are you here?"

"I have a set a little later."

"Come on, Mosh," Ashton said, a smile playing at the corners of his mouth, a bottle of beer pinned between his fingers like a champagne flute. "Why really?"

Incredulous paused, but something in the aura of the man was calming. Peaceful. "Okay, something bad is going down. Something not… normal."

"More than usual?" Ashton smiled and glanced around at the patrons. Incredulous tilted his head just a little. Just a small yes.

"Why, Mosh. I thought you were above all that. All our superstitions. You're ready to come to the Lord?"

"Ash, this is serious."

"Alright, alright. But you should know that you can fuck with devils all you want. You're not going to win. The power of Christ is all that wins, brother."

"Okay," Incredulous said.

It wasn't what the singer had expected.

"Oh, I'm sorry, Love. Look, if you're searching for some dodgy shit, those vampires are a place to start. And I'll make sure people leave you alone. You and your Mortiis-looking friend."

"You saw him?"

"No judgement, brother. We all have our tastes."

"Shut the fuck up, Ashton," Incredulous Moshoeshoe smiled, cheersing in the air at his old friend. "And thank you."

"No worries, darling," Ashton shouted at the DJ's rapidly retreating back. "Don't let those bastards near your neck!"

Back in an alcove with the pastor, Incredulous sipped his vodka and cream soda and relaxed. It was good to be home.

Jon Power was feeling less comfortable. The make-up felt thick on his face like his skin was heavy. The music sounded evil, though most of the time his spirit was at peace with it. He couldn't tell the difference between most of the songs. Like a helpless racist in a room full of 'them'. The sensation was unfamiliar. He watched the dancing figures more in distant puzzlement than any kind of fear or judgement, which surprised him.

"Moshoeshoe!" he said to Incredulous over the music.

"Mosh! In here, call me Mosh, Orloch!"

"Who's… Oh, I see. Sorry. Mosh!"

"Yes?"

"We need to start asking questions. Investigating!"

"We will. Chillax."

Jon Power winced at the word and Incredulous grinned the grin of the postmodern language-abuser.

"Haven't you ever been undercover, sweetcheeks?" the DJ said, trying to sound Noir.

"Lots of times. Though nothing much is covered here." Jon Power's eyes followed a girl in a shiny black corset that, despite an impressive array of straps and buckles, did not have the wherewithal to contain her breasts, which hung in a friendly fashion over the front of it, black tape crosses over her nipples.

"Well, we just need to take it easy. These people don't like outsiders coming in and questioning them."

"Who does?" the pastor asked, remembering a few exposés focusing on Pentecostal churches.

"Yeah, but these people even more than most."

"Everybody hates a tourist. That Pulp guy said that."

"These people been turned into a freakshows too many times."

"Because of the whole coffin kid thing?"

"Yeah. People tend to misunderstand the scene. To turn it into a parody. It's a legitimate subculture, an aesthetic community, you know?"

"I get it. I'm from a weird minority myself."

"White people?"

"Christians."

Incredulous snorted, "In this country? Are you kidding?"

"Believing Christians who act like their faith is more important than a Sunday hobby, who let it affect their lives? What do you see more of, soup kitchens or angry Facebook campaigns? How many martyrs are you seeing? No. Not kidding at all. So, while I don't understand the attraction of all this satanic kak, I think I get it."

"Well, journalists and TV people and some of those Christians you were talking about don't. They come in here sometimes, like tourists. They turn us into a cartoon. Assume all sorts of freakish stuff about us just because we're a distinct community. It's disrespectful and unfair."

Jon Power nodded sympathetically.

"Come," Incredulous said. "Let's go drink some blood."

Are you the one that I've been waiting for?

Scientist had never given much thought to how he would die. Probably reading Twilight fan-fiction in the bath – something he had faith Houk would take care of before any press could be alerted. Houk was good that way. But tonight he was thinking about it a lot. Young at the talons of a giant bird or an angry mob. In prison (or an asylum,) a very old man.

He ran his fingers over the scratches on his cheek and hung back in the shadows. His eyes were wide and he was breathing hard. He worried that someone would notice him and tried to calm himself.

There's a moment when you know you are in the shit – profoundly and irrevocably in it, waist deep and sinking – the moment when your skeleton turns to water and your blood temperature drops like a currency value during a terrorist attack. Scientist Likota was experiencing that moment. Had been experiencing it for what seemed like days.

His absence from the public eye was beginning to be commented on. After all, Mandela was about to go for real. Tensions were high. Where would the poor and the dispossessed of the country look for help and guidance? The ANC? Unlikely. Aak de Nau and her lot? Not a chance. And if things kicked off, if the newly invigorated Broederbond came back, would the international community step in? Against a pro-business, pro-white, pro-America junta? Un-fucking-likely. His people would want leadership.

But it's hard to lead your people from a jail cell. Sure, Madiba did it. But Madiba wasn't jabbering about how a giant bird monster committed the treason. And anyway, Scientist was no Madiba. He knew that.

Caiaphas had told him to come here. Caiaphas told him to do a lot of things. In Scientist's experience, it was best to listen to Caiaphas. So, when he said "find my nephew and the white preacher he's hanging out with," Scientist said, "how high?" Or something like that.

Find the boy – Scientist had a name and a description, as well as the address of the club – *and tell him what you know.* Fine. Except this place was crawling with whiteys, like one of those anthills he remembered from his childhood. Not much of his childhood – Joburg's northern suburbs don't have many ant hills – but *veldschool* or some outing to learn about nature. He hadn't been paying attention. He remembered a white worm, its lair overrun with white ants. Something about 'survival of the fittest.'

Fittest. Good God. He did not feel fit at all. And someone was bound to recognise him. His flash suit, his all-over-the-media, the-firebrand-you-love-to-hate face. And these people would eat him alive.

Come on, Likota, he scolded himself. He always scolded himself by his surname. Posh schools do that to you. *Just go in.*

~~~

Herman Spieëlding was looking at the women. They all looked pretty, except when you got near them. Not that he had much chance to get near them. He'd donned a black nylon wind jacket and flattened his hair down from its more familiar quiff. He looked less like a businessman, more like an ageing bouncer. That was moderately good in terms of not standing out like a sore white supremacist thumb but didn't bring all the girls to the yard. He'd not have caught the reference even if it had. The Broederbond, as a rule, is not madly into hip-hop.

If you'd asked Spieëlding in private, he'd have confided that that wasn't a race thing. It was about age. Even the 20-year-olds in the Broederbond were 50 in their hearts. He had been since his mid-twenties, definitely. After a few years of Alternative Afrikaner rebellion, getting high at Koos Kombuis gigs, he'd come back to the fold. Old Afrikaans university? Old Afrikaans family? Degree in Theology and a post-grad in business and politics? The Broeders were bound to snap you up. Show you another way. An *older* way.

Initially, it was the secrecy. Yes, sir, the idea of promoting your race, your culture, that was attractive. But the sense of knowing more than everyone else, of being part of the country's secret history – that would appeal to any young man. Power.

In a changing, changed South Africa, that had been their downfall. A secret society dedicated to the promotion of a hyper-Calvinist niche within a niche of the white population? Where's the power in that? Older members had deserted – some with sad shrugs and explanations that things had changed, that business was business and racial purity was not a great guide for shareholder value. Others had just stopped coming to the meetings. Government positions – once guaranteed to Broeders – were hard to come by. A few years ago, in every part of the country, the Broederbond had been but a shadow of its former self. All but defunct. Hell, the *Masons* were doing better than them. Some chapters had even started taking in women, lightening up on the religious emphases. Going *bowling*.

The Broederbond had all but ceased to exist, some *hensoppers* forming a new, sanitised version with an adjusted name and *without* the palate for violence or real strength. They changed the name and made a monument out of a movement. The true Broeders carried on, but with the dogged hopelessness usually reserved for activists fighting a *good* fight.

Then Mandela got sick. Mandela "died" and they saw a dip. And then he wasn't dead. Shock and embarrassment and resentment rose in many, but especially the white Right. And resentment was fuel. Spieëlding knew how to make the most of it. And then Mandela got *really* sick. And the sickness *dragged*. And everything changed. White people who had thought of themselves as post-racial realised, privately, that they'd only liked one black guy, that Father Christmas figure with the funny voice who forgave them all their sins. As for the rest of his party, the rest of his *people* – well they were fucking this country up faster than Zimbabwe. And his numbers started to rise.

And every time Scientist Likota or Jacob Zuma did or said anything stupid, every time the all-too-comfortable white middle classes heard the have-nots call publicly for a bigger slice of the pie, the numbers went up. New chapters had to be established. Hell, they had even launched an app (password *and* pay-wall protected) to help with liturgies and rituals. Like the head of a secret service, he had neither confirmed nor denied his leadership of what was now being branded a networking society for business people with a cultural interest in Afrikanerdom. Even in openly admitted membership, it began to dwarf the sanitised, usurper version of the movement. The Broederbond was back. The unofficial opposition.

Their numbers had never been higher, but more than that, the motivation among those numbers was high. There was an energy, anger, a willingness to go further than they had ever gone before to make their country great again. They had people with real power among their numbers now. Not just peace-time power like the old days, but the power to fight. And they were eager to get started. Spieëlding was not madly keen on that – he could remember what war was like – but having powerful people in your ranks means they are powerful in your ranks – as well as in the real world. He'd allowed some preparation.

With rumours and occasional intelligence reports of Communists, black nationalists and revolutionaries making similar plans, he had fallen in line with the hawks. He hoped war wouldn't be necessary, but mutually assured destruction had worked in the Cold War, and he was a Cold War man.

And in the shadows behind this sink-hole of a club, thinking of Lucretia, not one part of that mattered to him now.

The voice on the phone had told him to be here. That Lucretia would be safe if he came. It was not the kind of place he'd want to be seen. Not good for the Broeder brand. But the voice had told him to stay outside, in the shadows of a side street.

The neighbourhood was "not good" – meaning "black and poor" – a classic inner-city location for white middle-class clubs, a neighbourhood where some arms caches had been found and spattered all over the news. Arms caches that did not belong to his people. He wasn't entirely comfortable.

Worse than the black neighbourhood factor was the cheap rent factor – with the class of white people it brought at night. Clubbers. The worst kind, too. Hipsters. Goths. Not that he'd have recognised the labels, but he recognised the types. White kids milled about across the street, cars slowed and stopped and taxis weaved madly 'round them on their way to the main rank a few blocks down. Workers from the other side of the city strolled wearily by and there were figures dotted all over the main street and the side streets.

Any one of them could have been his contact with the kidnappers. The guy, two doors down from the club entrance, leaning against the wall. The lurking silhouette ahead of him on the corner, watching the passing traffic. The apparent bum leaning against the steel shutters of a shopfront in the side street.

A voice said, "You came," and Spieëlding wheeled 'round, peered into the darkness that had been behind him.

⌒

Scientist jumped at the shout. A small, strangled thing, like you imagine lobsters giving when you drop them into the pot.

His nerves were shot. Sudden noises were likely to scare what little bejesus he had in him right the fuck out. Accordingly, he jumped, swore, spun 'round. Peering into the darkness he could only make out a shadow. It loomed. Struggling with something. A small cry again. Fuck.

Scientist Likota was not a hero. He had gone into politics for precisely that reason. Why work in a mine, or organise a union in one, when you could own shares in it? Secretly own shares, obviously – nobody needed to *know*. Of course, it was selfish. But he had always agreed with the divine Jane that selfishness had to be forgiven because it was incurable. In him it certainly was. Which was why he surprised himself at that moment by interrupting the mugging, murder or rape that was happening.

A large shape struggled with a smaller one. Perspective was warped in the dark. Were they further away, closer together than they seemed? The larger person couldn't be that big. Could they? Another strangled cry.

Perhaps it was being a victim of a frame-up. Perhaps just a fresh horror at the reality of violence. Perhaps he'd do anything to avoid the greater danger of going into that club. Scientist crouched down and picked up a brick lying on the pavement and hurled it, hard, at the looming shape. Fifty-fifty he'd hit the aggressor.

A stomach-turning crack and a loud, disturbing rustle were followed by a fast burst of air as the shadow whirled and grew.

"Well, that was stupid," Likota muttered, before gasping, "Fuck" again.

The wings were bigger than his mind could fully comprehend. They would have stretched across the entire breadth of the street without any problem. Scientist found himself making the calculation in his head, trying to work out the lengths of folds and relative perspectives before a voice inside him asked, not unfairly, *what the fuck are you doing, Likota? Run!*

But he didn't run. In the ambient light from the street beyond he saw the Lightning Bird's face – human eyes but grotesquely beaked, with ragged teeth like sharks' lining its curve. One giant talon was planted on the pavement, while the other held a man by the shoulders, a nauseatingly human knuckle, blown up large and leathery, encircled an older white man's neck. The bird began to flap its wings, each beat propelling it twenty feet down the road in a couple of seconds. Likota stooped to pick up the brick again and ran towards the bird. The winged form slowed, its wing catching on a Jacaranda tree, and he hurled the brick a second time. Another cracking sound as it hit the bird's wing. The white man dropped to the ground. Deep in Likota's brain, he registered something about hollow bones and flight, but before he could rush forward to pick up the brick or help the white man, his hands and teeth suddenly clenched up, along with every muscle in his body. A bolt of lightning convulsed him like a congregant at the front of one of those fucked up charismatic churches his mother had liked.

Sight and sound came in flashes.

A bird, like a man, hovering over him. Pain in his chest and arms. and the sense of being lifted. A gunshot, then another and another and another, and the sound of thunder. The bird trying to manoeuvre. Bleeding. Broken wing, tangling with the Jacaranda tree planted in the pavement and smashing, bashing into windows. The flash of lightning as the bird cleared the tree and blotted out the stars. The sound of gunshots as the shaking white man leaned against a tree on fire, emptying a gun into the air. The bird barrelling down at him and turning 'round. Rising up and disappearing. A crowd, rushing from around the corner. Relief. A slap.

Wait, what?

A slap.

"Wake up, man!" Spieëlding said, and then, over his shoulder, "Piss off, man, you people. Give this gentleman some room. You've all seen a bloody mugging before. Piss off. He's fine."

Spieëlding crouched closer to Likota. "Are you fine?"

"I… I think so…"

"Did you… help me?"

"Yes. I'm sorry."

"Don't be sorry," Spieëlding laughed.

"Oh, but I am," Likota said, sitting up and wincing. His body felt like it had been repeatedly fucked at the cellular level by an unloving prison guard with a grudge.

"That thing…"

"Yes. I saw it too. How did you… I mean, why was it… with you…?"

Spieëlding helped Likota to his feet, supporting his woozy, swaying frame with his shoulder.

"My daughter," he said. "I got a call, they sent a picture. She has been kidnapped."

"Kidnapped," Scientist said, eyes blank as a starless sky.

Herman Spieëlding didn't know why he was telling this stranger what he had not told the police.

"They said to meet them down the road, near the taxi rank. I was waiting here to see who they were. And then that thing was on me. If you hadn't…"

Scientist was still woozy but now standing. "Your… daughter?"

"Yes." Spieëlding held out his phone. The picture was of Lucretia. Her eyes were open, angry more than scared, though there was fear there too. She was in some kind of cage.

"Jesus," Likota mumbled, his legs giving way beneath him.

"You okay, chief?" Spieëlding asked, catching him. The black man in the suit said a word that made Spieëlding let him fall. Almost certainly by mistake.

"Lu…. Lucretia…"

Blood and honey

The Spillover Bar was tempting fate. Its 21 varieties of real blood (three of them geographically dispersed species of bat), mixed with a plethora of liquors in a variety of proportions was not a popular idea with all of Pretoria's citizens. When it had first opened, the *Pretoria News*, an ordinarily calm and reasonable paper, had run a fairly hysterical story about it, unable to decide whether hygiene, aesthetic, or spiritual concerns were most urgently worrying.

The name itself was intended to bait the squeamish and informed. The concept was calculated to horrify outsiders to the point that made the idea irresistible to those within the scene. But it was still a pretty niche idea. Uber Goths, the Black Metal fraternity of nastiness, and a small coterie of Satanists, black magic aspirants, and vampire fetishists all frequented it. But the health department was zealously keen to shut it down, and most people don't like to drink a lot of blood. It sits heavy in the stomach. Stock goes off.

Situated on the third floor, near the exclusive Goth and Darkwave dancefloor (and just a little further from the EBM,

Industrial Noise floor), Spillover was run on a concession basis, renting space from the club and paying a hefty percentage to the house on every drink sold. Refrigerated cabinets, lit beautifully from below, contained amphoras of blood in a gruesome rainbow of reds, with prominent labels as to their origins, both biological and geographic. The cabinet ran up to the ceiling and a row of stools, festooned with surgical tubing and antique medical bric-a-brac sat in front. It was only about half full. Or half-empty, depending on how you tended to view your shot-glass of plasma.

Either way, between tight profit margins and Health Department hassles, it was not a healthy business. Animal rights groups weren't in love with it either.

"Welcome to Spillover, gentlemen. What can I get you?" The bar lady was white, in her mid-twenties, and beautiful in that shark-eyed way athletic South African girls often are. Her lithe limbs and put-together attractiveness made one feel she'd be wonderful to fuck, in the way male mantises must feel when they first see females of their species.

"What's good?" asked Incredulous.

"Well, we have your standards, bovine, porcine, and, of course, little lamb," she smiled, "and snake – Cobra this week, though that is a little pricey, and three bats."

"Sounds delightful," he said. "I'll take a little cobra. My friend will have that too."

"Shots?"

"I'll have a Jaegerglobin." Incredulous said, "and my friend will have a Haemorrhagic Fever."

"A *what*?" Jon Power hissed in the black man's ear.

"Relax!" Moshoeshoe whispered back. "A Haemorrhagic Fever is mostly schnapps and lemonade. It's a cocktail with just a few drops of the blood."

"I'm not drinking it!"

"Oh, stop being such a baby. It's not that bad."

"It's a spiritual portal! I will not engage in pagan rituals, I told you this from the start!"

"Look, you're going to make a scene if you don't drink it. If Paprika was into bloodletting, then there's a good chance the guy she was with, the – " he whispered, "*bird* may have come here too."

"Moshoeshoe, you don't understand. I *can't*. The drinking of blood is a line I can't cross. I'm sorry."

He looked it. Many times, in his life of feeling more comfortable with unbelievers than believers, he had come up against the same problem. There's a point where people who don't share your religion simply can't understand why you draw the lines you do. He'd encountered it with Caiaphas more than once. Supporting the revolution came easier if you were a *real* Communist.

"Well, if you don't drink it, it's going to destroy your disguise."

"I'll sit and nurse it. Stir it. If it takes long, I'll spill it. Then we can leave."

"Fine," Incredulous said. "But you have better stir the fuck out of that thing. And spill it convincingly."

"Fine."

The bar lady in her vintage nurse's uniform brought the drinks with a smile and a substantial bill. Incredulous paid it.

"How's business?"

"Oh, you know, can't complain, hey. Nobody listens. We're making a go of it, but it isn't easy. This country is going to shit." She hesitated.

"Fucking right," Incredulous said and she looked relieved. "It's more like Zim every day, I'm telling you." You can't go wrong with that phrase and a large proportion of white South Africans.

"It's so nice to meet a person who thinks sensibly."

"Likewise," Incredulous smiled.

"So, why's business tough? Standard African shit?"

"Ja, that. But it's just the overheads, you know? It's a pretty small market I'm working in."

"You're not wrong," he said. "To be honest, I like the stuff, but I don't get the attitude of some of the people who indulge."

"I know, right?!" she laughed. "Fricken purity freaks. Oh, where's it come from, is it this species, was it fucking ethically farmed, *can I see a certificate of authenticity*. Flippin' pricks."

"In this economy? Are they flipping mental?"

"Exactly," she said, beaming. Nothing was more pleasant than speaking of unpleasant things with someone who agrees with every word you say. She leaned forward conspiratorially.

"I've got a good supplier. Brings me stuff through a diplomatic bag. No papers, no nothing. I almost wish I could tell people. Give some of these dickheads a taste of danger. I mean, that's what this is supposed to be about, hey?"

Incredulous nodded and sipped his drink. Jon was pretending he wasn't there, watching the PVC-clad EBMers strolling in and out of their dancefloor, the pulsing boom making his red cocktail ripple occasionally.

"Totally," Incredulous said, his eyes big and interested, his hand fingering a dread. "Hey, can I ask you a question?"

"You can ask me whatever you like," she said, leaning on the bar. Jon Power might as well have been invisible, which suited him fine.

"Do you serve… *human* drinks here? Maybe under the counter?"

Her demeanour changed. Her eyes shifted off to the side, in the distance, and she chewed at the inside of her cheek in irritation.

"Well, you can fuck right the hell off," she said, standing up straight again. "You Health Department pricks just don't give up, do you? I run a legal business here, with all the permits and all the hoops you set up jumped through every month. And still, you come here, trying to entrap me. Well, fuck right off." She turned around and started polishing a bottle marked 'Chimp, DRC'. It was two-thirds full.

"I'm not health department. I'm a DJ," Incredulous said as if she had made a ridiculous category error.

"Oh please. I know all the DJs here. And the only guest DJ they're expecting is…" Incredulous waited for it to click home and watched with satisfaction as her expression changed.

"DJ… Mosh?"

"Yes."

"Oh, I'm so sorry!" she fawned. She picked up a little bottle marked 'Horseshoe Bat, Yunnan' and checked its stopper distractedly. "I thought you were some government *doos*, you know? They're all as bad as each other, from Zuma down. Not one of them cares about the country. Helping their people. Just jumping on that gravy train, hassling people trying to make a living."

Jon Power wondered what 'their people' might mean in a post-racial South Africa. Or rather, he knew exactly what it meant. He hoped his make-up was hiding his feelings and continued listening to Incredulous' conversation with the down-trodden blood sommelier.

"I don't care about politics," Incredulous said. "But I am interested in what we were talking about."

"Ah, yes, of course. Um. Well, I don't carry that sort of thing, you understand. A lot of heat these days after all the stories in the news about muti-killings and stuff. You know. But I know some people. I have … made connections in the past …"

"Connections for whom?"

"Well, that would be telling," she smiled, coquettishly leaning over and brushing a dreadlock out of the DJ's face. "But don't worry. It's not for muti. All strictly upmarket."

"Ah, you can tell me."

"Ag, well, I guess you're fine, even if you …" she stopped herself.

"Even if I'm black?"

She looked horrified. 'Racist' really is the N-word (or, in South Africa, the K-word) for white people.

"No!"

She was standing up again, regretting uncharacteristic trust. "Sorry, man," she said, looking embarrassed and trying unsuccessfully to re-engage her flirting gears. "Let's talk about something nicer." She bit her lip and tried a smile. "I'm all above board, anyway."

"Ah, I don't mind this topic," he smiled.

"No, man," she said. "I'm done with that. Let's talk about you. And whether you're single."

The smile in his eyes disappeared like a cigarette coal stubbed out on the tongue of a sociopath.

He grabbed her wrist.

"Listen to me," he said. "I am not interested in fucking you and I am not interested in the code of ethics a fucking abattoir sleucer operates under. I want to know who has been buying human blood. I want a list, and if you don't give it to me, not only will I tell every scene-maker in this place that you are faking the product, I will have a word with the police about what you just told me. And maybe while I'm at it I'll start a rumour that the blood you sell to all these white kids comes exclusively from poor black kids. Maybe I'll tell my uncle in the RYM. You want that?"

The 'fuck you' in her eyes while she weighed up her options was louder than the music.

"Fine," she said and pulled a notepad from under the counter.

"And don't go all pouty. If I had offered you R200, you would have jotted down the list on a paper serviette."

"You didn't, though."

"I didn't think you were *upmarket* enough."

She scowled and handed him a page from the pad.

"This is one name."

"I never met the buyer. Just arranged things."

"She's lying," Jon interjected.

"You're sure?" Incredulous asked.

"Yes."

It was enough. The pastor may not have had the Sight in the way generations of Incredulous' family had, but he had something. He brought his face fractionally closer to hers.

"Well?"

"Who the fuck are you guys?"

"We're going to save this country," Jon said. She laughed, turning scornful shoulders towards him, if shoulders could be scornful, and then she stopped abruptly. The white man wasn't joking.

"You're crazy."

"I'm this close to calling my uncle, little girl," Incredulous said. Even people who didn't know Caiaphas were scared of Caiaphas.

"Okay, I've met the buyer. They contacted me by email and it was clear that they wanted to stay on the down-low. Anonymous. I worked through an agent." She had paused over the word. "She handles a lot of stuff like this for people who want the underground life but want a little distance. I only ever moved that kind of sample for one person. Her."

Sense of purpose

Spieëlding looked at Likota.
"What?"
"Lucretia."

At that point, Herman Spieëlding's brain experienced something akin to a backed-up mail server coming back online (a social media analogy would have been meaningless to him – email he understood). Three messages were previewed on the screen of his reeling conscious brain at once. I stared at his inbox.

> From, Self-preservation reflex
> Subject, What the hell just happened?
> Preview, Bird. Bloody big bird. No. Yes? Bird!

> From, Lucretia kidnapping
> Subject, He knows her name
> Preview, How does he know... Who is this guy?

> From, News and politics
> Subject, Scientist Likota
> Preview, Wait. Isn't that... It can't be. Wait...

From, Anger centre
Subject, Motherfucker
Preview, WWWMMMMRRRRAAAAARRRRGH!

"You son of a..." He had Likota by the lapels in his right hand. His left fumbled for the gun. It was pointless. He had emptied a clip into the bird. "You tell me what you've done with her. You tell me now, or..."

"No, no!" Likota said, struggling and flinching, expecting a fist or a gun butt or a bullet. His nerves were shot. "I love her."

"You? What?"

MAIL SERVER MESSAGE, SERVER UNRESPONSIVE. PLEASE CONTACT ADMINISTRATOR

Spieëlding let go of him and Scientist slumped and sighed.

"Why would I want to hurt my wife?"

Clouds swirled in the city's lurid glow. Cities that came into their own in the 70s always glow luridly. It's what they do. Something to do with pre-unleaded smog becoming forever part of the air. You can't hose down an atmosphere. Pointlessly washed cars honked below. The lightning bird perched on the top of the Volkskas building.

Locals never looked up the full length of it these days. Long-ago eclipsed in height, nobody noticed its sandy Jenga façade and illusion of thick horizontal black bars anymore. Proximity does that. You live in a mostly dirty, always busy city centre all your life and you learn early not to notice that a building looks like an 18th-century server-stack. Pretoria has always had a retrofuturist vibe. Or it will.

If anyone had glanced up, they would have noticed an odd malformation, the rectangular black corner somehow mis-shapen. Had they been in a helicopter or piloting a drone or high as seriously fuck, they'd have seen something like a gargoyle, sort of man-shaped, framed by huge, bent wings, feathers flicking and shifting in the warm breeze.

Dulu winced.

The bone in his left-wing was broken. Shattered by something as stupid as a rock. A man. He'd been feeling off for a while. His attention… His focus… No matter. Mistakes happen from aeon to aeon. A man with a brick. It had been centuries since anyone had tried to hurt him so primitively. It was almost nostalgic.

He unfolded the wing, extending the bones. Pain shot and surged through him and lightning crackled and fizzed around him, silhouetting and glowing his form all at once. A tramp sheltering in a doorway near the foot of the building far below looked up. Dulu watched the skin around the vagrant eyes crinkle as he squinted, a tic in his cheek twitch. He saw individual hairs move and prickle, sweat droplets emerging from the skin. The lightning bird inclined his beaked head towards the tramp. The wreck of a childhood uncrinkled himself like a ticket stub and picked up his blankets and bags. He shuffled away, his matted hair standing on end.

Dulu went back to stretching his wings, paying little attention to his panoramic view of the capital at night. Anger was surging in him like a storm.

Spieëlding sat heavily on the pavement next to Likota. The crowd was wandering away with a sense of disappointment. Both men seemed to be okay.

ERROR 404. WHAT THE ACTUAL.

"Um. What." It wasn't a question. Not just one question, anyway.

"I love her," Likota said, "And I had nothing to do with what happened."

"You love her," Spieëlding said.

"Yes."

"She's your wife."

"Yes."

"How long?"

"A year."

"No, man."

"Yes."

"But…"

"I know."

"You don't understand. I'm…"

"I know who you are. And what you are."

"She told you?"

"No."

"Then…"

"I have staff. I have researchers. I know the face, background, and habits of every lobbyist, power broker, and militia leader in South Africa. I'm not going to be taken by surprise."

There was an uncomfortable silence as both men reflected on the currently obvious weaknesses in that theory.

"So you know who…" Spieëlding said, hope rising.

"Actually, I don't."

"But you'll find out. Your people. Researchers."

"No, sir. I am cut off. I have to disappear."

Anger visibly rose in the white man again. His fists clenched and unclenched.

"Spieëlding," Scientist said. "I didn't have anything to do with your daughter's kidnapping."

"Then why are you hiding?"

"Because they're trying to frame me. They took genetic material at the abduction. Blood. Skin. They can place me at the scene."

"Who is 'they'?"

"Fuck's sake, man, I haven't the foggiest! I have enemies."

"Of course, you do. You're dangerous. An extremist."

"I'm a pragmatist. That's part of dialectical materialism. Being a pragmatist."

"I'm surprised you know how to say that word."

"Bit long for you?"

"No, man. I just mean …"

"I know what you mean. The firebrand buffoon. He shouldn't talk like this. Doesn't talk like this on TV."

Spieëlding was silent.

"I tried reasonable. Nobody listened. For years nobody listened. Then I watched an episode of Ali-G—"

"No, man!" Spieëlding exclaimed.

"Yes. Cohen knows a thing or two. And I thought fuck it. Somebody's going to be saying these things. Most of which I believe, by the way. And I'd rather it was me than some addled war veteran."

They were talking like two strangers at a bar near closing time rather than political opponents on a pavement after a monster attack. It pleased Likota.

"You're an opportunist."

"I'm a Dadaist. You're a trombonist."

"What?"

"Exactly."

"Look, you bloody Communist…"

"*Me*?" Likota shrieked, "Hardly! Socialist, sure, but…"

Spieëlding interrupted. "My daughter is missing. I'm not in the mood for games. She…"

"Is my wife and I'm as worried about her as you are." Scientist's voice had not a trace of flippancy. His face was grave.

Spieëlding was silent again. Revellers from the club shouted and they heard the distant laugh of breaking glass. He sat down next to Likota, leaning against the tree. It was still warm. Smoking slightly.

"Now, as I see it, you only have a few options," Likota said. "You can hold onto your old prejudices and see if they comfort you. Assume I'm lying. Beat me until I talk. Hand me over to the police. But you know what happens then. If people put together…"

"Our people will declare war."

"And then so will mine."

"What are the other options?"

"We work together to find her."

"Me. With you."

"I am the only one who has seen what you saw tonight," Scientist Likota said. "And I am the only other person on the planet who cares as much as you do about getting her back."

Spieëlding stared into the shadows.

"What do we do?"

"We talk to a man about a bird."

A distant rumble and a glow lit Spieëlding's face from above, casting weird shadows. Perhaps that was what it was, Likota thought, that he could see there. Not a kind of madness. Just shadows. Echoes of weather.

Dulu winced and stretched his joints like a newborn. Electricity danced over his wings, crackling in the rushing wind. He had recovered. It had hurt. It always did. But now he was healthy as a child. The city was spilt sugar on a black leather couch below him. And in amongst the grains, he could see all the tiny little ants going about their business. He focused.

There.

In a long, graceful arc, he started his descent, turning and turning. The noise deafened him and his head buzzed from the g-force, like trying to hold onto a rope, tethered to a central pole, sinking. Soon he was clipping satellite dishes on blocks of flats, frying the circuits as he did so.

The two ants he was looking for were walking into a building. As it happened, it was a building he knew very well.

She's in parties

S he wore a swastika armband and more PVC than any non-dominatrix had any right to. Her head was shaved in an undercut that left a narrowish strip on the top of her head, in the pattern of a popular male teenager in the 50s or a fashionable vagina in the 90s. Hers was woven into dreadlock hair extensions shot through with blood-red thread and electric blue wire. The effect was architectural.

She thought of the swastika armband as a nod to the past. Siouxsie Sioux had worn one as a statement. The content of the statement was unclear, but that it was a statement was beyond doubt. She felt it made her look, in concert with the rest of her ensemble, *legitimate*. Authentic. Real and really a part of this world, despite her advertising industry job. She felt it made her look not just like she belonged, but that she led.

What it made her look like was a dumbshit Nazi sympathiser, *obviously*. But the insecurity of your twenties is a special thing. Confident enough, as it is, to take risks and stand out, while still desperate to be noticed, respected, loved. Your twenties are very much like the rest of your life.

She was not a very discerning woman. But well-spoken, clever, and cruel enough, socially, to woo a broad range of people. When she was drunk, she could be a lot of fun, postmodern enough to puncture the pomposity of the uber-scene, bitchy enough not to identify with the less-than-ubers too much. She was a curator, really.

Jon Power instantly disliked her, eyeing the armband all the while Incredulous spoke to her.

"Lavia?"

She looked him up and down without hiding it. She approved of his frame.

"Yes?"

"Hi, I'm DJ Mosh."

Recognition flickered on her face. She offered a cheek to kiss. Jon Power rolled his eyes and she ignored him.

"Hi there. You're doing a set tonight. I'm looking forward to it," she said, sipping on a tall, pink drink. "I'm more into EBM, usually."

"Of course, you are," Incredulous said, still smiling. Conversations with elites of all kinds are always the same. Painted lips are for hiding teeth.

"Do you like the club?" she smiled.

Incredulous looked around. To someone unfamiliar with the scene or new to its tropes, it might have seemed alien, even hellish in its more animated corners. Several floors, rotunda'd about the main dancefloor, black walls and strobes and bodies – frenetic, convulsive dancing and an unending parade of extreme aesthetics. Incredulous felt at home. Not affectionate, particularly, towards the scene, but comfortable.

"It's lovely. Nice to see so many people at an Alternative club."

"Yeah, there were some lean years there for a while," she said. "But we've built it up. It's pretty underground now, but a big underground, you know? It's just about communications. There is always a market for this." She spoke proprietorially as if the dancers and talkers and drinkers around her were employees – she in the role of upper management on a semi-regular visit to the shop floor. "It's not my best event, but I'm happy with it."

"Oh, you organised this?" asked Incredulous, aware she had booked two DJs for one of the lesser floors.

She waved a hand in shy dismissal and smiled. "Anyway. How can I help you?"

"The Spillover Bar told me you could put me in touch with someone who could help me out."

"With...?"

"Something to drink."

She smiled.

"You don't like their selection?"

"I hear yours is better."

"It is."

"So..."

"I'm sure you understand that that shit carries with it some... risks."

"Of course."

"Well, I hope you don't take this the wrong way, I mean I know about you, but I don't know you if you see what I mean."

"Oh, Lavia. I think we're going to get to know each other a lot better, don't you?" Incredulous' face was tilted downwards, his eyes flicked up at her with crescents of white under the green of his contacts. Without making a show of it, he pulled her to him and kissed her, long and hard. When they parted, her hand was on his chest, a micro-expression of kittenish kneading. Alpha behaviour doesn't only work in the Hip Hop scene.

"Hmm," she smiled. "I think you're right. Come with me."

Striding off towards the EBM floor, she held Moshoeshoe's hand, extending an arm behind her like a child crossing the street with a younger sibling. A parade. Jon Power trailed behind them, brushing past lesser clubbers as they closed like the Red Sea behind the newly-formed power couple.

"This is Special K," she said, sliding herself and Incredulous into a little booth on the wall of a smaller dancefloor where strobes pulsed to hard electro. Special K's real name was Kobus. Racism is alive in the darker corners of the South African Alternative scene. Cultural pride in some elements of white South African demography less so.

K had a similar haircut to Lavia's, three long spikes porcupining under his lower lip. Piercings whose chilling effect on making out must have commuted the difference in commitment cred. A zero-sum mating game. K was an uber.

From under the table, he produced a cooler box. Jon had a similar one he took to rugby games.

"Is this what you're looking for?" Lavia purred.

"Is it?" Incredulous asked above the booming music.

Lavia smiled coquettishly, pulling a blood bag from the cooler and opening its tap into a shot glass on the table.

"Yessss…"

Jon Power's stomach turned and he, in turn, turned to look at the dancefloor's stop-motion techno freakshow. Incredulous took a sip. He felt a surge and a tingling, like other men must feel the effects of psychedelic drugs. It was human. His Sense told him that and a part of his being that he had never liked, never tamed, felt thirsty. He drank the glass and set it down gently.

"Another."

He could taste fear.

Jon Power was praying. Thinking of the girls – Beauty and the Aak de Naus and the countless women he had seen across the border, killed by evil. The stench of evil was in his nostrils, making him feel weak and helpless and angry. His eyes were full of tears. He prayed,

Lord God, forgive me. Lord God, be with me. Lord Jesus be with me. Holy Spirit protect me.

Moshoeshoe raised the third glass to his lips and stopped. He felt like electricity was passing through his body. He knew he was getting stronger. It was old magic, this. The girl was smiling. K watched silently.

"Where is this from?"

"Here and there."

"Ha."

"Do you care?"

"Not really." He wasn't lying.

"It must be expensive, handing it out like this."

"Not everybody gets it for free," she said, her hand traveling sinuously from his face to his crotch, kneading there a while.

"Oh, yes?"

"Yesssss," she said, biting her lower lip. Then his.

"What kind of people…" he asked, kissing her.

"People like you. People like me."

"Anyone specific, recently? Anyone regular?"

He knew he had fucked up as soon as he said it. She pulled away, pushing his chest hard with her right hand and closing the cooler with her left.

"What the fuck do you want to know for?"

"No reason, just…" he kissed her again but she was impassive.

"Bullshit. What do you want?"

Incredulous kissed her deep and focused his mind. His fingers made a sign and he could feel power working through him. She was unable to move and he could see in her mind. Revulsion at his race. A kind of submissive respect for his social position. Excitement. Anger. Fear.

He whispered in her ear.

"I want you to tell me what I need to know," he hissed. "Or you will never move again."

She was high enough to believe the longer threat and aware enough to know that he was binding her. Her eyes grew wide.

"Who? Who am I looking for? Who are you afraid to tell me about?" A kind of power was leaving him as he held her there. The power in the blood goading him to hurt her. Something else, something outside, like a hand on the shoulder, telling him the opposite.

The sound of her voice made Jon Power's skin crawl. A thin, rasping sound, as if spoken in desperate italics, *emphasising. Every. Word. Until. It. Felt. Mad.*

"His name is Kabila," she said.

Both men looked at each other, recognising the name, remembering the long nails, the distant manner. The fixer. "He comes in here sometimes. He's a big wheel in the PDFP. Something political. He likes the human stuff. Way more than most people. Way more than a glass. I used to sell him *bags* of human."

"Used to?" Incredulous was whispering into her ear, still biting its lobe, still holding her hand. He wasn't sure why except that she had pretty ears for a Nazi.

"He's been coming 'round less," she gasped. "But Jimmy said he was coming here tonight."

"The bouncer?"

"Yeah. He gets him in free. Dulu is connected. We call him Dulu. I don't know why. Everybody does. Dulu can do you favours."

Incredulous released her and she slumped forward. Special K ignored her, staring past the dancers as if he couldn't perceive anything outside his mind.

"Where does the blood come from?" Jon Power asked quietly. In his state, the question had not occurred to Incredulous.

"Mostly immigrants, I think," Lavia said, not looking up. "People coming from Zim. Nigeria. Congo. That kind."

"They give it willingly?"

The look on her face said she didn't understand why anyone would care. "Maybe? I don't know. They'll do anything for money. Yeah. Sure."

"If you lie, I will hurt you again," Incredulous said.

She flinched.

"I don't know, I don't know. There have been hints it's part of a *muti* thing. I don't know. I just ignore it. I just sell it, you know. That African crap isn't any of my business."

"Where does this Dulu hang out when he's here?"

She told him and gave him a description that confirmed the identity. They got up to leave.

Jon Power stopped, turned back and leaned over, and tore the swastika armband off her. He opened the blood sample and shoved the fabric into the red liquid. He wiped his hand on the table.

"Siouxsie's overrated," Moshoeshoe said. "Peek a fucking Boo. That's it."

They left her slumped at the table, Special K as much help as he always was.

Floorshow

The Ladybird book of building a dark alternative (if not purely Goth) DJ set, by Uncle Incredulous

You start with She Wants Revenge.

I know, I know. There are issues of legitimacy. First, he's a rapper, then he's doing the 80s Goth thing, plus he hasn't come up through the Scene. But seriously. Listen to the tracks on that first album. At least half of them are works of genius when he's not drowning them in sugar. Yes, the less important collaborator was involved in deeply creepy shit. But clubs don't pay royalties.

And yes, he owes more than a little to Joy Division, and lack the music-journo kudos of an Editors or Interpol – and they're not Goth either – but at least they're Indie. Who the fuck is She Wants Revenge? I know. Shhhhh. Give it a chance. You'll like it, I swear.

And now I feel like a 17-year-old talking his girlfriend into anal.

You start with She Wants Revenge because A) you want to, and B) this is how you build a floor.

More than other scenes, the Alternative world is schismatic and paranoid about liking the wrong stuff. It's not about fashion, as it would be in trendier scenes, but it is about tribe and belonging and identities not so much wrapped up in music as music woven with identity to form the fabric of being.

Or something.

Point is, a change of DJ poses a threat. Obviously, genuinely confident people with nothing to prove are not going to rush off the floor. But there are enough of the others, you know? And an empty floor is hard to fill.

You start with She Wants Revenge because the people who like the band will be so pathetically grateful that you did. They feel isolated and misunderstood in this aspect of their taste and they will give you the benefit of the doubt for at least two songs. Start niche. Niche is loyal. And you can use loyal to build a crowd. And "Nothing attracts a crowd like a crowd."

Yes, I know that's Soul Asylum. No, I don't care that they're basically Grunge and Roses. Good songs are good songs. Even if I can't play them in this set.

Some people like to start with a big track – a floor-filler, guaranteed killer, people rushing from all over the club like ants to your aural sugar. I say this is a mistake. Partly for the aforementioned reasons, but also because if you are the opening DJ (and sometimes you are), that's a whole lotta empty you have to fill with people. And the shy people won't come. Neither will the lazy people.

That's fine, as far as it goes – you will still have a very reasonable floor to start with. But two things will happen later that will make you wish you'd listened to me.

1. Half of those motherfuckers are likely to leave if you play anything even remotely less popular than your opener directly afterwards. And do you want to blow your wad of golden guaranteed

floorkilla in your first twenty minutes? No. Because you're not a cunt. So, when you play a very respectable b-list track, half of those sonsofbitches will walk out like you just dropped a Coldplay crooner. And anyone contemplating getting up to dance who is not in possession of a full set of fire-hardened brass balls will pretend they were walking to the bar near your dancefloor. And you'll have the stink of failure on you. Do you want that? Do you?

2. You're going to have to play that fucking slice of gold again tonight. Now, you may not think that's a big deal of badness. But you are wrong. We've all done it – played a track more than once in a night, or even – for shame – in a single set. We tell ourselves we're in a service industry and are giving the punters what they want. We tell ourselves that radio stations have high-rotation playlists, so club DJs can do it too. We tell ourselves it's not our fault, that we're the victims, and that victim-blaming is wrong. But we are lying pieces of shit and we know EVERY SINGLE TIME that a repeated song is a failure and a confession that hey I don't know very much about music and I could be replaced by a fucking Spotify playlist. We wash and wash but we never feel clean. Trust me on this. Don't do it. If everybody who wants to dance to that shiny new crowdpleaser doesn't get a reasonable shot at it, they will ask for it again. And even if you resist, eventually the manager, the owner, and the bouncers will be squeezing your balls and/or vag until you spin that motherfucker. And then you're doomed to crying in the shower and avoiding eye contact with better men. Don't do it to yourself.

So, assuming you pick She Wants Revenge (other niche gratitude-magnets are available – I've had decent success with under-represented Metal), what song? The natural choice is Out of Control, right? It's about dancing, it's about meeting someone and dancefloor sexytimes. Win, right?

Wrong.

Out of Control is great, but it's not a strong enough song. No, no. I don't want to hear it. You know deep down I'm right. It's a wonderful dance song – wait, let me finish – but it's not an opener. Playing it early is missing its potential. Wasting it. The beat-heaviness means it's easy to mix into some electro or industrial or even 80s stuff (which you'll need later), and it's ideal for that time of the night when they just want to dance to anything. Plus, the narrative of music-making for sweet, sweet suckface is wasted until the crowd is wasted, know what I mean? Wait 'til they're drunk and loose and watching each other through half-closed eyes on the dancefloor. Then hit them with Out of Control. It will be like porn. Good porn. They will thank you.

Now, in my heart, I wish I could say Red Flags and Long Nights is the way to go. It's the best on the first album and the first album is the best album. But it's just not poppy enough. Don't get me wrong, the fans will line up to polish whatever genitals you prefer, just because they never thought they'd hear it that loud, but you won't get them all on the floor, and that's what you need to do. I call it the Reverse Trump. Grab them by their non-socially-sanctioned-music-loving scrotes and drag them to your floor.

The song you do this with is Tear You Apart. And I can see the way you're looking at me. Disdain in your eyes and 'sellout' on your lips. And I hear you. Playing the single can feel gross and dirty and like when the 90s went so corporately wrong. But let's be honest, the bands we're dealing with here don't have singles in any real sense.

Nobody's playing this on any real radio stations since Elvis Hitler *(peace be upon him)* left the Tuks FM building. So, a single is just what we call the song you're most likely to like first. That's a big factor.

Two other factors. One, the Long Walk to Fucking Freedom intro. It thumps and clicks on so long it makes Bela Lugosi's Dead feel like it gets right to the point. That gives the fans a chance to be sure that they're not dreaming, that you're giving them a chance to dance to their band. On a dancefloor. An open dancefloor. Like some kind of beautiful goshdarn dream.

Factor Two is the chorus. "I wanna fucking tear you apart" is all the right kinds of sexy, violent, vaguely transgressive, and sweary to cut across a broad range of potential fans. Who wants to be seen as the kind of guy/gal who will tear a lover apart? You do. So do I. We'll be dancing. So, you start with that.

And here's the danger zone. Here's where it can all go wrong, as I said.

Song #2 is crucial, baby. Woohoo.

You can go with a big classic, though I would wait for the third track for that. Rather, go for another niche song, ideally one that isn't so different from the first track that it loses all the grateful people. Something that doesn't leave them feeling like this was all a glitch in the Matrix. Something with a slow build for running under that last refrain, so the dancers hear the beginning and prepare for it as he shouts his final "TEAR YOU APART!"

Your She Wants fans are gonna like them some drum machine joy, but they are also into the underrepresented. That's why I'd go niche again. Depending on how progressive your Alt club is, you could give them an Evil by Interpol. If no one there likes to admit to going as mainstream as Indie stuff like that, then this is one you save for late at night when they're drunk and making all kinds of bad decisions. If they're a bit less siloed (and if millennials make up a significant demographic, you're in luck), there will also be a few snobs and music Nazis who want to demonstrate how far above genre loyalties they are who will add to your floor.

But, all being well, you can give them the Evil.

You start it at the exact moment the music drops out under the vocals on Tear You Apart. It's a big, strong, 80s alternative bassline, and if nothing else it will confuse people as to what it is. Before the vocals kick in you have eight seconds of it. Tear You Apart finishes with about five seconds of free vocal. It's a catchy enough hook that three or four seconds of that dum, da-dum dum da-dee-dum will work to your advantage, the pure pleasure of a catchy bass hook.

And when the Interpol vocals start, they give you a gift with the word "Rosemary". It's always made the song feel darker, just with the horror movie connotations. Horror fans, like the dark Alternative community, don't mind revisiting the hits of the past. You may have noticed.

The danger moment is the four seconds between vocals starting and the beat kicking in. Beatless moments are always an excuse for people to leave your floor and you must not let this happen.

The way you keep them is, if you have the skills, by casting a spell. Small enchantments can daze people long enough to get them into the groove of a song, but fuck that noise. This is art. This is craft. We do it the hard way. We use smoke and lights, like decent, God-fearing, Anglo-Saxon Protestants around here, boy.

Hey. What are you looking at? Racist.

We hit them with the smoke machine when the bassline starts. Drop them into darkness for the crossover shout. And as they are left *with just that beautiful bass, you give them a slow-moving red light. Little beams. or something swirly. Nothing too hectic. And when that beat kicks in, you give them strobes and they'll be babies sucking at their mothers' titties, beatific smiles all over their mascara'd faces.*

The key will be not to let Evil go on too long. Open-minded they might be, but you don't want them to think for even a minute that they might as well be in a club where their vanilla friends (or, gods forbid, hipsters) would be entirely comfortable. That's not why they're here. You work those lights, you make them love dancing and you rush like the talented, crowd-sensing motherfucker you are to find a nice big fat whale of a dancefloor killer.

You'll know what it is if you've been in the club before. Or you'll be able to work it out. Don't trust the other DJs if you're new at the club or on a particular floor. DJs are insecure assholes with a need to be worshipped so deep they will use other people's art to satisfy it. I know it. I own it. This is postmodern art, my friend. We don't have to make it ourselves.

Point is, don't trust us. We are not interested in everybody having a good time. We don't want to 'see the community thrive'. There is a limited supply of glory and Mr. or Ms. DJ is so unlikely to help you it's pointless asking (and trusting any of us would be dumbshittery of the highest order).

Read the room. How elitist, how uber are these people? How much old stuff have they been grooving to? How mixed is it? Regardless, it's almost always safe to play Closer. A certain era of Nine Inch Nails never went out of fashion, and because our boy Trent never really got to be as famous as Marilyn Manson, people feel comfortable being less sniffy about him. Plus, "I wanna fuck you like an animal" in a song that is legitimately dark and self-destructive rather than an

RnB slow jam? Come on. Of such things are Alternative kid dreams made. We're not better than the mainstream. We love that shit. Just don't make us acknowledge that tasty, brutal fact, and we'll call you a genius. I love my scene.

Of course, your Rob Zombie Living Dead Girls *are fairly safe if people are not too obsessed with the new. And that could open the way to some* Manson, *if that's the kind of crowd.* Dead Girl *carries the benefit of that sibilant intro.* Dope Show *could lead you into some more GlamRock beats and even a Bowie track.* Sweet Dreams *will get you groans, but it will also get you fuckloads of people – just be sure to follow it with something hard and credible.*

Personally, I'll go for Sonne *by Rammstein. Here's why, Chad! The secret's in the ab-dominating, hair-repairing, age-defying patented formula! The semi-beatless intro gives you 16 seconds of counting in German. German, my friend. The language of Alternative legitimacy, so powerful that a bunch of homoerotic (in a body building/rugby-playing way) thugs can seem cool in the rarefied air of the Goth-Industrial scene.*

That intro tells everybody in the club that a Rammstein track is coming up. The metally kids who like it for non-German reasons get enough warning to run for the floor. And the riff? I don't give a shit how over guitars you are now that you're cool and wear PVC. That fucking riff is just immense. Plus, as it's a mid-career Rammstein track, you don't need to worry about old production making it sound less ballsy than Interpol. Cos, you know, that would suck.

Sure, it's not the biggest Rammstein track, but you want to save Du Hast *for later when they've drunk more. Picking this one gives you all the catchiness benefits, plus a smidge of cred for those who think non-singles are the same as being underground. People like to feel special while they dance. And while the dancing is all about the music, row upon row facing you and the speakers, interacting only with the band, the lights, the smoke, it doesn't hurt to pay attention to psychology.*

What Sonne gives you, too, is an opportunity to build up with increasingly frantic coloured lights, to a decent strobe explosion when the guitars kick in. And the female vox, faux operatic warbling that comes in later gives you not only something for the Goth girls to justify their backward leaning, pretend magic fingers dancing. Not just that, no. It also gives you the chance to mix into something more neoclassical like a Dead Can Dance or Miranda Sex Garden. Gotta check your crowd for that. If they're not old or tasteful enough, you could be fucked.

Safer in a right-of-centre Alt club is to go more testosterone. Korn could work if they're still listening to that (and you would be fucking surprised how many are). But equally, some real Industrial could do better. Just One Fix by Ministry is basically the template for all Rammstein riffs, so if you fade that in during the last 30 seconds of Sonne you could go in a harder direction. Classic industrial like that remix of Self Immolation by Fear Factory, Die Krupps, or KMFDM (doin' it again). They're all cool. They're all old, but our scene always has a 20-40 year grace window due to our inherent fear of not being legitimate or credible. Musical dues must be paid to prove you're serious. Old is okay.

At some point soon though, you are going to want to change the pace. Maybe a classic organic Alternative excursion, starting with Peek-a-Boo by Siouxsie, which sounds electronic enough in its intro to make it segue well. Which could naturally make space for the Cure, Lullaby if you're gonna take it dark and downbeat, Love Cats if not. Violent Femmes would work here, too, if you made the dancer's journey smooth enough. Also, it's a great opportunity to play some Sisters of Mercy. And why wouldn't you?

Alternatively, you could move from Rammstein to something more electro, but with a guitarry, harder edge. And One, maybe, or later KMFDM. Even old Apoptygma Berzerk or This Shit Will Fuck You Up *by Combichrist. But the aim is to move quickly from that to a nice EBM set, classics from VNV Nation, Covenant, and Apop (if you've not touched them down there yet), slipping nicely into some synthy sweet stickiness. This is a chance to play a relative newbie like* Not in Love *by Crystal Castles or some Wolfsheim, or any of the million darkish synth bands out there that the kids like these days. Fuckit, if you're feeling brave, you could slow right down for some Sigur Ros, or just slide into a classic 80s Synthpop flume of lushness. Yazoo, motherfucker. Men Without Hats. Alpha freaking Ville. And, ending with Depeche Mode could take you darker again. Ending with A-Ha could allow you to drop into some happier, boun-cier stuff, even some Punk or Grunge.*

But hey. Who am I talking to here? You know what you're doing.

Boy sinister

"I'm Team Edward. I know that's not cool. Everybody likes Jacob, you know? The whole tortured werewolf thing. *Ag shame*, your temperature's so high because of 'the change' that you can't wear a shirt. Bullshit. He knows he's hot and he's flaunting it. It's no different to some of these bitches 'round here with their boobs out all the time. How can people prefer him? He's always wanting to fight! Who wants a guy like that? Edward is beautiful. And kind. And he loves her at a deeper level. I mean, sure, he's a vampire, but then I've always liked vampires. Long before they started sparkling. Not that I mind. I like any kind of vampire. The classics and the new. I know you're not supposed to. You're supposed to be all cool, totally over the *Twilight* thing, but I like them all. Books, blogs, and movies. Stoker and Lee. Even Rice."

"I see…" said the vampire thoughtfully. He was sipping a spillover cocktail that looked much deeper and thicker than water.

"I mean, I like Sookie and the whole *True Blood* thing, too. Even though it became a bit of a soap, you know?"

Dulu nodded. Sipping, watching.

"It's so cool," she continued, very occasionally pausing to breathe and to sip on a bright blue drink people of a preceding generation of clubbers would have called an alcopop. "I mean that whole deep South of America thing. Voodoo and Cajuns and New Orleans and the Bayou, know what I mean? *Dark*. Have you seen *Angel Heart*? It's very cool. Got that daughter from *The Cosby Show* in it, but all grown-up?"

"Mmm."

"Ja, she's so hot, man. And it has the sexiest scene. Like a sex scene, you know. But there's blood pouring everywhere. And a fan. I'm not sure why. Maybe cos it's so hot." She laughed. "But ja, so much blood, and they are just having sex, you know? But it's not a vampire thing. Just Voodoo. But that's what I mean. It's so cool. Like Germany is cool and it has all these folk tales, you know? And Eastern Europe with the vampire myth. You know that's where it comes from?"

"No!" he mocked.

"Ja! It's true! That's where the whole Dracula thing is set. Now it's all full of communists or something. But they have that. The Norwegians have Black Metal and the black magic witch-craft Satanism stuff. The Japanese are all kinds of fucked up and cool. And then South Africa has nothing, you know? What's the best we've got? The ghost of Piet Retief? Haiti has zombies. We've got nothing!"

"You're very white, do you know that?"

"Thank you," she blushed.

Dulu chuckled.

"I'm not even wearing base. This is just how pale I am. I look dead." She smiled.

"Wow," Dulu said.

"I know, right?" she giggled. "Look." She slipped the strap of her rubber dress off her shoulder. "No tan lines. None."

"Impressive," Dulu said, drinking long and staring at the translucent skin, the veins and flesh below.

Inside him, something tightened.

"Hey, do you think the Cullens can tan? Or does the sparkly skin reflect light so much that –"

She stopped and smiled at the two people behind him. A black man was not that unusual in a club like this. Not these days. One dressed so badly was, though. More unusual was an old white guy. She wondered if they were gay cruising. And how they would know someone as cool as Dulu.

"You should leave," the terminally uncool black man said to her. He looked familiar.

"Why?" she asked, more to know than as an objection.

"We have something to discuss."

Dulu had not turned around at all. "Do we?" he said.

"Yes," said Herman Spieëlding.

Michelle kissed Dulu on the cheek and trotted towards a dancefloor playing The Cure, *Lullaby*.

Dulu turned. "You."

He looked from man to man.

"Fancy meeting you here," Dulu said.

∽

Lucretia opened her eyes, then wished she hadn't. Her stomach turned a somersault and she wished it would keep still. She ached all over and felt like hundreds of thorns were pressing into her skin. She wasn't wrong. She opened her eyes again and felt the blood drain out of her brain and to her extremities. Fight or flight. Never before had she wished so much that the second of those choices had been an option.

~

"We meet again," Scientist said, regretting it instantly.

"Am I James Bond?" Dulu asked. "Makes sense. Blow..." he said, nodding at Scientist, "And veld..." he said with a nod to Herman. "I'm assuming you remember me from the club that whore..." he said, but Scientist lunged at him.

Dulu raised a hand and Scientist felt the air thicken with a kind of magnetism, his skin prickling with sparks. He stopped.

"Not here," Dulu said. "Not ever. I can always see you coming. I can always fry your circuits."

"Where is she?" Spieëlding asked, knuckles and muscles and bared teeth in every word.

Dulu sipped his drink.

"You will rejoice to hear that no disaster has befallen that tasty little bitch," he said. He surprised himself by feeling a strange sensation when he spoke of the girl that way. A regret. Disloyalty. Strange. But not enough to stop him enjoying this odd little *tete-a tete*.

"Yet," he said and smiled.

Likota held Spieëlding's arm in restraint.

"What have you done with her?"

"What haven't I?"

Spieëlding took his turn to hold Likota back and Dulu smiled the smile of the confidently invulnerable.

"Look," Likota said, his best private school accent adding authority and a sense of reasonable friendliness to his words. "Tell us what you want. We have influence. You must know that."

"What I want?" Dulu mused, his face dead. "What I want is worlds. What I want is the return of centuries. I want the silence of a night not rent by automobiles and gunfire and ant-nests too large to slip in and out of, too large to control. What I want," he said, looking from one set of worried, confused eyes to another, "is emancipation. What I want is recompense." He took a long sip of his drink, the boom, and thud of a nearby dancefloor, the ducks' nest cackle of conversation-making white noise against the black walls. "What I want doesn't matter."

"What the actual fuck are you talking about?" Likota deadpanned.

The man in the dapper suit smiled. "What I have. And more."

"Don't test me ..." Likota said.

"I don't want anything you can give," Dulu replied.

"Then *why*?" Spieëlding said.

"I don't know. And I promise you, there is nothing you can do." The words were spoken without malice. Without an emotion either of the human men could recognise. Final as a stone slab sliding into place.

"We should just shoot this motherfucker right here."

"And then what?" Dulu said. "Two public figures like yourselves? Caught attempting murder? Together?"

"I don't care," Herman Spieëlding said.

"Neither do I," the lightning bird said. "And there is nothing you can do that can hurt me."

Again, the finality. It gave the odd pair pause.

"Where is she?" the old white man asked, the fight almost out of him.

"Knowing won't help."

"What have you done?"

"Things, things…" the monster said, absently, a sigh in his voice. He sipped, looking around, distracted.

"If you've hurt her…"

"If I've hurt her, what?" he asked.

The two men were silent. The club pulsed around them.

"There it is," Dulu said. "As it happens she's not suffering, not dead. Not experiencing much of anything."

"Why?" the father asked.

"I got her high."

High

Lucretia saw nothing but stars. Facing straight upwards in the open air, that kind of thing happens. Everything in her muscles and her mind was telling her not to lift her head again.

She did.

Fuck.

She slumped carefully back down again, squeezing her eyes shut.

Okay. So that's Pretoria. An irregular little window onto Pretoria. *All* of Pretoria. A fucking tiny scale model of Pretoria with fucking lights and minuscule cars and mountains and... And the goddamn moon. Not a model. *Fuck.*

She took a deep breath. Let go.

She turned to the left and felt a painful stab and whatever she was lying on give way, just an inch. The moment before an avalanche, when everyone stops talking about how great the powder is. Her heart stopped and restarted, sending shocks of fear through her whole body.

Still. Hold still. Open your eyes. Breathe.

Her vision acclimatised to the light and she could see what looked like branches. A mat of branches right in front of her. A tree? What kind of tree towers over the city like this?

Gingerly, she reached out an arm. It was scratched and bruised and bloody. Her fingers reached a mess of branches and sticks just as they resolved in her vision. Blotchy with black spots, the pixelation of the human eye at night. A wall of sticks and twigs, thorns, and some dead leaves. She touched a thin twig and it shuddered. Sent trembles through the surrounding tangle. Snow shuddering under her skis. She stopped breathing. Eyes open. Waiting.

The branches underneath her stayed stable. Just a vibration. *Highwire guitar string*, she thought, *high, why, g-string*. Giggle. She was in shock. Okay.

She lifted her head, eyes traveling up the chaotic, woven wall of wooden spikes and branches roughly twisted like broken fingers. Higher up, stars were shining through. Lower down, a gap in the mad lattice, about a foot wide, was what she had seen the city through.

Lucretia lifted herself, in what should have been a painful motion, onto her knees. Breaking skin as relevant as breaking fingernails. The pain receptors in her brain had reset for the task at hand. She looked around her. She was in a kind of hollow in a mass of branches. A nest.

What? Don't think about it.

She shifted her weight from side to side. Nothing. Stable enough.

Okay.

Through the thinner parts of the walls, the gaps, she could see the city. In her panic and fear, she had just known she was looking at Pretoria. *How?* She shifted around on her knees, noticing for the first time that she was not wearing much in the way of clothing. Silver classic G-string and a silver bikini-style top. Remains of some kind of kimono clinging to her arms and shoulders, shredded into a feathered cape.

I'm a fucking superhero. Woo.

Right. Where am I?

Hills. A conglomeration of light in one direction and another. Suburbs and arterial roads and what must be a highway. The Voortrekker Monument looking like an alien jukebox. A giant building much lower, much closer. Wait. UNISA?

The cubist aeroplane resting lazily on a hillside, watching over all the traffic entering the city was familiar to her, though not from this angle. She took a while to make sure she was right. And then calibrated. She knew where she was.

Oh, God.

The Telkom Tower. Lukasrand Tower. That big fucking tower near the Parks Board and the hospital that should still be called the Little Company of Mary but isn't. The giant communications tower. Bastard offspring of a monkey wrench and a record stylus, drawn in 80s computer screen blocks, its right-angled nodules and sheer towers defining the horizon for some of the more affluent suburbs of Pretoria's elite. In architectural terms, probably not that tall. In being stranded on top of it terms, fucking tall enough.

She was in a giant nest, an actual nest, big enough to take four of her, on the top of a huge microwave mast. Her head reeled and she couldn't decide whether she wanted to cry or to throw up.

She did the latter, raising her head afterwards to gulp for breath, and noticed a pair of shining black eyes watching her.

Jon Power was slumped against the bar, drinking a Castle. So uncool was the drink in this particular scene that the pretty little barmaid hadn't been sure they'd had it. But she tried and they did. This bar looked onto a mainstream floor, pumping out the tunes the scenesters were not interested in. Fewer ubers. Less latex. More classic metal t-shirts and little black dresses. Lots of Dr. Martens. People enjoying themselves.

An affable-seeming lanky 20 something with long, dirty hair leaned against a wall in floppy shorts, sheer leggings, and what looked like mining boots. He wore a "Danny is a cunt" T-shirt that seemed in conflict with his jovial bearing. He chatted to a woman of indeterminate age in a leather corset that ballooned her breasts up to her collar bones. Airbags deployed. Her hair was pink and loose and looked like a wig. Maybe it was. She laughed as much as women who want insecure men to like them often do, and when she did, her breasts jiggled and the boy hardly noticed the laughing.

The music wasn't bad. A couple of 80s Pop songs he recognised had made it into the set, for reasons he couldn't understand. His youth transposed onto a strange scene. Weirdly, the hairsprayed, overly-made-up, outlandishly dressed dancers seemed to love them. Actually, that wasn't so weird.

A very catchy song referencing lines from what Jon Power thought must be *The Silence of the Lambs* was playing and the dancers were laughing. Good-natured, wholesome fun, with serial killers. *Lekker*.

His spirit was uncomfortable, but not with the dancers or the music. Something else. Something else was wrong.

He prayed that God would use him. He quietened his mind. Tried to empty himself, to make room for Him. Peace welled up.

He sipped his beer and turned to a girl standing at the bar, rainbow hair, cleavage, and kooky eye make-up.

"What is this?"

"The music?" she asked, smiling. He nodded and she said, "Greenskeepers. Old YouTube thing more than a band. But the song is very cool. Funny, you know?"

"Ja," he said, unconvincingly.

"You're not a black metaller, are you?" she said, kindly.

"It's that obvious?"

"Not obvious. Not a secret. What are you? A cop?"

Jon Power made like Jack Reacher and said nothing.

"I don't mind," she encouraged. "My dad's a cop."

"I'm not a cop."

"What, then?"

"I'm a pastor."

"Cool."

It wasn't the response he was expecting.

"Is it?"

"Yes. Well. I'm a Christian, so I would think that."

"What are you doing in a place like this?"

"Same thing you do in the places you go, I expect."

"Good answer," he smiled.

"Thanks!" She smiled back. "Do you need anything? Can I help, I mean? Are you looking for someone?"

"I'm looking for two girls."

She made big eyes and a shocked expression. "*Pastor!*"

"No, man. Not like that." *What was it with charming Alternative girls?*

"I know," she giggled. "I get a good vibe from you. Not that there's anything wrong with polyamory. But I know. What girls?"

"They're in a band."

"'Round here? Throw a shot glass and you'll hit someone calling themselves a singer or a musician."

"Ag. Wait. What were they called? Um. Something to do with steam and the sea."

"Ah, Diving Belles," she said knowingly. "They're nice. I haven't seen them tonight yet, though."

"Thanks anyway, hey. What about DJ Mosh?"

"Oooh, he's pretty!"

"Ja, I guess he is," Jon Power laughed.

"He's supposed to be DJing on the other main floor about now. You want me to take you there?"

"Please."

"Can I buy you another Castle?"

"Sure."

"One Castle for Pastor of Bodom!" she shouted to the bar lady.

"What?"

"Don't worry," she smiled.

"You're very kind."

"You seem like you need to relax."

"Ja," Jon Power said, exhaling for longer than he thought he needed to.

"I could help?" she smiled.

"Kind," Jon Power smiled back, in a way that conveyed 'thank you, but that won't be necessary.'

But Communist Pentecostal preachers in their early 40s have been known to misinterpret signals from millennial gummy goths before. Probably.

⌒⌒⌒

The Hammerkop hadn't moved at all as she crept toward it. And it could see her. Eyes open, glinting like shaved onyx. In a part of her mind, her soul, that she had rarely felt before, she knew that it was just an extension of something. Something she could feel watching her. Feel enveloping her. Something damaging and comforting and easy to fall into. Some people are destined for this kind of love.

She shook herself from the reverie.

The bird was an eye set in warm, feathered sinews. It was perched on a metal tube. The tube was part of the pinnacle of the tower, a radio mast of latticed pipe about a foot in diameter and arranged in a triangular column. She put her hand on the edge of the nest, a couple of feet from the bird, and peered over the side.

The Hammerkop started flapping its wings and keening wildly, fluttering and beating at her, its bulbous head swinging and scything. Not massive, but big enough. A medium-sized dog, but with a sharp beak and long claws. And the ability to fly. And rabies. Absolutely no boops.

It flapped and pecked and screeched and wheeled chaotic about her face. It pecked at her eyes, her hands taking the painful force of the attacks, her body flailing instinctively backwards into the nest. The sky was empty above her. And below. Her stomach fell, sending cold, heart-pausing signals through all of her nerves.

Her pain receptors had woken up, her panic, too. The nest was swaying. She had no idea how strong the structure was and had no desire to fall the vertiginous storeys of empty to an eastern suburbs' death. Not for a flipping bird.

She crouched down in the centre of the nest again and the Hammerkop went back to where it had been playing sentry. Perhaps she should stay. Calm suddenly fell on her. From nowhere, from the sky, from far away, and not very far at all. She felt the presence again. For a long moment, she was not alone and she sat perfectly still. And then it passed.

Okay. She thought about her first boyfriend. His occasional anger, his need to know where she was at all times, the way he made her feel safe and afraid. She had been trapped in the air before. *Okay.*

What now? Any time she approached the edge of the nest, the bird went berserk. So, she'd have to avoid the edge.

Through a gap in the nest's wall, possibly uncovered by her scramble to get away from the bird, she saw a metal tube a good four inches in diameter. She had an idea. She'd never climbed before. Too preppy. But people change, you know? They try new things. Growth.

Slowly, she started pulling and snapping sticks around the opening. The little black eyes watched her without reacting, like CCTV.

Ten minutes into the beer, he started to feel weird. Initially, he just thought it was the place, the people. But it was more than that. Jon Power recognised the feeling.

The girl led him through the crowds of people like trees – under waving, dancing arms, between the boughs of bodies into an eerie, slow-motion grove of gyration and gesticulation. She was smiling and dancing and saying things to him. He could hear only a few of the words, as every now and then she'd zoom out, too far away to hear or properly see. He felt contented and a little confused.

Incredulous Moshoeshoe was there, above them, mid-ascension, his face lit from below by blue and green lights, his dreadlocks throwing shadows around like searchlights in the bush. He seemed happy. Everyone around him seemed happy. This girl seemed…

Gone. She was gone and that was okay. He drifted from group to group, either welcomed or gently ignored. People were smiling in his face and he could feel the music. Was riding it like a motorbike over familiar paths. Like a rhetorical groove, rising to an altar call.

People swung their hair, bent backwards at crazy angles, wet him with their spraying sweat and it felt like a sprinkler on a hot afternoon when he was a child. Jon Power had been high before.

You couldn't help it in Angola. And sometimes you didn't want to. Anaesthetic for the soul. And though he'd never taken whatever this was, it was not unpleasant. He was smiling.

Out of the garden of the dancefloor, then, as suddenly as he could perceive it, he saw a face he recognised. *Howzit*, he wanted to shout, but no one would have heard him, and anyway, he was too slow. Scientist Likota. Friend of the Movement. Not committed, it was true, but useful and important and …

He couldn't think. The music lifted him again and he bobbed as on a swell on Durban beach. No. Somewhere nicer. The Eastern Cape. Kenton-on-Sea. He rose and fell and felt the salty wind in his hair and watched a beautiful girl like Morticia Addams, from that movie, swim and spin around in her little circle of joy by the speakers. Endless seconds later and another face he knew. Less friendly. Broederbonder. Following Likota? *Shit.*

He motioned to Incredulous, high up in the clouds of the DJ booth, but the people around him started emulating his gesture, becoming anemones in a sea of mixed metaphors and haze. He was lost. Incredulous was a blue moon, and he was standing alone on a dancefloor of long grass, all swaying with the wind. He closed his eyes, listened to the beat of the wind, and swayed, beginning to disappear. The ends of his fingers had no nerves, his lips were numb. He began to feel happy, but when he opened his eyes, he saw a shadow pass across the moon.

⌒〜⌒

Lucretia shivered and smiled. The hole was big enough to fit through. The nest had been woven into the triangular column lattice. Serious tree branches had been wedged into the spaces between the sturdy poles forming a kind of wooden platform for the mess of sticks. *What the fuck kind of bird…?* An image flashed in her mind and she tried to push it away. *Not now.*

She stretched out to touch the metal, to see if she could reach. Her stomach turned and she felt her blood pressure fall as she peered out of the nest to the impossible drop beneath her. Again, the bird attacked.

Again, the wild air-beating with whirling wings. Again, the savage claws and beak and wild, mindless violence. The bird was her guard. Pulling back into the nest, she turned to face it, and it went back to its perch. Steadying herself, she extended her left hand, crossing the threshold of the nest. The bird flew at her again.

It took every molecule of will not to protect her face. She closed her eyes, dropped her chin, and allowed the bird to tear at her forehead and scalp. Pain filled her consciousness but she held still until the bird settled into a rhythm of attack, like a robot on a loop. Leather feet and nails like thorns hooked and tore, scratched, and cut her. Stinging, singing pain. Cells screaming at her brain to evade, avoid, escape. She held herself there, like a wife. Like a soldier under torture. Like a victim deciding to be a survivor, an avenger.

In a gap, blood pouring down her face, she made a grab for the feathered form, the downy neck. It thrashed and struggled and pecked and she tightened her fingers around the neck. It was hard, like a veined, tendonned plant. She held it like that boyfriend used to like, while he pulled her hair until she cried. She let her fist work up the neck until she felt the knob of a head, and started using two hands. Like he liked. She struggled to pull the hard, beaked skull away from the body. The mad, screeching creature kicked and tore at her face and her arms strained slowly apart, head and neck. Steady, ripping a curtain, pulling a Christmas cracker.

A click and a crunching rip, slow and catastrophic, and the bird went limp and surprisingly heavy in her hands. *Leaving that motherfucker was the best thing she had ever done*, she thought. *The beatings had been worth it.*

She dropped the empty bird through the opening. "Bye-bye, Tweetie," she muttered, listening to the pleasing clang as it hit the metalwork on its long way down.

Then she decided to put her training to good use.

In Dulu's mind, the scene he'd been watching suddenly switched off. It threw him for a minute, disoriented him. He sensed his familiar's life-ending without grief, but with confusion, concern. That hammerkop had been with him since Kinshasa the last time. Almost 50 years ago. Home.

He'd been the only *Sapeur* with an exotic pet. His black and red plumage then had been translated into something more extravagant and beautiful in people's minds. Amazing how human self-defence perceptions crossed boundaries of time and culture. But how he detested the conservatism of the early Teenthousands. One could not walk around like a dandy with an extravagant bird without expecting a beat-down. He missed the old days. The clubs. The friends. The bird always with him. It had been a most open companion then. A familiar familiar. For a familiar.

He thought on these things without warmth. *If she escaped, would the plan be ruined? Perhaps. Perhaps not.* There was enough tension on either side, with the old man about to pass. The death, at the hands of the radicals, of the daughter of a right-wing leader. Well, that was a guarantee. *Would it be as good if she died in a fall?*

She certainly would die in a fall if she was trying to escape. Trained men fell. A woman – and that kind of woman – she had no chance.

Her father was a man of spirit – this he had seen in their earlier altercation – he had left the boer and his politician friend lightly stunned with a small burst of his power. They had toppled as if drunk, steadying each other like drinking buddies. They would not try again. And if they did he would see them, he would stop them, as he had so many like them before. These two were weak and stupid and probably gone – or leaning against each other, dazed and confused like an interracial farce in this place of too-loud music. Ebony and Insobriety.

He smiled and thought again of the woman, surprised at himself. She was stronger than the others. Stronger than any before. In another world, another life…

But it didn't do to think about these things. Better to disdain. Less bitter to despise. We all have our allotted roles. We all have a job to do.

He was thinking this, standing on the stair to the dancefloor, when a quart of Black Label broke on his skull.

Out of control

Strippers make great climbers. Fact. Particularly if the climbing involves sliding down an almost regulation pole, from a great height.

Lucretia had made the heart-stopping drop from the nest to the tower proper and started climbing down the outside, rung by rung. But several terrifying slips, precipitated (as it were), by the condensation on the 'round, painted steps, had made her rethink her strategy. Slithering through a triangular gap and clinging like a scantily clad koala to the central pole, probably a cable conduit, she found herself looking at a panoramic cityscape, brisk winds burning her eyes and the ice-cold steel and desperation burning her thighs.

Inch by inch, foot by foot, she clamped and relaxed, as she had done a hundred thousand times before, a billion stars leering at her, willing her to fall. She thought of her father.

Incredulous Moshoeshoe was deep into the groove of his set when he saw the fracas begin. A dancefloor has a pattern, waves, and ripples the subconscious can predict when viewed from above. A disturbance, as in an ant nest or a commuter stream, is an instant minor chaos explosion among the ordered fractals. The DJ notices it immediately and assumes it was one of the classics: a passed-out dancer, a dropped-bottle spilling its contents in a hazardous puddle, or a good old-fashioned fight. He saw all three. A good-looking black man in a beautiful suit lay on the ground, a growing puddle of beer and blood spreading like a rash around his head, a less well-dressed pair, black man and a white man, were leaning over him, grabbing hold of his limbs.

The little scene attracted a crowd, and soon the self-appointed policers of clubland had swung into drunken action, shoving and jostling the two men. Incredulous deployed a messy mix to a guaranteed floor-filler, hoping to drown the conflict by sheer force of dilution.

He failed.

He was about to switch to another tactic, the slow, moody track, all darkness and smoke, when out of the corner of his eye the patterns of the fracas changed again. The group of late-night vigilantes were still struggling with the two men, the prone figure was still on the floor, but another figure had arrived. Incredulous recognised him immediately as the pastor. He was swaying drunkenly and had started to bend double over the victim when the image seemed to swim in Incredulous' vision. The shape on the floor became indistinct. Almost as if it was growing.

Thirty metres doesn't sound like it's high. Not enough to win you medals or anything. It feels more impressive, however, when you're atop another 157 metres of building. And even without that, it's significantly taller than the average club pole. The thigh gripping slide had been successful though. Lucretia's legs were on fire from the friction and she was shivering with cold, but she had made it down to a concrete ledge. She clambered out of her terrifying Mecano prison and looped her arm through one of the triangular spaces to catch herself when she slipped. Which she did.

Hanging there, in space, above the concrete block off which she'd almost certainly bounce to her death if she fell, she thought she should have had a tiny King Kong in her hand. The idea flitted through her mind like an aeroplane in a black and white film. Even go-go dancers indulge in whimsy.

She knew in her bones that the presence, the underwater part of the iceberg that was the hammerkop, was looking for her. And she felt a pull to where it was. A lodestone of abuse.

She prayed for the first time since she was a child. *Please help me.*

⌐━━━━━━╝

A small scuffle had broken out around Spieëlding and Likota. Exactly the kind of scuffle they could have done without. The two men stood back to back, shoving, shouting, and occasionally punching onlookers who hadn't liked the vibe of two obvious outsiders attacking a dude for no reason. Some of the more fresh-from-the-farm kids in Slayer T-shirts and blue jeans were focusing on Scientist. White liberals, excited for an opportunity, finally, to come to the aid of a black man in a fight, were pouring rage, scorn, and beer out on Hermann. Almost all of them were drunk.

Almost.

One girl stood apart against a matt-black wall, watching. A woman, really, but people always saw her as a girl. Slender, long-legged, and fresh-faced, in a tight black vest top that proved bigger wasn't always better, and beautifully tight blue jeans, clinging to her body like very fortunate paint. She had long, dark blonde hair, unstraightened like she'd walked to work on a breezy day, gapless fringe, eyes as blue as you imagine water to be when you're young.

It's good, sometimes, to describe a writer. As an act of reciprocity, if nothing else.

The writer had pupils so large they made grown men lose their train of thought entirely. Pupils that took in everything, even if her soft pink mouth and long fingers never said a word.

Something she saw now in the melee (she would use the term melee if she wrote about this, but only ironically) gave her pause. There was something off about the men at the centre. Like a tiger in the Kruger Park, or a reasonable man at an AWB rally.

Those two faces.

She pulled out her phone, took a couple of pictures, and searched them.

Then she started tweeting.

Lucretia dropped to the concrete slab and stumbled, almost going over the edge. The surface was cold and rougher than it looked. Her legs were like jelly from the effort of clinging to the pole. Her face was torn and bloody from the sentry bird's attacks. The rest of her body was scratched and grazed by the mass of sticks she had been nestling in. Her feet were bloody from leaving the nest. Again, her father came to mind.

She wrapped an arm around the metal tower protruding from the concrete slab, fearful that the wind rushing around her would punch her out into the cool, dark air.

A tiny ladder, like one on a child's bunk bed, was bolted to the edge of the slab and dropped disturbingly over the side, into nothingness. She tried desperately to remember the structure. *There were offices or labs or something in the big, thick bits, right? Was there once a restaurant up here? Maybe.*

Maybe, maybe, maybe. Fuck. She couldn't do it. She couldn't fathom it. *A nest? A bird? What was that?* What was the feeling she had in a part of her she'd not felt since she was a girl, pulling her magnetically into the city? She knew it wasn't watching. But it wanted her near. *Why?*

It wasn't possible. Birds don't come in size super-mega-extra-monster-large and walk into dressing rooms and deposit women in nests on top of landmarks and all this was just a psychotic break. *Right?*

Right?

And if it wasn't …. Well, shit. If this was real, if this was not a psychotic break – and who hallucinates the discomfort of g-string creep? – then she was the victim of something fucking horrible. And she had had enough of that. She had been dragged into something she didn't want, something she had no control over, something that she didn't understand and was never given a choice about. She was going to be the victim. Again.

Fuck. That.

Fuck that bird. Fuck the genetic mutation that made it or the voodoo bullshit that animated it or the fucking freak in a bird costume and a jet pack that brought her here. Fuck the Broeders and her dad and the fucking Vivaldi club and having to hide her marriage. Actually, fuck Scientist, too, with his fucking need for secrecy and his public image and all his shit-stirring and never being there for her. *Fuck all of them.*

She let go of the metal and crawled painfully on all fours towards the ladder.

How the hell do you get onto the ladder without falling off it?

She turned around and inched backwards towards the edge. A cold wind rushed over her feet and her ass offered itself to the world. She chuckled. *Pretty standard night, really.*

Not for the first time in her life or on that night, she stepped out into the void.

Allegedly, dancefloor tragedy

I t started trending almost immediately.

Is this the head of the Broederbond and the head of the RYM, fighting on the same side in a bar-room brawl? ran the headline accompanying her picture on Awks.co.za, the site the blonde girl wrote for. #BroederFromAnotherMutha started trending soon afterwards, but was quickly overtaken by #BroederBarney and, finally, as web wits started speculating as to what could make allies of such seemingly incompatible men, #EveryoneHatesGoths. It was, at first, an amusing night on social media.

As the evening progressed and more pictures, more reports came out, the Twitterati became less amused. Horror stole over that corner of the internet.

Incredulous watched the shape change and grow, a large shadow that seemed to blot out more and more of the floor as if several lights were fading at once. People were still dancing, but their number was thinning. As the shadow reached them, more and more were stopping. Turning.

The lightning bird spread its wings. Flapped once or twice, pulling a booming sound from the air, the rush knocking glasses off tables and making more people turn. There were screams and an equal mix of running and standing rooted to the spot, as the black and red Impundulu beat its way awkwardly into the air.

Lightbulbs exploded. Electricity was crackling everywhere, making hair stand on end and metal piercings tingle and warm. The lightning bird was still struggling, its massive wings battling walls and tables and bodies to push itself into the air above the crowd. Below it, an old white guy and a man who looked like that Scientist guy from the Radical Youth Movement were the only ones rushing repeatedly towards the creature, being pushed back by the force of the air, blows from the wings, and something else. One would try to distract the bird while the other circled 'round, heavy broken bottle in hand. But the bird would always notice, sending bolts of electricity into the attacker, tazing him down for crucial minutes as it regained more and more composure and strength.

In its grudging, violent struggle to gain height and advantage by rising up the three-storey atrium that was the main floor, the Impundulu's wings swiped four or five people from the viewing decks over the edge, sending them plummeting to the dancefloor below. In the thunderous noise of wings and frantically buzzing air, nobody heard their collisions with the already sticky ground.

"She was screaming as she fell," tweeted @gummygoff1999 later, "but I never heard her hit. RIP Candice. #FemmesForever".

A phalanx of men, black, white, 'coloured' and 'Indian' (these things are important in reporting South African news), started to advance on the lightning bird. Some stood beneath it, others raced up the stairs, colliding with those trying to get away from the insane scene at the centre, taking up positions on viewing decks, climbing speaker stacks. Most were hurling missiles of varying sizes and degrees of usefulness, from bottles and chairs to shot glasses. They bounced off the bird almost before they hit it. The air around it seemed to shimmer.

Occasionally one of the clubbers would produce a handgun. Bouncers are not made of the same stuff as airport security, however much their attitudes coincide. But no matter how stealthily, no matter how slowly they raised their Glocks and Norincos, the bird would catch sight of them before they could fire. A muscle-bound metaller with hair incongruously in a top-knot turned instantly black, his clothes smoking. His eyes evaporated, an old Tokarev dropping to the ground next to his body. The air reeked of nitrogen, burning nylon, and cooked meat.

A barman with a shotgun dropped the moment he entered the lightning bird's field of vision, managing more than most, letting off a shot that knocked the bird back for a minute, dropping it several feet. The barman's body steamed. A woman with an undercut and a face full of metal took a running jump from a balcony, landing on the Impundulu mid-air and scrabbling to hold onto its feathers, its vulture neck, stabbing it repeatedly with a small blade mounted on a ring. 'Heroic' is a word not often enough associated with female acts of violence in our culture.

'Ineffective' is also a word. As is 'burning'. Quickly she began to scream, her blade and piercings glowing red, then white, the pain becoming too much.

As she let go, the bird halted her fall, catching her in a large talon and snapping off her head, as if opening an ampule of morphine or nerve gas. Dulu thrust his beak deep into the wound of a neck and drank. There he became stronger. Healed.

What followed was a frenzy of blood.

Jon Power, still high, still confused, but trying manfully to be of help, was pulling stunned bodies off the dancefloor as the flapping, swooping thing made repeated passes at the moving and immobile forms, tearing them apart and drinking. There was a stink of iron over everything, overpowered, when a truck full of police burst in, by a thicker stench of smoking. Burning.

Twenty, thirty, fifty dead. Blood and burning and the almost total darkness of dead circuits and lightless corridors, broken only by spasms of lightning and electric flashes. Stills of scrambling, running people, clawing and trampling each other, trying to get out and ending, like desperate rats in Minos' labyrinth, exactly where they didn't want to be. Blinded by the white light, jolted and stunned and opened like fruit.

Spieëlding and Likota lay twisted together like lovers, regaining consciousness, their palms burnt and their ears ringing. The lightning bird slammed down on the ground next to them and leaned in, close as a trusted uncle. Sinister as the same. Likota tried to stand. He could smell the souring blood on its breath, feel the warmth of its body. The occasional spark and crackle played along its feathers, giving him nightmarish impressions of matted down, red eyes, the grotesque shoulders of something softly post-reptilian.

Likota stood up, his face a few fizzing feet from the lightning bird's beak. It cocked its head to one side, the blood-glow of its eye, regarding him closely.

"Do it, Big Bird," he said firmly. "Do your fucking worst."

The monster growled, "Who do you think you are?"

"Prometheus. Fuck face."

"Um… What?" which was a strange word to hear from a giant, vampiric demon-fowl.

"You can head back to Sesame Street, or you can…" he paused and lifted his head. "Suck. My. Liver."

Spieëlding rugby tackled him to the ground just as the giant beak snapped in the air where the classics-referencing revolutionary's throat had been. Likota opened his eyes to see Incredulous Moshoeshoe's grinning face next to Spieëlding's, illuminated by the arcs of electricity playing between the monstrous feathers.

"Greek myth smack talk?" Incredulous said. "Really?"

Likota smiled weakly. "Private school."

"Come on!" Spieëlding said, dragging Scientist and Incredulous behind him, straining to see enough to find his way off the dancefloor.

All three of them crashed into a dazed Jon Power.

The Impundulu raised itself above the floor, its body singing with energy and strength and its mind now ringing with triumph. A big man, about to swat a fly. The bird climbed the hot black air to the ceiling, its perfect vision showing every detail of the panting pastor below in the darkness. Pupils impossibly wide. Eyes focused in the dark. It flattened its wings against itself and dropped, at terminal velocity like a kingfisher, towards the tangle of irritations. Dulu saw in utter clarity every face, every throat, almost a full panorama, slowed by centuries of speed and physical superiority. He dilated his pupils fully, counting hairs on the heads of his prey. Hissing frame by frame towards them, calibrating an arc of scything vengeance. The humans moved slowly, oblivious. *This is the end.*

Incredulous Moshoeshoe made the room explode with light.

Blazing brightness, off the spectrum, conjured from the power behind the air. One day it would have a name. It would have metrics. Now it was just magic.

He'd been watching, studying the monster as it thrilled and killed and tore the place apart, seeing "between the shadows," as his grandmother had called it. He had seen the creature's eyes, taken advantage of its assumption of total superiority, the arrogance of slow living.

He willed a great explosion of light from between things and from the past and from above and it made every black surface white. The bird, blinded, disoriented, crashed headlong into the ground, feet away from them, stunned and tumbling and skidding, tearing through the wooden bar on the edge of the floor like it was kindling, smashing a wall of clear bottles, pouring vodka and white spirits into a growing pool.

Jon Power lay in darkness, alcohol filling his nostrils and the clamour of shouts and moans from the other men echoing around his head. He was too tired to pray with his mind. His lips formed words in languages he did not understand but that his God would know.

Moshoeshoe disentangled himself and looked between the shadows at the pastor. His energy was fading, his ability to see now lessening as his power drained. He dropped back into darkness. Behind him, he thought he heard the lightning bird stirring, but he couldn't bring the vision back.

And then, out of the darkness, there came another great light.

Cerebral song

Goethe got it wrong. He always did. Ossenfelder, too. Though he was closer.

Yeah, I read. I've had time.

The question, then, am I a vampire? Am I evil?

The answer, No.

Yes. But, no.

I am not dead. Not one of the clever categories of dead so popular in the late twentieth century, not one of the simple categories in the nineteenth. Eighteenth.

And I don't hate God if that's what you're thinking. Though I have no love for him. Not anymore.

I went through my phase, of course. We all do. Or, at least, we should, if we are not already convinced that he exists. The lifelong atheists, they know him. They've seen him. And they are so afraid that they must keep him away with cattle-prods and misapprehension of what science is for, and barely concealed terror. Harris and his friends have white knuckles. You can see them, under the smugness.

I lost my love for God when I realised I would never die. It sounds childish, I know. But, you know what else? Fuck you. You live for hundreds of years on this continent, in this body, contending with… with…

Forget it.

I stopped loving God when I realised he did not love me. That the pathetic importers of the Christian religion (which had made so much sense to me when it arrived, which had captivated me, even as it sought to disabuse my people of the notion of my existence) convinced me of that much, along with their monotheism. God was primarily concerned with humans. And I was not a human.

I think if I were not vampiric, I would be a vegan. But I think the rules are different for us. Us, you know? Those within, not the parasites without. You know who I mean. What I mean. The birds and reptiles, crocodile men, and the hyaenas. The animals. It is okay, I think, for us to kill each other. To feed on each other. To feed on them, too, the men.

I remember, when I loved the Lord, how I would love to read about the lion and the lamb. How it would make me weep with guilt and hope. I loved the vision of that God, that world where none of us (us, within) would be designed to murder.

That was a long time ago.

I am who I am. And I will never die. I don't age. I don't fade. I drink the blood and heal and grow more youthful and more strong. Even as those who own me grow older, weaker, more maddened with bitterness and fear. I am the first taste of real power some people ever have. And it doesn't do good things to them.

I mean not just the ones who I control, of course. But you've guessed at that, no? You've watched and thought it out? What is this to me, after all? I am not a monster.

Ha.

But of course, I am.

And one of my disciples gave the drugs to the Christian, and look at him. Worthless. And all the others with their brutal confidence, where are they now? Celebrating.

I like to let them think I cannot see them.

I like to encourage them to put up a fight.

I like to play with my food.

We are all following orders.

That's what the Nazis said. That other great European monster, white-skinned and always smelling of the grave. Fearful of the cross, of the spice of cultural contamination, of refracted light. And in a sense, they were. But the orders were their own. The speeches were their own, the rallies and the symbols and the leading of the scapegoats onto trains, these were not one man's ideas. They had crowned him. They had sculpted him from shame and denial and the anger of children, and then they listened for his voice. They followed. They followed him right into the grave.

I am following orders.

I did not create my king. I don't have a king.

Neither of our victims are virgins. That's another thing the writers all got wrong. There is no innocence that we are feeding on. That's a fantasy attributed and searched for by masturbating puritans and bored filmmakers. That is not African. And Europe so long in the past forgot its innocence you cannot claim that 1939 (or Vlad before it) took anything that hadn't dissolved long before.

I'm meandering.

I'm killing time until time… You know.

I'm bored, too. And sad that there is nothing in this crop that makes me think for just one second that I might not make it through tonight. No one to free me.

And before you say it, I am not a man, either. So, suicide is beyond me. Hegel got that right. No beast will sacrifice its life for nothing but an idea. And I am beast.

That your God told you about. And I have come to destroy. And I can never die.

Don't believe what you're told. I have no equal. There is no predator above me on the apex. I am the sharp corner of that pyramid. And I'm doomed never to lose.

They are all so stupid.

Bird without wings

Lily was holding a zippo aloft, filling the room with gentle, warm light. Like she so often did. She looked to him like the Statue of Liberty. Incredulous embraced her and she smiled.

"You guys okay?"

"I am," he said. "My buddy here…"

They all looked at Jon, who was still muttering incomprehensibly on the floor, motionless and oblivious.

"Yeah, he's fucked," Lily said. "What's he on?"

"Nothing, as far as I know."

"You sure?" she asked, holding fingers in front of the pastor's face.

"Does it matter?" Likota asked, aware of raised voices and flashing lights outside, unaware of his current presence on Twitter. He was standing a little way off. Bloodied, but upright. "We should get out of here!"

"Where's Alice?" Incredulous asked.

"She's getting people out. There's a scrum out there," Lily said.

"I'm Scientist, by the way," Likota said, offering his hand.

"I know your name," she smiled. "Though I feel like I may have an incorrect impression of you."

Likota smiled too. Spieëlding was about to tell them to hurry the hell up when a sound of scraping glass and crunching bone from the splintered bar made them turn. A growing dark void, sparking with electricity, loomed against the gloom, struggling noisily up.

The lightning bird spoke, clear and loud and undramatic, "Okay."

"Shit shit shit," Spieëlding said.

The voice again, "That's it. I'm done."

"No, you're not," Lily said simply, tossing the lit zippo into the pool of vodka and immediately regretting it. That zippo was expensive. Why do people do this, like they're matches? Her irritation at herself changed to satisfaction almost immediately.

Flames engulfed the bird, which thrashed and slipped in panic as the fire turned the flickering carnage orange, thunder exploding, and bolts of electricity firing off in every direction. The ethanol mingled with the deeper, older oils of the bird's plumage, and the heat they generated was excruciating.

The Impundulu's feathers melted as it beat the air, sparks and smoke and sickening ashes showering the scene already slick with blood. It crashed to the ground.

The flames died down to a flicker, the bird looked like it was stuck together, covered in oil. Burning oil. It twitched in spasms as it spoke.

"You think you've achieved anything? You can't kill me."

"You don't look as strong as you were, friend," Hermann Spieëlding said, his voice cold. "Maybe you should tell us where she is."

"Where who is?" asked Alice, rounding the corner and stopping dead at the sight of the monster.

"I'll mansplain later," Incredulous said, and she nodded, transfixed.

The lightning bird laughed. Small bones protruded from its smouldering skin and the effort made it shudder and shake. It was a hollow sound.

"Your daughter is dead," the Impundulu said. "She is deceased. She is an ex-daughter."

"What?"

"You don't like the classics?" the bird laughed, its skin rolling in pain like a coiling python.

"What?"

"You really don't know, do you? When your followers learn what has happened, it will begin."

Spieëlding kept his face blank, clenched his jaw.

"You have failed," the patriarch said.

"How so, racist? And what makes you think I care?"

"I'm not…" Spieëlding caught himself and the bird smiled with its eye. "I know this man is not to blame. I know he is –" Spieëlding paused. "He *was* her boyfriend."

Another death rattle laugh.

"Her husband," the bird said.

"Dude," Incredulous whispered to Likota.

Spieëlding kept the tremor from his voice.

"I know he has nothing to do with it. You have failed."

"*I* have failed? This has nothing to do with me."

"You're delusional."

"You can torture me all you want. It will get you nothing. Nowhere."

"You're right," Spieëlding said. "You have nothing useful to tell us. This will be the kindest thing." He bent and raised the barman's shotgun at the bird. Before anyone could have intervened had they wanted to, he fired, force and pellets ripping through hollow bones.

Nobody spoke for a long time.

The body lay still, bleeding quietly. The fearsome power of the bird now a shadow. His raptor power seeming poultry now.

The sirens and murmur of crowds that had been seeping into the room grew suddenly louder and several flashlight beams intruded in on the room, creating solid cones in the smoke and steam.

Caiaphas Molefe's voice boomed.

"Jon Power! Scientist Likota! Where are you?" The shout echoed in the room and ten men, bigger even than Caiaphas, followed the torch beams, each one armed with a submachine gun and night vision goggles. Caiaphas walked proprietorially behind. He took the scene in, motioning two of the behemoths to bar press and police from the door. All meekly obeyed. Molefe himself was known to some of them. The drill was known to others.

"What the *fuck* is that?" he asked. "Don't tell me. I don't believe this shit anyway."

"Hello, Uncle," Incredulous said. "Don't worry. I'm safe."

"Eyta, boy," Caiaphas said, noticing him. "Where is my friend?"

"Over here." Moshoeshoe motioned to the man still praying in tongues on the floor.

"Is he in shock?" Caiaphas asked. "Is he hurt?"

Incredulous shook his head. "I think they spiked his drink."

"Bra Jon!" Caiaphas shook Jon Power with rough affection. "You okay?"

He was fully absorbed in shaking the pastor out of his reverie when a sound from behind the group made him swing 'round. Scientist Likota had walked closer to the lightning bird. Perhaps to look at it, perhaps to check it was really dead.

It wasn't.

Incredulous Moshoeshoe felt the cold rush from his core to his skin.

Likota's head was bent at an angle that made the DJ's stomach turn. Blood was gushing in torrents from a hole torn in his throat and the bird was drinking. Visibly strengthening. It made Jon Power think of hummingbirds he'd seen in the bush. In slow-motion on nature films.

Caiaphas cried out to his men and before Incredulous could stop him. A few of them formed a closing crescent on the bloody scene, as one they fell to the ground, rigid with current. One or two others convulsed, pulling their triggers and sending several 'rounds into the bird. The wounds seemed to mend as soon as they were made, the bird draining the last of Likota's blood and sloping awkwardly towards the prone paramilitaries like an oil-drenched cormorant, its eyes glinting, electricity crackling.

Jon Power began praying more loudly, almost shouting, glossolalia pouring from him like water. Then he fell silent.

"Everybody?" he said, loudly and clearly, as if he'd been conscious all this time. Completely clear. "Run."

They obeyed, breaking into a sprint, Caiaphas in front, surprisingly quick on his feet, Jon Power and Hermann Spieëlding bringing up the rear.

The explosion caught Jon and Spieëlding in the back, propelling them through the doorway, crashing onto the others.

The bird was getting stronger. The pounding of its wings, the noise of exploding circuits and breaking glass, furniture in a turmoil of air and gravity, the screech of the bird and the roar of its voice – all pursued them as they ran.

The place was a warren. Small dance floors and chill areas, little passages. A network of sticky black playgrounds for the morbidly fashionable. They skated from room to room, now led by Molefe's men. Crashing sounds receding behind them suggested the lightning bird was hampered by small corridors.

Spieëlding and Power brought up the rear. Moshoeshoe, Molefe ran with Lily and Alice and Caiaphas' two remaining buffalos.

Flashes and the sound of voices reached them and Caiaphas slammed on the brakes, his men doing the same, stopping the group.

"What the fuck, man?" Alice shouted, glancing over her shoulder behind her. "Move!"

"Not this way."

"Why?" Moshoeshoe shouted at his uncle.

"Because the press is out there. Twitter is fucking exploding with this shit. And when it all calms down and they find a story to explain it all away – LSD in the aircon or something – then we're going to be left with the ritualistically murdered body of the head of the RYM. How long do you think it will take to put that together with Mr. Broederbond here?"

"If they're out there they already know," Jon said.

"Twitter. Only kids take it seriously. Indie news blogs. If we flood the narrative it will be fine. *If* we don't get actual press photos of *Witbaas* over here."

"I don't care about any of that," Spieëlding said. "I need to find my daughter."

"You don't care about your reputation. Your wellbeing. Fair enough. Neither do I, ballbag," Molefe said quietly. "I'd gladly let my boys execute you right here. But that won't help. You cannot have been here. Not with the other news."

"What other news?" Jon Power said, leaning against a faux Geiger mural, panting.

"Mandela is dead."

Jesus Christ

Jon Power was unaware of himself. His surroundings. Or, rather, he was aware but unconcerned. The drugs in his system had dragged him into an abyss and something within him had started swimming upwards, rising between the dolorous narcotic like a gentle but insistent finger between folds of brain tissue. Not an inner voice. Something external but familiar, sympathetic. Spirit. He cried out.

Fuck.

Fuck fuck fuck. What.

What?

What? Where, how? What?

Fuck.

Calm.

CalmcalmcalmcalmcalmcalmcalmFuck.

Wait. Help.

Yes, help.

Help me.

Lord, help me. Jesus.

Jesus Jesus Jesus Jesus Jesus Lord Jesus please help me.

Lord Jesus please, fuck, please God, help me.
Lord Jesus, please. Lord Jesus, please. Forgive me.
Forgive me, Lord, forgive me, forgive me, forgive me, Lord save me.
Lord Jesus, please. Lord Jesus please, Lord Jesus please save me.
Save me.
Please.
Help.

And slowly, not instantly or in any way that could be pointed to as clear certainty, his mind entered the warm shallows.

He could hear small voices, thin voices, feel his body moving, he had seen something outside him, and his head had broken through the surface as if propelled, as if compelled to say,

"Run."

And then he had slipped back under, praying still. Praying more from mind as well as spirit. Holding hands still with the larger Spirit, but praying more as a man.

I love you, Lord. I love you, Jesus. Help me, Jesus Christ, my Lord. Help me Lord Jesus, please.

The words were the second wave.

When the narcotic had been strongly on him like a net, and his mind had been bound, his spirit and the Spirit inside him had entwined, and something deeper than language had reached out beyond the void, into the Deep.

His physical mouth had moved and words, understood perhaps by angels, perhaps by no one – just the mind's verbal centres spasming in shock at a profound communication brushing past them – words had spilled out.

I love you, Lord.

He was calmer. Clearer. Outside him, they were in a shining room.

Lord, help us.

Lord, please.

Jesus, please.

Tell me. Fill me. Use me.

Talk to me.

His body felt light, as if he were rising, his feet shuffling on sticky lino, cement. And peace poured into him and filled him up and reached into the least peaceful places and saturated him and he knew what to do.

Surely not.

But, the answer came, Yes.

But how? I don't know.

And he knew the answer was to do what he had been told. That he was not God. That he was in no position to lecture. That righteousness had one source. That he had to do the unthinkable and to do that he needed to say the unthinkable.

Lord, I do not know.

Do it. Trust.

Yes, Lord.

He rose out of the depths, out of the shallows and into the world, into his body. Into the breathing, speaking, thinking universe and began to engage. To listen to sounds in the air. To people. To prepare to do what needed to be done.

God in an alcove

They stopped on the metal floor. Not the Metal floor, which was bigger and easier to get to, but one of the myriads of little sub-floors for sub-genres.

This one was for 'Rivetheads' – a term some Industrial fans had once, hopelessly, tried to make popular. Architecturally, it was an afterthought, an adjunct to the passage to the bathrooms and accessible only through a side door from one of the chill rooms. It was now just a storage area. Industrial was, for the scene, dead as a source of new music. Crates of beer and old lights were stacked everywhere. It smelled old. Glow-in-the-dark paint had been daubed inexpertly on the walls, charged by UV lights wired into the floors, giving the room a green pallor. Like those plastic stars we used to stick to our ceilings and look at in the dark.

The floor was literally metal. The walls were lined with metal, the bar was tiled in metal, cheap, puckered in those little double leaf-shapes that make fire-escape floors ten percent less slippery, and had once been polished to a high shine. Caiaphas set his men to pulling up some of the panels and barricading the door with them, piling beer crates against it.

"Put all the lights on either side of the door," he told the buffalos, "That thing sets off circuits. They will be our alarm if it gets close."

"What are we going to do if it gets close?" Lily asked.

"We're not going to let it get that far," Spieëlding said. "We have to take the fight to it."

Caiaphas did not respond. He had long ago given up on arguing with white men of a certain age. His finger itched.

The others were sitting on the cold metal floors, leaning against walls, stunned.

Madiba, dead.

All of them were silent. Still. Finding it hard to think. Almost all of them.

Spieëlding paced up and down, thinking of Lucrecia.

"People!" he shouted. "We need a plan!"

"We wait for it to leave. It's never going to find us here." One of Caiaphas' buffalos had spoken, the words coming out between heavy breaths as he and his partner pulled at floor plates with their immense arms, sending rivets pinging like popcorn. "It will find an exit. We just wait for that."

"No." The word was spoken by Jon Power and Incredulous together.

"No, we don't let that thing live," Incredulous said simply. "We don't let it go out there."

"Agreed," said Spieëlding.

"Well, then, what are we supposed to do? You saw what it did to my men," Caiaphas Molefe said.

"We must keep it here until we can kill it." Jon Power was clear and direct. Unhurried in his speech.

"What?" Alice was shouting. "Are you insane? How? Did you see it?"

"Ja, Dominee, I think you need to think this through," Incredulous said. "I was watching it. It has some kind of incredible vision. Eagle eye shit. Even in the dark. It will see us coming and it will electrocute us and tear us apart and drink our blood like it did Likota's. And then it will just get stronger. Plus, she's right. It sounded like fifty people outside."

"Can you keep them out?" Jon Power asked Caiaphas.

"Yes."

"Can you keep it in?"

"I think so."

"How?"

"Distraction. Ammunition, running, harrying fire. They used to call my unit the Guerillas that never missed," Caiaphas smiled a little too brightly. Forcing confidence like a soldier must.

"How long?"

"Dawn."

"That will be enough. Can you get us in and out?"

"You. The boy. Maybe the women. Nobody knows them. This guy—" he nodded at Spieëlding, "Too risky."

"He can help you and your men fight it. Keep it busy. Keep it here until we get back."

"Then what?"

"God has told me how to destroy it," the pastor said.

There was a long period of quiet as everybody tried to take this in, then shifted uncomfortably.

Even in desperate and life-threatening situations, social discomfort is one of the most powerful forces in the world. Embarrassment echoed around the ironclad room.

"I mean…" Incredulous said slowly. "Maybe you need to rest…"

"I don't. God told me how to beat it. I know it sounds ridiculous, and to be honest, I'm not a fan of the idea myself, for many reasons. But it's what the Lord wants."

"You…" Lily said, gently. "You were pretty high…"

But Incredulous saw the look on Jon Power's face. Felt something strange in his senses. Said, "No. He's fine now. Look."

"But he said…"

"There's a giant fucking vampire bird out there, snapping people in half and drinking them like Yogisip, shooting lightning out of its balls!" he said. "You want to draw the line at believing in God?"

Lily slumped back. "Truthiness."

"Jon," Caiaphas said. "What are you thinking?"

"Can you hold this place tonight?"

"Yes. Meningitis. Gang fight. Gang fight *and* meningitis. Meningitis gangs, fighting. It will take a few calls. And some of my men outside, but the press are not so expensive these days, and they will be covering the old man's death."

"Good."

"It can only be until morning, though. When people start waking up, I won't be able to hold them off. Even the police will need to look like they are doing something."

"Until morning is all we need."

"Are we still listening to this guy?!" Alice asked. "He's high! We need to be making plans! We need to get out of here!"

"I trust him," Incredulous said simply.

"It's not me," Jon said. "It's God. Don't trust me. Trust God."

"Fuck that," Incredulous said. "I've stretched to the possibility that he exists and that he spoke to you. Or something approximating him in your experience spoke to you. But I'm not trusting anything here except that I know you're not a complete dipshit."

"You're too kind," Jon Power said.

"Almost constantly. It's like a sickness with me."

Jon Power smiled.

"He's one of the good guys," Incredulous said to the room. "And if anyone else has a plan to defeat Vampire *Knersus* that trumps a strong conviction that the ruler of the universe is passing notes to the pastor, I'll hear it now."

Nothing.

"Okay, then," Incredulous said. "How?"

"Well, that's where it gets complicated," Jon said slowly.

"What is it? How do we do it? What do we need?"

Every face in the room was turned towards the pastor. He spoke slowly. Unwillingly.

"Well, that's the thing. I don't know where to get it. Or if it's even *real*."

"Let's assume it might be! Hit me up with some details!" Incredulous said. "Stop talking like a stoner and give us the vision. Come on, Jon of *Pot*mos."

Alice interrupted, "Must you?"

"Sorry," Incredulous said. "I resort to puns when I'm freaked out."

"It's very annoying."

"Alright," Jon said, ignoring them. "We need to find…" he paused. "What I have been told to find," he paused. "I was told," Jon Power said very slowly, "to find a tokoloshe."

Amphetamine logic

"I take it back; he's still fucking high. We're fucked."

Molefe and his men fell into conversation, the women as well. Spieëlding started to cry.

"I'm serious," Jon said.

"Seriously fucked," Alice said.

"In every part of his head," Spieëlding muttered to himself.

"You don't trust me."

"Of course not!" Alice said.

"But you believe."

"Not in this. Not in this interventionist, charismatic, drug-fuelled, and let's not forget, profoundly animist bullshit, no I don't."

"Pray."

"We don't have time…"

"*Pray.* If you don't feel peace about it, we'll find another way."

Caiaphas Molefe stared in disbelief as the steampunk closed her eyes.

"Bra Jon," he said, not unkindly. "Is this how we make decisions now? By consulting the spirits?"

"Caiaphas, my friend, I know..."

"It's cool, bra. Do what you need. But do it quick, ne?"

"Oh come on, uncle." Incredulous said. "You are *not* going to pick now to develop a sympathy for the Lord."

"Boy," Molefe said, shoving his nephew down onto a pile of old, disgusting beanbags. "I'm just trying to ascertain..." He didn't finish his sentence.

Incredulous Moshoeshoe pulled himself to his feet with a creak of leather and PVC and punched his uncle in the face. Hard as he could.

"I'm not your boy."

The larger man shook his head and raised a hand thoughtfully to his lip, where one of Incredulous' many rings had caught and cut him. He examined the blood in the glow.

"You're going to have to learn to hit harder than that if you're going to make a habit of that, Incredulous," the larger man said. Then he smiled, nodding an acknowledgement – I see you – to the younger man. "Now listen."

To Incredulous' irritation, he found his rage subsiding. He felt better. Maybe there was something in this expressing yourself in violence thing that parts of his family had always been so fond of.

"Yes?"

"This girl is praying. I don't trust it any more than you do. So let's be..." he paused. "Scientific."

"How?"

"Throw your bones."

"That, if you don't mind me saying so," said Lily, "is barely a better class of bullshit."

"Alright, Mike DeGrasse Tyson," Incredulous said, "chill out with the aggressive scientism." Immediately, he looked ashamed of himself. "Sorry."

Caiaphas gave his nephew a look somewhere between disappointment, pity and disgust. "Who was your niche for that?"

"Sorry, sorry!"

"Good grief," Spieëlding said.

Incredulous went on. "I thought you didn't believe in the old ways," he said. "Grandma always said you hated 'that hocus pocus animist crap.'"

"I do. But look around you, b—"he stopped himself. "Look around you, Incredulous. Bets are off. And I've seen you do things. Give me a chance to figure this into my dialectic. Find out if he's right."

Incredulous shrugged at The Catholic steampunk fingering her rosary, at the wild-eyed Pentecostal pastor and the Dutch-reformed fascist. He nodded to his uncle and the impassive cadres of undetermined spiritual or secular bent. "Fuck it. This is South Africa."

He looked at his uncle. "How soon could one of your guys here get something from the bag check?

"How soon do you need it?"

⌐══╛

Twenty minutes later another cadre arrived with Moshoeshoe's old black satchel. He started pulling out feathered headdresses, leather riempies, the alleged Shaka spear, assorted shells, stones, and bones.

Caiaphas' men took several steps back, nervously. Not paid-up materialists, then. Or maybe memos about superstition just didn't often make it to the noticeboard in the gym.

Incredulous kneeled on the bare concrete where the two heavies had pulled up the metal plates, made a sign, prepared his mind, and summoned the meagre reserves of that strength he could not quantify or explain. Then he threw.

There was a long pause. Only a minute and a half, chronologically, but a time much bigger and broader in reality. Caiaphas and Lily shifted uncomfortably. Jon looked blank. Uncomfortable too, but for different reasons. The buffalos tried not to watch Incredulous but didn't seem to be loving the sight of Bechdel-Smith crossing herself blindly in a corner either. Longing more for the simplicity of fists and guns than uncomfortable with the addictions that too often held the proletariat in mental chains.

And then both pilgrims arrived at their answers.

"He's right," Incredulous and Alice said at the same time.

"I don't know why, but I think God is with this," Alice said.

"The bones say tokoloshe," Incredulous said. "I've never seen it so clear. Hell, I've never seen it at all."

Another long silence. The buffalos had the look of men who thought they'd rather take their chances with whatever was crashing in the corridors, then realising what that was and preferring the tokoloshe. Then 'rounding back to the original option. On and on, in a loop of bewildered (but apparently vindicated) superstition and a blind need to fuck something up.

Caiaphas said, "Alright. You go find a …" he hesitated, hating himself for even having to say the word. "A tokoloshe. I'll call for reinforcements."

"Don't let them in its field of vision, uncle." Incredulous said. "In the darkness, I saw its eyes. They are the bird's advantage."

"And not being the size of an elephant but being able to fly and shoot lightning out of its dick?"

"There is that," Incredulous conceded. "But it can see in incredibly low light. The smallest details. Its vision is why we're always four steps behind it."

"It's a raptor," Jon Power said, decades of bird-watching in the bushveld was finally of some operational use. "Like an eagle. Or an owl, actually. Incredibly sharp vision. Like infra-red binoculars," he said, nodding to Caiaphas and the buffalos. "If this thing is anything like those birds, it will be able to see us clearly in what looks like complete darkness to us."

"Well, that's useful," Incredulous said. "Because tokoloshes are supposed to have a kind of advantage there, too."

"That's great," said Jon. "But where the hell do you find one? What even are they? I thought they were the bogey-man."

"A tokoloshe is not a boogeyman," Incredulous said, deflating. "It's way worse. Weirder."

"In what way?"

"It's a tiny little man, just a few feet high, but with a cock the size of a donkey's."

A long, silent pause, pregnant, but with something unnatural.

"What?"

"Yup. Sorry."

"This is what half of this country is afraid of?" the pastor asked.

"It sounds appealing to you?"

"No…" Jon Power allowed, thoughtfully.

"Well then. Keep your white South Africa middle-class privilege to yourself."

"Take it easy, Khoisan X-Box," Caiaphas chuckled.

"So, we're just going to assume that all this shit is real?" Lily said. "Like science doesn't exist. Like logic and reason are just old-fashioned?"

There was a roar from deep inside the club. The filaments in the lightbulbs at the door glowed as if to make the point. Everyone got it.

"Fine," she said. "How does a tokoloshe help us?"

"Yeah," Alice said, taking her hand and laying her head on her girlfriend's shoulder. "What's the deal with these magic dick-midgets, Incredulous?"

"They hate that word," Lily said. "Say 'dwarf' or 'Little Person."

"Really?" Alice said.

"It's like the K word for them."

"Oh no," Alice said, looking genuinely pained. "Okay. Good to know."

"Magic dick-midgets…" Caiaphas chuckled. "I'm out. We're going to lay down some covering fire and some smoke grenades and get some big boys in here. I'll see you fuckers in the morning. Don't be late."

Jon Power wondered what 'big boys' could mean as he watched Molefe and his crew start to dismantle their makeshift door.

"You. Racist poes." Caiaphas indicated Spieëlding. "You're not going anywhere until we are sure this is over."

"But… I thought…" the old man said.

"Got problems taking orders from a black man?"

"I've got problems taking orders from liberals," the Broeder replied.

"Fuck liberals. Always. Are you ready to fight?"

"Yes."

"Yes, what?" Caiaphas boomed agreeably.

"Yes, sir!" Spieëlding shouted, a small smile playing at the corners of his mouth.

"Good."

The barricade taken down, Caiaphas and the buffalos lumbered into the bowels of the club and towards the distant sound of banging and scraping. The buffalos looked happier, fingers on triggers. Caiaphas was already barking orders into a ruggedized radio. He paused and turned back.

"My people have been looking at the plans of this place," he said to Incredulous. "If you head down this corridor and take the first right, you'll reach a delivery entrance in an alley." Caiaphas indicated a passage to his right. "My boys will be there in five minutes. They know to expect you. I expect you gone after that."

"What are you going to do, uncle?"

"We," he indicated the buffalos, "are going to make sure that thing is on the other side of the building so that you don't have to mess up your hair getting out. I don't think it will lick its wounds much longer."

"Thanks," Incredulous smiled.

"No problem."

The big man and his bigger friends receded into the flickering light of the club.

"Well," said Alice. "Now what?"

"Now we find a tokoloshe," Incredulous said.

"I suspect that will be hard," she said.

"Harder than you think. They're supposed to be invisible."

"Are you kidding me right now?"

"Nope."

"What the…"

"They're not always invisible," he said. "But in any context, I'd encounter one – a spiritual, magical context – they'd be wary. They'll be camouflaged. Ngakas and witch doctors hunt them. The fat of a tokoloshe is very valuable for magic. We'd need to find one in a non-magical context."

"Well up until tonight, I thought that was every context. What contexts are tokoloshes found?"

"I only know the magical ones," Incredulous said, trying to go to yellowmoepels.co.za on his phone and finding it fried. From memory he recited, "They possess a stone. When they put it in their mouths they turn invisible. And most of the time, they are doing work for a witch of some kind. They are usually enslaved. Like a lot of magical creatures."

"So, do we even know if they take physical form?"

"The lore suggests they do. There are stories of them playing with children, who take them for another child."

"That's gross," Lily said.

"No, they love children. And not like that."

"Okay…"

"So," said Alice, "where do you find a four-foot man with a gigantic dick?"

"Actually," Lily said, quietly, actually raising her hand to speak. "I think I know."

Red Light

Club Perineummm was on a Jacaranda-infested street in Waterkloof, one of Pretoria's wealthier suburbs, all leafy lanes and gigantic houses. It wore discretion like a platinum cock-ring. No signage outside, just a 'P' where the house number should have been, illuminated by a slot-machine array of lights.

Discretion is a relative concept. For certain types of suburban establishments, it means not standing out. In Waterkloof these days, not standing out means flaunting wealth like your neighbours. Like, enough to make an investment banker reach for his college copy of *Das Kapital* and start shouting about how elites are a cancer at the heart of our society.

The revolution will not be metastasised.

This five-storey block of white cheese had a gatehouse for security guards, which contained just one – though this was no minimum wage employee. Tall, good looking, in a suit and alert, he smiled warm and courteous when their taxi pulled up, its yellow light glinting off his pale cheekbones.

"Good evening."

Lily handed him a card and he smiled. Lily didn't.

"Are these gentlemen your guests?"

'Gentleman'. The popular white South African code for 'black man I must pretend to respect'.

"Yes." She didn't look at him, ignoring him as if he were homeless and she was a douchebag. It was odd.

"Very good," he said, cranking up the obsequious smiliness a few more notches. "Please come in. Parking bay 14."

"This is a taxi, idiot," she said. We won't be parking. Open the gate."

He did.

The building was somewhere between a millionaire mausoleum and a casino, tall palms and coloured lights on columns. Bombastic giant windows and eagles on plinths. A nouveau riche festival of features. Architectural bukkake. Four storeys of solid, wealth-advertising hugeness, dripping with the yoghurt of disposable income.

A white woman with a perm opened the front door for them. She was wearing an evening gown and pearl earrings. She showed them to a bar in a little lounge with mirrors on the walls. Lily hardly acknowledged her.

In terms of interior design, it was like a Greek temple, roughly fucked by Donald Trump. Low marble coffee tables, soft white leather sofas, and plush, cream carpet, like a testosterone-enhanced regrowth of shaved grey hair. The cleaning bill must have been astronomical. And, as if to answer Jon Power's thought, a handsome man in his late 40s with blond hair and a tan came in and started clearing away glasses. Wiping tables. Jon Power thanked him and he smiled. Perfect teeth. Years of orthodontic work. Expensive, like his shoes, his suit. A white man, who looked more like a rising star exec than a cleaner.

With exaggerated clumsiness, he dropped a glass. It didn't break, but the noise was disturbing in the silent lounge. He scowled with frustration at himself in the mirror. Greying temples pulsing. *Fear?* Incredulous was interested, but couldn't tell.

"Sorry," the executive cleaner said, eyes downcast. Moshoeshoe was about to tell him not to worry about it when Lily jumped in. Or *on*, really.

"Sorry isn't good enough," she said, with exaggerated coldness. "You think sorry makes up for it?"

"No," he said, eyes still down. There was something in his voice. Alice, Jon Power, and Moshoeshoe said nothing, awkwardness bristling from them. Trying to look away.

"You should apologise," she said. "but not just for this."

"Babe –," Alice tried to interrupt, but Lily continued.

"You should apologise for being a worthless, inadequate excuse for a human being."

"Seriously, babe…"

"How are you going to make it up to me?" Lily said to the executive cleaner.

Incredulous, Jon and Alice shifted uncomfortably, not understanding.

"I… I could kiss your shoes?" Eyes up for the first time. Hopeful. That certain something in them.

"Ah," Incredulous said, relaxing a little.

"Oh," said Jon.

"Ew," said Alice.

"I don't think so," Lily said. "You'd like that."

He nodded.

"You aren't getting a reward, you little sub creep. Nothing like that. Go to the kitchen and clean every single cup and saucer in there. It's not hard work. And try not to steal anything."

Grey Temples looked up at her, waiting to be dismissed.

"Go."

And he went.

"Ah," Incredulous said again.

"Yup," Lily said. "I used to work here. For a bit."

"You never said," Alice said, with just enough interest in her voice.

"Yeah well, it wasn't long. When I was a student. It was all a little boring, to be honest."

"I find that a bit hard to believe," Jon said.

"Truly," she said with a little smile. "This is a very expensive place. If people want to get whipped or made to walk on all fours or lick riding crops, there are plenty of places that do that. This place specialises in a more profound form of humiliation."

"So, there's no sex?" the pastor asked, relief dawning on his face.

"Oh, no, there's sex. If you want it. But you know the BDSM scene."

"I thoroughly don't," Jon Power interjected.

She smiled.

"Perineummm specialises in privilege-fucking."

Blank faces all around.

"It's not fucking in the simple sense," a new voice said. They all turned to face the woman who had spoken. Tall, black, thin, simply dressed in jeans and a t-shirt, but a sense of command somehow filling her sneakers and overflowing from her cropped, natural-styled hair.

"We fuck our clients sometimes, but mostly we fuck *with* them. With their sense of entitled expectation. With their expected position in society."

"So…" Jon said.

"So, most of them are white males." She looked at Jon. "Of a certain age. Hi," she offered a hand. "I assume you're not here for our services. I'm Martha."

"Pleased to meet you."

"Indeed."

"You were explaining…"

"Yes. Mostly men like you, but richer, much richer. Some white women. Some new black elites, though far fewer. And we give them all the experience of real humiliation they crave. Of being in the position of people who work for them. Maids. Cleaners. Secretaries. We have a lot of domestic situations. Which also helps keep our overheads low." She smiled. "Of course, we have some embassy trade. This being a capital city and all."

"Really?" Lily said, interested. "That's new."

"Oh hello, Lily. Long time. Yes. We expanded. Mostly to British clients. Maids and the like are old hat for them."

"So, what's their darkest desire, humiliation-wise?" Incredulous the émigré asked, interested too, now.

"NHS waiting room. Hands down."

"Wow."

"Yeah. Anyway, I'm assuming you're not all here for sex? Or anything else on the menu?"

She looked pointedly at Lily.

"No, sorry, Martha."

"It's okay, my dear. You know you're always welcome for a visit." Martha shot a look at Alice, then back at Lily. "And you're always welcome back for longer if you'd like."

"I was wondering if you would let us talk to one of your guys."

"Who?"

"Tsumbe."

"Just talk?" Martha smiled.

Lily laughed. "Just talk."

"Why?"

"A few weeks ago, Diane told me this one thing that only made sense to me tonight."

"Diane? She called you?"

"More like, WhatsApp'd."

"Hmm. And she told you what?"

"About a thing with one of your clients a while back. And about Tsumbe."

"That was perfectly legit," Martha said, suddenly annoyed. Animated.

"I never said…"

"They were *children*! If Tsumbe hadn't done it I would have."

"I know, I know. I'm not saying anything was wrong. Just that I've never really known Tsumbe to get that… upset."

"Oh, yeah."

"And Diane said that when the police came here, Tsumbe disappeared. Like magic."

"He's a small guy, Lily."

"Yes, but Diane…"

"Yes, yes. It was weird. He didn't want to talk about it. Not even to me."

"And not to all the others."

"You know why, Lily…"

Jon interrupted, "Why what?"

"Why he wouldn't talk to the others. Some of our staff are from… *humble* beginnings, shall we say. Rural. That sort of thing. Just a few of them, well… Some things that persist. Beliefs. Tsumbe's stature, his… gifting. Well, it makes some of them uncomfortable. And to be honest, he has made little effort to integrate with them. They steer clear of him."

"Why?"

"Hasn't Lily told you?"

Lily shook her head.

"Tsumbe's a dwarf."

"Oh, come on. That can't be a thing. We all watch Game of Thrones, right?"

"Dwarves are fine," Martha said. "No prejudices like that here. It's just that Tsumbe… well…"

"Well, what?" Alice said, trying to distract herself with the question.

"Tsumbe's a *big* dwarf."

Sex Dwarf

Three hundred and forty-eight weeks, six days, and nineteen hours ago that day, Pretorians had woken to the sound of Clint Bells, a moderately talented talk radio DJ specialising in middle-class white aggression and jokes about lesbians, doing a feature called *The Full Piel* on his morning show.

Tsumbe Kgolokgolo preserved the memory of the day – not, as one might be tempted to imagine, because of the shame and embarrassment involved in having such personal details aired and shared by a boorish bigot with a radio show. Not because of the no small measure of laughter aimed at, or around him – being a little under four feet tall since he was 14 had taught him skin-thickening techniques of the highest order. Not even out of a misplaced sense of pride – something for which any man in the circumstances could be forgiven, no?

No. Tsumbe Kgolokgolo remembered that day's *Full Piel* because it was the day his life changed forever. A coming out, of sorts. Because the *piel* being discussed and guffawed over was his.

"Man, it's a little embarrassing, hey," the caller's voice had said, a little hesitant but egged on by the jackal-hyaena laughter of 'Clint's Bints'. "He was this nice guy. Maybe a little short for me…"

"How short are we talking?" Clint Bell had sniggered.

"Well, quite short," she had said shyly. "But that was when he was sitting down."

"But when he stood up you discovered something, didn't you?" Clint Bell used a phoney English accent and if he had put the kind of effort into actual journalism that he put into getting embarrassing details out of callers off-air, he'd have had some worth as a human being. Journalism, however, had never attracted him. Too few tits in South African newspapers.

"Ja."

"Come on, my girl, tell us! Tell the listeners!"

"Well, when he stood up, I saw he was short."

"Come on! How short are we talking here?"

"My nephew is six," she'd said. "He was a little shorter than that."

An explosion of laughter, quelled by Bell.

"But that wasn't the only thing you discovered about him, was it?"

"No…"

"Tell the listeners…"

"Well, I was quite drunk…"

"Of course you were…"

"And he was quite handsome."

"They always are when you're drunk!" Sound FX of dogs barking, pigs squealing, whale noises. The studio menagerie's cackles and howls.

She continued. "We went back to my place. He was really small. Like a dwarf small ..."

"A hot little munchkin?" One of the menagerie.

"Well, ja. But ... but he wasn't small in *every* way."

"Oh, yes?" The menagerie was warming up. "A big boy for a small guy, was he?"

"Bigger than you've ever seen!"

The studio exploded in sound FX and laughter. After a while, it calmed down enough for Bell to say, "Details, woman. Details!"

"Clint, I don't know what to say!"

"Say, say!" the acolytes chanted.

"Like a baby's arm?"

"Bigger."

"Like a boy's arm?"

"Bigger!" She was giggling now. In the spirit.

"Like a *man's* arm?!"

There was a laughter-filled pause and then, perfectly timed, "Like a leg."

Enough of Tsumbe's details had been revealed by the end of the segment that when he arrived at work, his boss had let him go. The children's entertainment industry in South Africa is as deeply conservative as it is anywhere and Tsumbe's manager Laurie had used *all* her nonviolent communications training to break it to him.

"Soom, I want to take as long as you need so that you feel heard ..."

A white woman in middle age, with a background in communications in Sandton, she felt entirely comfortable adapting the names of black employees to versions that were "a little easier to remember" and contracting the names of absolutely everyone.

"I've already spoken to Sare, Nay, and Jenny," – Sarah, Naomi, and Lebohang – "and they were very upset. Not just about the …. revelations… but also that you would have to leave. They send their best wishes for the future."

Tsumbe hadn't argued. No outburst. No fight. No giving in to the long-held temptation to say "I'm going to call you Lerato. 'Laurie' is just a bit complicated." He'd just gathered his things and left, followed by a dozen speculative eyes, glistening with repression.

It had been the best job he'd ever had.

Tsumbe had loved children with a giddy gentleness and clear-eyed joy for as long as he could remember. And the length of his remembering was impressive, even for one of his kind. Hundreds of years. And in his frequent and necessary moves, through his many occupations and lives, through wars and slaveries and identities he had almost embraced as real and lasting, they had been the only thing guaranteed to give him joy. Moreso even than sex.

He found this generation hard. The uneasy mixture of worship and loathing of innocents, the seemingly infinite explosion of abuse stretching across the century, the paranoia that accompanied it and made an affection like his automatically suspect. *People.*

Moving to Pretoria from another rural hell, captivity escaped again by outliving the woman who owned him, he had taken advantage of the new waves of guilt lifting the previously disadvantaged above what they could have hoped for in the past.

He was now officially disabled and, as such, a progressive hire, even if he was occupying the position people of his stature had been occupying for centuries in courts, fairs, and circuses. It was 'for the kids,' and that suited him just fine.

And then, because of a one-night stand and a douchebag radio shock jock with a penchant for 'comic' songs and talking about outgroups, it was over.

The sense of *what now* – with its open spaces, inviting roads, and long dreaming moments of possibility – lasted only a few hours. Tsumbe had gone to a roughish bar in the CBD, near the giant snail shell that had always appealed to him (despite being the site of a racially motivated massacre a few years back). Near it, in the shade of the Volkskas building, was a small dive bar called FitzPatricks. Because in the deepest reaches of Mongolia and the most removed river communities of the Amazon where white people are but a myth, where money is yet unknown and knowledge of the world beyond the horizon is sparse, you will still find a fucking Irish-themed bar. In Pretoria they are legion.

This one was down on its luck, the faux four-leafs and *Guinness is good for you* signs dog-eared. FitzPatrick's was a lunchtime hangout for escorts at the ends of their shifts, bored drug dealers and a smattering of people traffickers and wet-work specialists.

Tsumbe had caused a minor stir walking in. That sort of thing still happens, even in our post-Dinklage world. His hair was in soul-glo ringlets, hanging over his cavernous eye sockets. He'd never liked haircuts. He'd strolled into the place, ordered a milk, and sat down.

Floating in the liminal space that always accompanies leaving a good job, he wasn't tense. But he never was. Head barely clearing the tabletops, vulnerable as a toddler, he moved with the confidence of an eight-foot MMA champion. Usually, that was enough. That day it wasn't. Because the universe says fuck you, that's why. *Bad day? You don't even know. Have this. Suck it, little man.*

And if he had been a man, it would have been quite bad.

"Hey, lofty!" a rangy coloured *skorrogo* with prison-dead eyes in a hoodie shouted over a Black Label.

Tsumbe had given him a bro chin-lift from his table and contemplated his phone.

"Hey, Jim!" the skorrogo shouted across the bar to the man cleaning glasses behind it. "When did you start serving kids in here, bra?"

Jim "Mac" O'Kelly, a gigantic black man who looked like he existed exclusively on a diet of meat and beer, with the occasional rawhide whip thrown in for roughage, glanced up from the glasses he was shining and the staffie he was stroking with his foot. He was as concerned as the name he claimed was real.

"Fuck off, Jordan."

Jordan Kay the Skorrogo laughed a little too loudly and turned back to Tsumbe. A mixed-race boy who'd grown accustomed to bullying weaker lads at his fancy school, something of a big deal because of that and his abilities on the Rugby field. Less posh at the root than his school and even less posh now, having never moved beyond the cigarettes and vandalism phase of rebellion. In a couple of years, heartfelt messages from other former jocks who shared classrooms with him would be posted in Facebook groups set up, but would fail to raise the cash he needed. Boys he'd bullied would look him up and discover this, muttering "I win, cuntface," and smile smiles that they would take a while to become ashamed of. But at that moment he was alive and missing high school.

"Hey, little man!" Kay had shouted.

Tsumbe had ignored him and the big, rectangular-faced, skorrogo had got up to loom over Tsumbe's table.

"Hey! Bru! I'm talking to you!"

"What?" Tsumbe had answered.

Kay had taken this as encouragement and said something about dwarf-tossing. He'd then picked Tsumbe up bodily and walked outside, into the alley near the bins. This, too, was not unusual for the smaller man.

"What are you?" Jordan said, holding the smaller man above an industrial-sized waste bin.

Tsumbe said, "I can't believe you've never seen a short man before." He said it with a lisp, which can't have helped.

"'Man'?" Kay had replied, and laughed, holding Tsumbe above a bin. He was quite drunk. "And no. I mean, what *are* you? Like, a Xhosa or a Sotho or a Zulu or what. Hmm? I bet you're a Zulu. I want you to be a Zulu."

Tsumbe hung impassively in the man's giant hands, looking into his face.

"Tell me you're a Zulu!" Kay bellowed red-faced and inches from Tsumbe. He could smell the beer and cigarettes. See the veins in the idiot's neck.

"I'm a Zulu," he said quietly.

Kay dropped him in the bin.

"I've never been good at languages!" the big white boy shouted happily. "But now I can tell my friends that I know a little Zulu!"

"You have friends?" a voice said from the bottom of the skip. Kay turned around.

"What did you say, you fucking midget?"

Tsumbe said nothing. Kay reached into the bin and picked the dwarf up with one hand, baby-style, shaking him violently with the other. The motion seemed to come easily, reflexively to him. The way he had no doubt been shaken as a child. In the holding and movement, his expression changed, confusion, interest, disgust.

"What the fuck…?" Holding the smaller man up by his shirt, his other hand recoiled from the nappy-hold. "Wait," he said, dawn breaking slowly over his acne-pocked Cro-Magnon face. "You're that *piel* from the radio, aren't you?"

Tsumbe just had time to grab the pebble from his pocket before his trousers were wrenched down in one move.

"Holy shit!" Kay shouted and dropped him in shock. A few of the pub regulars had strolled in a bored kind of way to see what was happening. They gasped too.

"It's longer than his legs!"

"That's some big dick, Harry."

"We're gonna need a bigger bin."

"Little *big* man!"

"We're doing westerns now?"

"Voetsek, man."

Kay dropped him back in the bin, laughing and pointing, a big dumb grin on his big dumb slab of a face.

Lying in the filth of the bin, his monster cock lying next to him like a twin, Tsumbe sighed. He put the stone in his mouth and dissolved from view.

Kay blinked.

"What."

He leaned in to see where the diminutive black man had gone, like the victim of a car theft will go and stand where they parked looking for the missing vehicle. He saw nothing but a brief shuffling of rubbish as if a weight were shifting on it. Then he felt a slap to the face. Saw nothing. But a wet, meaty slap. Once. Twice. And the sound of spitting, a wet mist. He bent there for a while afterwards, as if willing the invisible assailant to appear. Nothing happened. The rubbish twitched in a trail towards the edge of the bin and a dull metallic thud and then nothing.

As far as retaliations go, it would have seemed weak, even if it had been visible. Kinky, sure. But hardly a punishment. But that's how tokoloshe punishments work. They are stony. Invisible. Their enormity always surprises.

At that moment, an almost inconsequential number of Jordan Kay's cells were turning sour. Turning in on themselves. Turning rogue. A process had begun. The cancer that would kill him.

Tsumbe had regretted it almost immediately but forgot about it with similar swiftness. Pebble back in his pocket, walking down the crowded Pretoria street, one of the hookers from the bar had trip-tropped up behind him, calling out. She had seen. She asked if he had a job. If he liked fucking.

That was it. He had gone to the club, met Martha, and embarked on the second-best job he'd ever had. He'd made films. He'd made love. He'd made grown men and women wince. He'd made an obscene amount of money. Not enough for a gold Rolls, but enough to keep out of the way of unwelcome attention.

Until now.

Pornography

Nobody was really surprised when they saw it, not really, not at the subconscious level where ambitious things grow. Marvellous and terrible, at odds with its surroundings, deserving of better. But following what they had heard, what they had read. What they wanted to believe was possible – the way people believe about religion.

It was a magnificent cock.

It wasn't just big – though that it was, in heavy, brown, veined spadefulls – it was perfect. The platonic ideal of a penis, magnified for effect. Emanating from it was a sense of peace and rightness that always radiates from the aesthetically exceptional. An *honourable* member. It could have run for public office and won in a constituency of homophobes and lesbians. Some things are just beautiful in themselves. You don't have to be a geologist or climber to be impressed by the Victoria Falls.

Proportioned it was, but not to its owner. Its minder. Tsumbe had it slung over his shoulder. In an unfortunate but inescapable phrase in the minds of Alice and Lily, it dwarfed him. And in doing so, it seemed to bend perspective, make you second-guess distance and where you were, so that you had to reach out for something fixed and earthly to hold on to. People frequently fell over when looking at Tsumbe's cock. Have we spoken enough of the tokoloshe's genitals? We'll see.

"Tsumbe?"

"Lily! Oh, Lily, my friend, how good to see you!" The lisp again.

"And you, Tsumbe."

"How long has it been?" The dwarf was standing, stark naked, his penis slung heavily over his shoulder, staring out of a window. In a corner, a white woman in her forties was stripped to the waist and kneeling. A camerawoman sat on a stool, texting.

"Too long," Lily said. She and Alice had left the men in the lounge.

The woman on the camera put her phone away and cleared her throat. Tsumbe moved reluctantly from the window and into frame. The red light glowed life into the SD card and Tsumbe started opening a pack of jumbo condoms in a laboured way in front of his face. He grimaced a smile at Lily, shrugging, and the camerawoman cleared her throat until he got back into character. Serious-faced he examined a sheath that would have lost your John Holmeses and Ron Jeremies – even the nameless legions of underpaid studs of more contemporary fare.

"You hear the news?" Tsumbe asked, his small fist exploring the depths of an elephantine rubber.

"News?" Lily shifted uncomfortably, not wanting to get to it so soon, not used enough to this sort of thing anymore to feel comfortable in any way.

"Madiba," Tsumbe said. His eyes were glistening. "I never voted," he said, squirting half a litre of KY into his little hands and slicking up his penis, which he had placed in a toddler's high chair. "But he was a good man." With the back of one wrist, he dried the corner of an eye.

"Um. Is it okay for us to talk?" Lily asked.

"Oh, yeah it's fine at the moment. Yes, Loraine?"

The camerawoman nodded.

Tsumbe said, "This is a close-up. There will be music. What will it be, Loraine?"

"An old rock track," she said. She was chewing gum. "Wait, I'll check." Consulting a script, she said, "Bush. That's appropriate." She smiled at Tsumbe's unshaved-because-he-didn't-need-the-optical-help groin. "The song is called …" she scanned, popping gum as she went, which is a dying art. "It's called 'The Little Things That Kill'."

Tsumbe rolled his eyes.

Jon Power scanned the waiting room. He felt strangely hungry.

"Incredulous."

"Yeah?" Incredulous was watching a white girl in her early twenties. Brown pigtails and Wizard of Oz blue dress, several sizes short and tight. Something for the male gaze and the male gays.

"Incredulous, I'm hungry."

Incredulous laughed. "Stoners."

"Shut up man." An exaggerated stage whisper. "Let's go find some graze."

Incredulous Moshoeshoe had not heard the colloquialism in years. He smiled. "Come on."

They strolled through the corridors mostly unmolested, though not treated warmly – a light kicking from the nation's id. Seemed fair.

There were a few studios, some occupied, some not. Windows in the doors. Mostly garden variety BDSM, all that choking that porn fans seemed to like these days. Incredulous shook his head.

Jon and the isangoma strolled into a green room. Low chairs, low table laden with snacks. Jon Power started tucking into the koeksisters and slices of spinach and feta pizza in a way that gave *Incredulous* heartburn. The black man strolled around the room, looking around. Next to a too-floral couch was a decent-sized rock. Grey and jagged and a foot in diameter. Incongruous on the carpet. He poked it with his toe. Light. Super light.

⌒〜〜⌒

"Do you think it's true? Will there be a war?" he asked earnestly, tugging with ineffectual exaggeration at a monster condom, stretching it grotesquely over the slowly engorging head, like he was asphyxiating a bald stranger.

"I don't know, Tsumbe," Lily said with as much gravity as she could muster. "I hope not."

"Another generation sent to the trenches," he said. The white woman was dusting his now upright cock like a grandfather clock. Alice wondered whether the wordplay would make it into the final cut. And why puns seemed to help some men masturbate.

"That's what I wanted to talk to you about, really," Lily said to Tsumbe.

"Mandela? Father of our nation? Because I'm not sure I can talk to your white friends about him right now. Their respect seems… hollow." The white woman who was climbing his cock like a sex tree nodded to Lily in agreement. The camerawoman was texting again.

"Not Mandela. War."

"War…" Tsumbe said thoughtfully.

"I think we may be able to prevent it."

"'We'? You and..?" he indicated Alice, who had come in a while back and had been standing quietly, trying not to compare his cock to his legs.

"Alice," she said, extending a hand. He took it and smiled shyly. She wasn't sure why. "And our friends."

"Tsumbe, if the Broederbond and the RYM each had a public reason for immediate violence, what do you think would happen?" Lily asked. "If that happened now."

The tokoloshe shuddered. "The country would burn."

"And if you could prevent it?"

Tsumbe looked like he had just woken from a trance, looking at her for the first time. "What?"

"Can we talk privately?"

The white woman clambered down and said, "Go, buddy. We can finish this later."

"You sure?"

"Of course. I'll go see if there are any BME queens on the floor."

"Thanks, baby." And to Lily and Alice, "Sure. Of course. Come."

⌒〜ᵒ

Jon was still scoffing like a happy, post-weed piglet. THC stands for The Hungry Caterpillar. Incredulous bent and picked up the too-light rock. One of those safes people put their keys in if they have to share them or don't trust themselves to hold onto a bunch throughout the day. Thieves don't look for valuables in the garden. Good place to stash cash, too. He found the little catch on the underside and clicked it. Jewels? Child porn? Cash? Something weirder?

Biltong.

Well. Droëwors.

Why the actual fuck, Incredulous wondered briefly, would anyone hide droëwors in a secret safe? He drew out a long-mottled stick and took a bite. Ah, yes. That's why. Damn, droëwors is good. If you've never had it, you don't know. But seriously.

And this was unusually good droëwors. Incredulous closed his eyes.

⌒〜ᵒ

A few turns down a corridor and a few stairs, they found themselves in a blandly furnished room with an empty counter and an electronic display. As Lily, Tsumbe, and Alice walked in, the display clicked forward and a recorded voice said, *Number 47 to consultation room 7, please.* The ticket machine offered them number 77.

"The British room?" Alice asked.

"Oh, you know it?" Tsumbe asked brightly. "I thought it was after your time."

"Lucky guess."

"Yes. Well." Tsumbe had a Hugh Grant bashfulness about him, even when he had his penis slung once more over his shoulder. "Have a seat. Feel free to move the *Hello* magazines."

"Thanks."

"Look, Lily, what's this about? Heaven knows I don't mind making them wait, but I *am* at work."

"We have some friends with us. Can we invite them in?"

"I don't know, Lily. You know me and crowds…"

"Please. They will help me explain."

The dwarf, still naked, nodded, looked at the floor while pressing a button on the counter, asked a receptionist to send in the ladies' guests.

"Fuck this is good."

"I know, right?"

"I mean, I love this stuff usually, but whatever that girl slipped me…"

"Hey, I didn't get slipped jack…"

"Yeah, yeah."

"Is it rude to finish all of it?"

"Yeah."

"Whoops."

"Yeah."

⸻

Tsumbe's face lost colour and his knees seemed to buckle beneath him even before the door had fully opened.

"Ngaka!" he said in a strangled cry, slumping on a pouf. "And… what..? A Christian..? I don't…"

"Hey, it's cool, we don't mean you any harm," Incredulous said, spreading black-nailed fingers in the air between them.

"Do not be afraid," Jon said, wiping meat crumbs from his mouth with the back of a big, tanned hand.

"That's what the angel said to Mary," Tsumbe said with a defeated sigh. "It's what angels always say."

"Can you blame them?" Jon said kindly. "People look at them and assume they're gonna die."

"Not a bad assumption."

"True," Jon laughed. He was feeling significantly more cheerful.

"Um," Incredulous interjected. "Time."

Tsumbe regarded him warily. Like an impala looks at a lion. A sated lion, but a lion, still.

"What is it you want?"

"How did you know what we were?"

"You have guessed, I assume. So, what is this? A muti murder? You know I can kill you, right? Not quickly, I know, but I swear it will be painful…"

"Whoah whoah, Tsumbe, chill!" Lily said, taking his hand. "We're not here to hurt you."

"Then what?"

"We need your help. If you can trust us."

The tokoloshe looked around warily.

"If you've got the stones for it," Incredulous said, immediately regretting it. "Sorry."

"What are you talking about?" Tsumbe said.

"It's a lightning bird," Jon Power said, simply.

"And," Tsumbe said pleasantly, standing up, "I'm out."

Turn to stone

"Tsumbe! Come back!"

The tokoloshe turned, stopped at the door.

"Lightning birds? Are you serious? No frickin' way!"

"The country, Tsumbe!" Lily said.

"Fuck off," he said simply. "This country can go fuck itself. The country is still owned by settlers. The country is a sham."

"Oh, suck it up," John Power said, picking a less than ideal moment to speak up and get involved. White people do this a lot in South Africa, around the time talk turns to how much better things are. Instead of counting their blessings for not being Uhuru'd out of existence, some of them think that this is the time (it doesn't matter when, it's always the time) to give black people a lesson in *letting shit go*. Some people call it 'whitesplaining'. Not smart people, admittedly, but some do. And they have a point.

"This country is wonderful." The pastor was not wrong. But everyone took a collective breath as he said it. White South Africa has not done a quarter of the apologising it needs to, mainly because it spends most of its time asking everyone else to forget the past and move on. Jon Power, it turned out, was not going to meander along that particular road. "I mean, look around you. No Kaspers. No Group Areas Act. No soldiers in the streets. Sure, too much of the land is in white hands. Same with the wealth. But the Party is changing. The people are changing. Young black women and men are being radicalised daily. A spectre is haunting South Africa and it's the spectre of good times ahead," he said. "If we just stop being such pussies and start some serious redistribution, we could see justice one day. An African South Africa."

Tsumbe had not expected to be out-lefted by Whitey.

"Yeah, but…"

"I know," Jon said simply. "I'm sorry. And I of all people don't have a right to criticize. I've benefited too much from the injustice. But we can't give up hope. We can't let this thing destroy it all, not when we're so close."

There was silence in the room. Incredulous expected a rainbow bird to land on the white pastor's shoulder.

"Sorry," Jon said. "I just…" He paused and looked sheepishly at Incredulous, who just raised his eyebrows and shrugged as non-political a set of shoulders as ever sported a fishnet vest.

Jon said, "I just think there's a chance for this country. And I am okay with there being a civil war – I am – as long as the right side wins. But at the right time. For the right reasons. If there is no avoiding it. But this… this manufactured crisis, this manipulated conflict… It just isn't right."

Tsumbe paused by the door. He peered over his shoulder, over the bulk of his penis, at the faces in the room, and turned.

"Fine," he said. "Tell me about this bird." He sat heavily on a couch after scrambling a bit to get up on it and turned to the witch doctor.

Incredulous obliged, "We think it's an impundulu. A lightning bird, you know?"

"I know," the tokoloshe said, wearily. "I've come across a few in my time."

Incredulous raised an eyebrow.

"I mean 'encountered' a few," the tokoloshe said with irritation. "Do you know who its owner is?" he asked.

"What?"

"Well, you know. The master. The ngaka, the big magic cheese who's pulling the strings."

Incredulous frowned. "I don't think there necessarily is one. I mean this one seems mostly motivated by sex and a desire to kill…"

The tokoloshe interrupted, "Oh, here we go. It's an occult creature, so it's got to be motivated by some kind of magical Thug Life bullshit no one else ever experiences. We're all just monsters."

"Look, no one's saying…"

"Sure, no one's saying. No one ever says. They just put bricks under their beds and run from you when you walk onto a dance-floor and assume we're all bloodthirsty ghouls, when everyone knows ghouls are European, and act like every man under a certain height is a fucking tokoloshe!"

"But you *are* a tokoloshe!" Incredulous sputtered.

"Well, it still hurts!" the dick-M-word said with dignity.

There was silence again. This time more awkward.

"Look," Jon said. "All we know is that this bird seems to be picking off people specifically to cause a race war. A civil war. And we want to stop it if we can."

"'We'…" Tsumbe said.

"Yes, we," Incredulous replied. "'We' is still a thing."

"We *are*…" Tsumbe said absently, looking out of the window again.

"No, I mean…" Incredulous began.

"I know what you mean."

"Oh."

"Oh," the tokoloshe said. "What do you want from me? Give the blood budgie piles? Cause its crops to fail?" He sighed. "My magic is so fucking old-fashioned. So *slow*."

"We don't want your magic," Jon said with rather more force than he had intended.

The dwarf looked at him with fresh scepticism.

"Of course, you don't. Fucking Christians with your new god and your arrogance and your pretending that your power is somehow different, somehow isn't magic. Fuck sakes, I went to the soaking at Hatfield in the 80s. I know what that shit is. You could smell the magic happening there from fucking Limpopo. Or whatever it was called then." The dwarf was pleased to have something more familiar to talk about. Something he'd been meaning to say. "You plaster your symbols over everything, you do your rituals and you call it a 'relationship' because it's got a marginally greater potency than everyone else's. Because your spirit *shows up*. It's rude, it's arrogant and I don't know why people put up with it."

"Me neither," said Jon, "But what I mean," he paused, smiling, "is that we don't need that. We don't want you to curse anyone. We need your stone."

"My mouth pebble?"

"Yeah," Incredulous said.

"You want to go invisible?"

"Yes. The bird has amazing eyesight. We can't get close. We feel like invisibility might give us the edge we need."

"It won't."

Muscle in plastic

The tokoloshe spoke with a finality that entered the consciousness of everyone in the room, sought out their fear and stress centres, and shoved electrodes into them.

"Can't be done."

"What can't be done?" Alice asked.

"You can't kill a lightning bird with a gun. Or a knife. Or a brick or whatever you're planning on using."

"Why not?"

"You people have seen too many Dracula movies. Big Bird is like a vampire, sure. He drinks blood, he fucks the ladies. But he can't be killed with a piece of wood. This isn't fucking Bucharest. This is *old* magic. *Big* magic. You need magic to fight it."

"I tried," Incredulous said. "He's too strong. I can't…"

The tokoloshe waved his words away like so much clove-laden smoke.

"It's not that kind of magic. Come on. You're an Isangoma. What's the catch-all remedy for big magic problems? The big magic solution…"

Incredulous shifted uncomfortably.

"Don't be shy, kid, you know the answer," the tokoloshe lisped.

"I… I'm not… I mean, it's not a real…"

"Spit it out, Moshoeshoe!" Jon Power said, pronouncing his name precisely and correctly.

"Fine!" Incredulous shouted. "It's tokoloshe fat! The big ingredient in powerful spells and wards and charms is the fat of a tokoloshe. Ngakas are supposed to hunt tokoloshes and kill them for their fat. They catch other tokoloshes using the fat. It's supposed to help with virtually any spell. Add power."

The room was awkwardly silent again. It was becoming a habit.

"Yes," the tokoloshe said. "So, who here wants to kill me?"

Lily was already starting to shout no as Jon Power stood slowly up and Alice jumped between him and the dwarf.

"Whoah whoah woah!" Tsumbe laughed. "Put the gun down, Sam and/or Dean. Let's talk it through!"

"There is nothing to talk about," he said simply.

"Oh, but there is. Sit down. I need to fetch something from the kitchen."

"I don't know…" Jon Power said, but a look from Incredulous silenced him. He was as surprised as anybody. Trust grows in strange places.

Tsumbe went out and was gone for minutes that seemed longer than they usually do. But he returned, holding a plastic bag of something disgusting.

"That's not…" Incredulous said.

"Oh, yes it is…" the tokoloshe replied. "Liposuction. I got the idea from a movie."

"Fight Club?" Alice asked.

"Wow," Tsumbe said, shaking his head slow and grave. "What's the first fucking rule?"

"Ummmm…"

"I kid! Wow, you people are all so serious," Tsumbe said. "No, I got it from *Baseketball*. Fucking hysterical." He looked around the room. Blank faces.

"Okaaaay," he said. "Well, anyway, it's a useful sideline, financially, and it keeps the fucking ngakas off my ass. And the rest of me. Plus, in my line of work, and at my age, it doesn't hurt to keep in shape. And I hate running. It hurts my balls."

Everyone nodded in a "fair enough" sort of way.

He held up the bag. Thick yellow viscous liquid, laced with blood and bits of flesh. Tsumbe followed their eyes.

"Yes, it wasn't a great job. Back street. Makeshift. Never know who you can trust, you know? I prefer to be completely under."

They nodded.

"So, there's more of me than just the fat in there. There's…" he shuddered, "meat."

A collective 'ew' swept the room.

"So, what do we do with it?" Jon asked.

"Ideally you use it in a spell," the tokoloshe said. "But I doubt you have the time. I'd suggest the one of you who plans to do the killing ingests it."

Another 'ew', bigger than the last.

"Such wussies," he muttered. "Don't worry, I've got some stuff that will make it easier. And it travels."

Red Water

"Um," Incredulous said. "I am sure this is a silly question, but…" he paused and gave a weak, apologetic, hopeful smile, "You didn't perhaps mix it into a batch of droëwors?"

Tsumbe the tokoloshe gaped at him, speechless.

"Really… *delicious* droëwors…" Incredulous said, mostly to emphasise what the dwarf already knew.

"Oh, for fuck's sake," Tsumbe said, his eyes wide. "*How much?*"

"Maybe all of it," Jon Power said looking at his boots.

"Are you fucking kidding me?"

"No."

"*Why?*"

"We were hungry."

"The entitlement of you people will never cease to astound me."

"Hey," Incredulous said. "Less of the 'you people'".

"Yeah, because you're *so* black," Tsumbe said, witheringly.

"So how much did you guys eat?"

"Ja, no, literally all of it," Jon said. "Sorry, man."

"Shit."

The room fell silent for a few long minutes. Jon Power could still taste the droëwors on his lips and wished he couldn't. Was this the equivalent of eating food sacrificed to idols? Food *made of* idols? *Fat* idols? Gross, man. *Sies.*

"Which one of you is planning to take Megachicken down?" Tsumbe asked, wearily.

"Me," Incredulous and Jon Power said simultaneously.

Tsumbe was just mouthing the word "Awkward" when Lily interjected.

"Oh, bullshit. Macho nonsense."

Incredulous looked hurt.

"It is, Incredulous. You know it. There are four of us."

Alice said, "She's right. We should all have a shot."

Jon Power started, "Ladies..."

"Just shut up, Jon," Alice said. "We're not letting you do it on your own."

"This is all very touching," Tsumbe said, "but aren't you guys on a timeline?"

"Shit, yes," Incredulous said. "Do you have any more of that..."

Tsumbe sighed. "Yes. Wait."

He returned a few minutes later with a brown paper bag full of tokoloshe-fat droëwors.

"One stick should be fine. But you guys seem to have a bit of an appetite," he said, looking pointedly at Jon, then at Incredulous.

"Um," Lily said. "I'm a vegan."

"Well, then," Tsumbe said. "No saving the world for you. Classic."

"I'm not trying to be difficult, I know you're not…" she paused, "an animal."

"Ta."

"I just can't do the texture."

There was a collective shuffling of uncomfortable feet.

Alice said, "Sigh."

Tsumbe said, "Come with me."

They followed him to a kitchen, where a nice 30something white boy was wiping a countertop. Tsumbe grimaced apologetically at his guests and then grabbed the man's hand, jerking his face down, level with the dwarf's. He gestured to the floor. The white boy got on hands and knees and Tsumbe clambered onto his back. He patted the white boy's rump and the boy arched and extended, raising the tokoloshe slowly, like a stage riser in an opera.

At surface height, Tsumbe pulled a small blender towards himself and reached over to a pile of fruit.

"Strawberries…" Tsumbe said, like a celebrity chef. "Guava…" He didn't bother cutting off the hard edges. "Raspberries. Beetroot…" Some raised eyebrows but no mutiny. "Banana… Biltong…" Everybody grimaced at that. The white boy raised an incredulous head and immediately regretted it, receiving a slap. "Kale…"

Biltong was one thing…

"Eeeeewwww!" Alice shouted.

"Noooo!" said Incredulous.

"Why, Tsumbe, *why*?" Lily cried.

"Because it's good for you. And because you bothered me where I *work*."

"It is *not* good for you," Incredulous said.

"It's a fad," said Alice.

"Yeah," said Lily. "A gross fad."

"It's of the devil," said Jon Power.

"Do you want my magic fat or not?"

A grumbling consensus of *fine, if it's a choice between the country burning to the ground and drinking kale juice we'll probably take the kale juice*. Probably.

Tsumbe passed the red liquid around. It didn't taste too bad.

"Woah, not you, Christian!" he said to Jon. "You fell into the cauldron when you were a baby, remember? And you should probably chill too, ngaka."

"I'm not a ngaka."

"I'm not giving a fuck."

"Fair."

Dark Entries

Caiaphas was waiting for them. Spieëlding was standing behind, an incongruous white cadre.

"Greetings, brother!" he shouted to Jon Power. "And you, Incredulous."

He led them through the corridors to their stronghold.

"Any trouble getting in?"

"There were some people near the back door when we called, but they disappeared."

Caiaphas smiled. "Good."

"Your men?"

"Yes. Gunshots are honey and journalists are busy little bees."

"Bees aren't attracted to honey, they make it," Jon said.

"Fuck you, David Atten*bra*."

"Sorry."

"Anyway, these days the public are all fucking journalists in their heads."

"True," Jon said, turning towards the old white man. "You okay?"

"I'm fine."

"No word from your daughter?"

"No."

"And the bird?"

"Around," Caiaphas said grimly. "We've given it a good go, but I've had to call in more men. We've brought an arsenal, but every time we get close…"

"It sees you. We know. We think we can help."

"The tok…" he trailed off, feeling silly.

"Yes."

"Well, good," Molefe said. "My guys are the best, but they are broken. Room to room shit. Watching it transform. Watching it vaporise some of the strongest…" he paused and swallowed, collecting himself. "It has been a long night. I hope this idea…"

Spieëlding interrupted, "We need to do something. Lucretia…"

"That's not of primary importance, Herman," Caiaphas said. First names. It *had* been a long night.

"She's my daughter, you fat bastard!"

Caiaphas reared up, an elephant bull towering over a white rhino. "Listen, *doos*. This country is in deep shit right now and my men are busy trying to keep shit from boiling over out there."

"Mine too. But if she dies and people find out about Likota's connection, I won't be able to control all my people."

"A poor general."

"We're not all Stalinists."

"I thought Hitler had a good line in…"

"Stop it!" Incredulous shouted. "Uncle, is this helping? Mr. Spieëlding?"

The big beasts stood down, scolded by a child. Not-distant-enough gunshots and furniture being demolished in another room, small walls falling. It had been the regular, if not constant soundtrack.

"Besides," Incredulous said, "There's forensic evidence of Likota at Lucretia's crime scene. We've been sitting on it, Uncle, but you know we can't hide that forever."

Both men shifted.

"Mr. Spieëlding, are your men looking for her?"

"Yes. They think the kidnapping's racially motivated, but just a crime. If it comes out that it's political… Well, there are hotheads in my organisation. Young people. You know. Simple, idealistic, enthusiastic."

"Morons," Caiaphas said, nodding. "We've got them, too."

"Fucking kids."

"Yeah."

Every non-millennial hates millennials.

The young women and the slightly older Incredulous shifted in embarrassment. Jon Power said,

"We should go."

The corridors flickered with light, the occasional discharge of electricity, shorting circuits, small fires. Those sounds. Mostly it was dark, entering the gullet of an untamed animal. The air smelled of iron, burning, and stale beer. Nightclubs.

Caiaphas Molefe led the way automatically, a few of his buffalos with him, a few more bringing up the rear, Jon, Lily, Incredulous, Alice, and Spieëlding the filling of the sandwich. They walked in single file, like porters in an old Tarzan movie, like GIs in a Vietnam film. Like a polling station queue in 1994.

Jon Power thought of Angola. Different formations. A different landscape. Looking out for anti-personnel mines. Thought about the times they hadn't been good enough at spotting them. Incredulous Moshoeshoe thought about his boots. His feet were killing him.

From distant, flickering corridors came a minotauran bellow and some gunshots. Caiaphas's men. The lightning bird. Nobody said anything. The tramp of their feet on the sticky floor and broken glass made a coordinated crunch.

Roar. Bang. Click-click.

The sound became louder and louder until they were on the threshold of the large dancefloor. Hair stood on end and sparks fizzed around the walls. Caiaphas motioned to one of the buffalos and he put his head around the corner.

Light exploded seemingly from inside his chest, force ripping his ribs apart, heat evaporating the spray of blood in an acrid puff of smoke and steam, with the scent of burning hair. It was all the others could do to stop, recoil, not follow into the line of sight.

"Jesus," Jon Power said, unsure of the word's intention.

Jon Power motioned to Incredulous for the stone, took it from him, and put it in his mouth. The change was not instantaneous. He seemed to desaturate for a while. Initially, it was hard to see any difference in the flickering light. It could have been a different coloured gel over a par-can changing the hue of his skin. But there are no grey gels. Incredulous knew that. He would have used them on his dance floors. In his isangoma studio. This was like watching successive parts of the spectrum switch off, gradually losing C, then M, then Y, leaving only K. R, G, and B all dissolving into the walls.

Incredulous thought it was like watching a kind of backwards time travel, a photograph drifting from colour to sepia to grey, then, a gradual loss of focus, of sharpness. The last he saw of Jon was a kind of indistinct impression and then nothing. Nothing like the silver shimmer of Hollywood invisibility.

Like so much of the real supernatural, this felt normal. Dull, almost. But the pastor had disappeared.

"Holy shit," Alice said.

Caiaphas said nothing but looked uncomfortable.

"This is the best fucking thing I've ever seen," Lily said.

"Incredible…" Spieëlding muttered.

Incredulous asked the space where the pastor had been, "You there, Jon?"

"Yeff."

"What?"

"Yeff. I am."

Alice giggled.

"That stone a bit bigger than you thought?"

"Yeff." Testy.

"Does it taste funny?"

"Shulluff."

"Good, good," Incredulous laughed. "Let's do this."

Before he could leave, Incredulous handed something to the man made of air. Something old. Something he'd been carrying around for a long time. It dissolved into the invisible pastor's hands. For some reason, it felt right.

When you don't see me

"I suppose you will be getting away pretty soon," Caiaphas said to the space Jon Power had been occupying. There was no answer but a jaunty, laddish music passing between them. The white pastor was whistling as he headed for the dancefloor. Incredulous wasn't sure, but it might have been the Vengaboys.

Incredulous hoped everything he knew about omens was wrong. The rest of them held their breath.

Jon Power had his gun. He also had a very authentic-looking assegai. At least, he remembered it looking authentic when Incredulous had pulled it out. He couldn't see it anymore.

The bird was bigger. Much bigger. And the sight of it made Jon Power's skin spasm and contract with fear. Just his skin, though. Within him he felt calm. Glass crunching under his feet, the dark figure growing larger as he approached. *Perspective? Imagination?* He prayed. *Your will.* And then, after a moment, *But HELP.*

He was trying not to forget the plan they had discussed on the way. Ridiculous, of course. Simple as it was. But you know how it is when you're stressed and need to remember something and it's important and you're about to face a giant vampiric bird from the heart of pan-African myth and legend in mortal combat. *Yeah, yeah. #ThirdWorldProblems.*

The bird was looming and crouching at the same time, the matted feathers of its folded wings brushing the ceiling of the ground floor – the undertaker shoulders of a vulture, head low, craned into the central dancefloor, the three floors of open-air above it. It was eating.

The snap and wet chump of bones and flesh being torn and shaken loose. It grunted, with effort or hunger and shook its head in paroxysms of enjoyment. Jon Power felt sick, he walked slowly, carefully. His pockets were bulging with magic droëwors, a borrowed handgun in one hand, loaded and unlocked, a ceremonial spear in the other. He picked between the larger pieces of glass and wood, the deeper puddles of beer and blood. The surreal sensation of watching where he stepped without seeing his feet. With each step, he saw the detritus flatten and, through the soles of his *velskoene*, he felt the uneven surface. Like slapping himself in the face after the dentist, feeling in halves. It made him a little dizzy, but he dared not stop watching, existentially novocained as he was.

He closed his eyes for a second and immediately regretted it. He miss-stepped. He heard the loud crack as he looked down, too late, to see the shard of table leg, resting on a glassy fulcrum, snap. The bird stopped and turned. Its vulture shoulders flexed, its wings extending slightly for a second, red feathers briefly flashing. It cocked its hammerhead, eye swivelling, breathing heavy and loud, looking directly at Jon Power.

Or, rather, through him. Puzzled. Suspicious. Forever hungry. Jon stood completely still, the stone feeling heavy in his mouth, trying not to breathe. He inhaled as slowly as he could through his nostrils.

The bird looked in his direction a moment longer and then returned to feeding. Not for the first time, Jon Power was acutely conscious of the softness of his skin, the exposed nature of a throat, the brittle thinness of the human spine. Not for the first time, he thanked God for protecting him while still far from clear of danger.

He took another step. And another. The nauseating crunching becoming louder and louder as he approached. His hand was tight on the gun. The other tightened too around the stabbing spear Incredulous had given him. The shaft was smooth, almost soft-skinned. Ancient.

He had killed people before by stabbing, mostly with bayonets or Spydercos. Some general issue hand to hand combat knives. Once or twice, in grim memory, when he had run out of ammunition and had found himself in the rural beyond in a strange country, he had used an *assegai*. It had not been a pleasing experience. Not that killing ever was.

In this case, he'd have to choose his weapon quickly. Gun if all was lost. Spear if he was close enough, able to make several confusing attacks.

He gripped the weapons and tried to calm his mind. Combat required an empty mind. He crunched on. Slowly.

Eight feet away from the monster, he stopped. Jon Power had smelled blood in quantities before, too, but this was overpowering. He clutched the spear. An antique, Moshoeshoe had said. Creeping closer, he fixed his eyes on the bird. Its blood-drenched beak and talons, its clotting feathers. The row of what looked disconcertingly like teeth. Jon Power gulped down the spit that was running from his mouth and step, slow step, slow, slow step.

Five feet away from his target, his foot crunched loudly on the glassy floor.

The bird turned and reared. Its wings opened slowly, with a tearing sound, and Jon Power felt the pressure in his ears change and pop. The impundulu's chest expanded and it roared, vibrating the bones in his body.

"What. Is. This?" it bellowed.

Jon Power stood utterly still. Held his breath like a useless spear.

The bird took a step towards him, looking for the sound. He could smell the half-digested blood on its breath, the rich, animal scent of its body, a hint of electrical smoke, and ionised air. His legs cramped as he held his muscles taut, not wanting to shift even a millimetre. He tried to breathe shallow. Leopard crawl breathing. Stalking. He had done this before.

Well, not *this*, exactly.

The pain in his leg was not the only one, though. That droë-wors. Whether it was the tokoloshe protein or just the amount he had eaten in his post-drug nutrition-craving haze, it was going to have its revenge. And before that, it was going to announce its presence. From his throat. Through his mouth. He had never needed to burp so much in his life.

Hang on, Jon. Hold.

The bird approached. Shit. It was three feet away. Jon Power found himself scrolling desperately through years of bush knowledge looking for something about the avian sense of hearing. Smell. He came up with nothing. And the bird was getting closer.

Jon Power stopped breathing. The bird was just a foot or two away, low rumbling from its throat, its head swathing left and right, looking for the source of the noise. It stopped, its beak inches from his nose. He burped.

Loud and deep and gullet-shaking, an eruption of sound and repeating flavour, like a truly unpleasant volcano. Like a meat geyser. Like any one of a thousand disgusting similes, but with the added threat of imminent slaughter. The burp resounded and echoed as time slowed for an aching second, and the bird began to react.

Jon Power raised the handgun and fired.

Three shots, quick succession, a neat, broad triangle in the bird's chest. His memory of bird anatomy was sketchy at best. A breastbone like a pigeon seemed likely. But that was where the good stuff was.

The lightning bird screamed. It pivoted in confusion, thrashing around, looking for its attacker. Jon Power was close enough to see a pupil the size of a five Rand coin dilating to the diameter of a cricket ball and contract wildly as the enormous gory head missed him by inches. He waited for it to swing back, perfectly still. Empty. Aimed. Held. Fired.

The muzzle flash itself must have burnt the bird's eye. A horrific injury under other circumstances, but rendered irrelevant a nanosecond later, as the bullet tore through the soft flesh, turning the seared eye to steam and slop, shattering the bone of the socket in a wet explosion that sent the monster reeling.

The bird was staggering. Jon stepped forward, three quick paces, bringing him close enough again to feel the heat radiating from its huge body and feel his hair stand on end with electricity. He smelled nitrogen and iron. He fired again. Two shots this time. One hit it in the chest, penetrated, but as it reeled the second glanced off the back of the bird's skull. Jon Power noted in his mind that this was no longer a target and waited the few split seconds it took for the impundulu to turn. Waited. Waited. Almost. There.

He fired again, the familiar kick like a surge of power emanating from his palm. You can't fight the love of guns.

The bullet tore into the bird's face as it swung past him. He saw no exit splash.

He also saw an eye socket that was wounded and bloody, but nothing like the smashed pulp he had seen earlier. The bird was healing with sickening speed. All that blood. He saw also that it had fixed his position.

Jon Power barely had time to jump. An explosion of light came out of the bird-like a bow wave, like the first blast of an atomic bomb in a propaganda film from his childhood. Incredulous Moshoeshoe watched it rush towards the space he imagined the pastor to be. Willed the power from between things to lift the man of God, propel him faster than the lightning. It seemed to work.

Jon Power felt the electricity in his calves while he was still in the air. Hot-cold fingers clawing up towards his heart, his whole body jolting and spasming from just the edge of the wave of charge. His handgun fired. Either the muscles in his hand had contracted or the lightning had set off the round in the chamber. The gun was hot in his hand. He smelled smoke from the assegai. He was still in the air.

The bird swung towards him and seemed to recharge again as Jon Power, still invisible, dived through the air. He knew before he connected that he would land on his stomach. And what would happen?

He hit the floor in a weird splash and clatter of cluttered sticky wooden chairs. His stomach flattened on the ground. The stone flew out of his mouth as the impact punched the air from his lungs. Skittered and clattered across the floor towards a door on the far side of the dancefloor. The pastor undissolved. The bird reared.

❦

She stepped out onto the road. Cut up, undressed, disoriented, and alone, one could easily have mistaken her for just another victim of an habitually violent patriarchy. But one would have been wrong. She felt nothing like a victim.

❦

The bird rose, scattering feathered ash and blood and pieces of meat as it shook its giant wings. Jon Power lay in a stained heap in the corner of the dancefloor, the looming black form becoming a tower of threat above him. Wings extending. Red flashes underneath glowing. Electricity crackling.

It moved more lightly than seemed reasonable. Hollow bones. Dressed in feathers, made of magic. Caiaphas Molefe ran out from the shelter of the doorway firing wildly and shouting.

"Come get me, you fucking pigeon!"

The impundulu barely turned towards him, flicked him away with a burst of lightning that sent him bowling into a wall. It stepped inexorably on towards Jon Power. Fired a burst that put the 'light' back in lightning and kicked the white man around, losing him his weapons and making him convulse a little. The pastor was lying on the ground, gun beyond him against a wall. Spear between Incredulous and the bird. The inevitability of what was about to happen weakened Incredulous' legs. He felt sick.

The lightning bird stood over Jon Power, briefly burying him in hollow shade like a cormorant. It lifted one large talon, balancing its weight on a huge wing, pressing on the filthy floor. With the clawed talon, it lifted the prone figure of Jon Power.

Incredulous willed a burst of light exploding from between the molecules of air, between the monster and his friend. The bird reeled briefly, blinded. But Jon Power didn't stir. The Bird shook its head, a bolt of lightning searing the wall next to Incredulous and sending shooting pains through his arm, knocking him to the ground. Draining him.

The bird lifted the white man to its beak.

⁓

There was a crowd. They barely looked at her. Nighttime in Pretoria. Weird shit happens, motherfuckers. Girls get hurt. She snaked through them as if they were moving in slow motion. Drawn to the place. Sensing what she was looking for, there. She tried to go in, but two huge men barred her way. She didn't talk. Didn't interact with the cop cars and environmental health signs and random partiers. She skirted the building.

At a back door, there was just one man. He was talking to a woman.

Incredulous Moshoeshoe summoned all his will, all his gift, and tried to materialise force out of the ether. He was almost empty. Like vomiting when there is nothing left inside. Like scratching at the inside of an orange skin for juice.

The bird staggered slightly as if it had been punched by a small, invisible child. It laughed.

Incredulous had never felt so tired. So drained. He slumped against the wall and closed his eyes. His pocket started to move from the inside like there was a creature living there. Wait, what? He opened his eyes. Lily was pulling pieces of droëwors out and stuffing them into her mouth.

"You're a vegetarian," he said.

"Vegan!" she hissed. "I feel like I've probably mentioned that before. And shut up." The words distorted by the meat in her cheeks. "He needs help."

"We can't…"

"We have to try!"

"You'll be killed!"

"It doesn't matter."

"It does to me."

She stopped for a second. Kissed him on the forehead. Swallowed and headed into danger.

Incredulous felt welded to the floor with exhaustion. He looked over to where Alice was crouched, watching her girlfriend go. She was playing with a string of beads protruding from a fold in her corset.

He caught her eye. Her face was blank, the way the faces of the people on the home front always are. Her lips were moving. Lily was making her way from alcove to bar to the upturned pool table, dashing between bits of flimsy cover, making a winding way to the pastor and the impundulu. The bird had stopped. Its beak hovering over the man, as if waiting for something.

Lily looked tiny. Insanely exposed.

Alice crawled over to Incredulous and took his hand.

"Can you help?"

"I tried. I don't think I can."

"Okay," she said. "Pray with me."

"Look, I…"

"I know. I don't care. Pray with me."

Incredulous closed his eyes and squeezed her hand.

The woman was middle-aged, power-suited, out of place in Pretoria Central late at night. Super out of place here. It didn't matter. Lucretia didn't wait to hear what they were arguing about. She walked swiftly towards the distracted cadre, increasing her pace as she approached him. The last few paces she almost skipped, bouncing in a final leap that let her almost climb the giant of a man to get up to his face, like running up stairs. She head-butted him hard on the bridge of the nose, forcing him backwards with her weight and velocity, landing hard on his chest, breaking several of his ribs. She kicked him in the face twice.

She didn't look back at the businesswoman or the unconscious guard. She walked on. In.

She could feel it waiting for her.

Who the hell knows if prayer works? The faithful believe, at best, that it can. And might. Unless their theologies are so out of whack with 2,000 years of Christian history that they have reduced God to an animist force or a magical lever to be pulled. The mainstream of Christian thinking – for it was Christian prayer Incredulous Moshoeshoe was engaged in – see God's hand as unforceable. They can ask, they can beg, they do so in faith and with the best motives, and the answer, if any comes at all, could be no. It so often is, from prayers for healing to interventions in the life of a child, a country.

But, to those who believe, it is not the same as simply leaving things to chance. Good prayer is a proportionate request for the odds to be shifted in your, or someone else's favour. Great prayer is confident that the one being prayed to is already predisposed to making good things happen.

Incredulous' prayer was neither confident nor proportionate. He simply asked God to let the girl live, to let the pastor live, to let them win.

Lily would be dead ninety seconds later.

Tumbling out from behind a low wall, she rolled in an arc, partly sheltered by an upturned table and a beer crate, picking up the assegai as she went. In one motion she seemed to bounce, unfold and land on her feet, bending and twisting like a snake. That is what years of goth dancing teach you, if you do it right. What it doesn't teach is how to fight.

Lily had done years of Tai Chi but never been as devoted to it as she'd have liked. She remembered enough of one stabbing weapon (was it a spear? A sword? That death-fan?) to adopt a good stance and make a few feints at the bird. But no martial art teaches defence against lightning. The bird, still seeming to wait before the kill, looked up at her, with its huge, now repaired pupil dilated. Incredulous Moshoeshoe thought he saw it smile. The bird dropped Jon Power and turned towards Lily. Whatever was preventing him from killing Jon, seemed to have frustrated him. And seemed not to apply to the girl.

Lightning burst with disproportionate force – if proportionate use of lightning is a thing – and instantaneously melted the rubber of her dress and set her hair smouldering. Her heart stopped before the flash had receded from Alice and Incredulous' retinas.

The bird swept forward, mad, flapping its wings and rising in the air, grabbing her body in both talons and snapping her in half, blood washing over the floor, over the dropped pastor, over the assegai. Huge bites, the bird took, massive chunks of flesh and clothing, hair and bone, and all the things that moments before had made Lily herself – swallowed greedily. Noisily.

The blood, the jolt of being dropped, a cry of grief and horror – something shook Jon Power awake.

He rose, baptised in blood, white eyes, white knuckles, off-white teeth. He picked up the assegai where Lily had thrown it as she died. Red and slick and full of a feeling he had thought was dead in him, he walked towards the monster.

The impundulu was still eating.

Jon Power walked right up behind it and cleared his throat.

The Witch

The monster turned around, saliva and sinew and blood running from its beak, its chest still heaving from the effort of the feast.

"I could kill you," it said simply.

"Do it," the pastor said.

The bird hesitated. Jon Power took a step closer. The bird's breath was hot on his face. Dulu shook his head. His eye contracted. If there was a way to read emotion in its unmammalian eyes, then Jon Power felt it, frustration and rage. He took another step towards the created thing. Pressed the spear gently into the monstrous torso, looked into the bird's eyes. The spear tip hadn't even scratched the bird.

"I've worked it out, Gonzo."

"What, little man?"

"You aren't *allowed* to kill me."

"Ha!" the bird exclaimed. Haughty and unconvincing.

"All this time we've been chasing you, like you're the bad guy," Jon Power laughed, looking away. "You're a monster, sure.

But you're no more responsible for any of this than a gun is responsible for a massacre," Jon Power said.

"You sound like the NRA," the bird deflected.

"Oh, don't get me wrong," Jon Power replied, turning back as if talking to a beggar at his door. The relaxation of automatically diminished respect. "You will need to be put down. Like we sometimes used to put useful dogs down if they become dangerous. Like guns sometimes just need to be put in a big pit and burned so hot they stop being guns."

The bird laughed again.

Jon Power continued, "I just want you to know that I know what you are. You're a slave."

"European. Of course, that is your understanding. It is all you've ever understood. This is Africa. You have no sense of the bond between a queen and her…"

"Oh, fuck off," Incredulous interrupted. He had stepped out of the alcove. He was shaking with hate and grief. "You're a house boy." To Jon Power, he said, "It's true. In the stories, Impundulu are controlled by a witch or ngaka."

"Careful, boy," the bird said to Moshoeshoe. "I am forbidden from killing only one of you."

"So, I can do whatever I want," Jon Power said.

The bird's leathery skin, around its eyes and throat, twitched as the pastor stepped forward. The monster seemed to shrink.

Dulu the lightning bird started to speak.

"I … I … am not allowed to kill you, but I can …"

Its words were interrupted by the assegai being thrust into its soft belly, deep enough that Jon Power's hands were buried up to the wrist in hot, wet flesh. Blood poured out as he twisted the shaft, felt muscle contract around his hand, and give way, shredded. The blade was sharp. Strong.

The bird took seconds to register what had happened. Jon Power pulled the assegai out with a sucking pop, raised the blade, and swung it in a tight arc, slashing the bird's throat. Neither wound began to heal.

"What…" the lightning bird choked and spluttered. "I don't understand."

"Tokoloshe fat," Jon Power said simply.

"No…" the impundulu said. It was shaking. Crumpled to the ground.

Incredulous Moshoeshoe strolled up to the bar and got a cellar of tequila salt, walked slowly over.

"Hey, shitbird" he said. "I've caught you." He poured the entire contents on the bird's tail.

The vampire-bird detonated.

The explosion threw Incredulous Moshoeshoe across the dancefloor, sent Jon Power flying back towards the doorway, to where Alice sat motionless and blank. Both men were pinned to the walls, held by arcs of light that crackled and spat. The rest of the lightning earthed harmlessly into the ground.

Caiaphas Molefe, dazed and hurting in ways he'd never experienced, was watching from a side corridor when he saw the figure of a woman pass by one of the doorways.

"What the fuck," he whispered to one of the buffalos. "I thought the perimeter was secure!"

They shrugged.

"Come!"

Caiaphas and his men jogged off to the outside world with its health officials, police and propaganda. He was formulating a plan B, in case the boys didn't make it.

On the dancefloor, there was the kind of quiet you sometimes get directly after a thunderstorm.

"I cannot kill you," the bird said. "But I can cause you so much pain." It coughed. The arcs weakened, the men slipped down their walls. With an effort, the bird increased the voltage and they stabilised. Both were contorted in visible agony.

They seemed to hang for eternity and then it all ended.

A voice from the doorway, flinty and cold.

"Stop."

The bird released them immediately.

"I was not…" the bird said, bowing its head.

"Shut up," the woman said.

"He is alive…"

The woman made a gesture towards the bird and it fell to the ground, shaking and screaming.

"Idiot," she said. "You have created an incident. You have made a mess. You knew it and you did it anyway. Honestly, I don't know what I'm going to do with you."

She sounded like a suburban mother. She was one. "You will suffer for this."

"But…"

"Shut up, Dulu!" The sound of the word was louder than a human voice. Incredulous Moshoeshoe felt cold in his senses. Power radiating from the woman.

"Ms. Aak de Nau," Jon Power said, pulling himself up against the wall and standing unsteadily. Limping towards her. He was sure he had broken several bones but felt nothing. He expected that to wear off with the tokoloshe meat and the adrenalin.

"Reverend Power," she said, coldly. "You have helped to make this mess."

"Sorry," he said. And remembering something Incredulous or one of the girls had said to him, "Not sorry. Hashtags."

The woman snorted. "I had hoped you would fail. I thought you would."

"Hashtags." He wasn't sure he was using it correctly, but he didn't mind. He was drawing her attention away from the corridor behind her.

"You believe in sacrifice, don't you, Power?"

"Yes."

"Well, you were going to be one of my lambs. For the good of the country."

"War is not good for a country."

"There's a saying, pastor. To make an omelette, you have to start a race war." She laughed at her joke. Which would have been an indicator that there was something wrong with her had it not been for the whole megalomaniacal sorceress thing.

"Doesn't sound familiar."

"Well, it was something like that. This country needs purging. The experiment has failed."

"Because people like you never really gave it a chance."

"Oh, please. I worked to get where I am. Why don't they?"

They, Jon Power thought, the entire sentiment and the word very familiar from similar arguments over the decades.

"Because you opposed it, every time it looked like things might change."

"Oh, spare me the sermons, pastor. You're drenched in blood. Soon everyone will be. And good will come of it, as good always comes from sacrificial blood. The time is at hand."

"You're…"

"Insane? Such a cliché. You disagree with me, so I'm insane. You think my vision is too radical so I'm insane."

"I was going to say you're in sin," he said simply. "Repent."

The witch laughed. It echoed around the room.

"I am so far beyond your petty vision of the Kingdom, Reverend Power. I am a prophetess. I am Jael. And this monster, this magic – they are the tent peg I am going to drive through the skull of impurity and the unnatural order in this country. This creature, this magic, and the coming war."

"Mother of the nation…"

"That is how I will be seen when the tide of blood recedes, yes. And it's true."

"A pity about your daughters."

"Alida was a whore. A fornicator unequally yoked. I was teaching her the ways. I would have passed on the country to her. But she disobeyed me. She went with this… man…" she gestured to where the bird had been. In its place lay the figure they had met in the Kruger Park. His skin and his suit seemed woven together, imperfectly, as if caught halfway in the process of evolution. Junk DNA and feathers, tears where the assegai had entered. He was grimacing with pain.

400 | Incredulous Moshoeshoe and the Lightning Bird

"You never…" he pleaded.

"Shut up," she said, making another gesture that caused the monster man to scream. "You knew. And you did it anyway. And I thought we could move past it, but you have demonstrated tonight that you cannot be trusted. We have done enough. The war is coming. But you are a blunt instrument. And I have no time to sharpen you, animal."

"The whole trying to cause a race war thing I can almost deal with," Alice said from her spot by the wall. "But the mixing of metaphors has got to stop." She smiled the smile of the delirious grieving. "Just saying."

"Chanel was not a whore," Incredulous shouted. Jon Power remained quiet, his jaw clenched.

"No, but she was always rebellious. Involved in occult…"

"Are you fucking kidding me?!" Incredulous shouted. "You're a witch!"

"It doesn't matter." The sentence was pronounced with finality. "The old man is dead. The RYM boy is dead. The Spieëlding girl, too. If you imagine for a second that the newspapers will go with any narrative but mine, you are dreaming. Dulu!"

The bleeding man stood up.

"A new command I give unto you," she smiled. "Kill them."

Dulu took a deep breath.

Jon Power and Incredulous Moshoeshoe both involuntarily closed their eyes. A thudding sound, not as loud as either man's expectation, echoed weakly against the dancefloor walls. As one man, they opened their eyes.

Aak de Nau was on the ground. A very beautiful woman neither man had ever seen was standing over her, wearing very little.

She was bloodied and dirty and panting calmly. She radiated strength. She had the remnants of a quart of Castle in her hand.

"She talks too much," Lucretia said. "And I'm not dead."

Dulu was looking stunned too.

"But…"

"You?" Lucretia said, lifting the jagged edge of the bottle towards the bleeding birdman. Recognition flickered in her eyes, then died. She dropped the bottle and just stared. Entranced.

Dulu turned towards the pastor and the isangoma.

"You heard her," Incredulous said. "She's going to kill you. Torture you."

"Do you want that?" Jon asked.

"You people," Dulu said. "Always pushing. Always using."

"She *is* going to kill you," Incredulous said.

"Nevertheless. I must obey."

Jon Power slumped. Out of options.

"I must obey," the birdman said. "But she is not awake right now to hurry me."

"What?" Incredulous asked, looking up.

"I may delay. A Little. Until she awakes."

And Aak de Nau began to groan and stir, a shaky hand reaching up to her scalp.

Lucretia bent at the waist as she swung, disintegrating the bottle entirely on the back of Aak de Nau's head.

Incredulous looked at Jon Power. They both looked at Lucretia, beyond her, to Alice. They picked up the assegai and the gun and as one man shouted,

"Run!"

Love you to death

A **note from Incredulous' grandma**
That boy doesn't listen to me. These boys these days never do. In my day, that kind of disrespect would have been beaten out of a child. But my daughter. Her husband. They were 'progressive'. And look what that progress has got the world. This country. Haai.

That boy Incredulous, who never took the things I taught him about the ancestors seriously and never really listened about our true religion – until he could turn it into a business – haai, it makes me want to spit.

He never believed me about Shaka's spear. The first one. The one he made with the great Zulu wizard. The first of its kind, cast and beaten perfectly and cooled in blood. It is a special spear. He kept it I think because he thought it was old. Because it might be worth something. Some money. And perhaps it is. Perhaps. But it is a powerful blade.

But that is not all that helped them to injure the lightning bird so. Not on its own. Even with a magic blade, the impundulu can heal from any wound. It is why it was created. To take life from others and itself be impossible to kill.

Except.

Except it had vices. Too many years walking as a man. Like Incredulous. Like too many of these young blacks who think they are white, who forget who they are because they talk of 'Struggle'. The lightning bird became greedy and twisted like a man. Its thirst for blood was beyond what it needed, which led it to drink the blood of thousands of people over the years. Some are still alive. Some are alive, but not well.

This bird contracted Aids, one time. This bird, with all that blood, it was not a surprise. But it did not notice. Did not know. It was strong. Its diet was good and it was rich and it could heal so quickly. This is what it was made for, I told you.

But when this bird ate the white girl – the strange one with the strange clothes who attacked it so bravely – it ate the tokoloshe in its pockets, in her stomach and veins. And that is very strong magic.

The magic that helps an impundulu repair its body was boosted and confused with the magic from the tokoloshe, like this red bull these kids are drinking always – like cocaine. A white drug. It made the bird's blood strong. And the Aids was in the blood. And as fast as it healed itself, so it also strengthened the virus. The bird was already dying, fast, when the Christian stabbed it, made it weak enough to kill – though the Christian did not kill it. Christians, too, are weak.

This is what happened. But if you ask my grandson he will say I am an old woman. What do I know?

What do I know? All the hidden things. What do I know?

And would I lie to you?

Last Dance

As they ran, they could hear the impudulu's wings begin to beat. Aak de Nau had awoken. Dulu had transformed again. The Lightning bird was coming.

To Incredulous Moshoeshoe, the flickering filthy walls of the endless abandoned corridors reminded him of the first-person shooters of his youth. To Jon Power, they just looked like the same wall, endlessly repeated. It's funny how different psyches can perceive the same thing in the same way without realising it.

In the bowels of the club, they found themselves on the old industrial floor again. There they devised a plan.

The lightning bird was limping. Staggering. People talk about blood pouring, but they usually mean dripping or running. Here, blood was pouring out of the lightning bird as it stood on the threshold of the cluttered little room. Alice, Jon, and Incredulous were hiding behind a wall of lights, furniture, and panelling.

The bird was stooping to crane its hammerhead through the door. Eagle eye side-on, scrutinising.

"They are here, ma'am," it growled.

Aak de Nau pushed past the bird, not reacting at all to the hot wetness splashing on her, nor to the smell of iron.

"There's nowhere to go," she said. "Just give up."

Silence.

She turned to the bird.

"Dulu."

The lightning bird shuffled, spilling more blood. It splashed on the white woman's shoes like vomit on a Saturday night. Its head disappeared behind the door again and then emerged. In one giant talon, it dragged Lucretia out, lifted her with some difficulty, pushing her up against the wall.

"I'm sorry," the bird whispered. Lucretia strained a little and then went limp. Horror and resignation. Sisyphus must have had that look on his face the ten-thousandth time he was crushed. Prometheus would have had more to relate to.

"Come out, progress-inhibitors!" the politician shouted. "Come out from behind your walls, from behind your self-righteous posturing and your scruples!" She was the ring mistress without the top hat. A market stall fish wife providing her own ice. "Come out, little men! Or I will have my pet snap this slut in half."

The bird shifted uneasily. To it she said, "Oh don't be so easily impressed. She escaped you. Big deal. It's not a miracle."

Lucretia put a soft hand on the talon. The bird shuddered and then seemed to relax.

Jon Power came out first, hands up. He stepped far back into the rivet-head room. He spoke quietly. The trick of the bully. He had been an officer. Aak de Nau unconsciously stepped forward. The bird came with her.

"You can't do this to the country," Jon Power said quietly, and then softened his tone. "Please don't do this."

Aak de Nau laughed. "I am doing this *for* the country!"

"But think of Chanel. Of *Alida*." He whispered the name. Aak de Nau took several steps forward, annoyed.

"Don't you talk to me about…"

Incredulous Moshoeshoe stepped out, several paces to the left of the pastor, and several more forward. Dangerously close to the witch and her familiar.

"I knew her," he said, also quietly.

"You didn't know anything," Aak de Nau said, turning towards him.

He stepped, backwards, a pace to the side deeper. As if he was intimidated, cowering. He said, "No, I *knew* her." He laughed.

Jon Power had skirted around behind them and was edging towards the doorway. Alice had crept out and was following. As she stepped towards the pastor, her bootstrap caught the edge of a light. A small 'ting'. Incredulous heard it at the same time as the bird.

The isangoma shouted, "I fucked her so hard. She loved it a little rough. A little strange. A little," he gestured to the bird, "*dark meat*." He shouted the words. Aak de Nau did not turn around towards the ting. The bird had inclined its head towards Jon Power and Alice. Its huge eye focused on them. Blinked once, slowly. Then it turned back to focus on Moshoeshoe. Lucretia was stroking the leathery skin of its claw. The blood was pouring slower. Dulu was looking sick.

Aak de Nau laughed. "Do you think that means a thing to me?" she shouted. "I'm not the prig I have to pretend to be.

'Family values' are just a platform," she said, making air quotes, the universal indicator of the truly dangerous madman. "I don't think my daughters were virgins and I don't care who fucked them," she said.

"That's very enlightened," Moshoeshoe said. "What do you care about?" He was letting a woman back him into a corner, not for the first time.

"This country."

"Interesting. So, what do you want from me?"

"I want to kill you and your friends and let the country begin to burn. For cleansing."

"Your bird is sick," he said. "Are you sure he can?"

"He does not need to live much longer. It is almost done."

"He is almost deceased," Incredulous said. "He is about to shuffle off this mortal coil and join the choir invisibule."

"What?" Aak de Nau said.

"You don't like Python?"

"*I* do," the bird said.

Aak de Nau looked perplexed.

"Kill them, Dulu," she said with finality and pulled out her phone.

I walk the line

*M*y bones feel hollow.

That's to be expected, of course. But more, today. Now.

I obey and obey and obey. The destiny of a cubicle-farm tenant. The destiny of battery men, who dream of free-range slavery. Men.

We've spoken about this before. I am not a man. And the Untermensch morality this pastor preaches, the amorality of the isangoma and his scenester supplicants are so… unsatisfying. It's all so unsatisfying. Hundreds of years and thousands of people punctured like Liquifruit. I'm still thirsty. All the time.

You understand I'm speaking metaphorically. And while I am no more responsible for my actions than the bank teller forced to give up the cash is guilty of theft, I have not fought. I have not opposed. Am I culpable as a death-camp guard? Or the guard dog?

I am barbed wire. And I am rusty.

I want to say that, as far as it has been my choice, I have done the right thing. Tried to be a good man. Not a bad monster. Something in-between. No regrets, you understand. Not really. Would I have done anything differently? Perhaps. Probably not. But could I have been more? Could I be more alive if I picked a side? Committed? I'm so tired.

I feel I'm at that point that actual people reach, suddenly aware that the narrative of 'yes, but I'm a good person' has not been true for a long time. What do you do? Where do you go from there?

And when you encounter something, someone, that is good… I mean good for you. Beautiful. Good… It is hard to explain and I am so tired.

I'm tired of the dark laws that bind me like spells. Obey. Obey. I am tired of being left behind by speeding history, tired of everything I love decaying while I live beyond them. I'm tired of the struggle. Mostly I'm tired of this crazy white bitch and tired of hurting girls like this one. Cradled in my hand.

I have to obey.

But I can pick my speed.

Leave me for dead

Dulu dropped Lucretia with an air of impatience and careless brutality. Threw her, really. She didn't land on any of the sharp edges, wasn't flung in the way of danger. She tumbled softly out of the door and the lightning bird drew himself taller, stretching. Still bleeding. He coughed a bubbling wet fizz and extended his wings.

Aak de Nau said, "Some time today, Dulu," not looking up from her screen.

"They are too spread out. I am not strong enough to tear them apart."

"I don't care," she said.

"They will hurt me."

"Do it. And quickly. Use your lightning."

"Yes, ma'am," he said. She was still on her phone, face blue. Eyes flickering, finger swiping, and typing. A busy woman.

Dulu watched Alice and Jon Power make their way to the door. He nodded. Smiled. And winked at Moshoeshoe, glancing at his boots and his spear.

Incredulous was briefly confused. Shrugged. Charged.

The bird did technically try to kill the isangoma. He gave every volt and amp of himself, releasing it in an unfocused detonation of electricity. Light and charge expanded from him in a sphere, ball lightning made larger. It expanded from the bird's chest and stopped as it touched the floor. The metal floor.

The lightning ran in waves and sheets all around the steel-lined room. Every surface conducting unimaginable levels of charge. The air screamed.

Incredulous Moshoeshoe managed to stay upright, stay running, and passed through the wave of electricity that made his piercing hot and his hair sizzle. The charge did not make it through the three inches of rubber at his soles.

They gave him grip and speed and made his final launch at the bird's chest a little more powerful. He plunged the assegai into its sternum, felt gristle crack and tear, felt the blade scrape against bone, and deflect into soft tissue. Felt the hot wetness of a wounded abdomen, still moving and heaving, swallow his hand far past the wrist. He looked into the bird's face, so close to his. It was smiling.

Incredulous let go of the wooden shaft and stepped briefly back, turned slowly around. He had felt the shock, but his rubber boots, their thick platforms, not for the first time, proved to be worth the obscene amount of money he had spent on them.

Aak de Nau had been wearing sensible flat pumps.

Her heart had stopped before she hit the ground.

Her eye sockets were black where her eyes had evaporated. Her clothing had melted to her body.

The lightning bird himself had shaken and convulsed with the charge, barefoot as he was on the metal surface, separate as he was from the lightning that lived independent of him after being loosed. Feathers smoking, he had collapsed. A used boa. A carnival costume, discarded in a skip.

Both bodies, witch and familiar, lay in smoking piles on the glowing, buckled floor.

Incredulous was standing alone in a cave made of lava.

"Well, shit," he said.

Jon Power was standing in the doorway, safely on cement and paint and a light and ancient layer of beer vomit. He stepped gingerly into the red glow.

"Well done."

"He wanted to die."

"I'm glad."

"No, I mean, our plan would never have worked."

"I had faith."

"Yeah."

They made their way out of the warren of the b-grade dance-floors, towards the side exit. Lucretia was completely out of it, mumbling incomprehensible things. Alice had her arm around her. Grief is a blanket. It's big enough.

"I can't believe that's all over," Jon Power said.

"It isn't, you communist fuck," a voice said from the shadows.

"Oh shit."

A Strange Day

A white guy who looked like he'd been built from the discarded parts of a university rugby team stepped out of the shadows. He wore a panelled shirt in blues and khakis. He wore *velskoene* and long brown socks. He wore short shorts. He held a gun.

Behind him, fourteen others, slightly bigger and better armed, reared up.

"We saw you on the web before the government conspiracy to hush it up," he said. "Our brothers in Komatipoort called. They would like a word with you."

The men bristled with weapons. Guns. Barrels like seed spikes under a microscope or a tangle of sticks in the veld. The organically casual attitude of people who had hunted before they walked. Enough of the weapons were trained on the pastor to make a mess were they to go off, but Jon Power wasn't worried about any but intentional shots. Guys with lead in their blood and warm liver on the tips of their tongues were usually pretty good about gun safety.

"Come with us," the leader said.

"And who are you, back at the ranch?" Incredulous asked.

The man twitched. Addressed his answer to the white man. "*Veldcommandant* Japie Strydom," he said. "*Broeder Weerstands Span Drie.*" He switched to English again. It was halting, but respectable. "We have some questions we would like you to answer. In private."

Jon Power sighed. "Look, guys, what happened there was not my fault. You get that?"

"We don't care."

"It was an exorcism. Things happen. The family messed with some magic that..."

The big white man laughed.

"This isn't about that, *poes*. They've been watching you. You've been channelling funds to agitators and communists. You are an enemy of your race and enemy of the God you claim to serve."

"Ja, *poes!*" The echo came from a bigger man, the one with a smaller penis. A classic henchman's henchman if ever Incredulous had seen one. The bully's friend, the torturer's assistant, the less attractive cheerleader who demands more cruelty. He had a face that had been punched a lot. But not enough, as far as Incredulous was concerned.

"Jesus told us to love our enemies," Jon Power said, but without much hope it would work. His sentence went up at the end, like a question. The answer was swift.

"Ag fuck off, man."

"Ja, fuck off!"

Incredulous started to say, "Listen..." And was punched in the face by a fist the size of a leg of Karoo lamb. He fell sprawling and got slowly up. "This has got to stop happening to me," he muttered.

Jon Power assessed the men. Untrained in any formal sense, but big as Toyota bakkies, all of them, and hyped up on nationalism, mampoer, and South African media, if his guess was right. *Dangerous.*

"Guys, haven't you got more important things... I mean, tonight...?"

"We have orders. And if it's going to get hectic, then following orders is going to be more important than ever."

"Bru," Incredulous said, "You have no idea what we've been through tonight."

The leader turned on Incredulous, looked at him for the first time. Like he was inspecting a piece of animal scat in the bush. Not good animal scat. Disappointing animal scat, that he'd not had much hope for but had still somehow found a way to fall short of expectations.

"You," he said, pressing a gun-barrel-sized finger into the isangoma's chest, rocking him back on his heels, "should shut," he paused to push him again, "your" and again, "mouth," he dropped his hand and smiled broadly. "Boy."

"That was an error," a voice from the shadows said. It was followed by the chopped roar of a powerful handgun going off in an empty room. Every human being flinched. Flinching wildly was the man standing in front of Incredulous, who jolted awkwardly as bits of his brain jostled with shards of skull to exit the space they had been occupying a nanosecond before.

"Woah!" Incredulous shouted.

Before the rest of the broeders could react, Caiaphas Molefe had stepped out of the shadows and capped two of the Afrikaner nationalists, point-blank shots, muzzle in their faces, surprise and indignation in their eyes.

Before he could take a third shot, one of the truck-sized men had gun-butted him and he fell to the ground. The remaining broeders split their attention between checking on the corpses of their fallen comrades and holding Molefe down. One of the corpse-checkers stepped over, cocked his handgun, and stood over Molefe, motioning for his friends to step away.

"That's enough," another voice, differently accented, shouted from the shadows.

"Woah!" Incredulous shouted again. Violent farce impressed him. He was only human. And born in the 70s.

Herman Spieëlding stepped out of the shadows (which, Incredulous thought, must have been capacious).

Moshoeshoe said, "Any more of you in there?"

Spieëlding ignored him. He said to the man holding the gun, "Do you know who I am?"

The man blinked. Looked around. Back at Spieëlding. He nodded.

"Then lower your weapon."

The man obeyed.

"You… you were AWOL, sir," he said.

"I'm your leader. I don't need to ask anyone's leave. At best, I was AWO." He pronounced the word "eh-woah". His subordinate smiled. He did not. "What is your business with this man?"

"He shot one of my men, sir."

"Yes, I saw."

"So, I was going to execute him."

"On what authority?"

"Sir?"

"On what authority were you going to kill him?"

"Sir," he said, a little confused, "we saw him murder…"

"I said I saw."

"Sir, I do not understand."

"I'm asking…" he paused, raising his eyebrows at the man.

"Van Heerden, sir."

"I'm asking, Van Heerden, why you feel it acceptable to kill a criminal like this rather than calling the police."

"Sir, you can't be…"

"I think you will find, Van Heerden, that I can be whatever and however I want to be."

"Yes, sir."

"And also, Van Heerden," he said, "that our group stands for law and order. Against the wave of crime that is ruining this country."

"Yes, but, sir, he…"

"I don't want to hear it, Van Heerden. Has war been declared?"

"Sir, no, but it will soon…"

"Van Heerden, what is your name?"

"Sir?"

"What is your name, Van Heerden?"

"Van... Heerden..?" He seemed suddenly unsure.

"Not Spieëlding, then?"

"No, sir."

"And what is the name of the leader of our movement?"

"Sir, you have been…" He trailed off. "Spieëlding, sir."

"So, perhaps, as the leader, I might be allowed to decide when this turns into a war?"

"Yes, sir."

"And when it is war, will you be executing any enemies you capture in the act of killing one of our brothers?"

Van Heerden felt like he was on firmer footing here. "Yes, sir! Only then, sir!"

"Wrong," Spieëlding said, raising a handgun and putting one small hole and one very big hole in opposite sides of the man's skull.

"Seriously!" Incredulous shouted.

The rest of the broeders seemed less unsure of themselves, more like they just didn't want to be there. Like animals standing perfectly still as the shadow of a predator passed by. Spieëlding helped Molefe to his feet.

Caiaphas brushed his clothes off. "Sorry about your guy," he said.

"No worries," Spieëlding said. Neither man smiled. "Who's in charge here now?"

A skinny little man looked back and forth and stepped reluctantly forward.

"I guess it's me, sir."

"What was your mission here?"

"To apprehend the pastor and race traitor Jon Power, sir, and to return him to the Komatipoort branch."

"Why?"

"I got the impression, sir, that we had received pressure, sir." The skinny man had seen behind the orders. Thought about things. He'd either go far or be beaten to death.

"Pressure," Spieëlding said, thinking.

"Yes, sir."

"Who from?"

"Someone important, sir."

Spieëlding nodded. "And what was the accusation against the pastor, exactly?"

"He had been investigated as a supporter of communist agitators, posing as a Christian."

"Pastor," Spieëlding said to Jon Power, "Who is Jesus Christ?"

"Son of God, died for our sins, rose again, will come again to judge the living and the dead," Jon Power said.

The head of the Broederbond turned back to his subordinate. "He sounds like a Christian to me."

"Sir, we have evidence…"

"As do I."

"Sir, he has been supporting *elements*…"

"Is this true, Pastor?"

"Yes."

Spieëlding paused. "Oh."

"Sorry." Jon Power gave a thin-lipped smile.

"Okay," Spieëlding said slowly. "Why?"

"I'm a bit of a Communist."

"But still a Christian?"

"Yes."

"I don't suppose…" Spieëlding tried, "in terms of race loyalty, you have… ?"

"None. Sorry."

"Okay." Spieëlding paused a long time. His men shifted awkwardly. "Well, he's exonerated. Fully."

"Sir, we will have to inform our branch head."

"I am the only head you need to worry about."

"But what if he doesn't believe us?" The skinny man thought ahead. Thought of his skin.

"I will talk to him."

The skinny man bit his lip, hesitated, and said, "When, sir?"

"What?"

"I only mean that if he thinks we have disobeyed an order, and it turns out to be war, sir. I just mean that he might react fast. And I know you are busy, sir. You must have a lot on your mind."

"Why would you say that?"

"Word is out that your daughter is missing."

"No, I'm not," a voice said from the doorway. Incredulous started violently.

Spieëlding went with it, suppressing every paternal instinct in him except those that sought the systematic repression of other races. He remained calm.

"See?" he said to Skinny. "And I will talk to him, this superior of yours. Where is he?"

"He's at the Monument, sir."

"The Voortrekker Monument?"

"Yes sir."

"But that's a big RYM gathering today. They're doing a celebration of the old man. What could he possibly be…" He stopped, going several shades paler. "Are they…?"

"Yes sir."

"What?"

"A bomb."

Detonation Boulevard

"Right," Spieëlding said slowly. "Can you call them?"

"No, sir. He's gone..." the skinny man glanced uncomfortably at Moshoeshoe. "...dark."

"When?"

Skinny checked his phone. "Forty minutes?"

"You have a car?"

"Yes sir, but the traffic outside... The press... Finding them... We will never get there in time."

"I have an idea," Lucretia said. "Oh, and... Hello, Daddy."

There is nothing on earth faster than a South African taxi. Not cheetahs, not, it could be argued, Formula One cars. Not in the real world. Not in traffic. They bend time and space. They curve 'round corners and seem to squeeze past, through, and under cars and trucks and pedestrians that crowd Africa's most beautiful country's cities. And they do so at high speed, crammed with people, blasting very loud *Kwaito,* House, and Hip Hop.

The five of them – Incredulous, Caiaphas, Lucretia, Alice, and Jon Power, hung onto anything they could reach, looking longingly at the unused seatbelts. Lucretia's father sat in the front. Because, of course, he did. The driver turned 'round, gave them a big, part-gold smile, and said, "You want to go fast, eh?"

Caiaphas nodded.

"Why?"

"We're trying to save South Africa."

"Eh! Okay. Then this makes me a hero!"

"If you get us there in time."

"Don't worry about that, my man. I can be your hero," he waggled his eyebrows, grinning, "…baby." With which he slouched down in his driver's seat, his relaxed posture lulling them into a false sense of not being utterly fucking terrified. But only briefly. They took off like a rocket fired from a bullet train.

The familiar white shade of a Gauteng taxi, either in its old Hi-Ace form or the new, bigger regulation vehicles, is an iconic symbol of the lawless, fearless, peerless spirit of everyday South Africa. It's how people get around. Though not, on the whole, white people, who mostly do not understand how it works. It's not a taxi like a London taxi is a taxi. It's more like a bus. But not so much like a bus that it operates as a bus. There are routes, hand signals, and understood tariffs that whitey does not know. And whitey, in his assumptions about black South Africa, is taking a longish time to learn.

There are notable exceptions, of course, but Jon Power was not one. And he was one of the good guys.

"Is this a good idea?" he shouted to Incredulous in a voice he had only ever used before in troop helicopters.

Incredulous was having trouble answering. The view out of the windscreen was like a spacecraft in hyperdrive. Cars swerved into view and swerved out, hooters blaring and fingers lifted in salute. But they were rocketing on. The driver looked supremely calm. He slouched back in his chair, one hand on the wheel, matchstick in his mouth, a look of zen belligerence on his face. He'd been offered a bonus and had every confidence he'd earn it.

He did.

They pulled up at the entrance, a little way from Fountains Valley and the highway, faces aching from the smiles they had been forcing, immensely grateful to be on stationary ground again. Caiaphas Molefe, who did not have much cause to travel in a taxi these days, dropped to his hands and knees and kissed the ground like a pope. Which was kind of what he was around here.

Walking in, the giant sandy jukebox of the Voortrekker Monument loomed over them. It was illuminated still by base lights, but the glimmering of the first white hints of dawn was changing its colour, suppressing its shadows. Soon it would blush like the sky, but for now, it was a slab of stone, cold and unsympathetic to the crowd of indigenous provenance nearby in its meeting kraal.

The kraal itself had caused a stink recently, when it had been consecrated to some animist and ancestral spirits, in keeping with the uneasy pluralism that South Africa sees through rainbow lenses. Local, mostly white Christian groups, had protested the insensitivity of such a ceremony at a site consecrated to thanking the one true God for allowing white settlers to slaughter heaps of indigenous aggressors.

424 | Incredulous Moshoeshoe and the Lightning Bird

Jon Power found the place unsettling. Not just the sense of other, older religion and its spirit haunting the place. The Lord knew he had made some peace with that over the last weeks. It was the stronger, pervading sense he felt in his spirit of what the place had been originally consecrated for. Named for the triune God but reeking far more of allegiance to a place, a nation, a race. It made the pastor deeply uneasy, as idolatry in a church always did.

The rally was hotting up. RYM supporters are not, as a whole, cool-headed intellectuals. The word 'firebrand' is used more often to define them, which is lazy European shorthand for anyone who believes in something I do not, a little too strongly. But looking around him, Moshoeshoe could imagine these guys setting fire to shit.

They were angry. Someone on the stage was shouting. An air of combustible aggression permeated the gathering. Jon Power, Incredulous Moshoeshoe, Spieëlding, Mrs. Likota, Caiaphas, and Alice were in the throng, almost completely ignored, barring the occasional moment someone noticed the white faces and did a double-take. The presence of Caiaphas, even for those who didn't know, in detail, who he was, lent a certain amount of credibility. He was a big man, and he carried himself with a sense of assurance. Wherever Caiaphas Molefe was, you suspected from the look of him that he was running the show. You were usually right.

The man on stage said a name that made the little group stop.

"Scientist Likota..." he repeated, "is dead." Roars of disapproval from the crowd. "I know, I know. But that is what people are saying! Murdered by Boers."

Herman Spieëlding swallowed in the way he wished the earth would swallow him and gripped his daughter's hand. She had thrown on a coat, but a woman with Lucretia's natural walk and aura of sex would seem utterly naked under a coat even if she was wearing woollen leggings and a balaclava. As it happened, her legs were very bare. It was a measure of the crowd's agitation that not one of the men paid her much attention at all. Still, she felt nervous. And uneasy. Which may have been because she was holding her father's hand for the first time in about 15 years.

"So, what do we do?" the man on the stage said to the crowd, quite calmly. "Do we just let that happen? Do black lives matter in this country? Have they ever, since the settlers arrived?"

The crowd thundered. Alice was walking like a zombie, not paying attention to much. Lily was gone. She'd seen a thousand movies where the love interest had been killed and the hero had moved swiftly to conclude an elaborate plan of revenge. Alice didn't know how those people could stop crying long enough to even start. Everything was empty. She followed the pastor and the DJ-witch doctor and the militant kingpin and the racist in a haze of grief and exhaustion. Only the noise of the crowd intruded. It felt like catechism, when she was a child, imagining the crowd, demanding the death of Jesus. Those shouts, fists, she thought, idly, are the essential image of humanity. She turned to her left to say so and stopped. Christ, she missed Lily.

"That is why, comrades," the man on the stage was saying, "It is time for us to make war. Tonight. In whatever way we can. They will call it a riot. They will call it 'damage to property,' they will call it," he paused a beat, and spoke more quietly, "indiscriminate killings. They will call it terrorism." He spoke up again, almost shouting, never losing his composure, "We will call it the liberation we have been waiting for all these years!"

The crowd cheered. It was good stuff. And fair, motivationally speaking. But it made Caiaphas Molefe very angry. He ploughed through the ululating, cheering, or clapping throng – not universally working class, a lot of students, young professionals, and intellectuals in the ranks – and was stopped at the stage by a compere and a couple of heavies. Their resistance was beautifully brief. Incredulous and the others had just got close enough to see Caiaphas whisper something in the compere's ear when he turned distinctly pale and ushered Caiaphas onto the stage.

The man who had been speaking was quietly dressed, well-spoken, wore glasses and a light checked shirt. Chinos that said, 'I'm a reasonable guy. I read. I go to parent-teacher conferences. I make a respectable salad.' Caiaphas Molefe punched him in the face like a motherfucker. Or, rather, he punched him eventually. First, he stepped on stage and thundered down on the gentle-looking man in a manner that suggested ears flapping, trunk raised in trumpet, and tusks poised for some A-grade goring. The beatific smile touching the corners of the speaker's mouth as he enjoyed the agitation he was whipping up disappeared as recognition grabbed hold of the pit of his stomach and twisted. Caiaphas may not have known the speaker's name, but the speaker knew Caiaphas.

Stepping away from the mic, he said, placatingly, "You saw the news, comrade. It is time."

"I'll say when it is time," Caiaphas said in the man's ear, gripping his arm tight enough to leave bruises, smiling for the crowd.

"But Scientist…"

"I watched Scientist die this evening. It had nothing to do with the Boers."

The man perked up a little, ambition filling his cheeks where fear had emptied them.

"So, then we need a leader…"

"Listen, you bourgeois cunt, Scientist Likota may have been a fraud, but he did everything he could to make sure we didn't plunge into a mad fucking war." Caiaphas stepped towards the mic without letting go of the arm he was using as a stress ball. "Amandla!" he shouted to the crowd. They shouted back. He stepped them away again.

The man had had enough. "You take your hands off me right now," he said, "or I will shout traitor and these scumbags will necklace you faster than it takes to put out a Stompie." The man was getting more stressed and as he did his voice took on a higher register. His words a more childish tone.

"Puns? Really?" Caiaphas said, letting go.

"Anyway, isn't this what you wanted?" the man said testily. "I know who you are. What you have been preparing for. This is it."

"This is not it. This will be about race."

"Race is bigger than everything else in South Africa." He sounded like a junior high school debater, like most identity politics nerds do, eventually.

"Class is bigger than everything else. Everywhere." Caiaphas was beginning to believe this guy wasn't even a communist.

"Your mom is bigger than everything everywhere."

And *that* was when Caiaphas punched him in the face.

A few things happened very quickly at that point. More security man-mountains than Caiaphas could take woke from their work-rhythm semi-comas and flew at him. At the same time, the crowd rushed the stage, more in confusion than anything else – *we're moving? Okay*. Three or four seconds later, Caiaphas had been dragged to the side of the stage, some distance off, and the security goons were looking around for some sort of instruction. The crowd was edging them further and further, ebbing the mass of humanity away, leaving Herman Spieëlding, Jon, Alice, Lucretia, and Incredulous exposed, an odd little group. They were attracting attention. It also left a group of four white men in black clothing nobody could ever mistake for Goth, carrying a small kit bag. They wore the expressions of nude bathers exposed by a suddenly retreating tide. They knew a tsunami was about to hit them.

Jon Power shouted, "Bomb! They've got a bomb!" pointing at the men, and the crowd dissolved and resolved into streams of humanity running towards exits. The broeders separated off, predictably, and ran as one, perhaps according to plan, perhaps by instinct and love, towards the Monument. It loomed like a multistorey Wurlitzer. Spieëlding and Jon Power ran after them. Lucretia, Alice, and Incredulous went to Caiaphas' aid. Always with the girls, Incredulous. Always, since childhood.

⁓

Jon and Spieëlding ran for the sound of crashing and breaking, the panicked sound of new terrorists digging themselves into a corner. The monument was dry and dark. Cold.

A voice from the depths said, "Traitor."

"This man is a traitor!" the blackeyed orator, once again vertical, shouted to the throng arguing around Caiaphas, who was thrashing and occasionally throwing gigantic security men off him like water off a ridgeback.

"Idiot!" a senior functionary who had walked over to see what the kerfuffle was about, shouted. He was not afraid of bombs. "This man is the head of MK Underground."

The thrashing stopped, the security guards loosened their grips and looked, a little wide-eyed, around them for guidance. The crowd took a step back. It's one thing to watch a big guy get lynched. Even an important guy. But when you hear that he could command legions of cadres, like avenging angels, to kill every single man of you, it gives your average lynch mob pause. Not always, of course, as the Christians know. But usually.

"He killed Scientist Likota!" the orator cried, sensing a disturbing turn in the tide, feeling the ache in his face more keenly than when he had the upper hand.

"My husband," Lucretia said, quiet and clear, "died fighting alongside this man."

A confusion of voices erupted and bubbled with exclamations. *He was dead. There had been a fight? Fighting whom? So the war had started, then. Wait, her what?*

"Let him get up," the orator said. "We must attack now!"

Caiaphas clambered up with about as much dignity as he could muster. "No," he said. "We do not attack first. We are a defence movement. We are here to protect the gains we have made, to assure the direction for the future. We are not a faction. We are not..."

"Terrorists?" the orator interrupted. "It is a bit late in our history to become squeamish, friend."

"Terrorism I like," Caiaphas said, "as much as any other strategy, comrade. But our friends in Hezbollah learned the hard way how toxic it is for a movement when they lose focus on who they are fighting, and why."

"Hezbollah seems strong to me."

"Sure. But after the last shitstorm with Israel, they had *Christians* supporting them. Ordinary Lebanese. The nonpartisan. Because they had never trained their guns on anyone but Israel. And then they got involved in all that shit a few years ago and the popularity plummeted. It will be a decade before they have that opportunity again."

"Do you think, given the state of Syrian support and the changing Tehran..."

"Hey! Nerds!" Alice shouted. "Not to interrupt your fascinating debate, but there is a bomb on the grounds, people who think it's time to make war are trickling out of this place without hearing the truth and the woman who meant more to me than anything in the world is dead and I would very much like that not to have been for nothing." She stopped. There was silence. "Please."

The orator, shaken from some kind of trance, dashed up to the mic.

"Comrades!" he shouted. "Order!"

The crowd that had picked out the broeders and moved in a single wave away from them stopped its milling and reeling.

"We have a friend here, someone many of you know, though perhaps not all because of the secret nature of his work for the movement," his voice echoed off the stone. "He has a message for you."

The crowd went silent and Caiaphas Molefe stepped up to the mic, pulling a dazed-looking Lucretia Spieëlding with him.

"Comrades! This is Scientist Likota's widow."

⌒〜〜⌒〜⌒

"Traitor," the voice said again. A young white man stepped out of the black, his tread starting its echo as his voice still faded. "You have betrayed your race, betrayed your faith."

"My faith is in God," Jon Power said simply.

"And yet you are yoked with an occultist."

"Bud," Jon said, "the woman directing this whole bloody mess is not what I would call a good evangelical."

The man stared at Jon emptily, blank hate on his face, a heavy kit bag hanging from a strap in his left hand.

"How long do we have?" Jon asked.

"Not long now."

"So, you had better be going."

The man's partner seemed to agree, he laid a hand on his arm, pushing him towards the exit. Jon Power and Herman Spieëlding stepped aside.

"No."

"No?"

"No."

"If you stay here you will die."

"I will never die. God has my soul."

"God is love," Jon said.

"God is bigger than love."

"Would he want you dead?"

"His will be done."

The crowd was not loving Lucretia. Her voice was shaky and it was clear under her coat that she was not wearing very much, which simultaneously titillated and undermined her credibility with some in the crowd. Because patriarchy.

"Listen to me!" she struggled. "Scientist was a good man, and he believed in your cause. I know..." Derisive laughter from the crowd. "I do. He did. But he wanted to prevent a senseless war. A war that was being manipulated into existence by Elena Aak de Nau."

"How did she do that, then?" a voice shouted.

Another said, "Take it off!"

"She... I don't know, I think she..." Days of exhaustion hit her like a train. She started to cry. "She did it with a kind of... Like a sort of..."

"What?" a voice jeered. "Speak up!"

"Show us your tits!"

Lucretia folded a little in herself. "A kind of magic."

The crowd exploded into laughter. Loud, booming, rhythmic.

"There… there was a giant bird…" she muttered to herself as Caiaphas put his arm around her and shepherded her away from the mic.

"You're a giant bird!" a voice from the crowd shouted.

Caiaphas reeled 'round and grabbed the mic.

"You shut your fucking mouth, boy, or I will remove every tooth in your skull." Silence fell like magic. "Shit happened tonight that you would never understand. I… I am not sure I do."

He faltered in his resolve and the crowd sensed weakness. The spell was broken.

"What, like a giant bird?" a heckler shouted. The crowd erupted again with laughter – crueller now and edged with danger. They were advancing. A menacing tide.

"Show us your bird!" a voice shouted. Caiaphas shuffled backwards on the stage. The orator looked worried. They were moving forward with purpose. No longer individuals. Mobs have single minds. Mobs are not good people.

A sound like large, beating wings, rolling like thunder atomised them again. It stopped first one, then another, and another of the crowd. They looked up into the brightening sky. It was getting closer.

⌒⌐

"Oh, stop this nonsense!" Spieëlding said. "I am your commander! I order you to disarm that bomb and step away."

"Then that proves it."

"What?"

"You have been compromised. My only commander is God. And God demands that we fight for our nation, for his truth."

The man was young. Maybe 22. Short blonde hair, not the biggest guy. Never picked first for rugby. No flash of intelligence in his big blue eyes.

"It's over," Jon said. "You can't achieve anything. You'll kill a few white guys. That's all. Likota is already dead and the crowd out there is too far for you to harm. The only thing you're going to do is damage your own monument."

The man's mouth twitched and his eyes started to glisten in the weak light. He seemed to be thinking. Or trying to stop thinking. He looked around him in a way Jon Power had seen many times before, on borders, in cells. The man's eyes welled up with tears. He was seeing nothing around him but failure and impotence.

"Well, you two are traitors," he said.

"But it would look like a victory for them," Spieëlding said.

The man looked up, away from his inner thoughts to Spieëlding's face as if seeing him for the first time.

"Yes, it would," he said.

Spieëlding said, "Oh no."

"You know what?" the man said. "The Muslims are right. They could teach us a few things." He laughed, tears spilling down his face. The lightness of having nowhere else to turn lifting him.

"What are you talking about?" Spieëlding said.

"He's talking about suicide bombers," Jon Power said flatly.

"No, son," Spieëlding said, genuine concern flooding his face. "That's not our way."

"I don't care," he said and reached down into the bag.

～

It's hard to describe what happens to a crowd when a mythical bird approaches by air. It disperses and regroups, dissolves, and reconstitutes. To the bird, it looks like fractal patterns in the movements of ants or bees or fish on a high-budget documentary. Like finches. On the ground it looks like it has no pattern – just running and yelling and stopping and staring and more mindless running – but there *is* a pattern. There are patterns anyone can see. One day we'll map and predict them, interpret what they mean about us and about time, the way ancients used to read the same things as omens. But that's still a hundred years away. Right now, it just looks like pandemonium.

The orator just stood and watched as the bird loomed larger and larger until it was huge and black against the dawn sky, impossibly large. He kept on waiting for perspective to resolve it to a normal size. It never happened. The bird swept down and landed on the stage, rather more clumsily than one would have expected from its beautiful arc to land. It crashed and stumbled and the orator braced for the stage to collapse under the immense force and weight, but the bird rolled and shrank and seemed to shift in his focus and a man, black and well dressed and bloody, limped to his feet, the red lining of his coat flashing like sparks as he fastened the top button of his French coat.

Dulu took two steps and crumpled, coughing, racking, spitting up blood so painfully it had to be his own. Caiaphas Molefe stepped in front of the human shadow of the monster. The bird did not electrocute him. Just said,

"Please."

There was something in the way the word came out that made Caiaphas step back.

Dulu paused. Then took a few steps towards Lucretia. She did not move. Just watched him. He took a few more. Until he was very, very close. His aquiline nose almost touching hers.

"Hi," he said.

"Hi."

"You left me."

"You were going to kill me."

Dulu took a breath. Not angry. Almost embarrassed. He looked at her, turning his head to the side, regarding her with his right eye, then his left.

"I'm sorry."

"Why?"

"I don't know." Dulu coughed again and his face contorted, grimaced. His skin was pale. Grey. Blood was still running from him. Every movement painful slow.

"Why are you here?" Lucretia asked.

"I don't know." The sapeur reflection of the lightning bird said. He smiled, a little sadly, like older men always do with young, beautiful women. "I have nowhere to be. No orders. And you are here. It felt right."

"How did you know I was here?"

"Don't you want me to be?"

"You killed my husband. And so many other people."

"I know."

"Why are you here?"

The birdman looked around him for what seemed like the first time. The crowd was silent, gathered, still, watching them speak.

He said, "I'm dying."

"You are indestructible."

"Usually. Not now. That spear… And that meat…"

"You're dying."

"Yes."

"And you want to die here?" she said. "The Monument?" She frowned.

"No," he said, never taking his eyes from her. Pupils locked. Darkness reflecting darkness.

"With me," she said.

"Yes."

"Why?"

"I don't know. You've heard me. Felt me looking for you. I don't know."

"You wanted to kill me," she said again.

"You know that isn't true," Dulu said, a wince making its way from his side to his face. "I never wanted to, I had no choice."

"Why did you want to find me?"

"I have imprinted on you, I think."

"Oh, God," she said. "Is that from *Twilight*?"

"I'm a bird. We had it first," he smiled. "Did you ever see *Fly Away Home*?"

"Yes."

"It's like that."

"You want me to teach you to fly North for the summer."

"I want to die near you."

"You killed my husband."

"I know," Dulu said.

"Why?"

"I find it hard to respect the feelings of lesser species." He coughed and laughed. "Even as a person, I am not a good person. I'm not asking you to love me."

"What then?"

"Be with me. Talk to me. Be *with* me."

"You're going to die."

"Yes," Dulu said.

"How long do you have?"

"Not long."

"Are you ready?"

"No."

"Why?"

"I don't want to, not like this. Not slow, trickling out onto a stage in front of all these people, in this..." he cast an eye around, "this place."

Lucretia looked towards the Monument. She didn't know how, but she could see inside it.

"If I came with you, would you try something?"

"What?"

"Fuck something up. Something beautiful and wrong."

"Alright," he said. The trust of the torturer. The oppressor. Some victims could ask you anything. "I don't want to die."

"But you will."

"Yes."

"So, make it matter. Destroy something pointless. Tear down a lie."

"It's all pointless," Dulu said. "I don't take sides. I don't care."

"Do it for me," Lucretia said.

Dulu smiled. Nodded once, slowly, never taking his eyes off hers.

"Show me."

***

The bomb was tiny. Embarrassingly small. Small like Pele could advertise it. Small like Donald Trump's hands. Jon Power almost laughed. He didn't, though. Partly because small bombs can still kill you, particularly when you're standing right next to them and also out of politeness. The man was distraught.

"I'm sorry," the young man said. And something in the tone of the word tripped a switch in the pastor's mind. Took him to a time before he was a pastor.

Jon Power barrelled Spieëlding towards the exit like a very enthusiastic gallery security guard at closing time – a long, running shuffle. The man with the blonde hair nodded to his friend as he stumbled and looked down at the bomb. Said a short, Calvinist prayer. He was slowing down. Strong. And Jon Power was finding it harder to shift him. The young man had his hand on the call button of the old Nokia attached to the pipe. With his other arm, he elbowed the pastor in the face, connecting with the bridge of his nose. The pastor fell, and prayed a monosyllabic prayer in tongues, hope failing.

The man – the boy really – did not push the button. He was distracted by a loud beating, a rumble in the air.

Lucretia put her arms around Dulu's neck and whispered in his ear. He smiled.

The lightning bird burst through the doorway and blotted out the trickle of sun from the ceiling. The air roared around him, dust and papers and leaves and discarded hope whirled around the cenotaph. The bird was enormous. It carried a passenger, clinging to it, holding onto its neck, half-clad like a Boris Vallejo painting.

The broeder with the bomb stood still and mumbled, "Six wings... covered with eyes..." The lightning bird thundered its feathered limbs enough to rise to the centre of the great stone building.

Lucretia shouted, "Pastor, get out! Dad, I love you!" She was smiling.

The young Afrikaner nationalist seemed to wake from a reverie. He gripped the bomb more tightly and looked up.

Lucretia shouted down to him, "This is for Scientist. He was a good man!" She added, "He hated this architecture!"

Lucretia kissed the bird on the cheek and the man pushed the button on the Nokia a fraction of a second after the impundulu detonated. Entirely. The force drowned the blast of the pipe bomb, drowned out all light, all sound, and then filled them with an excess. Speed and fire and lightning; nuclear force.

In an instant the monument disintegrated, briefly expanded in its original shape, and then, pulled back by electrostatic force, imploded on itself. Burning roof and tower. Broken walls. Leaving a void in the historic landscape.

A few hours after this

"You can't bring down a monument that size" has taken its place in the lexicon of crazy along with "Jet fuel can't melt girders" and "The flag is waving! There's no wind on the moon, doofus!" The combined weight of Caiaphas Molefe and Herman Spieëlding's propaganda machines had made sure that any criticism of the official story was treated like the most pathetic of conspiracy theories.

The new reality was that a right-winger, disillusioned with his movement and with the way the white opposition was being run had teamed up with the daughter of its head – a stripper who was angry with her daddy. They had blown up the Voortrekker Monument as something between a protest and a sulk. Most people don't know enough about explosives to argue. And those who do, learned their lesson at 9/11, whatever their views.

The clean-up efforts had started the next day, RYM supporters who had been left hurt or stunned and stranded at the site picking up rubble and helping to sort stones for the inevitable rebuild, side-by-side with Afrikaner nationalists of all stripes. Men in khaki. Women in *kappies*.

There was bemusement, awkwardness, comments about settlers and mutterings about mixing races, and then, at the end of the day, 12 churches from all over Pretoria and larger Tshwane brought braais and meat and salad and *pap* and fed the four thousand people who had shown up to help. There was bitching, one or two fights, and some hairy eyeballing, but for the most part, it was good. *Braaivleis* brings a lot of people together. That is its power. It's kind of like suffering, but less healthy.

A joint funeral was held for Elena Aak de Nau, Scientist Likota, Lucretia Spieëlding, and an unnamed adviser to the Aak de Nau camp. A moment of national mourning, taking in political violence, outbreaks of disease, and living in a dangerous but beautiful country. Archbishop Tutu delivered a unifying homily. The orator returned to the stage he loved and preached peace, because preaching is the important thing to some men, not outcomes. The Old Man was invoked enough to give the recently deceased backache.

The death of a coloured Steam Punk singer didn't make the news at all. Another woman sacrificed in a country of violent men.

The country did not descend into unusual violence and chaos. Not this time. Not more than they could handle.

Caiaphas Molefe continued to prepare, though. But Jon Power stopped bankrolling him. Which was fine, because Caiaphas had moved out of the shadows fairly permanently when he stepped out onto that stage. He was fast becoming something of a celeb. An official politician. An elder statesman of the radical left who had the advantage of a sense of humour and being able to string a sentence together. Donations, for men like that, are not hard to come by.

Jon Power continued to give most of his money away, and still to the Movement. Just not to weapons. Not to war. Some bursaries, some orphans and widows' benevolent funds. A little to a church that still believed in the supernatural. And he went back into deliverance. Faced the old enemy. All of his insecurity had died. He knew who he was. Not a good man, but redeemed, and a lot more chilled out than before. God can use people like that.

Herman Spieëlding, however, had a change of heart. Not so much a turning from war to peace, but a decision to take more control of his organisation. He wouldn't have thought of it as Stalinist, but he would have been missing a trick. And slowly the Broederbond returned to its roots as a weird little Calvinist cult giving the Masons a run for their nepotistic money. Cultural concerns. Language glorification. Networking.

Alice mourned for Lily for a long time. She left her job as an analyst for the security services and became a lecturer in history and geopolitics, down in Grahamstown, there was, for a while, a very respectable steampunk scene. She also met a beautiful Catholic girl, who never replaced Lily, because Lily never could be replaced, but who she became very fond of, and who loved her for years and years. And it was good.

Incredulous Moshoeshoe never changed his business cards, despite their literary inaccuracy and political incorrectness. He did focus his practice though. Supernatural detection, the ridding of monsters, subculture stuff. He wasn't depressed anymore. He listened to less Goth, it's true, but he also spent more time with his family. More time in the country, sitting with older healers, listening to their stories. It's easier to take seriously the religion of your ancestors when you have seen a figure from its legends die. This is true of all religions.

Incredulous Moshoeshoe believed. His belief was in no way required, but he did. Comfortably, thankfully, patiently. He was learning. He was willing to be there. No longer pining for the blacklights and the business of London. Family dissolves those desires.

Jon Power saw him occasionally. Consulted on cases. Asked for the isangoma's help in understanding some aspects of magic and myth. Uncomfortable things that seemed less threatening somehow, after everything. He liked Moshoeshoe. He liked to work with him. Which was a predictable end, but pleasing.

Jon Power wouldn't have called them partners. That would have been ridiculous. Heretical, even. And Jon Power was, at the end of it all, not a heretic. But he found as the years passed, that his orthodoxy had softened, smoothed its edges. Loosened its grip a little. He wasn't sure how to reconcile the occult ritual and languid pantheism of the isangoma's newfound path with his own. But he found as they spent time on cases, in bars, that his path remained straight and, yes, narrow, but that its edges blurred a little bit. And at no point did the Spirit tell him to stop.

This was all much easier with proximity. Not a lot of people have seen what Jon and Incredulous had. Not many could share it. So, it was a good coincidence, fortuitous, even, that they lived so close together. It pleased them both. It was a beautiful place. Mpumalanga is where God lives, after all.

Glossary of South African, African, and subculture terms

Ag shame – an expression of pity. 'Poor you' or 'that's a shame'.

Assegai – South African spear.

AWB – Afrikaner Weerstands Beweging, or Afrikaner military movement, a far-right paramilitary group with a three-armed swastika made of 'holy sevens' as its symbol.

Bakkie – a pickup truck.

Biltong – like beef jerky – dried, spiced meat – but better.

Blerrie – 'bloody' but pronounced with a heavy Afrikaans accent.

Boer – literally a farmer, but also an old-fashioned reference to the Afrikaner race.

Boytjie – little boy. Afrikaans diminutives often include '-tjie' (pronounced 'kih').

Bra – brother, as in 'bro'.

Braaivleis/braai – barbecue but better. The South African form of barbecue, with more chops, steaks, boerewors (a traditional Afrikaner sausage now beloved by all South Africans, even vegans), and less rain.

Broederbond – a secret society of Afrikaners that operated within the South African government before and during Apartheid. As exposed in a book called *Super Afrikaners*, the secret society was responsible for members being in almost every post of authoritative significance in South Africa, from school principals to Prime Ministers.

Broeder Weestands Span Drie – Broederbond Defense Team Three

Bru – like 'bra' (above) but for assholes and Capetonians.

Bundus – the middle of nowhere, the wilds, the uncivilised parts of the country.

Bushveld – like Veld only with more bush. And trees.

Dominee – pastor in Afrikaans churches, usually of the Dutch Reformed tradition.

Doos – cunt in Afrikaans.

Dorpies – diminutive of 'dorp' – a town.

Droëwors – sausage biltong. Dried spice sausages, usually thin long sticks. Delicious. If you have never had the pleasure, you should stop being a wuss and try some.

Eskom – National grid power company for South Africa.

Gibbs – Martin Gibbs was for decades synonymous with quality photography in Pretoria.

Hammerkop – literally 'hammerhead' species of medium-sized fishing bird, brown in colour and common in the bushveld.

Hensoppers – 'hands-uppers', a nickname for Boer soldiers who surrendered, collaborated or defected during the Anglo-Boer war. An epithet for capitulating Afrikaner supremacists.

Howzit – classic South African greeting, initially white, now in more popular use. "How is it?"

Isangoma – male form of sangoma, a witch doctor, herbalist, spirit diviner.

Ja – 'yes' in Afrikaans, but used across many languages.

Kak – shit. Bullshit.

Kappies – Traditional bonnets worn by Afrikaner pioneers and still favoured by some old-school Afrikaner nationalist women at demonstrations.

Khoisan X – the adopted name of noted black militant leader Benny Alexander, PAC leader.

Kierie – a *knopkierie* or *kierie* is a stick, usually with a knob at the end, generally used as a weapon.

Klipdrift / Klippies – a brand of cheap blended whiskey, best drunk after several other kinds of whiskey, and an essential part of bushveld drinking.

Knersus – 80s South African tv character, a kind of pterodactyl monster always trying to eat a cute fluffy bunny. Fucked up shit of the best children's tv kind.

Koeksister – traditional Afrikaans sweet pastry drenched in syrup. Diabetes in the form of a 3D infinity symbol.

Kwaito – South African township electronica, influenced by hip hop and classic sub-Saharan disco.

Lekker – originally an Afrikaans word but adopted across languages to mean a combination of appreciation, affirmation and enjoyment. Kind of like 'Nice' when said in response to the number 69. *Lekkers* are sweets. *Lekker* means tasty and also enjoyable. *Lekker* is a lekker word.

Liquifruit – brand of South African fruit juice, often available in a box, punctured by a straw.

Madiba – The family name for Nelson Mandela, adopted by the nation as his affectionate name.

Miesies – Madam. Mrs. What domestic workers, mostly black, have habitually been instructed to call their female employers (mostly white). Males have habitually been called "master". I'm not kidding. It has become far less popular, along with the uniforms and headscarves that were for years a standard feature of domestic arrangements in South Africa.

Moffie – offensive term for a gay man, the equivalent of 'fag'.

Mos – an untranslatable emphasis word in Afrikaans. Equivalent is 'in actual fact', but that doesn't really express it.

Muti – ritual magic. Muti killings for human body parts to use in witchcraft are not unknown.

Ngaka – a more sinister type of witchdoctor, often employed to lift or cast curses, less involved in community healing than sangomas.

Pap – maize meal, cooked until firm and eaten traditionally in South Africa with an onion and tomato sauce and braai'd meat.

Penny Heyns – a great South African swimmer.

Piel – penis in vulgar Afrikaans slang.

Plaas meisie – farm girl.

Poes—like *doos*, but funnier.

R500 – five hundred Rand, Rand being the currency of South Africa.

Riempies – little cords of leather.

Rooi gevaar – literally, red peril. Anti-communist slur.

Roomse gevaar – literally, Roman peril. Derogatory term for the Catholic Church among some conservative South Africans under Apartheid.

Sapeur – Congolese term for a group of dandies who dress lavishly and inhabit their own subculture of cool, mostly in Kinshasa clubs. Dulu spent his best years as a Sapeur dandy.

Sies – exclamation in Afrikaans of disgust or shaming.

Skorrogo – scumbag, criminal.

Snor – Afrikaans for moustache.

Stoep – a verandah.

Veld – fields of savannah grassland.

Veldschool / veldskool – school in the fields, an awful traditional introduction for school children to the wonders of nature, often with weirdly militaristic and ultra-nationalistic overtones during Apartheid.

Velskoene – plural of velskoen – literally, skin shoes. Rough leather shoes favoured by traditional Afrikaners.

Verlig – directly translates as 'enlightened' but really means liberal to a degree.

Witbaas – white boss.

Author bio

JW Langley grew up privileged and dissenting in Apartheid South Africa, raised by parents so tolerant and liberal they left him no choice but to become a Christian. This act of rebellion coincided with reading Literature, Psychology and Philosophy at university – subjects he neglected in favour of playing alternative music on the radio and in nightclubs. In 2004 he moved to the United Kingdom for a year – and sort of forgot to leave. He has worked as a writer and manager at a 200-year-old missionary society, written for religious and political publications in print and online, and has had his poetry published by *The Rialto* and *Rattle*. He currently identifies as a straight male communist, but nothing lasts forever.

Lightning Source UK Ltd.
Milton Keynes UK
UKHW040133020922
408189UK00003B/1032